Andre

Andrew Michael Hurley has lived in Manchester and London, and is now based in Lancashire. His first novel, *The Loney*, was originally published by Tartarus Press as a 300-copy limited edition, before being republished by John Murray. It went on to sell in twenty languages, win the Costa Best First Novel Award and Book of the Year at the British Book Industry Awards in 2016, and is in development as a feature film. *Devil's Day* is his second novel.

Praise for *Devil's Day*

'A master of flesh-creeping menace . . . Hurley doesn't need the devil's help to grip you. His taut writing does that for him. Nature's routine cruelties are caught with a fierce accuracy that Ted Hughes would have admired' *Sunday Times*, Books of the Year

'Andrew Michael Hurley is adept at making his readers' spines tingle' *The Times*, Books of the Year

'The devil is everywhere in this deliciously creepy second novel from the author of *The Loney* . . . Andrew Michael Hurley combines the eerie power of folk memory with a much more modern manifestation of horror and the final pages are among the most unsettling you'll read this year' *Metro*, Books of the Year

'This is a story with pull. Its lively, building sense of evil is thoroughly entangled with the assumptions of the way of life depicted, that apparently timeless relationship of the smallholder and the moor' *Guardian*

'A work of goose-flesh eeriness . . . Hurley's work is like a reincarnation of novels such as John Buchan's *Witch Wood* or the stories of M.R. James. His prose is precise and his eye gimlet' *The Spectator*

'Beautifully captures a bleak landscape and the feeling of something evil and unknowable in the moors, the hills and the byways . . . lithe and lyrical' *Sunday Express*

'This impeccably written novel tightens like a clammy hand around your throat' *Daily Mail*

'The follow up to *The Loney* deploys myth, landscape and the tropes of horror to chilling effect' *Financial Times*

'Hurley is a fine writer, with concerns that place him a little to the left of the literary mainstream, a remove that makes him extremely interesting' John Boyne, *Irish Times*

'*Devil's Day* is evocative and unsettling, exploring the potency of tradition, place and allegiance in a brutal rural environment' *Daily Express*

'Makes for impressively uncomfortable reading' *TLS*

'The nebulous presence of the Devil is evoked so palpably in this novel that at times I hardly dared look up when reading for fear of seeing him grinning at me from the chair next to mine' *Literary Review*

'Chilling and captivating; read at your peril' *Stylist*

Devil's Day

Andrew Michael Hurley

JOHN MURRAY

First published in Great Britain in 2017 by John Murray (Publishers)
An Hachette UK Company

First published in paperback in 2018

1

A CIP catalogue record for this title is available from the British Library

ISBN 978-1-473-61988-3
Ebook ISBN 978-1-473-61989-0

Typeset in Adobe Garamond by Hewer Text UK Ltd, Edinburgh
Printed and bound by Clays Ltd, Elcograf S.p.A.

John Murray policy is to use papers that are natural, renewable and recyclable products and made from wood grown in sustainable forests. The logging and manufacturing processes are expected to conform to the environmental regulations of the country of origin.

John Murray (Publishers)
Carmelite House
50 Victoria Embankment
London EC4Y 0DZ

www.johnmurray.co.uk

For Jo, Ben and Tom

The shepheards life was the first example of honest fellowship.

George Puttenham – Arte of the English Poesie

In the wink of an eye, as quick as a flea,
The Devil he jumped from me to thee.
And only when the Devil had gone,
Did I know that he and I'd been one.

An old Endlands rhyme

The Blizzard

One late October day, just over a century ago, the farmers of the Endlands went to gather their sheep from the moors as they did every autumn. Only this year, while the shepherds were pulling a pair of wayward lambs from a peat bog, the Devil killed one of the ewes and tore off her fleece to hide himself among the flock.

Down in the farmlands, he flitted from one house to the next, too crafty to be caught, only manifest in what he infected. He was the maggot in the eye of the good dog, the cancer that rotted the ram's gonads, the blood in the baby's milk.

The stories began to reach the ears of the villagers in Underclough further up the valley, and while they were not surprised or sorry to hear that the heathen folk of the Endlands were being persecuted by the Owd Feller, they petitioned their minister to do something for their own sake. But he was frail and elderly and, unwilling to tackle the Devil on his own, he asked the bishop for an assistant, by which he meant a substitute.

The priest who arrived with his crucifix and aspergillum was a young man sceptical of his summons; he would think of himself as a missionary, he decided, a bringer of light to this dark valley. These people were no better than the gullible savages of the colonies who found spirits in everything from the clouds to the dirt. They deserved his pity.

But when he saw the animals decaying before his eyes and the blood dribbling from the wet-nurse's teat, his nerve faltered and the Devil brought a blizzard to the valley that lasted for days.

The cottages in the village choked under drifts that grew to the windows and stores of wood and peat that should have lasted all winter were quickly gone. Across the bridge, the church was lightless and cowed and in the graveyard the dead were buried a second time as a bigger swell of snow blew down the valley and across the farmlands. Man and beast were forced to share the same warmth. Piglets and gun dogs slept on the hearth rugs. The tup steamed in the kitchen.

Days were late to lighten and quick to end and people began to die. The older folk first, coughing up their lungs in shreds like tomato skins, and then the children, burning with fever.

But the worst of it, the very worst of it, they said, was that it was impossible to know who the Devil would visit next. He left no footprints in the snow, there was no knock at the door. It was as if, they said, he was the air itself. The stuff they breathed.

The villagers of Underclough blamed the farmers of the Endlands and the farmers began to wonder if they'd brought it upon themselves; if there had been some sign that they'd missed and left to fester like an open wound. Hadn't a jackdaw flown into the Curwens' house one evening in the summer and clubbed itself to death on the walls? Hadn't the Dyers' children seen a hare digging up bones in the graveyard? Then there was that warm Saturday in September when Joe Pentecost, drunk on port and pride, dropped his glass as he made the toast at his daughter's wedding breakfast. They'd all laughed at him, forgiven him his moment of clumsiness and thought nothing of it. Yet now, they argued over the ritual that would have sponged away the bad luck with the spilled wine. But no one could remember what to do; only fragments of old, cautionary stories came to mind, that made them throw their cats out into the snow and sprinkle their doorsteps with salt.

Whatever they did made little difference in the end. Thirteen people from the farms and the village died that autumn. Their bodies were wrapped in blankets and left in outhouses and back yards until they could be taken to ground soft enough to bury them.

Briardale Moss

No, tell me a different story, says Adam. I know that one.

All stories in the valley have to begin with the Devil, I say.

But there must be ones I haven't heard before, he says. You know hundreds.

These last few years, I've acquired a reputation for telling stories just like the Gaffer, my grandfather. Though there are some that Adam wouldn't want to hear. Some that I'd be better off keeping to myself.

Come on, he says. Tell me one from when you were my age.

Later, I say. We came here to shoot snipe, didn't we?

He nods in that funny way of his and strokes Jenny's back with one hand, keeping the other firmly locked in mine.

You'll have to let go, Adam, I say. Otherwise we can't do anything.

He relaxes his grip but still stands close to me, within smelling distance, angling his head so that he can hear the lapping of the marsh water.

It's a cold spring evening and the last of the daylight is starting to leave the Moss, slipping out of the valley and on to the moors, receding westwards to the sea. Dusk has already taken the colour from the fells and made the sound of water loud in Fiendsdale

Clough. Somewhere in the gloom, the river moves against the banks it cut in the storms we had early last month and winds away to the black mass of Sullom Wood. The air feels skinned. But Adam's been a good lad and not said a word about it. Like all boys of his age, he prides himself on his toughness. The ability to endure without tears is a badge all sons want to wear for their fathers. Still, I know that he's asking for stories because he wants distractions. I know that he's trying his best not to show that he's scared of being so close to the water.

Remember what I told you to do? I say, dropping one cartridge and then the other into the Browning that Dadda passed on to me. The over-and-under with the walnut stock.

Now? says Adam.

I'll tell you when.

Another couple of years and I should have been teaching him to shoot on the Moss. I was shooting at twelve. Woodcock and pigeons and pheasants. Things we could eat. Adam will never fire a gun, of course, but that doesn't mean to say he can't make himself useful. He can still raise the birds from their hiding places, he can be my beater.

The butt against my shoulder, I put some space between us and when he hears my voice further away than he expects it to be, further away than he would like, he says, Daddy, and holds out his hand for me to take.

I'm still here, I tell him. You're all right. You're nowhere near the water. Do what I told you to do. Go on.

He keeps his face in my direction for a moment longer and then starts to clap his hands.

A quirk of acoustics makes it sound as if the noise is coming from the fells and drives the birds out of the coverts towards us. It's a trick Dadda taught me and one that was handed down to him by the Gaffer, who learned it from his old man, who'd learned it from his and so on, back and back. To be honest, I wouldn't be surprised if fathers and sons have been coming here for centuries to hide in the dusk and shoot their supper out of the clatter of wings.

Louder, I say and Adam nods and now the echoes start to lift the teal and oystercatchers from the shallows, sending them weeping over our heads. A heron climbs, unhurried, and then the snipe burst out of the rushes and undulate low over the marsh, their reflections blurred on the water into little brown scythes. I put the barrels slightly ahead of them, losing one when it blends into the deepening shadows and taking the other on the second shot as it gives itself away against the white of the rowan trees near the gate. Adam's shoulders jolt at the crack of the shotgun and the snipe startles in mid-flight and arcs to the ground somewhere in the field we've left fallow this year.

Keep hold of her, I tell him, and he grips Jenny's collar tighter before she can dart off to pick up the bird. She needs to unlearn her worst instincts.

Make her sit, Adam, I say, as I break the shotgun and shake out the empty casings. Let her know who's in charge.

He runs his hand down her spine and pushes her backside to the ground. The light drops again, and a stronger gust of wind bends the reeds. The Moss ruffles. Jenny blinks and waits.

Send her then, I say, and Adam makes the noise I taught him, a kiss of the teeth, and lets Jenny go. She sets off, wriggles under the field gate, giddy with the scent, and brings the bird back in rags.

Adam can hear her and smell her and she presses her forehead to his palm.

Drop it, he tells her, touching the bird in her mouth. When she won't, he tries to work his fingers between her teeth.

No, I tell him. Across the nose.

He touches the side of her face with one hand and with the other gives her a hesitant tap that only makes her growl.

Harder, I say. Otherwise she won't learn a thing.

A downward belt on the snout and she does as she's told. She'll remember the pain next time. She'll anticipate it in his raised hand and open her mouth as soon as he tells her to. She's a bright girl. Gentle and good-natured on the whole. It's enthusiasm rather than malice that's decapitated the snipe.

Leave it for the jackdaws, Adam, I say. We've enough.

Hand in hand and muddy to the knees, we go slowly back along the lane to the farmhouse, as Jenny runs ahead and waits and runs again, torn between obedience to me and sniffing out the frame of her territory. Adam carries Dadda's old leather game bag over his shoulder and can't help putting his fingers inside and touching the mallards I shot earlier. The smell of their blood and the smell of the water is still on their feathers. When we get back to the farm, we'll pick out the pellets and let them hang in the scullery until the morning. And then I've promised Adam I'll teach him how to draw them and get them ready for the oven.

Is it dark now? he says. It feels colder.

Nearly, I say. Mam's put the lights on.

Are there any stars out yet? he says.

A few, I say. Orion. The Plough.

He knows their shapes. I've held his hand and traced them with his finger.

Is the moon fat or thin? he says.

Fat, I say. Full fat.

A bloated, astonished face, like a dead man under water.

Where is it? he asks.

Behind us, I say. It's rising over the Three Sisters. It's making our shadows long.

A different night and he'd have asked a dozen more questions, but he's tired and every step through the gravel is awkward, purposefully so. He won't admit it, but he wants me to carry him. At least until we get to the tarmac.

Here, I say, and to keep him occupied give him the shotgun to hold.

He hooks it broken over his arm, as heavy to him as a couple of lead pipes and turns his face to my voice and grins. Despite everything, he's in no doubt that this is all he wants. As soon as he was born, the farm was his; just as it was mine when Mam gave birth to me. He feels his grandfathers at his back and imagines his sons walking before him. I'd been exactly the same at his age. But then I lost my way.

Tell me a story then, he says. Tell me one about the Gaffer, not the Devil. We've got time for one now, haven't we?

The problem is that in the Endlands one story begs the telling of another and another and in all of them the Devil plays his part.

The Endlands

I'd always known that when the Gaffer died it would be sudden, like a lightbulb blowing out and blackening the glass. But, even so, when Dadda called one night with the news I couldn't help but feel shocked that he was gone. Shocked and suddenly very far away from the farm.

I was living in Suffolk then, freshly married, and teaching at a boys' school on the edge of the fens. It was hard to get back to the Endlands more than two or three times a year, so I generally mucked in when another pair of hands was needed the most: Lambing at Easter, or Harvest in the summer, or at autumn time when the sheep were brought down off the moors. In fact, Kat and I had been packing to go up and help with Gathering when Dadda phoned a few days before the October half-term. And we still would, of course, only now there would be a funeral first.

Even though the circumstances were unhappy, Kat was excited about seeing the place where I'd grown up. With the nursery always being so short-staffed in the holidays, she hadn't been able to come with me to the Endlands before and had only met the other farming families – the Dyers and the Beasleys – once, on our wedding day back in the June. Come to think of it, she hardly knew Dadda very well in those days either. After we'd got engaged, we'd driven up to meet him in Derbyshire a couple of times when he happened to be over that way selling off some of the four-shears, but it had only been a quick cup of tea and a sandwich between lots and he and Kat got no further than small talk about the farm or her parents.

He hadn't said one way or the other, but he seemed to like her well enough. Not that I was asking for, or needed, his blessing. Now that I'd left the Endlands, who I married had no bearing on the farm. Yet at least he'd made the effort to meet her.

The Gaffer hadn't come, of course, and the first time Kat laid eyes on him was at the Registry Office. Even so, when I told her that he'd died, she was as upset as everyone in the valley and all the way up on the train she asked me about him, disappointed that she would never get to know him now.

'Sorry if I've been bombarding you,' she said, as we clunked to a standstill at the last station. 'I'm just interested.'

'Well, don't do the same with Dadda,' I said. 'He won't want to talk about him. He'll just want to get on with things.'

'I know,' said Kat. 'I have been through this before.'

'This is different,' I said.

'Denial's pretty common, John,' she said, as we stepped down on to the platform. 'Little Emma Carter talked about her dad as if he were still alive for at least six months.'

About a year earlier, the father of one of the children at the nursery had died and Kat had thrown herself into helping the family cope. She'd assisted them with organising the funeral and written letters to the insurance company and the bank on Mrs Carter's behalf; but mostly she'd busied herself with the domestic chores often shoved aside by grief. She made sure that the house was clean and that they ate well; she put out the bins and fed the cats.

She'd invited the Carters to the wedding but they mustn't have been quite ready for large social gatherings just then and had sent a card instead. A hand-made thing that the postman had to knock to deliver. I'd been painted as a stick man in a top hat and Kat had wings and a halo.

Every day in the run up to the wedding she'd come home with another two or three creations that the children brought in for her, the pipe cleaners and glitter and scraps of voile coming loose in transit. They were all more or less the same – a church, confetti, a big yellow sun – although one showed a little girl crying as Kat and I held hands.

'What's up with her?' I said.

'Oh, God, that's Olivia Brown,' said Kat, looking up from chopping onions. 'I had to spend half an hour this morning trying to convince her that you weren't going to take me away.'

Girls, especially, were fiercely possessive over her, drawn first to her prettiness and then to her sororal affection. It was on her knee that they sat to cry, her sleeves they snotted on, her hair they plaited with their jam-sticky fingers, her hands they clung to when it was time to go home.

Children quickly and intuitively put her at the centre of their lives, and even though she was a lot older than the ones Kat looked after at the nursery, Grace Dyer had been just the same at our wedding reception. She was Liz and Jeff's only child, the only child in the Endlands at that time, in fact, and quick to latch on to anyone who gave her the slightest bit of attention. All night long she'd been Kat's shadow. They danced together, kicked the balloons, sat with two straws in a glass of lemonade, talked into each other's ears when the music was loud. And when Kat had had enough of her shoes and went alluringly barefoot instead, she let Grace wear them for the rest of the night until we left to go to the hotel near the airport. When everyone gathered on the street outside the King's Head to see us off, Grace was the one who waved for the longest as the taxi pulled away.

'I hope she's not too upset,' said Kat. 'I did try to let her down gently.'

'About what?' I said.

'I don't know why,' said Kat, 'but the poor thing seemed to think that we were going to be moving into your dad's farm now that we're married.'

'What did you tell her?' I said.

'That we'd go and visit her as soon as we could,' said Kat. 'What else could I say?'

'She'll hold you to that, you know.'

'I don't mind,' said Kat. 'She's lonely.'

'From what I hear, she doesn't exactly do herself any favours,' I said. 'She's not good at keeping friends for very long.'

'From what she told me, they pick on her at school,' said Kat.

'She gives as good as she gets.'

'Don't be mean, John. It happened to you,' she said. 'You know how horrible it can be.'

She looked out of the back window and plucked her thumb against the teeth of the plastic comb Grace had given her. It was a present that newly married women always received in the Endlands. If Kat could keep her hair free of knots on her wedding night then she would be pregnant before the Harvest Moon.

'I thought we were going to wait a while?' I said, nodding at her hand.

'I don't think Grace will let us,' Kat smiled. 'She's desperate for me to have a baby.'

'Only so she'll have something to play with whenever we see her.'

Kat waved back one last time as the taxi rounded the corner. 'Well, what's wrong with that? She's a sweetheart,' she said. 'I'm going to miss her.'

And she had.

She'd sent Grace a postcard from Spain and on the long, sweaty bus trip to Granada decided that when she next saw her she would give her the locket she'd worn on our wedding day – the something old her mother had presented her with before she took her seat in the Registry Office.

But now she was carrying an even better present with her to the Endlands, and she was looking forward to giving Grace the news especially.

Kat's parents had been ecstatic, of course, particularly Barbara, but I'd warned her not to expect Dadda to react in the same way. He wouldn't proffer names or start making plans to paint the spare room with jungle animals.

~

Here at the end of the line, the cloud was low on the hills that looked over the shops and terraces and a cold wind cut down the street. Clitheroe was the nearest town to the valley and in the summer folk came to look around the castle or walk along the river, but by this time of year, between the jangle of the ice-cream vans and the Christmas lights, there was a drabness about the place that was inescapable.

Kat sat on a bench with her little blue going-away case between her feet and picked up the newspaper that was lying next to her. The headline was about two children who'd been attacked by dogs on a council estate in Burnley, the younger one only a year old. In the photograph that filled the front page, the little girl held her brother on her knee, her chin on top of his head as he played with a plastic dinosaur. From what I could gather, the police seemed to think that the dogs had been set on them deliberately.

Without saying anything, Kat folded the paper and put it back where she'd found it. She looked down the street and touched her belly. Little by little, it was becoming real. At six weeks, he – Kat knew that it would be a boy – was no bigger than a split pea, but there were eyes of a sort; a spine; fleshy buds that would turn into arms and legs. A few months from now, she would sense the first flutterings inside her, and then it wouldn't be long before the baby started to assert itself with heels and hands.

We waited until the station clock passed the half hour and I was about to suggest we walk around to the bus stop and see if there was still a service out towards the valley when I heard Dadda's Land-Rover coming up the road.

A flash of the lights and he swung in behind a row of taxis, the engine trying to judder its way out from under the bonnet. He'd had the thing for years. It was older than I was, driven to within an inch of its life like one of those poor Spanish burros Kat and I had seen bearing overweight tourists up to the Alhambra. A cracked headlight was held together with sellotape and the blue livery that made me think of filing cabinets was blistering at the edges. Thrift had always been a stern mistress with Dadda, and while he could patch up his heap with parts from Abbot's he wouldn't replace it.

'Sorry,' he said, when I opened the back door. 'I've been at Halewood's. You know what he's like. You go in for one thing and he tries to sell you two of summat else. Is there enough room?'

'Just about,' I said, and wedged my duffle bag and Kat's case in with the dented toolboxes, assorted boots and gloves, empty feed sacks, chains and ropes. Like an extra passenger, the straw-shit smell of the farm sat in with the junk as it always did and Kat pretended not to notice as she squeezed in next to me, closing the door on the third attempt.

'How are you, Tom?' she said, leaning across me and shaking Dadda's hand.

She knew him better than she made out; she knew that he'd have been embarrassed if she'd hugged him. She was good like that, Kat. Good at reading people, knowing how to make them feel comfortable.

'I'll be all right once the ram's better,' he replied.

'He's still not well, then?' I said.

'I think he's on the mend,' said Dadda. 'But it's hard to tell. Leith says to keep an eye on him.'

And I had no doubt that that was exactly what he'd been doing; every hour, knowing Dadda.

'Mum and Dad send their regards,' said Kat. 'They were so sorry to hear about the Gaffer. He really made our wedding day.'

Only after he'd downed a few pints, mind, and given up sulking. Then there was no stopping him. He'd still had everyone singing at two in the morning while the bar staff cleared up around them. He was a real character, everyone had said. Someone they wouldn't forget in a hurry.

'Aye, well, folk go when it's time,' said Dadda. 'That's all there is to it.'

He checked his mirror and then pulled away from the kerb and Kat looked at me. He was exactly as we'd both expected him to be and I was glad. If he'd been tearful and talkative, I wouldn't have known what to do.

~

We crossed the Ribble at Edisford Bridge and headed out on the long straight road towards the valley. Autumn was well settled here and the hay meadows were full of crows and stubbled earth waiting to be turned. Sycamores and beeches crumbled a little more with each heft of wind. Standing water shivered. Every field had been stripped back to the first decisive touches of husbandry, and the corrugations of old ridge-and-furrow stretched away to hedgerows and coppice woods.

This was the countryside that I thought about when I stood at the back of the classroom at Churchmeads and longed for the holidays to come. Before the Gaffer passed away, I'd been feeling restless for some time. I wasn't particularly unhappy in what I was doing – the boys were generally pleasant and keen to learn – but I found myself thinking about the Endlands more than I used to. I'd left when I was barely older than my Upper Sixth-Formers, and overhearing them in the quad boasting about their imaginary conquests of girls from Queen Mary's, or watching them picking at their acne in the debating club, it had begun to feel like a decision I'd made when I knew nothing about life at all. Like every teenager, I'd been itching to leave home at the earliest opportunity and hadn't even thought that there might be a cost. But a young man has certain prerogatives, doesn't he? Selfishness. Ignorance. Myopia.

If Kat had ever had similar desires to beat her own path, she'd suppressed them better than me. She was well-rooted in Suffolk and her little square of Suffolk at that. Not that she was a native (she'd been born in Harrow when her father was the stand-in vicar at Holy Trinity), but she'd lived in Dunwick since she was eleven and thought of the fields and their Constable cumulus as home. She liked being able to *see*, she said. Too much of England was hemmed in for its own good.

Clarity was measured by the churches we could name from the bedroom window. When it rained, the Reverend's place of business on the other side of the village was about all we could make out, but on good days we could cast our eyes as far as the flint tower of St Hubert's, the horizon beyond it grey where level soil became level sea.

Come the Flood, I said, we'll be set adrift. But she'd already made plans to elevate the house on stilts, she said. Won't make a difference, I said. Since the ice sheets melted, I told her, the country's been tipping on a fulcrum somewhere near Derby, the north rising, the south sinking. Give it twenty years and I'll be rowing to work, I said. We'd better migrate while we can.

She could tell, I think, that the jokes were lids on deeper wells, though she never asked me if I was happy. Probably because she knew what the answer would be.

Whenever we talked about the valley, Kat always thought of it as the setting for a part of my life that was well and truly over. Somewhere as peculiar and charming as the past. A place where she would always be a visitor and happily so. Not somewhere she thought she would ever actually live. But I was certain that when she saw the Endlands for the first time, she'd change her mind. She'd see that the place was as precious as the baby she'd be holding in her arms next Harvest.

~

On the quiet lane, Dadda put his foot down and pinked his wedding ring on the steering wheel.

'See if you can find my lighter, John,' he said, and in rummaging through the old receipts and carrier bags on the dashboard I came across the box of hollowpoints he'd bought from Halewood's.

'Christ, Dadda,' I said. 'What are you going to shoot with these?'

'I've seen deer on the moors,' he said.

'Deer?' I said. 'Are you sure? I thought they were long gone.'

I hadn't seen deer since the summer I'd left the village school.

'What's wrong with having deer on the moors?' said Kat. 'I don't understand.'

'We can't have them getting in with the sheep, love,' said

Dadda. 'They bring disease with them. I've already one animal sick. I don't need any more.'

'So what do you do?' said Kat. 'Scare them off?'

Dadda took the lighter from me when I found it under an old packet of eucalyptus cough sweets.

'It has to be a bit more permanent than that I'm afraid, love,' he said.

'You mean you kill them?' said Kat.

'Aye,' said Dadda. 'We find that works best.'

'Don't they belong to someone?' said Kat.

'What if they do?' said Dadda. 'They still need getting rid of.'

He changed gear and banged his fist against his sternum as he coughed. His *lungs* were back, then. Every year they returned at this time, like the Icelandic geese that congregated on Briardale Moss.

'You're not going up on to the moors with that chest, are you?' I said.

'It does sound nasty, Tom,' said Kat.

'I've had it worse and survived,' said Dadda.

'Even so,' I said. 'You'd better get yourself to the doctor's. I'm sure you'd be able to make an appointment tomorrow morning before the funeral, wouldn't you?'

'I've too much to do,' he said.

'Well, why doesn't John ring?' said Kat. 'He could get the doctor to come to you instead.'

He glanced at her and gave his head a little shake. He didn't like doctors much. He never had. The only doctor that had set foot on the farm lately was the one that had pronounced the Gaffer dead.

'I'm all right,' he said, and lit the roll-up that he kept behind his ear.

His hair, his face, they'd always smelled of tobacco. Tobacco and straw and the sweetish brew of damp oilskin and sweat. The scent had soaked deep into him and even after scrubbing his hands and face with the block of carbolic soap at the kitchen sink it wasn't long before it rose to the surface of his skin again. I liked to think that in a crowded room, I could have sniffed him out in a minute flat.

The cab filled with smoke and he coughed himself hoarse before winding down the window. He always smoked too much anyway but seemed to have a roll-up permanently on the go at this time of year. October was the start of the breeding cycle and the future of the flock depended on so many things that were mostly beyond his control: the sheep had to have survived the spring and summer without falling into bogs or contracting diseases; the hay needed to have matured in the barn; the ram had to be keen and the ewe willing. Those problems he could eliminate – like the red deer – were dealt with as quickly as possible.

He barked again and Kat nudged me. But it would have been pointless to try and change his mind about seeing someone. The valley made placid men stubborn, just as it made ageing men older. Especially in the autumn.

I've noticed it myself these last few years at Devil's Day and Gathering. Adam laughs at me when my shoulder creaks and calls me granddad. I worry about cartilage. I read the labels on tubes of ointment in the hope that they'll live up to their promises. There are aches and pains that keep returning as if they want something from me. The Gaffer was just the same.

When I was a child, the cold and damp sometimes used to stiffen his legs to the point of bedrest and I would be sent up with hot sweet tea that he medicated with a slug of scotch from the bottle under his pillow.

'Give us your hand, Johnny lad,' he said when he saw me looking for his injury and wedged his fag in the corner of his mouth as he untucked his shirt from his trousers.

'Feel that,' he said, and pressed my fingers against his hip. When he moved his leg, the ball and socket grated as if sand had got into the joint.

'What happened?' I said.

'A ram broke it,' he said, his fag jiggering as he spoke. 'It had a skull like a fuckin' wrecking ball. You make sure you always keep both your eyes on a ram, Johnny lad.'

The Gaffer had been knocked about more than anyone else in the valley. Not necessarily through carelessness – although one or two scars were the results of loud nights at the Croppers' Arms – but because he was of a generation that used their hands more than they used machines. He cut down the ash trees in the coppice with an axe. He used the hand-held shears that his father, Joe Pentecost, had once used, the blades still stiffly sprung after a hundred years. And not long after he'd been married he'd had to start wearing his wedding ring on his right hand after most of his holy finger, as he called it, was chewed off by one of the Beasleys' cantankerous sows.

The course of nature had eventually returned the ring (if not the knuckle bones), and he'd rinsed it under the yard tap and put it back on.

'That's horrible,' I said.

'Your grandma would have done worse than the pig if I hadn't found it,' he said.

I'd never met Grandma Alice – she died long before I was born – but from what I'd heard she was the only one who'd been willing to try and keep the Gaffer on a short lead. A proper hill woman. Hard as horn.

'You'll have hands like this one day, Johnny lad,' the Gaffer said. 'You'll be able to look at them and know that you've worked hard.'

I wanted that more than anything. I wanted hands that were different to those of the kids down in the village. I wanted nail-less fingers, welts along my heart-line, a thumb that snapped like a cap-gun when I moved it, bones that told stories. By the time I went to grammar school I had three good scars: one between my finger and thumb, one above my brow from Lennie Sturzaker's fist, and one on my elbow that I could only see in the mirror.

Kat looked out of the window as she rubbed her thumb against the calluses. She'd always liked my hands. Soon after we first met, she'd looked them over inch by inch like a palmist, finding something in the pleats and wounds that assured her of a happy future.

I suppose by today's standards it would seem as though we'd got married pretty quickly: less than eighteen months from our first drunken meeting at Amanda Stewart's thirtieth to the exchange of rings. But it didn't feel rushed at the time, and if any of our friends thought otherwise then they didn't say so. There just seemed no reason for us to wait. Another year or two wouldn't have made us any more certain about what we wanted. Over the last couple of months, though, I'd started to notice the way Kat looked whenever we happened to pass a wedding. It was the same look she had now as we drove through the hamlet of Whitewell and she watched someone sweeping up confetti and leaves from the lych-gate of the church.

'That's pretty,' she said.

It was a note of regret she'd picked up from her mother, who'd spent the whole ceremony forcing herself to smile and thinking that Kat – a vicar's daughter, for heaven's sake – should have been walking down the aisle of St Leonard's to the swell of the organ and the echo of old stone rather than giving herself to me in a council building next to the Co-op.

Of course, she thought I'd been the corruptive influence in it all, and couldn't (or wouldn't) see that she might have had a hand in it herself. As soon as we'd announced our engagement, Barbara had started directing the wedding day and, to wrest back some control, Kat told her one evening at the dinner table that she needn't worry any more about deciding on the hymns or readings – we'd already been in touch with the registrar at the town hall and had a slot booked for June the fifth. A slot? The word stuck in Barbara's throat. We'd booked a slot? It sounded like we were going to see a ski instructor rather than getting married.

She'd cried all the way through the clafoutis she'd made for dessert and then on and off for the next six months until the taxi came to take her and the Reverend to the Registry Office. Outwardly, Kat asserted that this was what she wanted to the last, but as we sat on the leather benches waiting for our turn, I could tell that she wished she'd never started to plough that particular furrow. To be honest, I think she would have given anything to have been married in church. Lace, bells, a choir in ruffs. All that.

'You and Mrs Pentecost had a church wedding, didn't you?' she said to Dadda.

'Aye, love,' he said.

'In the village?'

'At St Michael's, aye,' said Dadda.

'John's shown me pictures of his mum,' said Kat. 'She was very beautiful.'

She wasn't. Not beautiful, as such. But Dadda gave her a sort of smile and put his eyes back on the road.

Kat began to say something else then stopped short when we came out of the trees and the ravine to the left was exposed. There was nothing to stop a car from shearing off into the white stream below but a flimsy barrier of wire and wool tufts. But Dadda had driven the road in all weathers, at all times of the day and night, and took the bends unfazed by the drop.

The wind got stronger the higher we went and I felt Kat's hand tighten on mine. By the time we'd come to Syke House – the sullen, red-brick mansion set back from the lane in a knot of horse chestnut trees – it had risen to a gale and sent branches and leaves skittering off along the Cutting, as the road from here on in was called.

For three miles, or thereabouts, it wound northwards through the hills before it came to Wyresdale and dropped down towards the market towns and the byways that led to the ports along the coast. A packhorse route that had been here for centuries, even though the passage through the hills was bleak and boggy.

'Ah, but folk are like water, Johnny lad,' the Gaffer said. 'They always find a way through. No matter what's underfoot.'

The road had always been at the mercy of the weather and he remembered the Cutting being nothing more than a dirt track that softened to butter in the autumn, and in the summer kicked up dust that marked its meander in a thick brown haze. After even the briefest of rainstorms, the top layer of it would run like a river and horses would have to trudge the miles knee-deep, dragging the carts like sledges. In the worst winters the valley could be cut off for days. After the Blizzard, it was weeks before anyone got in or out. By that time, what had happened there, what the Devil had done, was already fable.

~

To this day there's no road sign to the village of Underclough or the few houses of the Endlands. Anyone who needs to come to the Briardale Valley knows where they are, and if a stranger asks for directions then they're told to turn between the abattoir and the three beech trees that keep that part of the lane in permanent shade.

They were each at least eighty or ninety feet tall, elephantine and twisted, old even in Joe Pentecost's time, the Gaffer used to tell me. He'd given them names too.

'But once I put them in your head, Johnny lad,' he said, 'you can't let them out again. Trees are funny about things like that.'

I'd kept my word. I hadn't told anyone. Not Dadda. Not Kat. I've not even told Adam, who at ten – the age of curious digging – would feast upon the knowledge. Perhaps the names might conjure up something to help him picture them. I mean, what does he think a tree looks like? How can he imagine height? I've lifted him up and sat him on a branch and he's listened to the wind blowing in the topmost leaves, but for all he knows the trunk that he touches might carry on rising into the clouds, like the beanstalk in the fairy tale.

From the mouth of the valley it's at least a couple of miles to Underclough and there's nothing much to see at first. A few broken walls. That wooden trailer that's been rotting away for years. It's quiet enough for a weasel to take its time crossing the lane. The grass and the bracken is never cut or tamed and thickens each year with the brambles and the sedge.

Kat looked out of the window as the cloud drifted over the crags like battle-smoke, shrouding and revealing the holly bushes and the rowan trees that grew in the clefts. It began to rain in needles and then wheatstraws and Dadda set the wipers going in a shuddering arc.

The lane came closer to the River Briar as it flashed past in spate and stuck close to the banks all the way to the village. When the first buildings appeared, I could tell that Kat was disappointed. I think she'd expected to find Underclough nestled in the valley, not dark and cramped like something buried at the bottom of a bag. She hadn't imagined it would be so overgrown either, so loud with water, nor the fells above too steep for anything to cast a long shadow.

'It's quite sweet, really, isn't it?' she said, though she didn't need to be polite for Dadda's sake. He'd have been the first to agree that the place was run-down and abandoned. The lane had become potholed and grassy, and on the other side of the river the old woollen mill – *Arncliffe's* to everyone in the valley – had been derelict since the Gaffer was young. It had started life as a humble cottage industry, and even though the addition of weaving sheds and an extra storey by subsequent generations had made it the largest building in Underclough, it still looked small beneath the fells.

'Oh, that's such a shame,' said Kat, looking across the river. 'I'd love to have seen it running.'

But she'd come more than eighty years too late. The sheds hadn't been in operation since the Great War, when they turned out yards of khaki serge and thick, durable blankets for the military hospitals. In the years that followed, with half the workforce dead and the empire countries with cheaper labour and looms of their own, the company that owned the mill floundered and went into receivership. Some time back in the twenties the roof had collapsed, and the pediment into which the Arncliffe name had been engraved lay in pieces on the ground.

Since then, from what I know, it's changed hands half a dozen times and there have been plans now and then to level the site and build houses. Or, more recently, when it became fashionable to live in the remains of industry, to turn the existing building into apartments. But nothing ever happens and year by year it falls further into disrepair. Its windows are all covered in steel plates now, but back when the Gaffer passed away they were open to the elements, having been broken one after the other by the village kids.

The river under its looming presence was whisky-coloured and thick on the banks with the nettles and hogweed that had, as always, gone wild in the summer and overgrown the millrace.

Crumbling now and green with moss, the brick-built structure had once siphoned off some of the water down a steep drop to power the wheel, which was still intact even if it only now collected the detritus that the river carried here, or what the villagers threw in. Decades of silting had also raised the water level, so that the steps quickly disappeared into a stagnant well that undulated with branches and leaves, beer cans and crisp packets. I'd always stayed well away from the river by Arncliffe's. Fall in and you'd struggle to get out again. Hands and feet would find no grip on the slimy brickwork. And your last breath would take in a mouthful of fag ends and turds.

I hadn't told Kat – why would she have wanted to know? – but the summer I'd left primary school they'd found Lennie Sturzaker there one afternoon rising and falling with the debris.

Along with many of my classmates, he'd lived on New Row, the terrace of eighteen workers' cottages on this side of the river. Like everything that had been built here in the valley, the houses were made of a brown sooty brick that the damp air made darker still. Mind you, they'd been forward-thinking types, the Arncliffes, and a small allotment had been set aside at the back of each so that the mill workers could grow their own vegetables and raise a fruit tree. A few were still used in that way, but most had been left to go to seed or flagged over for the sole purpose, it seemed, of giving hard-standing to rusting motorbikes and broken ovens.

There was a permanent smell of coal fires here and the smoke from the chimneys rose through the rain and lingered as a cindery mist in the trees. On days like this, the streetlights came on early and folk stayed at home, leaving the village to the jackdaws, which had always nested here in great numbers and made more noise than the river.

A gang of them took off from the bridge as Dadda approached and flapped away to the roof of Beckfoot's. Bay-fronted and painted in a mutton-coloured gloss, the butcher's hadn't changed much since I used to come down with the Gaffer when he had pheasants or snipe to sell. He wouldn't ever get very much for them, enough for a few games of gin rummy in the pub on Saturday night, but it was a good excuse to probe Alun Beckfoot about the village rumours that had found their way down to the Endlands. Who'd done this or that. Who'd been seen in the Croppers' Arms. Who was on his last legs. Who was always at number eight when her husband was on nights. If they looked over at me while they talked, then it was an indication that I shouldn't be listening and I moved to the other end of the counter to watch the Beckfoot brothers in the prep-room hacking and slicing behind the threadbare plastic strips. They did everything so quickly that it was hard to understand how they managed to last a single minute without severing something vital. And yet I never saw any of the Beckfoot family bleeding or bandaged. Alun, especially, had hands that didn't look as if they'd been anywhere near a meat cleaver or a bone saw. He had hands like a woman's, in fact. Pale and hairless with slender fingers that would have better suited a piano player. That they were so pristine was astonishing, especially given his lazy eye. But then I suppose that a clumsy butcher doesn't stay a butcher for long – and perhaps his affliction had forced him to take extra care with the knives.

'He's got the lamb for Devil's Day, has he?' I said, watching Beckfoot switching the sign from OPEN to CLOSED, and Dadda nodded.

'Aye,' he said. 'The Gaffer took it down last week.'

'I'd never heard of Devil's Day before I met John,' Kat said to Dadda.

'No, well, you wouldn't have done,' he said.

'And it's when Bill plays the fiddle, I hear,' said Kat with a smile. 'I can't imagine him doing that somehow.'

'We're all expected to perform,' I said.

'Even me?' said Kat.

'You can sing,' I said. 'I've heard you.'

'I don't know the songs they sing here, though,' she said.

'You'll pick them up quick enough,' I said.

'I bet the Gaffer enjoyed it, didn't he?' said Kat.

'It's a day for the children,' said Dadda, 'so I dare say he did.'

'Come on, Dadda,' I said. 'I've never heard you complain on the night.'

'The whole thing's daft,' he said. 'I don't know why we bother with it any more. It's a waste of a good animal.'

The stew that we had on Devil's Day was always made with the meat of the lamb that was born first in the spring; male or female, it didn't matter. As soon as it slithered out into the straw it was ear-tagged with a red label so that it could be easily picked out of the flock when it got closer to the time. Then we'd take it down to Beckfoot's and he'd cut its throat and leave it to hang for a week before he butchered it. The rump was diced for the pot, Beckfoot got a leg, and whatever was left over split into thirds for the chest freezer at each farm, enough for several meals over the winter. Kat said that it sounded as though everyone went into hibernation here. And it was true, I suppose. Come November, Dadda didn't leave the valley all that often. There was no reason to do so. The larder was full, the scullery dangled with rabbits and birds, and anything else he needed he could get from Wigton's.

'Is this the place you were telling me about?' said Kat, wiping away some of the condensation so she could see the village shop. 'God, you're right. It's just the same as Granny and Grandpa's.'

It was one of those corner cornucopias that anywhere else would have long since fallen by the wayside, as the place Kat's grandparents once owned in Felixstowe had done. Its windows were covered in a uriney cellophane to stop the goods from fading in the sunlight, though they ought to have been more concerned about them fading with old age. The display looked exactly the same as it had always done: toy boats, fishing nets, trashy Westerns on a stiff carousel, jigsaws – so many jigsaws – of castles and harbours and soft-focus kittens; boxes and boxes of Hornby train track and every type of bridge and locomotive, enough to fashion a complete pre-Beeching fantasia.

The Wigtons' son, Davy, had been in my class at school. Always red-cheeked and sweaty, he worked as a cleaner at the abattoir, shovelling up innards and collecting sheep heads in a trolley. From what the Gaffer used to tell me, he was still as put upon as he had been at the age of eleven by Sam Sturzaker and Jason Earby and Mike Moorcroft, those classmates of ours who, like him, had gone to work at the slaughterhouse as soon as they'd left school. Pigton Wigton, they called him, Piggy Wiggy. They'd drop an eyeball in his tea, leave a trotter in his coat pocket, slip a sow's ear into the sandwich that his mam wrapped up for him every morning. Pigton Wigton. Piggy Wiggy. Mummy's Little Piglet.

But they couldn't say much when they all still lived with their parents too: the Sturzakers and Earbys next to one another on New Row; the Moorcrofts in the second of the Nine Cottages, which sat between Wigton's and the school. They were some of the oldest buildings in the village, the Nine Cottages, and it was hard to imagine that they'd ever looked any different: sagging and flaking and meek as alms-houses. Each tiny plot separated from the next by a fence of varying height and material, replaced or repaired with whatever had been to hand at the time of need. Most of the front gardens were overgrown and children's bicycles and plastic toys sat deep in the weeds, making the last two houses seem out of place with their painted facias and little rectangles of clipped grass. A pair of old boys – Laurence Dewhurst and Clive Ward – stood in their dripping doorways talking to one another as they drank tea and smoked. When they saw us driving past they both looked and nodded, confused by the sight of Kat in the Pentecosts' Land-Rover, as they were confused by any deviation from the normal way of things.

Nothing changed in Underclough. Nothing happened. Not really. The headlines that came and went from the *Lancashire Gazette* newsboard on the street outside Wigton's only reiterated what everyone here already knew: that elsewhere was always a place where the worst things happened. Take those two little children in Burnley, mauled by dogs.

The rest of the village went by and Kat smiled as she saw for the first time what I'd been describing to her ever since we'd met. We came to my school, Dadda's school, the Gaffer's school, a brownstone barn with a cockerel weathervane and a bell on the roof. The playground was noiseless and strewn with puddles, the windows of the Infant classroom plastered with sugar-paper autumn leaves and pumpkins, silhouettes of stealthy cats and witches riding broomsticks. Halloween was a few days away and the village kids would soon be out trick-or-treating, the little ones working their way along New Row and the teenagers lighting bangers in the graveyard. We'd never bothered with all that in the Endlands. We had Devil's Day instead.

Kat turned in her seat and smiled. It amused her, I could tell, to imagine me as a little boy barely older than the ones she looked after at the nursery. 'It's lovely,' she said. 'It's so tiny.'

It was true. Whenever I came back here, I wondered how the

yard had ever contained us all at breaktimes. And the field, I was certain, had once been wide enough for athletic prowess to be demonstrated or disproved.

It had been because I'd beaten Lennie Sturzaker by a country mile that he'd collared me after school one afternoon and given me a black eye to save his shame. He'd have swollen the other one too, if I hadn't extracted myself from his wrestling hold and run off through the graveyard. Threats and promises came after me but I was quickly over the railings and down in Archangel Back, that short alleyway of grassed-over concrete between the church grounds and Sullom Wood.

It was always the place – and still is now – where the older kids in the village went to smoke and drink and do things to each other that sounded painful. Perhaps in an effort to dissuade the next generation from doing the same, we were given warnings at school now and then about Archangel Back being church property and that if we were to go there we'd be trespassing and the police would be called and so on, but no one took much notice and no one in authority ever came. It was hard to imagine that anyone really cared about St Michael's any more at all. In Dadda's day, folk were married there and the villagers held their babies over the font, but I'd only ever known it used for departures.

The stump of a bell-tower made it more of a chapel than a church, and as we drove past, it looked even more dilapidated than it had in the spring. Wet, rotting leaves had turned the slates green and the flashings at the top of the downspouts had been left half-peeled by thieves who had either come ill-equipped or had been scared away before they could strip off the lead. There might have been a commendable, last-stand defiance about the place – it was still there, it still squared up to the Croppers' Arms like an old adversary, as it always had done. But perhaps unsurprisingly, the pub had fared better in this war of attrition and the hanging baskets of ferns lauded it over the weedy plot of tombstones where, the following morning, there would be a new addition.

It was still hard to believe that the Gaffer was dead. That he wouldn't be there at the farmhouse when we arrived. That he had gone to join the other deceased Pentecosts, like his father, Joe, and his brother, Philip, whose name was spattered with lichen on the war memorial with a dozen others. Still, it seemed right that a Pentecost was fixed there, as a reminder that what lay beyond the stone cross belonged to the farmers. Here, the Endlands began and the lane ran into the gloom of Sullom Wood.

At this time of year, the place was almost silent, the leaves and sodden windfall gently mouldering in the ditches. It's how Adam knows it's the end of autumn, that smell. That and the sound of me chopping wood in the yard. That and the taste of the blackberry jam we always make in spades for the larder. And in those days, I tell him, the Wood in autumn was the kingdom of Owd Abraham, the Beasleys' boar. An inelegant but industrious gardener who would snout up the rootballs of ferns and chew the bracken so that, come the spring, the trees in the ash coppice would have room and light to grow. Not that we ever saw much of him. As the season wore on, he roamed deeper and deeper into the trees, looking for acorns and mushrooms until Angela came to collect him a few days before Christmas.

About halfway along the lane, Dadda slowed to a halt as smoke drifted out of the trees and he explained the real reason for his cough.

'We had a fire here yesterday,' he said. 'Further in, next to the river.'

'Jesus, Dadda. Why didn't you tell me?' I said.

'What difference would it have made?' he said. 'You weren't here, were you? Anyway, it's out now.'

'It doesn't look like it,' I said, watching the smoke moving between the trunks.

'It's just smouldering,' he said.

'Was it a bad fire?' said Kat.

'I don't think there's ever a good one, is there?' said Dadda.

'I mean, was there much damage?' Kat said.

'Enough,' Dadda replied, looking out of his window. 'It took us most of the afternoon to dampen it down.'

'You tackled it yourselves?' said Kat. 'Did no one call the fire brigade?'

'The place would have been nowt but ash by the time they got all the way out here, love,' said Dadda.

'How did it start?' I said.

'Bill's convinced it were the Sturzakers' lad,' said Dadda.

'What, Vinny?' I said. 'Well, it wouldn't surprise me.'

Whenever I came back to the valley, I'd often see Vinny Sturzaker being yanked along New Row as he took one of his granddad's huge mastiffs for a shit by the river. He was only ten but he could stare with contempt and derision as well as any of the teenagers that hung about Archangel Back. He was light-fingered, too, and whenever he went into the village shop Mrs Wigton guarded the front counter, while Mr Wigton straightened magazines and bags of washers or whatever was close to where Vinny was making a pretence of browsing.

'A child wouldn't do this,' said Kat. 'Surely they wouldn't.'

'If Vinny Sturzaker's anything like his dad,' I said, 'then he'd have lit the match and not given it a second thought.'

'You sound like Bill,' said Dadda.

'Well, who else would it have been?' I said.

'I don't know,' said Dadda. 'It might not have been anybody at all.'

'Has no one in the village said anything?' I asked.

'Betty Ward reckons she saw Vinny going into the Wood,' said Dadda. 'But that doesn't mean owt. She reckons she sees a lot of things, doesn't she?'

'Maybe she was right this time,' I said.

'God knows,' said Dadda. 'Anyway, it's over with now. I can't waste any more time worrying about it when I've the sheep to gather.'

A gust of wind sent spatters of rain and beechnuts punking down on to the roof of the Land-Rover and he set off again. Kat held my hand and didn't let go until we were out of the trees.

Here, the lane ran past the Dyers' place, with its long barn of honking geese and moaning Ayrshires, and into rougher, open ground. Dadda had told me that it had been raining on and off here all week, sometimes in storms that lasted a day. The Endlands looked saturated. By the roadside, the brown ferns sagged and the reedbeds heaved, and beyond them the Briar was wide and brawling, almost touching the underside of the concrete bridge that led up to the Beasleys' farm. It had already flooded the edge of the field where they'd once kept their horses – that trio of elderly stallions that they couldn't bear to see go for glue or fertiliser. They'd belonged to Jim, rather than Angela, like all the decrepit animals he gave sanctuary to when he was alive. All through my childhood, the Beasleys' place had been home to limping dogs and blinded donkeys, earless cats and, for a time, a scabby peacock that we could hear wailing from our side of the valley. The Beasleys. I use the plural out of habit. There was only Angela left with that name.

The Pentecost farm was the last of the three smallholdings. A cream-coloured cottage, a lambing shed, an outhouse and a hay barn all clustered around the bye-field used for flushing and tupping. Everything dwarfed by the fells behind.

For generations we'd kept sheep, just as the Dyers had always bred geese and dairy cows, and on the other side of the river the slope up to the Beasleys' place had been named Swine Hill after the gingery Tamworth pigs that had nosed the mud there for as long as anyone could remember.

After Dadda's farm, the lane continued past two small hay fields and came to an end at a metal gate. Beyond that was Briardale Moss, a mile-wide stretch of reeds and marshes that led to Fiendsdale Clough and the path up to the moorland pastures.

And that was the valley.

~

The turning to the farm was sharp and Dadda slowed to a crawl before he spun the wheel and crackled through the loose stones to the gate.

'Get it open then,' he said, and Kat and I stepped out into the rain.

Dadda's two dogs emerged barking and jumping, more teeth than terrible like all collies, and slunk through the bars. Musket he'd had for a number of years now – a good lad, sharp and obedient, quick to chastise the younger Fly, who the Gaffer had bought in the summer to replace old Tubs. But she was too immature, Dadda had told me on the phone the week before, happier to piss about than work. And in the background, I'd heard the Gaffer setting him straight. I think that would have been the last time I heard his voice. Two days later he was dead.

Fly came sniffing at our ankles and Kat backed away with one hand on the wall, as if she were going to clamber up and perch on the top. She didn't trust dogs. As a child, she'd been bitten by her aunt's Alsatian at the Young Apostles Club and the scars were still there erotically high up on her inner thigh like scattered grains of rice.

Kat had always hated the YAC (as it was billed on the poster pinned to the church notice-board) but had no choice about going every Wednesday night. It was Barbara's pet project, to give herself something to do while the Reverend was chairing the roof restoration committee or leading the discussions at Share and Care. She'd formed the group with her elder sister, Ellen – twice married, off men, stuck on her own with a sickly dog that had to be taken everywhere she went and three boisterous sons that she hoped God would fill with quietude or combust with a lightning bolt: either would be fine. In all, a dozen children or so came to the vicarage each week and once they'd finished singing hymns or acting out Bible stories and they'd been sent off into the garden, the session generally devolved into an opportunity for Barbara to despair over her daughter's oddities. There was the collection of dead flies she kept in a Tupperware box. The savage haircut she'd given herself the day of her nativity play (but at least she was a shepherd and not an angel and the mess could be hidden under a tea towel). The habit she had of playing the Reverend's Mahler records at full volume whenever anyone important came round.

Then, when she ought to have been searching the garden for signs of spring (and God's love for the earth) with all the other children, she was down to her knickers in the greenhouse trying to dress Auntie Ellen's dog in one of Daddy's ties to play weddings. No wonder she'd been bitten.

Of course, it wasn't really the peculiarities themselves that upset Barbara – all children are eccentric in one way or another – but the fact that Kat wielded them so knowingly. The Reverend said that he'd told her time and again that the more fuss she made the more Kat would antagonise her, but this only made Barbara feel worse. She couldn't understand what she'd done to deserve her little girl's hostility. Why her daughter would plan, actually plan, to embarrass her in front of other people. And how could she so happily cut off her nose, or hair, to spite her face?

'You know, I think Barbara was quite shocked,' the Reverend said to me one afternoon as I helped him weed his allotment, 'that Katherine turned out to be like her.'

They tried their best to get on, Kat and Barbara, but like all people who are too similar to one another it didn't take much for them to fall out. The evening we'd heard the news about the Gaffer, Kat had called her to let her know and ended up rowing on the phone. The living room door slammed shut and when Kat came heavy-footed up the stairs I knew better than to ask what had happened straight away. I let her have a bath, as she often did when she wanted to calm down, and then, rubbing her hair with a towel, she came into the study where I was marking a batch of *Macbeth* essays.

'Mum doesn't want me to go to the farm,' she said.

'Why not?' I said.

'Why do you think?' she said, looking down at her belly.

'What, because you're pregnant?' I said.

'Isn't it ridiculous?' said Kat. 'What does she think's going to happen, for Christ's sake?'

'She's just worried about you,' I said. 'First grandchild and all that.'

'Don't defend her, John,' said Kat. 'She'd have me quarantined from now until my due date if she had her way.'

'Come on,' I said. 'She's not that bad.'

'I'm not exaggerating,' said Kat, patting her chest dry. 'I worry about her, the fuss she makes all the time. I wonder if she's got some kind of disorder. Seriously.'

From the sound of it, Barbara had imagined Dadda's place to be permanently swathed in a pestilent vapour, one lungful of which would be enough to dissolve a foetus like a salted slug. It was an impression she'd formed after sitting next to him at the reception, I think. She hadn't noticed me watching her, but whenever Dadda answered her questions about the farm, her eyes had flicked to his hands, intrigued by their potato colour and how he could be so unconcerned about eating with them. But they'd been perfectly clean. The muck was under the skin.

Musket nosed at Kat's hands and Fly barked and turned in a circle, excited by the smell of someone new.

'Go on,' said Kat, nudging her with her knee. 'Go on.'

Dadda leaned out of his window and shouted both the dogs away to their kennels. Kat stood back and I pushed the gate through its scale of squeals and moans until it came to rest against the Gaffer's old Ford tractor, which was now more rust than metal.

In fact, most things here were suffering from the corrosive urges of nature. Babylonian greenery hung from the gutters; a downpipe had broken free of the twine that was holding it to the wall and shattered; the lean-to that Dadda and the Gaffer had built one summer had rotted out of all usefulness. It was exactly the same at the Dyers' and the Beasleys' too. Living on the farms was one endless round of maintenance. Nothing was ever finished. Nothing was ever settled. Nothing. Everyone here died in the midst of repairing something. Chores and damage were inherited.

Kat watched as Dadda drove through the open gate and parked by the house. With the engine off, there was nothing to hear but the sounds of the river, the birds, the wind, the rain. As I closed the gate and we walked up the yard, the downpour turned heavier still, obscuring the valley we'd driven through and the ridges above. Between the cobblestones ran a delta of streams brown with straw and slurry. Water dribbled from the sills, discharged from spouts, swelled the drains, pounded up a mist that stank of dung. On the fellside above the farm, Gutter Clough lived up to its name and spilled past the house towards the river.

Kat held her hand over her nose and stepped quickly around the puddles as Dadda came over from the Land-Rover. The three of us dripped in the porchway and Dadda closed the door on the rain.

'Go in,' he said. 'It's open.'

No one ever locked up in the Endlands.

The Gaffer had only been gone a few days, but the place already strained with his ghost. The hallway was steeped in the sharp cologne that he used to pat on to his stubble before he went to the pub and the tobacco he used to smoke – Old Holborn, usually, and sometimes a little sprinkle of whatever the teenagers had on them in Archangel Back.

'I wouldn't hang your coat there, love,' said Dadda, nodding at the stand next to the telephone. 'It'll smell.'

Kat unpegged her denim jacket and looked at me, wondering what she should do with it, and followed him into the kitchen.

'Mind your step,' he said, indicating the pool oozing out from under the sink. 'I thought I'd fixed it but it's still weeping from somewhere.'

He put the hollowpoints on the dresser and threw down a couple of towels to soak up the water. Kat smiled as well as she could and looked around the kitchen at the cracked plaster and the dusty ornaments. The clothes steaming on a wooden rack. The piles of clutter. She was thinking about Mam, I could tell. A woman's touch, she was thinking.

'The beds are set up for you,' said Dadda. 'Take your things upstairs. The others will be here soon.'

~

Whenever anyone from the farms died, everyone gathered together on the night before the funeral. Dadda wouldn't have stopped them coming, of course, but hated to be fussed over, and once the first arrivals, the Dyers, had appeared, he absented himself and went to check on the ram.

I could hear Bill and Laurel bickering as they came down the hallway, though they were all smiles by the time they got to the kitchen. With a brown paper bag in her hand, Laurel held the door open for her husband, who came in with a large tray of roast goose. They were both in their best clothes: she in a dress dotted with little rose heads, he in the green wool suit he'd sported at our wedding.

No matter how long I was away from the Endlands, Bill never looked any different. Bearded and bear-like. Teeth rabbit-brown from the fags.

'All right, John?' he said, and went to put the goose down on the sideboard before shaking my hand. 'I can't believe the owd sod's gone, can you?'

'No,' I said.

'Mind you, eighty-six isn't bad, is it?' he said.

'For here, it's a bloody miracle,' I said.

'And he went while he were working,' said Bill. 'It's how he would have wanted it.'

'I'm sure you're right,' I said.

The customary exchange of assumptions about the dead over with, he came to what he really wanted to talk about.

'Your dad's told you about the fire, I take it?'

'He said you thought it was Vinny Sturzaker?' I said.

'I don't think it were him,' said Bill. 'I know it were him, the little bastard.'

'What will you do?' I said. 'Go and see him?'

'If your owd man lets me off the chain, aye,' he said, winking at Kat.

'How are you, Bill?' she said.

He wiped his fingers on his jacket – the grease off the tin was all right for me but not her – and planted a kiss on her cheek.

'You're looking well, love,' he said and kept hold of her shoulders until Laurel asked him to go and fetch the potatoes out of the truck.

'You tell him to keep his hands to himself, Katherine, love,' she said. 'And how are you, John?'

'Bearing up,' I said. 'It feels strange him not being here.'

She held my arms and smiled. Since her Jeff had got out the month before, Dadda said she was happier than she'd been in a long time, but the years of worry had taken their toll and there was a gauntness about her that made her look much older than she was. Her sight was getting worse, too; the thick glasses she wore made much of the mole on her eyelid and emphasised the bags.

'We're all missing the Gaffer so much here,' she said. 'It's like summat's been torn out of the farm.'

'It must have been a shock to you,' said Kat. 'Even though he was an old man.'

'It were, love,' said Laurel. 'But at least he'll have found some peace now.'

She smiled at Kat and brought the little Christ she wore round her neck to her lips.

Laurel was an oddity in the Endlands; no one but her had any interest in religion at all. The children of the three families might have been attending the Catholic primary in Underclough since it had been built, and gone through the Three-Cs of Confession, Communion and Confirmation, but only because it was easier than travelling miles to a different school. In the same way, a Christian burial was just a necessary bit of theatre that meant the dear departed could stay in the valley.

But I had to remind myself that this was all still quite new to her. Twelve months earlier, she'd been as godless as the rest of them in the Endlands. Her Damascene moment had come when Betty Ward had taken her to hear a talk at the town hall by an ex-convict who had been steered into a life of charitable deeds after a ghostly visitation in his cell. He had already donated a kidney to a man in Blackburn and now he was running a marathon to raise money for famine victims in Somalia.

Prayer, he said; that was what had changed him. It had been the whispered wishes of the Christian world for men like him to be saved that had brought the spirit of Padre Pio to Strangeways. Prayer worked. He was the proof. And Laurel, for one, had been convinced. There was hope for her Jeff yet.

With her new-found faith, Dadda had happily let her assume the responsibility of organising the Gaffer's funeral. She had selected the readings and the hymns and typed up the Order of Service, which she was especially keen to show Kat, who, being a vicar's daughter, would be able to validate the choices she'd made.

'I thought we'd start with "Abide With Me",' said Laurel, smoothing out the crumpled sheet of paper. 'And then "The Lord is My Shepherd", after the reading from John. You know the one, I'm sure. "In my father's house are many rooms"?'

'Yes,' said Kat, 'I know it.'

'The bidding prayers I wrote myself,' said Laurel. 'I don't know what you think.'

She was fishing for compliments and Kat took the bait.

'They're lovely,' she said, 'really heartfelt,' and Laurel smiled and blessed her and told her how pretty she was before being called to open the kitchen door by Bill.

'He's whining like a bloody baby out there,' he said.

'Well, you wanted to bring him,' said Laurel and turned to Kat.

'It's our Douglas,' she said, helping Bill carry the dishes to the table. 'We didn't want to leave him at home on his own.'

Douglas was a tetchy old Rottweiler that was always at the Dyers' gate baring his teeth no matter who came to their farm, friend or foe. He was more than capable of looking after himself, so why they'd brought him with them I couldn't imagine.

'Is he all right?' I said. 'He's not ill, is he?'

'No, he's fine,' said Laurel. 'It's just with the fire yesterday, well, you can't be too careful, can you?'

'Your dad would do well to make sure his doors are locked, John,' said Bill. 'I did tell him to. Anyone could walk through that gate.'

'Anyone?' I said.

'I mean the Sturzakers,' said Bill.

'You're not worried about little Vinny, are you?' I said.

'You haven't seen what he did to the Wood,' Bill replied.

'It's just a precaution,' said Laurel. 'Until we find out what happened.'

The Dyers went down into the scullery together – Laurel to fetch the blackberry wine and Bill to try and drag Dadda away from the ram – and started arguing again. They could never agree on the simplest of things and the meekness that had come with Laurel's conversion had started to grate on Bill more and more. She'd lived in the valley for thirty years, but had never seemed a farmer's wife at all.

Not like Angela Beasley, who came in now, swelling her orange roll-neck jumper. She was a large, breasty woman. A mother hen, grown rounder each year since her husband, Jim, had died.

'Here he is at last,' she said and smoothed the skin under my eyes with her thumbs, looking for damage and finding plenty as usual.

'Christ, has she been feeding you?' she said, nodding to Kat. 'There's nowt of you, lad.'

'She looks after me very well,' I said. 'Don't you, Kat?'

'I do my best,' said Kat.

'The pair of you look like you need a good meal inside you,' said Angela. 'Especially you, lady.'

'Well, that's what I've come for,' said Kat. 'Fresh air and a good appetite.'

'And hard work, I hope,' said Angela.

'Of course,' said Kat.

Angela took hold of her hands and looked at her fingers, slim and white as roots.

'Will they do?' said Kat.

'She's stronger than she looks,' I said.

'That's just as well,' said Angela, standing back and studying her. 'Mind you, I think I'd better fetch over some of Liz's owd clothes.'

'It's all right, I hardly ever put this on nowadays,' said Kat, pulling at her lemon-coloured dress. 'I don't mind if it gets dirty.'

'I'm not worried about that,' said Angela. 'You can get yourself as filthy as you like. It's just that you're not going to be much use to us if you're freezing to death, are you?'

'I've brought some sweaters,' said Kat.

'You put your good clothes back in your suitcase,' said Angela. 'You won't need them here.'

Other voices came from the hallway and Grace appeared at the kitchen door.

'Hi,' said Kat and kissed her on the cheek. 'It's so good to see you again. How have you been? Nice lipstick.'

Grace said nothing and kept her hands by her side. Kat smiled and frowned and then tried again.

'You've got taller,' she said, holding her hand above Grace's head. 'You'll shoot past me in another few months.'

Grace humoured her with a nod and started picking at the edges of the flesh-coloured plaster on her palm.

'War wound, is it?' I said and she ignored me and carried on, chewing gum as she leant against the door frame.

Despite her first experiments with make-up, she was looking more and more like Angela every time I came back to the valley; the moonish features and coppery hair had skipped a generation and landed firmly on her. She was in her final year at the village school and glad to be leaving. She'd never got on with the other children, especially Vinny Sturzaker. I hadn't told Kat, but not long after we'd seen Grace at the wedding, he'd twisted her arm so hard in a playground fight that he'd almost dislocated her shoulder.

'Come on, Grace, shift,' said Liz, giving her a nudge from behind.

With a glance over her shoulder at her mother, Grace did as she was told and sat down glumly on a chair with her arms folded. Kat smiled to reassure her that she understood what she was going through. If she didn't want to talk, then that was fine.

This was Grace's first proper experience of death and it had unsettled her. She'd adored the Gaffer and he'd doted on her, as he did with all children born in the Endlands; they were assurances that when he went the place would carry on. But it wasn't just that the Gaffer was dead. The way Liz looked at her, I could tell that Grace was in trouble about something.

'Are you in the dog-house today?' I said, and she looked out of the window.

'Oh, just ignore her,' said Liz and shifted the large plastic bag of ivy she was holding from one hand to the other so that she could kiss me.

'Did you hear about the fire in the wood?' she said.

'It sounds like you had a job on your hands,' I said.

'It's just as well it was on the riverbanks and we had water handy to put it out,' said Liz. 'Otherwise I don't know what we would have done. Aren't you cold in that, Mrs Pentecost?'

Kat looked down at her dress. 'I'm fine,' she said.

'Have you lost more weight an' all?' said Liz.

'I don't think so,' Kat replied, putting her hands where Liz was staring and smiling with the anticipation of telling everyone that she'd soon be swelling in that very place.

'You don't need to starve yourself any more, you know,' said Liz and dumped the ivy on the sideboard. 'You're married now. You got him.'

'You certainly did,' said Laurel, coming up from the scullery with the wine and patting my shoulder. 'And make sure you keep him, love. They're all good men, the Pentecosts.'

'I know,' said Kat.

'It were such a lovely day, your wedding,' said Laurel. 'And you had the time of your life, didn't you, Grace? Dancing all night.'

Grace looked at her and then went back to peeling off the corner of the plaster.

'Leave it alone, Grace, for God's sake,' said Liz. 'You don't want it getting infected, do you?'

'Come on, miss, make yourself useful,' said Angela, flapping open the large rectangle of plaid that was used when everyone came round to eat. Grace got up and began to smooth the cloth over the table, still not talking to anyone, and Angela put her hands on her shoulders and started to sing.

Oh, the day is done, the harvest's won –
The apples and the hay.
The leaves will wither on the bough,
And all will fall by Devil's Day.

'The Gaffer sang those owd songs so well,' said Laurel.

'Aye, he sang them in tune,' said Liz, and Angela stuck out her tongue and carried on.

Hang the lamb and pour the wine,
Play the fiddle bold
Devil sleep upon the fire
Until the sheep are in the fold.

Adam knows the story behind the song. We tell it every year on Devil's Day. It's important to remember why we do what we do, I say to him. It's important to know what our grandfathers have passed down to us.

After the Blizzard, once they'd buried the dead and things started to return to normal in the valley, it was agreed that the Devil must have gone back to the moors. And so, for several years, the farmers kept their sheep down in the Endlands and out of his reach.

But there was only so much land that could be used for grazing. The Moss was dangerous with its sucking marshes, and corralling the ewes in the hay meadows or in the fields by Sullom Wood eventually churned up the earth so much that nothing grew. After a few years, they had no choice but to take the ewes and their new-borns back to the high pastures and let the fields in the valley rejuvenate.

There was much debate about what ought to be done. Would the shepherds have to stay on the moors all summer in case the Devil tried to take the sheep? And if he did, what could they do about it? Thirteen people had died in the valley. When the Devil was determined, it took a brave man to stand in his way. And if the Owd Feller was asleep, who was to say that he wouldn't wake up and disguise himself again?

It was Joe Pentecost, the Gaffer said, who suggested that they wake the Devil themselves, an idea that was met with derision at first. But the thing was, said Joe, for all his cunning the Devil had given away his vices when he'd come to the valley and by those things they'd trap him.

So, that autumn, before they gathered in the sheep for the winter, they lured the Devil down off the moors – the smell of stewing meat and blackberry wine, the sound of singing and the see-saw of a fiddle bringing him spellbound to the farmhouse like a snake charmed by a fakir's flute. All night they'd kept him there, until, drunk and bloated, he curled up on the fireplace and slept.

The next morning, once the sheep were safely in the bye-field, they turned the Devil out of his bed of embers and the dogs chased him along the lane. He fled through the Moss and up the steep scramble of Fiendsdale Clough, where he leapt from rock to rock and disappeared on to the moors. He spent the rest of the autumn cursing the farmers, but cursing his own gullibility more. When the winter came and the snow began to fall, he climbed down into a hole under the peat and slept until the following year, when he was woken again by the Endlanders and their singing, too sick with hunger now to care if he was being tricked.

Grace finished laying the tablecloth and Angela thanked her and cupped her cheek.

'Oh, cheer up face-ache,' she said. 'It's forgotten about now, isn't it, Liz?'

Liz inclined her head to the scullery.

'Go and see Granddad Tom,' she said. 'Go and give him the ivy.'

Grace looked at the bag and shook her head.

'You picked it,' said Angela. 'You deliver it.'

It was always the children's job to cut the ivy for the Ram's Crown. And it had to be ivy. The Devil hated evergreens.

'Come on,' said Liz. 'I think you'd better do as you're told after today's performance.'

Angela handed the bag to Grace and kissed her on the forehead.

'Go on, sweetheart,' she said. 'Make it up to your mam.'

'Being helpful always makes you feel better,' said Kat, and Grace looked at her and twisted the bag closed.

'I wish Daddy was here,' she said.

'He'll be back on Devil's Day,' said Angela. 'He said he would be.'

'That's ages off,' said Grace.

'Three days,' said Angela. 'It could be worse.'

'Why can't he come home tonight?' said Grace.

'He's busy,' said Liz.

'Doing what?'

'Deliveries,' said Liz. 'You know what Daddy does. Stop pestering me.'

'Three days,' said Angela. 'It'll soon pass, love.'

When Grace had gone, Liz said, 'God, I could strangle her at the moment.'

'She's taken the ivy, hasn't she?' said Angela.

'I'm not talking about that,' said Liz. 'I'm talking about what happened at the house.'

'That?' said Angela. 'I think you're making more of it than you need to.'

'It weren't you who had to spend an hour picking bits of glass out of the bloody carpet, were it?' said Liz.

She caught my expression.

'Oh, you tell him, Mam,' she said and went to light the candles on the table.

Earlier that afternoon, Angela explained, Grace had taken a hammer from the toolbox under the sink and smashed up the mirror on the back of her bedroom door.

'Hence the injury?' I said.

'It looks worse than it is,' said Angela.

'Grace did that?' said Kat.

'Does that surprise you?' said Liz, blowing out the match. 'Stick around.'

'It's her age,' said Laurel. 'She's coming up to the change. They all turn a bit unpredictable, especially girls.'

'It's nowt to do with her age,' said Liz. 'She's just being a little cow.'

'She's upset about the Gaffer,' said Laurel.

'She's missing Jeff, too,' said Angela.

'Aye, and don't I bloody know it?' said Liz. 'I tell you, if she asks me one more time when he's coming home, I'll swing for her.'

'Don't have children if you don't want to answer their questions,' said Angela. 'You never stopped when you were her age.'

'It's every day, though, Mam.'

'She's only a little lass,' said Angela. 'You can't blame her for wanting to know where he is, can you?'

It had been a couple of months before Lambing that year when Jeff was sent down with Sam Sturzaker, Vinny's father, for emptying the safe of the amusement arcade in the town one night. They hadn't got away with very much (enough, went the rumours, to almost cover the cost of the petrol they used to get there and back), but even though the theft had been poorly executed, the judge had apparently taken a dim view of the fact that it had clearly been planned. He'd given Jeff twelve months and Sam, who had stolen the keys to the premises, got eighteen. And Grace and Vinny suddenly had something in common.

When Jeff had been released early on probation, a friend of a friend of a friend managed to beg him a job as a delivery driver for a brewery. It meant that he worked long hours and he was away a lot, but at least he *was* working – idle hands and all that – at least he was sending some money back to Liz. It was a shame, Laurel said, that he couldn't be here for the Gaffer's funeral, but that was the kind of sacrifice a working man had to make sometimes. It was normal. They were a normal family now.

In one way or another, Liz and Jeff had been together since we were children, and were closer to each other than I ever was to either of them. Liz would do her best to involve me in their games, but Jeff had always made me feel like a spare part. He and I were bonded by the fact that we were both from the Endlands but that was about it.

I think everyone, but especially Laurel and Liz, felt guilty that they hadn't done more to set Jeff on a better path when he'd been a boy, but the truth was I liked it when he got himself into trouble at school and at home. I enjoyed the look on Liz's face when he tried to impress her with a pocket full of sweets he'd filched from Wigton's, or the way she so expertly shoved him aside when he tried to pin her to the floor in kiss-catch. Filthy from the wet grass and embarrassed in front of the jeering kids from the Infants, he'd have no recourse but cruelty and he'd twist her skin and flick her ears and tell her that she looked more like a boy than him. But no matter what he did it was never so bad that he couldn't make her laugh five minutes later in a way that she never laughed with me. Jeff was just Jeff. He was the offence and the apology, even now.

'Might you have ended up with her, if you'd stayed in the valley?' Kat had asked me the first night of our honeymoon.

It wasn't a serious question, she was amusing herself. If I'd chosen her, then Liz clearly wasn't my type. Quite stocky and stooped, with big hands.

'Liz?' I said. 'No.'

'Didn't you like her in that way?' said Kat.

Even if I had, it wouldn't have mattered. Before I'd gone off to university, in the last few days of the summer, I'd found Jeff and Liz on the banks of the river in Sullom Wood. She had her knickers puddled around one ankle and Jeff was going at her like a jackhammer.

~

Bill fetched Dadda in from the ram's pen and they emerged from the scullery with Grace moping after them, her hands in the pockets of her jeans and scuffing the loose flaps of lino with her trainers.

'Come on, love,' said Bill, ushering her into the kitchen. 'Go and sit down. Let's eat while I've managed to prise Tom away from his bloody tup for five minutes.'

'Finally,' said Angela, pouring Dadda a glass of beer. 'That ram of yours must be sick of the sight of you.'

'Leith told me to keep an eye on him,' said Dadda. 'I'm only following vet's orders.'

'Aye, but you'll be sleeping in the bloody straw with him before long,' said Angela.

'It's not Tom's fault,' said Laurel. 'If the Gaffer was still here, then they could take it in turns, couldn't they? Oh, it is going to be hard for you on your own, isn't it, Tom, love?'

'All right,' said Bill. 'I don't think he needs reminding, does he?'

'He's not on his own anyway,' said Angela. 'Since when were anyone on their own here?'

'You know what I mean,' said Laurel. 'It won't be the same, will it?'

'I'll manage,' said Dadda.

'Well, I suppose at least you've an extra pair of hands for Gathering this year,' said Laurel, smiling at Kat as she picked out the cutlery from the drawer in the table.

'Aye, but is Mrs Pentecost prepared to get her hands dirty?' said Liz. 'That's the question.'

'I don't mind that,' said Kat. 'We had an allotment at home.'

'An allotment?' said Liz, sending a smile around the table as she took a knife and fork off Laurel. 'Well, that's all right then.'

'You'll be fine, won't you, love?' said Bill.

'So long as we feed you up a bit,' said Angela, removing the lids from the dishes of vegetables.

Dadda stubbed out his roll-up in the ashtray on the sideboard and wheezed into a cough.

'Oh, Tom, listen to you,' said Laurel. 'You sound awful.'

'I'm fine,' said Dadda.

'You're not fine,' said Laurel. 'You need to get yourself to the doctor's. Bill will take you in the morning, won't you, Bill?'

'For Christ's sake, stop mithering him,' said Bill. 'We're burying his father tomorrow, we've not time to bugger about going to the doctor's, have we?'

'But how are you going to carry the Gaffer into church, Tom?' said Laurel, putting her hand on his arm as he sat down. 'A virus can make you as weak as a kitten.'

'Are we going to eat or what?' said Dadda. 'I thought you lot were starving?'

Laurel uncovered the goose and it steamed and sweated.

'Looks good, Bill,' said Angela.

'It's been fattening all summer, this bugger,' said Bill, standing up to whet the knife on the steel.

Under the table Kat squeezed my hand.

'Oh, don't give any to Kat,' I said.

'Don't you like goose, love?' said Laurel.

'I don't eat meat at all,' said Kat.

'Didn't you notice what she had at the reception?' I said.

'No, love,' said Laurel. 'I can't say I did.'

'It were that stuff that looked like the pigs' porridge, Laurel,' said Liz, and Angela laughed.

'Grace tried it, didn't you?' said Kat. 'You liked it.'

Grace glanced up from her plate and nodded as she buttered a slice of bread.

'You don't even eat fish then, love?' said Bill.

'Nothing that was once alive,' said Kat.

'Christ, John, don't tell her where your dad's taking the lambs next month, will you?' said Liz.

'How long have you been like that, love?' Laurel said, her face full of concern.

'A few years,' said Kat. 'I watched a documentary. I'll just have some of the vegetables, it's fine.'

'It's no wonder there's nowt of you, lady,' said Angela.

'I can make you summat else, if you like,' said Laurel, lifting herself out of her chair. 'I'm sure Tom will have something in the pantry you can eat, won't you, Tom?'

'Really,' said Kat. 'Don't worry about me.'

'But I do worry,' said Laurel. 'I don't want you going hungry.'

'I won't go hungry,' said Kat. 'I had something on the train.'

'Leave her be,' said Bill. 'She knows her own mind, don't you, love?'

He smiled and poured her a glass of blackberry wine. A larger measure than anyone else's.

'No no, not for me,' Kat said, and I could tell that she was thinking that this was the moment to give everyone the news. But Bill just winked and carried on pouring and then Laurel changed the subject.

'What will you do about the Wood, Tom?' she said. 'Will you have to cut a lot of the trees down?'

'Let's not talk about that tonight,' said Angela. 'We're meant to be thinking about the Gaffer.'

'I were just asking,' said Laurel. 'We can't leave it as it is.'

'We're doing nowt, until we've heard what Vinny Sturzaker has to say,' Bill said.

'I've more important things to do than interrogate little lads in the village,' said Dadda. 'And I'm not going round accusing folk when I've no proof.'

'Quite right,' said Angela. 'You don't know it were Vinny, Bill.'

'But Betty swears that she saw him heading off to Sullom Wood yesterday,' said Laurel.

'Betty Ward's full of it,' said Angela.

'Look, everyone knows that the Sturzakers don't teach their kids right from wrong,' said Bill. 'They never have done.'

'Jackie does her best,' said Laurel.

'Jackie?' said Bill. 'She's as witless as her bloody husband, that woman.'

'It can't be easy for her, though,' said Laurel. 'Come on.'

'I blame the school,' said Liz. 'They never do owt about Vinny. You know they tried to make out it were our Grace's fault that he nearly broke her bloody arm?'

Grace looked at her sharply. She obviously didn't want to be reminded.

'When was this?' said Kat, touching Grace's hand. 'What happened?'

'It were summat and nowt,' said Angela.

'Mam, she could barely move for a week,' said Liz.

'Her and Vinny were both as bad as each other that day,' said Angela, giving Grace a look before she could argue.

'That's what they said at the school,' said Liz.

'They do what they can, I'm sure,' said Laurel, turning to me. 'Teachers can't discipline children like they used to, can they, John?'

'Have you seen the place where he works?' said Liz. 'He doesn't have to.'

'We get our share of villains,' I said. 'Believe me.'

'I'd like to have put Vinny Sturzaker in front of Mr Rose,' said Bill, cutting the first slice off the breast. 'Remember him?'

'What were his cane made of?' said Dadda.

'It weren't bamboo, I can tell you that,' said Angela, showing Grace the scar on her palm.

'I know it sounds cruel,' said Laurel, as she took the lid off the potatoes, 'but I think it does a child good to be frightened sometimes.'

Kat looked at them as they spoke, wanting to say something. She'd told me often enough that the nursery wasn't without its problems. It wasn't all singing and painting rainbows. But she believed that children were innocent parrots of their mothers' and fathers' prejudices. Wickedness wasn't innate.

Well, she hadn't seen what Lennie Sturzaker used to do to me.

No, some children are like pigs in a wood. Weaknesses to them are as pungent as truffles.

~

He must have sniffed me out at an early age, because I can't remember a time when Lennie hadn't cornered me at break or after school. There was, of course, a rivalry between the village kids and the Endlanders that went further back than even the

Gaffer could remember, but Lennie didn't ever pick on Jeff or Liz. Mostly because Jeff had clowned his way into immunity and Liz was a girl – if she were to use her fists on him, he wouldn't be able to hit her back.

On the other hand, I was fair game. A drip, a poufter, a soft-arse. At playtime, he'd bar my way with a hand against the wall and knock up his chin.

'All right, Pansycock? Bet I can make you cry.'

Sometimes he tried – a quick knee or knuckle – and sometimes Liz would come and shove him away, and then it was, what? You need a girl to fight for you, Pantycost? Sometimes his brother, Sam, would call him away to play with Mike Moorcroft and Jason Earby instead. They couldn't understand his fascination with me, not when there was better sport to be had with Davy Wigton, who was permanently on a hair trigger and seemed to cry if they even so much as looked at him. Whereas I did nothing.

Perhaps that was why Lennie wouldn't leave me alone. Or perhaps he was using me to prove himself to Sam, who called him Thunderbelly or Blubber and pulled his shirt-tails out of his trousers to show everyone the rings of fat. Sometimes Sam would jump out from behind the bins and make everyone laugh by knuckle-scrubbing Lennie's hair, cropped suede short because of his susceptibility to headlice. Sometimes they'd arm-wrestle in front of the girls. Sometimes they'd fight in the playground and Sam would always win and leave Lennie bent double and gulping for breath. Those were good days, when Sam humiliated his brother. But it didn't always work in my favour.

One lunchtime, a week or so before the end of the summer term, I'd found myself pushed by Sam to the edge of the field along with Lennie, the whole school behind us shouting, *race race race*. First to the churchyard wall and back.

I took it at a pace that made it seem as if I were trying but one that was also slow enough to give Lennie a chance to win. But even then he couldn't keep up, and I'd touched the wall and was on the return leg before he'd even got halfway. When he finally reached the other side, he threw up in the cut grass and everyone laughed.

It was hard not to enjoy the cheers and the hair ruffling that came my way for winning. Hard not to be satisfied in seeing Lennie sitting cross-legged on the field with his back to everyone, picking the heads off the daisies.

After school, he'd waited for me in the gloom of the lych-gate and grabbed me from behind, his thick white forearm around my neck, and his fist finding its way through my scrabbling hands. He might have been fat, but he was strong with it, and his knuckles made my skull ring. When he caught the edge of my brow the skin split instantly and, not expecting so much blood so soon, he loosened his grip a little and I twisted out of his arms and ran through the graves. At the wall I scrambled over the railings, almost impaling my balls on the spikes, and dropped the last few feet on to the concrete of Archangel Back. Looking up, Lennie appeared and I climbed the fence into Sullom Wood, leaving him wheezing and coughing.

It's odd to think that he only had a few more weeks left to live then. I used to wonder what he would have done if he'd known.

~

As we ate, the kitchen window became steamed up from the discussions Dadda and the others were having about the Wood and the villagers, the coming weather, the summer's yield of hay. It was talk that, like them, rarely left the valley, and Kat struggled to follow the conversation as it ricocheted from one side of the table to the other.

Grace hadn't said much either, apart from one or two thank yous that Liz had prompted in a tone that made Kat feel sorry for the girl.

'Here,' she said, reaching over and patting her hand. 'I've got something for you.'

From the pocket of her cardigan, she brought out the locket and held it up by the chain for Grace to see.

The deliberation that had started about Dadda's sickly ram petered out, and Laurel put on her glasses.

'That's beautiful, is that,' she said, holding the locket in her palm. 'Aren't you lucky, Grace?'

'Well, you said how much you liked it at the wedding,' said Kat, standing behind Grace to do up the clasp. 'I wanted you to have it.'

'You didn't need to bring her owt,' said Liz.

'Oh, it's not much,' said Kat. 'I'll never wear it again. Someone might as well get some use out of it.'

'What do you say?' said Liz.

'Thanks,' said Grace.

'Not that you deserve owt at the moment,' said Liz and Angela told her to be quiet.

'I've left it empty,' said Kat, when Grace prised apart the two halves of the shell. 'So you can put something special inside.'

'Isn't Auntie Katherine lovely?' said Laurel.

Grace stared at her present and nodded.

'You might look a bit more grateful,' said Liz.

'She's said thank you, hasn't she?' said Angela.

'It's the face on her, though,' said Liz. 'We've happier looking pigs.'

'I've brought something for you as well, Tom,' said Kat, before an argument could start. 'It's from Mum and Dad.'

Dadda left his roll-up in the ashtray and took the card off her.

'I'm afraid it was either doves or sunsets, or both in this case,' said Kat.

'No, it's very good of them to send it, love,' said Dadda.

'Let's see,' said Laurel.

He passed it to her and she read what the Reverend had written.

'It's a lovely passage is that,' said Laurel, handing it on to Liz. '"I will lift up mine eyes to the hills." Very appropriate.'

'It says here that you're welcome at the vicarage any time, Tom,' said Liz. 'If you have a shave you could go for high tea. That's what you lot have in the afternoons, isn't it, Mrs Pentecost, when the rest of us are working?'

'Give over,' said Bill. 'She's not posh, are you, love? John wouldn't have married her if she was.'

'I'm sure I remember you going to grammar school, John,' said Liz.

'He went to grammar school because he's got brains,' said Angela. 'Not because he's posh.'

'Aye, but look where he works,' said Liz. 'Mr Pentecost moves in much higher circles these days, you know.'

'Is it a big house your father has?' said Angela.

'No, not really,' said Kat, even though it was. A Victorian pile set back from the church by a long, striped lawn, where on summer evenings the blackbirds in the willow trees sang as bright as cutlery.

'Do you still get along with him all right?' asked Laurel. 'Even though you didn't marry in church?'

'Yes, what does Daddy say about it all?' said Liz.

Oh, Daddy was a modern man. It was Suffering St Barbara who thought Christendom would fall now that Kat had made her vows in front of a civil servant. No, the Reverend knew that the world had many distractions for young folk like us. He knew that it wasn't exactly fashionable to go to church, he knew that each new generation was more likely to come to Jesus via a maze than a set of stairs. I shouldn't worry about what Barbara thought. She didn't understand the complexities of the contemporary spiritual path as well as he did. Five years of running the teen group on Friday nights, you see.

All this confided to me in the summerhouse one afternoon not long after we'd been married, his hand on my arm, as we watched Barbara coming across the lawn with a tray of drinks and Kat and her younger brother, Rick, following her and mimicking her cautious steps.

Back at home, Kat always reverted to being a little girl again. She allowed herself to be scolded and criticised by her mother, and liked to play and argue over cryptic word games with Rick, who called her Kit-Kat and seemed like a little middle-aged man despite being still at school. He was destined for a clutch of first-class A-levels and then his pick of ancient universities. He was one of those people who seem to absorb information as easily as oxygen, and whenever the Reverend steered the dinner table conversation away from the domestic dramas of the wider family towards literature for my benefit, Rick had always read whatever we discussed. Joyce didn't faze him. Chekhov he knew. Donne was a doddle.

'I used to believe in God,' he told me one night, as he sketched a picture of King John at Runnymede. 'But then I read *The Waste Land* and I watched him die.'

'Die?' said Kat. 'That's three points to me.'

'No it isn't,' said Rick, without looking up. 'If I'd used the word *disintegrate*, then maybe.'

'Cheat.'

'Cheat? Now, *that's* three points.'

'It can't be.'

'Fraid so, Kit-Kat.'

And so they'd go on, playing as if they were little children.

Whenever we came to visit Kat's family, it was obvious that she would never want to be far away from them, even if her mother corrected her on almost everything she said. But that kindly hand the Reverend so often placed on my arm, was a bestowing of duty. It was up to me to wean her away from the quiet, ticking rooms of the vicarage, away from Barbara too. The Deacon, as he called his wife, meant well, but she didn't need to be consulted (even in thought) on every decision Katherine made. A bit of distance would do them both good.

But then we'd found out that Kat was pregnant and that was that. Her mother was already making plans for when we came to stay with the baby, and had already picked some names. Rory, she liked, or Lachlan, or Iain, perhaps, after her father – the supplementary 'i' something the boy could carry through life to remind him that he was one eighth Gaelic. Or Boyd, maybe, or Fingal, she said as she came round the table with the coffee pot after dinner. She did her best to present them as suggestions.

~

After we'd eaten, it wasn't long before the photograph albums were brought out of the cupboard under the dresser. Angela laughed at the old pictures of Liz, Liz laughed at the old pictures of me, all teeth, ears and dishevelled hair. Though by the time I was mid-way through grammar school, the dark brown curls had unfortunately gone. As I'd got older, it had been Joe Pentecost's genes that had surfaced most strongly, giving me his prominent Adam's apple, his mousey double crown, a pair of stringy legs.

Before she turned the page, Laurel kissed her fingers and

touched the picture of Jeff that was next to the one of me, the Jeff she'd once known as a cherubic thing of five.

'He were such a bonny lad,' she said.

'Aye, and now look at him,' said Liz.

'Oh, he's still got his looks,' said Laurel. 'We all married handsome men, didn't we, Angela? Your Jim were a good-looking feller. You've got his eyes you know, Grace.'

Laurel rotated the page so that Grace could see her maternal grandfather startled by the camera flash one Boxing Day, his nose as red as Mr Punch's from the brandy he was drinking. He'd been a strongly-built man with thick, sandy hair and the kind of cheekbones that a matinee idol would have coveted. His soft, grey eyes lived on in Grace, as Laurel had said.

'This is a nice one of him too,' said Laurel, finding another shot, where Jim was crowned with a yellow paper hat. 'He looks quite happy, doesn't he?'

Had he been planning it that day, though? I wonder. As he'd sat there silently eating the pork from the pigs he and Angela had been rearing all summer, had he known what he was going to do?

'Here, I don't suppose you'll have seen these ones of John's mam, will you, Katherine?' said Laurel, opening one of the other albums.

Mam had been caught in a moment of work, standing thigh-deep in a yard full of ewes at Gathering, her hands gripping the horns of a four-shear destined for the auction market. They'd have been married about six months then, Mam and Dadda, the same time as us. Mam would have been about as pregnant as Kat, too.

Rather than beautiful, she was what folk in those days would have called handsome: a bright, square face and a nest of springy hair under a fishing hat that seemed to be permanently fitted to her head. She had strong wiry forearms and the rest of her was quietly sturdy under the Fair Isle sweater and dungarees. The same smile was there in every picture, broadened further in the one of her holding me in swaddling blankets.

Kat leaned closer, trying to imagine the photographs that would soon exist of her like that. The joy she would feel. The completeness.

I had to remind myself sometimes how young Mam was when she had me. She would have been just nineteen, something that had always startled Kat. And it was planned? she'd asked me more than once. It was, of course. That's how the Endlands had survived for so long, I told her. Planning. There were enough surprises in farming, we didn't need to make any of our own.

Mam might have been barely out of school, but in all the photographs she never looked as if she were new to adulthood. In the ones when I'd first been born, especially, there was a certainty in her happiness. This was her life and there would be nowhere else she would want to live and nothing else she would want to do, even though she had no farming in her blood. When Dadda met her, she was serving behind the bar in the pub by the auction market in Garstang. If she'd been able to settle here, then why not Kat? What was the difference? Grandma Alice was hardly what you'd call farm-bred, either. She'd been brought up in the village and worked in the weaving sheds at the mill for years before she married the Gaffer. Yet she became as inured to the Endlands as the rest of them and her former life was all but forgotten.

It would be hard at first for Kat, no doubt, but the farm would eventually seem like home. And she'd appreciate the many helping hands when the baby came along.

Laurel separated the last two pages, the cellophane crackling, and there was a picture of me and Mam when I was about three. Duffle-coated and wellied, I sat on her knee helping her bottle-feed a new-born runt lamb, as she grinned for the camera. Big eyes, smooth skin, clean teeth. She'd stayed so young, while Dadda and the rest of them had grown old.

I felt Kat take hold of my hand under the table again. No matter how much she argued with her mother, she was still close to her, she still liked to lay her head on that blousy bosom, and it upset her to think that I'd never known Mam at all. She couldn't understand why I wasn't more affected by her absence. But it was hard to feel anything very much for someone I didn't remember. I'd only just had my fourth birthday when she died and the things that little boy once felt have dispersed like steam.

'Ah, now here he is,' said Angela, propping up the album she had open so that everyone could see the photograph of the Gaffer.

It had been taken during Lambing a couple of years before and had caught him studying the new-borns intently. The suit jacket that he wore around the farm – the one he'd been married in – was gone at the elbows, and on the back and shoulders it was so soiled with grease that it had an iridescent sheen to it, like a starling's feathers.

He had been a slight, bony-faced man, quite short too, with grey stubble like iron filings. His right ear was pierced with a thin hoop almost overgrown by the skin of his lobe. The closest he'd ever get to a halo, he always told me. Yet everything fell towards his eyes, which, even as he got older, stayed an almost unnatural intensity of blue. Something close to lapis lazuli.

'Pretty owd bugger, weren't he?' said Angela.

'Aye, and didn't he know it?' said Bill.

'How do you mean?' said Laurel.

She was feigning innocence for Kat's benefit – she didn't want her to think ill of the man now that he was dead – but like the rest of us, like the whole valley, she'd heard the stories about the women who had fallen for those eyes of his when he was a young man.

Even as a craggy old boozer, they still loved him. On Saturday nights at the Croppers' Arms after he'd finished playing cards, the women from the abattoir would get him to sing all the Endlands songs and put money in the jukebox so that they could dance with him. He was their minstrel, their clown.

'He were devoted to Alice,' said Laurel. 'They were married for thirty years.'

'He were scared of her,' said Bill. 'That's not the same thing.'

'But they went through a lot together,' said Laurel. 'They both lost family in the Blizzard, you know, Katherine.'

'Yes, so John told me,' said Kat, giving me the slightest of glances. I'd told her that folk here had long memories and that yesterday was never quite detached from now. It might have come decades before, but the Blizzard still haunted the valley, especially down in the Endlands, especially at the Pentecosts' farm.

You see, because the Devil had disguised himself among the sheep, the Gaffer told me, we were the first to notice that there was anything wrong. The lambs that had grown strong and weighty on mosscrop over the summer began to die for no reason. The dogs went blind and their eyes teemed with white worms. The mushrooms that the farming families always collected from the Wood in autumn now brought on seizures and the Gaffer's newly-wed sister, Emily, who had laughed the loudest when her father had spilled his port-wine, fell down in convulsions and swallowed her own tongue.

Hers had been the first body the young priest was shown when he came rattling up to the Endlands on his bicycle, his accoutrements in the basket on the handlebars.

He put on his stole and read the last rites and humoured the family's talk about the Devil, though it came as no surprise to him that in a place like this the explanation for these occurrences was one of superstition rather than rationality. Yet, it was easy enough to see what had happened. The lambs had simply picked up some disease from the moors and passed it on to the dogs. And the mushrooms, well, these people had obviously mistaken one species for another – it was easily done, he understood – and fried up a pan of toxic gills and stalks by accident.

But then the family's hay barn caught fire and burned even as the rain poured. And he saw the bottles of blackberry wine drained overnight. And he saw how the meat in the larder was taken down to the bone before his eyes and the bones notched with teeth marks like those of a dog. For days, the priest was always a step behind as the Devil sprang from one thing to the next. When he was splashing the Dyers' drooling bullock with holy water, the Owd Feller was already studding the Pentecosts' ram with tumours; when he pressed his crucifix to the ram's brow, the Devil had gone off to turn the milk that the Curwens' infant son was suckling into blood.

When the child died, the priest's courage failed, and he left on his creaking Triumph as the Blizzard came sweeping into the village. The looms in the mill were silenced and the doors were closed, and the workers sent home early to their cottages. The upper floors of the terraces soon became too cold to use and so the families huddled in their front rooms instead. But the fires that they lit devoured the wood too quickly, as though the heat were being sucked up the chimney by something on the roof, and before long they were burning whatever they could lay their hands on. Grandma Alice, the Gaffer told me, had watched her father and her brothers breaking up every piece of furniture they owned, even the bed in which her mother had died, coughing up blood clots on to her pillow.

Once the photograph albums had been put away, Kat seemed as though she was going to finally make the announcement about the imminent Pentecost baby. But the opportunity was lost when Laurel set down the bag she'd brought with her on the table and rustled open the paper.

'You go first, Tom,' she said. 'I think that's right, isn't it? It's been a while since we had soul's cake. Not since poor Jim.'

She smiled sympathetically at Angela and Dadda took out the square of sponge and put it on a plate. It was plain and slightly burned and smelled strongly of eggs. He broke off a piece and passed the plate to Angela, who did the same and handed it on to Grace. She let go of the locket and pulled a corner away, cupping her hand to catch the crumbs. There was enough for each of us, including Kat, who copied what the others had done and looked uncertainly around the table.

'Do you want to say owt, Tom?' said Bill, as he took the last piece and tipped the scraps into his palm.

'I don't think there is owt much to say, is there?' said Dadda, and Laurel reached over and touched his hand and then everyone ate their cake in silence.

I nodded to Kat and she put the piece she'd taken into her mouth, her eyes narrowing as she tried to chew it as politely as she could. I'd warned her it would be dry. It always was. We weren't supposed to enjoy it as such. It was a confection of solemnity.

The Gaffer once told me how it was when he was a child and someone died in the Endlands. The relatives of the deceased would blacken one of their mules from tail to lips with wet peat and send it wandering down the valley to let the other families know that death had paid a visit. When the mule was found, it was washed in the river and taken back to where it belonged. And with them they'd bring bread and meat and soul's cake. In those days, the Gaffer said, the body was not considered unclean or frightening and before it went to the undertaker's the loved one was laid out in the front room for touch and kisses. Yuck, says

Adam. But think of it like this, I say: Death would have plenty of time with them. The least we could do was let them stay in the house with their family for a little while longer.

Special candles, thick as leeks, were placed at the head and the feet, and the floor was strewn with salt and rosemary. And then the soul's cake would be laid on the chest over the heart and the living would each take their share. Not a speck could be left, not hidden under shirt buttons or between the fingers of folded hands. It was the privilege of the dead to pass on with all their sins eaten away. The burden now rested with the living.

Everyone began to reach across the table to Dadda and he smiled and thanked them and the conversation resumed.

'Well, it'll be good to have another singing voice tomorrow,' Laurel said to Kat. 'You'll know the hymns, won't you, being a vicar's lass?'

Kat tried to answer her and swallow at the same time but ended up choking.

Laurel rubbed her back, then patted it more forcefully and after edging her chair away from the table Kat coughed up the sludge of the cake into her hands.

'I'm sorry,' she said. 'I'm so sorry.'

'Here,' said Angela and handed her a tissue.

Liz poured her some water from the jug on the table and held it out for her to take.

'Thank you,' said Kat. 'I don't know what happened.'

Laurel smiled and rubbed her back again. 'It's all right, love,' she said. 'Don't worry about it. Did you feel sick or something?'

'Maybe,' said Kat.

'Perhaps it were what you had on the train?' said Bill.

'Perhaps you just need a few decent meals inside you,' said Angela.

'It's not that,' said Grace, opening and closing the locket.

Everyone turned to her. It was the first time she'd spoken in an hour.

'What then?' said Liz.

'It's because she's going to have a baby,' said Grace.

'How did she know?' said Kat, when everyone had gone and Dadda was back outside with the ram. 'I thought you said you hadn't told anybody?'

'I haven't,' I said.

'Well, you must have done,' said Kat.

'Perhaps Grace was just guessing,' I said. 'Because you were sick.'

'I wasn't sick,' said Kat. 'I was being polite. The cake was just so dry, I couldn't swallow it. And it didn't seem like she was guessing to me.'

'I didn't tell her,' I said, when Kat scrutinised me again. 'Anyway, it doesn't matter, does it? They were all happy for us.'

'It just would have been nice if we'd been the ones to tell them though,' said Kat.

'I'm sure Grace didn't mean to upset you,' I said.

'I know she didn't,' said Kat. 'I just don't understand how she knew.'

'You said she wanted you to have a baby,' I said. 'Maybe it was just wishful thinking and she got it right?'

'No,' said Kat. 'She knew.'

'I thought you women were supposed to be intuitive?' I said.

Kat gave me a sarcastic look and drank the rest of her tea.

'Still, she didn't seem all that excited, did she?' she said. 'I can't believe how different she is from the wedding.'

'I think you caught her at her best that day,' I said.

'How do you mean?'

'She can be a bit of a handful,' I said.

'But I'm sure she doesn't normally go around smashing things with a hammer, John.'

'Of course not,' I said. 'I'm just saying that Liz struggles with her.'

'I'm not surprised,' said Kat. 'I mean, look at her home life. It's hardly very stable, is it? And she must be ever so lonely. Didn't they ever want any more children, Liz and Jeff?'

The intention had always been that Grace would grow up with a farmful of brothers and sisters but after she'd been born nothing would grow in Liz beyond the first trimester, apart from a little boy who'd come out with half a heart and lived no longer than a mayfly.

Grace had only been eighteen months old at the time and so they'd never told her, of course. She didn't need to know about any of that. But it meant that she'd grown up thinking that her parents had deliberately chosen for her to be unallied, unable to conspire with siblings, even in fun.

'I think they tried,' I said and Kat nodded and looked down at her stomach.

'I don't want him to be an only child,' she said, smoothing her hand over her dress.

'Kat,' I said. 'I thought we'd talked about that.'

'About what?'

'About calling it a him,' I said. 'We don't know that yet.'

'He is a living thing, John,' she said. 'I didn't think you were so superstitious.'

'I just don't want you to be upset if things don't work out as you want them to,' I said.

'If we have a girl, you mean?' she said.

'No, you know what I mean, Kat,' I said.

'You shouldn't say things like that,' she said.

'Now who's being superstitious?' I said.

'He's meant to be born,' said Kat and pressed my hand to her belly. 'We deserve him, John.'

'I know,' I said and she kissed me and asked me to take her to bed.

The stairs went up from the corner of the kitchen, steep and narrow and brightly lit by the bulb that dangled from the landing.

Dadda's bedroom looked over the yard and the Gaffer had had a view across the bye-field and down to the lane. His door had been propped open to let in the air and I could see that Dadda had already stripped the bed and removed the mattress. He had probably dumped it behind the hay barn with the old tyres, out of sight and mind. The waste would have sat uncomfortably with him, but I suppose there was something more objectionable about keeping a dead man's bed in the house.

Eventually, everything the Gaffer had once owned would have to be sorted, thing by thing. Decisions made without sentiment about what was junk and what was useful. Packing away a life is a slow, fragmented affair. Everyone is outlived by objects, everyone bequeaths an uncurated museum to the living. It must have been the same when Mam died (where did that Fair Isle sweater go? That hat?) but I don't remember.

'Will you miss him?' said Kat, resting her head on my shoulder.

She knew how it had been between us, even if she didn't really understand why he'd been so cold with me. But I'd told her: in the Gaffer's mind, if you turned your back on the Endlands then it was better that it stayed turned. He hadn't disowned me as such

– perhaps that would have been easier – he'd just become indifferent about my life. He hadn't called me Johnny lad since I'd left to go to university almost ten years earlier. If he answered when I phoned, he'd put me straight on to Dadda, and whenever I came back to the farm to help, he treated me like a novice. I got in his way. I exasperated him.

We'd invited him to the wedding, but I'd told Kat not to expect him to come. Of course, as it turned out, I was wrong, and she'd had her optimism vindicated when he appeared with the rest of them. But even so, he'd sat with his arms folded all the way through the ceremony and afterwards lingered on the peripheries smoking while the photographer (Kat's short-tempered Uncle Neil) waved folk in and out of shot. As the day wore on, however, and his fourth pint was down to its last two inches, he seemed to thaw a little, especially when Kat waved him over to where she and I were standing at the other end of the bar. Like all women, she couldn't help but laugh at his jokes and stare at his eyes. And the Gaffer had enjoyed her attention, the way she touched his arm as she spoke, the way she admired his suit and ran the back of her hand down his tie. When she moved off to talk to the Colchester cousins, he watched her all the way across the room.

Blowing out smoke, he nudged me and said something, but the band had taken to the stage and so I couldn't hear what he was saying until he put his beer breath closer to my ear.

'I said you're a lucky bastard, John,' he said. 'Don't fuck it up.'

And then he polished off his pint and went to side-step to an Elvis song with some of Kat's aunties. They'd all loved him, of course.

~

The attic room had been given over to storage when I left the valley and the pair of z-beds were surrounded by boxes of my childhood books that wouldn't fit on the shelves. A run of well-thumbed *Beano* annuals from 1966 to 1973. Ladybird books on flags and Vikings and *What to Look for in the Country*.

Books were always my department. They were what I'd spend my pocket money on at Wigton's. They were what I asked for at birthdays and Christmas. And now and then the Gaffer would come home with a box of second-hand paperbacks that he'd bought off someone in the Croppers' Arms. Not all of them suitable for an impressionable twelve-year-old, I have to say.

As she got undressed, Kat cocked her head to one side and looked at the books on the shelf that sat under the skylight. Stories about giants and bears and adventurous dogs.

'We should take some of these back home,' she said. 'For when the baby comes.'

'Or we could leave them here,' I said.

'For when we visit you mean?' said Kat.

'I suppose so,' I said.

'We can come whenever you want to, you know,' she said. 'I'm not going to keep you locked up in Suffolk. Anyway, I like it here.'

She smiled to herself as she chased her reflection in the mirror that Dadda had strung from the roof-beams like something in a budgie's cage. A woman was coming to stay, he'd thought, and women wanted to know what they looked like. They expected to find a bedroom pretty, too, and so he'd given her the piss-pot with the flowers on.

Kat shivered as she got under the blankets and moved closer to me, crossing the crack where the two beds met and getting into mine. It seemed strange that I was lying there in my childhood bedroom with a wife, a pregnant wife, looking at the same books that had always been there on the shelves, listening to the sounds outside in the valley that never changed.

It had stopped raining now and what had fallen on the moors all evening came tumbling down the clough. Beyond that, the voice of the river seemed larger than it really was, as if it were flowing close to the window and yet distantly too. Sound moves strangely in the Endlands. Adam always says so. It can't lift itself over the walls of the fells and so it flutters from one side of the valley to the other like a bird trapped in a room.

'What would the Gaffer have thought about us having a baby?' said Kat. 'Would he have been happy for you?'

'I'm sure he would,' I said.

But more than that, he'd have been thinking what I'd been thinking since the doctor had confirmed that the two faint lines on the testing kit were telling the truth: that the child belonged to the Endlands. That Kat and I had a duty to come back and live here.

She wrapped herself around me, her hand on my shoulder blades, one cold foot rubbing my shin.

'Poor Grace,' she said. 'I hope our boy has a happier life than hers.'

A vixen yelped in the trees by the Beasleys' bridge, hollow with hunger. And further away I thought I heard the moaning of the stags on the moor.

Funeral

These last few days, I've been telling Adam about the maps that the Gaffer used to draw. Every October before Gathering, he'd take the book from the kitchen dresser and reset the boundaries of our land.

The maps had been made on large sheets of baking paper, so that each year the new could be copied, with whatever amendments were required, from the old. The whole of the valley was drawn out, from the two beech trees to the old wall on the moors where our pastures ended.

He'd deal with the village first, carefully tracing the position of the houses with a pencil that he stopped to sharpen between drawing New Row on one side of the river and the Nine Cottages on the other. Each little rectangle was labelled with the names of the occupants, and births and deaths were indicated by addition or absence. Look back far enough and there were names that no one in the village had any more: Clifton, Bullsnape, Calder, Mitton. Families that had moved elsewhere or come to an end with marriage, like the Curwens, who disappeared from the maps when Angela's father, Henry, died and the farm passed to her and Jim, whom she'd married two years before.

I suppose it must have been quite a momentous occasion really. The Curwens had lived in the valley for a long time, and along with Joe Pentecost and Vernon Dyer, Henry had been instrumental in buying the Endlands from the landowners in 1920. After that, the maps had been drawn up each year around the anniversary of the purchase.

In those years after the Great War, the Gaffer told me, when the toffs didn't have much money any more and the big houses were closed and they decided to cut their losses on what they owned rather than throw good money after bad, the Endlands had gone for a song. But even so, it must surely have still been beyond the means of three families of farmers, and down in Underclough there was a great deal of suspicion at the time about where they'd found the capital.

According to the Gaffer, accusations of poaching did the rounds – after all, no one had come to shoot in the Wood or on the moors for years and there was plenty of game to be had if someone was determined to steal it. But while knocking off a few rabbits or grouse might have helped to pay some small portion of the rent, it would hardly have been enough to buy the plots outright. And anyway, we weren't exactly habitual thieves. We just accommodated those who were.

The Gaffer remembered how butchers from Clitheroe and Burnley would come up at dusk with a few likely looking fellows with shotguns and slip Joe Pentecost and the others half a guinea for an hour or so in the Wood. The next day: pheasant and partridge and hare in the shop windows. Or young men, bored without war, would come with hunting rifles for the deer and were more than happy to pay for the privilege of having the Gaffer take them across the moorland to the choicest hiding places.

Yet, it still didn't seem to add up and whenever I pressed the Gaffer about it, he said the same thing.

'They're ours now, Johnny lad. That's all that matters.'

And he'd inch his chair closer to the table and sharpen his pencil again.

It was in drawing the borders of our land that he took the most care. The plots of the Endlands were not made of neat rectangles or straight edges, but sutured by the ragged lines of the cloughs. They were the remnants left by the Norsemen, who'd come to the valley centuries before and been the first to settle here. They were people of high places as well as people of the sea and when a Norseman staked out his land for the first time, the Gaffer told me, he started at the ridge and worked his way down to water.

'The three farms, if you look closely, Johnny lad, are all like that,' he said. 'We're living like the Norsemen lived.'

And so the Endlands were ringed by a wriggling line that followed the ridge of Kite Fell above the Dyers' farm and on to Wolf Hill above ours. From there it went off over the moors to run along the Wall before coming back across the top of Long Edge that loomed over the Beasleys' place and dropped down to meet its starting point on the village side of Sullom Wood.

'No one can ever move that line, Johnny lad,' the Gaffer said, showing me the edges of the Endlands again. 'Don't ever let anyone try. That land were bought fair and square. Don't listen to anyone who tells you otherwise.'

Once the outline had been correctly copied, the Gaffer sharpened his pencil again and began to fill in the details. At the very end of the valley were the Three Sisters – Fiendsdale, Whitmoor and Bleaweather – a cul-de-sac of high fells that were split here and there by hernias of rock. And even the smaller features were important to document; all the curious corners of fields and marshes, like Sour Bend, that conical polyp of grass around which the river horseshoed on its way to Sullom Wood. Or Reaper's

Walk, which wasn't a lane as such but the hedgerowed levee between the two hay fields.

These things hardly changed from one year to the next, but there were other features that required surveying and this meant that the Gaffer had to go out with a notebook and a tape measure. Not only for posterity but for more practical reasons, too.

The banks into which the Beasleys' bridge had been built were slowly eroding and sooner or later they would have to be shored up. Likewise, the track over the Moss could be damaged by floods and we'd need to know where to build defences or widen the ditches. The ash coppice in Sullom Wood had to be properly managed, the trees counted and replaced if we were all to have enough winter firewood in the years to come. Ash had always been favoured over oak and beech. It burns well even when it's damp and green. A useful attribute when we're at the mercy of so much rain. It chokes the river and fills the cloughs so that they derail from their usual lines and the deluge comes sweeping down the fells towards the farms. Wooden barricades were built in the Gaffer's time and the overflow channels angled towards the river but they don't always work and they have to be maintained, of course, like everything else here. Every so often I put up new fencing panels and unsilt the drains.

We're shepherds of water as well as sheep, I say to Adam.

We always have been.

~

According to what I'd always been told, the Pentecosts had been here in the valley much longer than the other families. We were direct descendants of some of those tough Norwegian migrants. Why else had Joe Pentecost been so tall? Where had the Gaffer got his blue eyes from? Our line stretched way back. When

William the Conqueror doled out this portion of England to the Bonyeux-Lacys, we'd already been farming the Endlands for a century or more.

The Bonjour-Lazies, Adam calls them. Were they friends of the king? he asks.

You didn't get two names unless you were, I tell him.

Were they rich? he says.

Rich enough to give away their land to the Church, I say.

Great sweeps of it. Acres and acres. It paid for a safe passage into heaven when the time came, but they were probably glad, too, that someone else was tending this northern backwater for them.

There were decent flushing meadows down by the Ribble – and these the abbey stocked with sheep whose fleeces ended up in the market places of Bruges and Venice – but the moorland valley was next to useless. The oak groves and beech clumps were too thick to be cleared for fields and the high pastures only fit for rough-coated ewes that were best cared for by the shepherds who already lived there. The monks didn't like to go up on to the moors. There was something unwholesome about the place, they said. There were strange shapes far off on the ridges and sometimes noises under the peat. When they came to collect kindling and fuel for the abbey's fireplaces, they wouldn't go too deep into the Wood either. There was something worse than the wolves in there, something that always seemed determined to follow them out into the open.

That was why they'd built the chapel. Not only as a shelter from the wind and the rain, but as a gatehouse. Whatever pursued them out of the trees would surely shrink back when it saw that God was present in the valley.

It's hard to imagine, I say to Adam, but in those days, change was geologically slow, and one generation of Pentecosts was no different to that which preceded or followed. They farmed sheep for their mutton and their coats, made their small contribution to the Church's coffers, and lived poor, short lives. Century after century.

Of course, the wool business was shaken every now and then by war and taxes like every other, but not enough for it to fall apart, and not enough for men to stop growing rich. Even when friend Henry came along and dismantled the abbey by the Ribble with such thoroughness that the foundation stones were taken up, there were new pockets waiting to be lined. The Bonyeux-Lacys might have been ousted (or executed for their treason in the Pilgrimage of Grace) and the monks chased from the fields, but the Protestant Ashetons were there to take their place, and their sheep.

They'd become even wealthier than the abbey, the Ashetons, not least because they were canny businessmen. They'd been quick to poach the Calvinist weavers escaping the spikes and screws of the Inquisition. Quick to buy up land in Lincolnshire and Norfolk, where they could pasture sheep for worsted rather than woollen and see a bigger return. Having said that they extracted a healthy revenue even from the shaggy fell sheep of their northern moors, turning their fleeces into the coarse cloth that the poor were forced to wear by law.

It was on these profits that they'd built Brownlee Hall over in the Wyresdale Valley, where the Cutting came down into prettier flatlands. We'd been taken there from school one day by the aptronymic Mrs Broad for our topic on local history and herded from musty room to musty room, watched over by the huge portraits of those nib-bearded merchants in stockings and vair.

The Ashetons had done brisk business for a century or more, until the Civil War robbed them and every other wool merchant of their workforce and then a run of hard winters and wet summers wrecked their northern grazing land. The farmers in the Endlands carried on, but the family left and headed south to live and die in a warmer county.

By the time the last Asheton, Matthew, passed away in 1805, the family's wealth had dwindled, and as each generation had sold off a little more of what they'd once owned, there was nothing left but Brownlee Hall and the Briardale Valley estate.

Having no heirs of his own, Matthew handed on everything to his nephew, Edgar Denning, a wine merchant in London. But he had no interest in a mouldering house or two hundred acres of boggy heather and just as the Ashetons had done when they fled to the Cotswolds, he collected what was owed to him without ever making the journey north.

That's not to say that he tossed the heirloom aside as if it were a broken watch. He was shrewd enough to know easy money when he saw it, and took the opportunity to introduce himself as our new landlord by putting up the rent and then again the next season. For years, the farmers petitioned him to think of the Endlands as one plot, rather than three, so that the lease might be set at a lower rate and the responsibility of paying it shared. But for one reason or another, though always financial, the request was consistently refused.

So the three families found ways of making sure that each could afford to live. Every autumn, a few sheep, pigs, cows and geese were set aside and when they were butchered the meat was evenly distributed. Whatever was poached from the moors or from Sullom Wood was sold in quick, clandestine exchanges on the next market day in Clitheroe and the money divvied out three ways to help with the rent when Denning's man came knocking.

Nothing changed when Joe Pentecost and the others bought the Endlands in 1920. Everyone still looked out for each other. We shared what we could. No one bought what would be freely lent. Fences were there to contain the animals rather than keep out the neighbours. If anything, the three families became closer, making the Endlands virtually self-sufficient, as it still is now. The world outside the valley might well collapse but we wouldn't necessarily feel the ripples here. And that was what had been given to each generation since Joe Pentecost's time, that opportunity to live by our own hands, the freedom not to have to dance at the ends of someone else's strings.

But a farmer in the Endlands was only ever a custodian. Nothing ever belonged to anyone, but was always in the act of being handed on. It's the same now, I tell Adam. The Endlands are always teetering, and it's up to those who come after us to hold them steady. No one here spends money on insurance policies; we have children instead.

~

Kat had a restless night and only settled properly in the early hours of the morning. I left her sleeping and went downstairs, finding the map book open on the kitchen table. Dadda had made a start on tracing the new page but, as usual, he'd been called away by another job. I found him in the scullery, which smelled as it had always smelled (and still does now) of turpentine and softening apples and the cat-piss of ever-damp shoes. A place for oilskins to drip dry and game to hang until it was ready to be skinned and gutted.

The window at the end was smeared with moss and shadowed by the straggling damson tree outside. Dadda had been meaning to cut it down for years to let in more light but had never got around to it, and I knew why. It reminded him of Mam, as it did me. One of the few solid memories I have from that long ago is watching her standing on a paint-flecked stepladder reaching up into the branches for damsons and her heels lifting out of her slip-on shoes.

Through the braces of limp, glass-eyed rabbits that hung from the ceiling, Dadda sat on a low stool with the Peek Freans biscuit tin of brushes and polish next to him on the floor. He had his hand inside one of the Gaffer's boots and was coughing loudly as he dug out the dried mud from the sole with a penknife.

'Why don't I do that, Dadda?' I said. 'You go and get yourself ready.'

He stopped for a moment, looked at me, and then turned his attention back to what he was doing. It was pointless of me to offer. The son always cleans his father's boots.

On the shelf above the paint tins, they were all lined up – fathers next to fathers next to fathers, back to old Arthur Pentecost, who'd been shepherding in the Endlands when the Ashetons were still collecting our tithes. His boots were colossal things, held together with hobnails and still skull-hard at the toes. The laces had perished but for a sprig still threaded through the bottommost eyelets, brittle as a dried worm.

The other two farms were the same. Everyone had their shelf of old boots so that no one would forget what had been preserved and passed on to them. How much work had been done on our behalf to keep the farms for us.

'Who did Mam's boots?' I said, finding hers leaning against the others and scuffed at the toes.

'You did,' said Dadda. 'You sat here for hours at it. I couldn't get you to go to bed. The Gaffer found you asleep on the floor.'

'I don't remember,' I said.

So little comes to me from that time now. The cork heels of Mam's shoes on the top rung of the ladder. A drift of jam sugar spilled across the oilcloth on the kitchen table. She and I in the hay meadows watching the lapwings. Like salt boiled out of water, these things remain. Everything else has evaporated.

'He'd have been made up, you know, the Gaffer,' said Dadda, working polish into the leather. 'About you and your lass.'

'And are you?' I said.

'Of course I am, John,' he said.

'What's up then?' I said.

'Nowt.'

'Come on,' I said. 'I know there's something. If it's Grace, we didn't tell her, you know.'

'It doesn't matter to me,' he said.

'Is it that we told Kat's parents first?' I said.

'Why wouldn't you tell them first?' he said. 'You live within spitting distance of them, don't you?'

'I don't want you to feel put out,' I said.

'If I start to feel put out about things like that, John,' he said, 'then I'll know I've too much time on my hands.'

'It's just that they were round at the house and it seemed strange not to say anything.'

'John, I don't mind,' he said.

'*They* would have done,' I said. 'Especially Barbara.'

'I take it she were happy?' he said.

'What do you think?'

He laughed humourlessly. 'At least you'll have plenty of help,' he said.

'We'll have plenty of interference,' I said. 'Here we'd get help.'

'I think you'll be hard pressed to tell the difference, to be honest,' he said. 'Laurel and Angela will be over here every moment of the day whenever you come to visit.'

'I meant if we lived here, Dadda,' I said.

Picking up the other boot, he glanced at me.

'Are you making some tea?' he said and started scrubbing at the sole.

While I waited for the kettle to boil, I sat at the table and looked at what Dadda had drawn in the map book. He'd got as far as outlining the Endlands and traced each of the farmhouses. Under 'Pentecost', his was the only name listed now. On its own it looked defenceless. Easily rubbed away.

He'd cut the conversation off before it had started, but if Kat and I were to move here, it wouldn't be simply for our sake and the baby's, but for his too. Not out of pity. Pity was about as useful in the Endlands as jealousy. I just didn't want to see him struggling. There was too much for one person to do. Drawing the map had thrown up several new jobs already.

It was obvious why he'd come to a stop with the pencil. He couldn't go any further without checking the extent of the fire damage in Sullom Wood. It had become one of those things in the valley that needed to be measured, just like the ash coppice and the culverts on the Moss, and the path high up above the Beasleys' farm – a bad weather route that had allowed folk to get along the valley before there was a tarmac road. Years of erosion had broken the track so that it surfaced and disappeared as if it were stitching that had been pulled loose and the whole line had been fragmented for so long that each section had acquired a different name. Above Sullom Wood it was known as the High Walk, and when it passed above the Beasleys' farm as Sow's Head. Beyond that it was simply the Corpse Road and ran on for miles into the moorland.

To call it a road at all is something of a misnomer. At best it's nothing more than a mowing through the heather – *a coffin's width* was the concession granted by the Ashetons in the document displayed at Brownlee Hall – prone to becoming overgrown or buried in snow. But it had once been well used, the Gaffer said, given that St Michael's was vulnerable to flooding no matter what barricades they set up to hold back the river. When the water broke through and swamped the graveyard, the newly dead would have to be carried over to the other side of the moors to the village of Abbeystead in Wyresdale, where the church had been built on a hill and the waiting soil was dry. It was a journey of almost six miles and would have been arduous enough on the flat, but the navigation of steep inclines and stretches of deep black peat sometimes led to the coffin being dropped down a ravine and splintering open and the body rolling out limp as a puppet. Or it might fall into a bog and, being irretrievable, left to sink, with a cobbling of rocks on the nearest patch of dry ground as a tombstone.

If they were unfortunate enough to ever have to use the Corpse Road, folk tended to set off in the early morning so that they could get to Wyresdale and back in a day. Sometimes they did, but sometimes the weather would come down so suddenly and with such force that they would have to leave the coffin and come back for it.

'Is that true?' I said. I didn't like the idea that someone would be left all alone on the moors, even if they were dead.

The Gaffer crossed his heart as he always did whenever I asked him that question.

'Aye, it's true,' he said. 'They'd find a bit of shelter for the box under a peat-hagg and cover it over with heather and build a little cairn so that they knew where to find it when they came looking. I must have told you about Stanley Clifton, Johnny lad.'

'No.'

'He were only little, about your age. Got his head crushed in a loom,' said the Gaffer, and demonstrated what had happened by pulling the sides of his face in opposite directions and making a cracking noise in the back of his mouth.

'It were when they had the floods the year after the Blizzard,' he said. 'You've seen the photographs, haven't you?'

'Yes,' I said.

They hung on the wall of the Croppers' Arms next to the grubby still-lifes of fruit and spaniels. Sun-faded black and white images of the lane in water deep enough for a rowing boat, while the headstones in the graveyard looked as if they were floating like marker buoys.

The Cliftons had been walking for an hour when the cloud descended and the rain came in a solid sheet. There was nothing they could do but leave their Stanley and head back to Underclough.

'When they went up the next day,' said the Gaffer, lighting his fag, 'the coffin were empty.'

'Empty?'

'Aye.'

'Where was Stanley, then?'

'The Owd Feller had taken him, hadn't he?'

'Taken him where?' I said.

'Nobody knows,' said the Gaffer. 'They never found him.'

'Are you sure that's true?' I said.

'Don't you believe he's up there, the Devil?' he said, and went to the peg by the door where his coat was hanging, the good herringbone number that he wore when he went to the pub. He felt around in the inside pocket and brought out a tobacco tin and handed it to me. The lettering was scuffed and dented, the lid held on with a rubber band.

'Go on, Johnny lad,' he said, sitting down and tapping the stem of ash into his tea cup. 'Open it.'

'I shouldn't smoke,' I said.

'There's no baccy in it, you daft sod,' said the Gaffer. 'Get it open.'

Inside there was a layer of tissue paper spotted with grease and mildew.

'I found it when I were your age, Johnny lad,' he said.

'What is it?' I said.

'Look for yourself.'

Under the paper was a small black hand the size of a baby's, curled in on itself like a burned spider.

'It's tiny,' I said.

But there was something else about it that I couldn't see at first.

'Count the fingers, Johnny lad,' said the Gaffer.

I did.

There were six.

While we waited for Kat to come out of the house, Dadda went up on to the fellside with a ball of twine and his pocket knife.

'Can't it wait?' I called from the Land-Rover. He waved me off and Fly followed him, sensing that he didn't have the appetite to chastise her today.

He hadn't slept much and while Kat had kept me awake as she fought with the bedsheets I'd heard him coming and going across the yard, checking on the ram, sawing something in the workshed, loosening a stubborn bit of machinery with a hammer and sending the offending part clanging on to the floor. And now, in the light of day, he'd noticed a broken railing that needed to be lashed back into place.

I watched him climbing through the chicken patch, the birds scattering as Fly sent them into gobbling half-flights, and thought that I saw him struggling a little with the gradient. Old age would come to Dadda sooner or later. How could it not? He still managed to carry things I couldn't have even lifted and he could walk pretty considerable distances, but the time would come when it wouldn't take much to knock the wind out of his sails: a twisted ankle or a persistent spell of pleurisy and it would fall to others to look after the farm. The Dyers and the Beasleys would do what they could, of course, but they had their own places to run, and Angela, Laurel and Bill were all getting older too.

Past the chickens' scrubland, Dadda reached for one of the fences to pull himself up. Not that it helped him much: nothing on the steep slope at the back of the farm was true. Gates and hurdles had been hand-built to follow the lumps and ditches and were always leaning one way or the other with the wind. Gales hit the fells here with great force and the stunted oak trees had been bent to the shapes of blusters and eddies. The last set of palings, where Dadda had stopped to cut the twine, gave on to wet, rocky terraces, where a few rowan trees grew, geisha white. Beyond that, there was only heather, ridge and cloud, where a pair of buzzards were winding up to the loft of the sky.

Kat stared up at them as she crossed the yard in her black coat and then folded her arms against the cold. She got into the Land-Rover, picking dog hairs off her tights and flipped down the sun visor to finish her make-up.

'There was no need for me to rush, was there?' she said, watching Dadda. 'What's he doing? He'll cover himself in mud.'

'Do you want to try and persuade him down?' I said.

'What was he up to in the night?' she said.

'You heard him too, did you?'

'Don't say anything,' she said, picking through her bag. 'But that's what had me awake for hours.'

'He's just keeping himself busy,' I said.

'He'll wear himself out if he doesn't take some time to grieve properly, though, John,' said Kat, drawing the tip of her kohl pencil across her eyelid.

'He is grieving properly,' I said.

He was grieving as folk in the Endlands had always grieved, by turning his thoughts to the farm and the valley and the welfare of the animals. The land didn't care if his father had died. It wouldn't wait for him to stop crying. What had to be done was much more important than what had to be felt.

'He just needs to slow down a bit,' said Kat.

'Well, perhaps he will, now that we're here,' I said, although I knew fine well that he wasn't going to hand anything over to us. Not when, as far as he was concerned, we'd be going back to Suffolk after Gathering. Whatever he delegated he'd only have to pick up again when we left. Trying to finish a job that someone else has started is always difficult; so much so that invariably they have to be started again. And he wouldn't have time for that when the weather began to deteriorate.

Once Devil's Day and Gathering were done, the place would descend into that brief season of sludge and mould between autumn and winter. There would be days of mists, days of gales, filthy days that failed to lighten. The legions of fungi would turn to pulp in the Wood and the birds would stop singing. And then all memories of summer days would seem suspect.

In fact, they already did, and when Dadda turned on to the lane and we set off towards the village, the Briar was as high as I'd seen it for some time. It easily outpaced us, rushing between the rocks and thistles in a tea-brown torrent as the previous day's rain came down off the moors. The concrete slabs of the Beasleys' bridge were several inches under water, and at Sour Bend the swell had cut away significant chunks of the bank, exposing the tree roots as thick, misshapen bones. When we came closer to Sullom Wood, the noise dissipated as the river veered away from the road and wound off to lose itself in the oak and beech and find the Greenhollow.

It seemed the right name for the place I'd discovered the afternoon Lennie Sturzaker split my eyebrow and I'd lost myself in the trees. Up until then, I'd always tended to avoid Sullom Wood, mostly because to get there from the farm I had to cross the field where Jim Beasley kept his horses. They were twitchy, temperamental things, especially Jim's favourite – the old wall-eyed stallion that stood alone on the far side of the meadow, exiled for his strangeness. I'd never liked horses much anyway. At the Lancashire Show I'd seen a man kicked by the mare he was leading around the parade ring and the memory of him trying to keep his eye inside its shattered socket had haunted me ever since.

Water troubled me too. I could swim quite well, and I'd happily play in the river further upstream, building dams or skimming stones or wading out to the little island of mud and marsh-marigold and claiming it for queen and country. But even though the water rarely lapped past my knees, if I stumbled over it didn't take long for the river to become aware of me, to sniff out my kicking and thrashing and lay on its many hands. In Sullom Wood, the Gaffer told me, the cutting was deep and narrow and the current much faster than it was on the floodplains.

But, like all the Gaffer's stories, the dangers were invitations as much as they were warnings. Go and see for yourself. You find out.

It was my valley as much as his. It would be my business to know everything about it one day. There was no profit in ignorance, and nothing had been kept from me when I was a child. I'd seen ewes bloated like balloons from the gas of the rotting, unborn lambs inside them. I'd watched the vet peel back the lips of the ram with orf to look at the bleeding, pustular scabs. I'd seen vaginal prolapses, coccidiosis, gangrenous mastitis. And more than once, we'd found a ewe crippled by a tumble in the heather and eaten alive by flystrike. These were just things that happened. They would happen again. There was no use in being frightened by the Endlands or anything in it: not old belligerent horses, not the river.

It was a thought I clung to as I thrashed through Sullom Wood, and realised I'd found the place the Gaffer had told me about. I heard the water well before I came to it. The cool of the spray moistened the trunks and rainbowed in the air. And then, almost catching me out, the woodland dropped away into a natural ha-ha of willow and silver birch, where the light under the nave of trees was green and dusty, like the skin of a pear.

Things fled as I slithered down through the dry mud. Birds dissolved into the undergrowth and the eel that lay curled up like a question mark just under the surface of the water shivered away in a ring of ripples. Nothing wanted to stay, not the damselflies or the dippers, or the kingfisher that unearthed itself from the dark, rooty banks on the other side and skimmed away with the current, burning a blue stripe into the air.

Kingfishers were thieves, the Gaffer told me. They'd stolen those pretty little coats and were always on the run. Catch a kingfisher and the reward would be gold or immortality or something even better. Whatever the prize, I followed them downstream, stumbling through the loose rubble of stones at the edge and making the strange clocking echoes that sound in places of rock and running water.

For a few moments they gathered, bobbing, on a low branch before they fled again, out over a waterfall where the whole of the river's width slipped from a shelf of blackened rock and tumbled ten feet or more in an endless crash. I had no doubt that what the Gaffer had told me was true. If I fell in here or I jumped, then no trace of John Pentecost would ever rise to the surface again.

I made a list of things that floated:

Spinning jennies.

Leaves and twigs.

Desiccated wasps.

The water-boatmen that delicately dimpled the membrane of the little, cut-off pool by the banks.

But a boy, even one of skin and bones, no. Bones that might well be shattered if there were rocks just under the surface. Of course, if I'd really wanted to know what was beneath the water, I could have easily sounded the depth with one of the long branches that had come off the trees, but I was frightened that I'd find it was deep *enough* and then there would be no excuse but cowardice.

~

When we arrived at the church, Bill was already there waiting for us with Wesley Burkitt and his son.

The Burkitts had been burying the dead of this wild corner of Lancashire for the best part of a century and Mythamwood, the village where they had their parlour (an unsettling bit of nomenclature that always made me think of séances or spiders and flies), had become synonymous with all things bleak and final. Elderly folk on their last legs were said to be halfway to Mythamwood, and it was where the Sturzakers threatened to send us if we grassed them up.

'Mr Pentecost,' said Burkitt, shaking Dadda's hand. 'My condolences once again.'

He was a tall, thin man, almost ideally pasty for his profession, with a rasping voice as though a speck of gravedust was permanently troubling his throat. In a Dickens novel, I always thought, he would have been called Tallow or Gritby. Sagacious, politic and thorough.

His son, who would make the fourth pall-bearer, seeing that Jeff was away, nodded from the back of the open hearse with a finely honed expression of understanding and discretion. I know your business here today. It is of the darkest matter. I shan't ask you to speak of it.

'And it's young Mr Pentecost, isn't it?' said Burkitt, shaking my hand now and bowing to Kat. 'My sympathies.'

Keeping my hand sandwiched in his, thinking me green enough to need his advice, he stepped closer to impart one of the secrets that he'd learned through a lifetime of dealing with the dead.

'I have to say, once the funeral's over,' he said, 'it does get easier to come to terms with your loss.'

It seemed that he was waiting for agreement before he'd let go.

'I'm sure you're right,' I said and he closed his eyes and patted me on the shoulder.

It's a strange expression – to come to terms with death. As if there are concessions to be bargained for and won. But death takes all.

From the church, Laurel appeared with the priest sent by the diocese to conduct the funeral. The last incumbent of St Michael's had retired years before I'd even started at the primary school and no one had replaced him. They wouldn't waste the money, not for the sake of a few old dears like Laurel. If she wanted to take the body and blood, she had to drive to town.

The priest smiled and offered his hand to Dadda and then me, thankful, it seemed, to be able to excuse himself from Mrs Dyer and the conversation about her Jeff and the rescued sinner she'd heard speaking at the town hall.

'There are already quite a few folk inside,' he said. 'I think most of the village has come.'

'Aye, well, they would,' said Bill, his hands in his pockets.

Funerals in Underclough were always well attended. Anything to spike the flatline of boredom.

Betty Ward and her husband, Clive, came up the lane and smiled at us as Angela arrived with Liz and Grace in Jim's old Hilux. It was as worn-out as Dadda's Land-Rover and the engine switched off in a kind of death-rattle.

The priest greeted Angela and Liz when they got out and blessed Grace on her head as she fiddled with the buttons on the cuffs of her dress – a woollen thing with a pleated neck and a cracked belt. It was a size too small for her but it was the only thing she owned that was black enough and smart enough for a funeral. She looked no happier than she had the night before, and wiped away the feel of the priest's hand when he wasn't looking, but she was at least wearing the locket that Kat had given her.

'It looks pretty on you,' said Kat and Grace attempted a smile.

It was clear that she was apprehensive about the funeral, and stood with her back to the hearse.

'Sit with me, if you like,' said Kat.

Grace shrugged and Kat went over and put her hand on her arm.

'There's nothing to be worried about,' she said. 'Just try and remember the Gaffer how he was.'

'I can't,' said Grace.

Kat bent down and rearranged her twisted collar. 'What you could do,' she said, 'is to try and picture him laughing. That usually works.'

'All right,' said Grace.

'You've got something in mind?' said Kat.

Grace nodded and unpeeled a corner of the new dressing that had been put over the wound on her palm. Blood had already seeped into the fabric.

'Here, I told you to stop picking at it,' said Liz, coming over and separating Grace's hands. 'It's no wonder it's still bleeding. It won't heal if you keep fiddling with it.'

She held Grace's wrist firmly and pressed the edge of the plaster back into place.

'We're going in soon,' she said. 'So behave.'

A glance at Kat and she led Grace away to where the others were standing.

The priest turned back the sleeve of his cassock to look at his watch, as some of the girls from the abattoir who'd enjoyed the Gaffer's company in the pub hurried under the lych-gate, their heels clicking on the pathway.

'We'd best start,' he said. 'I'm afraid I've another occasion of solemnity to attend this afternoon and if I mistime the traffic . . .'

'Are you ready, Mr Pentecost?' said Burkitt and Dadda pinched out his roll-up and nodded.

'You come with me, Katherine,' said Laurel, taking Kat's hand and kissing it. 'Heavens, love, you're freezing. Haven't you got any gloves to wear? You don't want that baby feeling the chill.'

'I'm fine,' said Kat. 'Don't worry about me.'

'You'd better get used to her,' said Bill. 'She'll mother you until you pop.'

'Is that what you think we do, pop?' said Angela.

'Eight hours I were in labour with our Jeff,' said Laurel.

'I were twelve with Grace,' said Liz. 'I certainly didn't pop.'

'All right,' said Bill. 'It's not a bloody competition.'

'They know nowt do men, Katherine, love,' said Laurel, putting a protective hand around Kat's waist. 'They've never been in proper pain. We have to stick together us lasses.'

The previous night, Laurel had been the first to throw her arms around Kat and pet her belly. The first to offer advice. The first to worry when Bill kissed her on the forehead and lifted her off the ground in an ursine embrace that threatened to crush the baby. Dadda was exactly as I'd thought he would be and patted me on the shoulder with the same sort of congratulations I'd received at the age of nine, when one of our rams won second prize at the show where the man had been blinded by the horse. Angela had been happy for us, of course – the comb Grace had brought on our wedding day must have worked – but promised Kat that she'd curse those slim hips of hers when it came to delivery. And Liz had warned her about the hell of cervical insufficiency, perineal stitches, sleep deprivation, anaemia and bleeding nipples to come.

And through the talk and laughter, Grace sat and said nothing. She seemed to find the fuss they were all making over Kat embarrassing and fended off the kisses that came her way in the general outpouring of affection around the table. But I could tell that she was more annoyed with herself than the others. She'd surmised that Kat was pregnant and had blurted out her assumptions too quickly and now she was upset that she hadn't kept the deduction to herself. What she'd really wanted to do was ask Kat on her own and for them to have enjoyed the moment together.

Perhaps Laurel was right about her age. I saw it every year in the First Formers at Churchmeads, that transition from happy innocents in new shoes to gloomy, gangling mutes or burgeoning sadists. The child in Grace was starting to leave and something else was taking over, a bully of a creature that broke things and got her into trouble or spilled secrets just because it hurt to do so. She was bored and frustrated, and friends had slipped out of her hands like fish for so long that it was easier just to hate everyone at school. It was only natural that she'd lash out. All children have it in them to be fierce. Even Adam had his moments when he was younger. He'd bite and scratch for no apparent reason. Sometimes he'd do it to himself too. It was nothing more serious than attention-seeking, of course. Look at what I've done. Now ask me why.

It was the same with Grace. Liz and Angela were always busy with the farm and though Jeff was out of prison now, he was still away from the valley more than he was there. That was why she'd taken a hammer to her bedroom mirror. She didn't want to be reminded that the only thing that noticed her any more was her reflection.

'Come on, mard-arse,' said Liz and waved at her to hurry up.

Grace followed awkwardly, pulling at her dress again and rubbing the skin where the straps of her shoes were tight. At the lych-gate, Liz caught her sharply by the elbow and shook it, making her cry out and run past Angela, who was waiting for them at the door of the church. When Liz came to the porch she threw up her hands and Angela thumbed at her cheeks and kissed her. The pair of them brought out handkerchiefs and went inside arm in arm. They were thinking about Jim's funeral, of course. Or trying not to. It had hardly been a happy farewell. Probably best forgotten. Despite eating soul's cake for the Gaffer the night before, I couldn't imagine that they'd ever really forgiven him for the way he'd soured the wake.

All afternoon he'd been on the beer and the scotch and laughed too loudly at his own jokes. When the girls from the abattoir came in after work, he chatted them up and cadged a few more drinks off them in return for singing the filthiest songs he knew. Dadda and Bill had tried to move him into the tap room but he'd refused and when Jeff put his arm around him and suggested he went outside for a while, he'd taken a swing at him and knocked the glasses off the table. Thinking that perhaps the Gaffer was just missing Grandma Alice, Laurel offered to walk with him over to her grave, but he told her where she could go and made her cry.

No one could stop him drinking and once he set the jukebox going, Angela and Liz went home.

I'd been in my final year at university then and come up from Norwich on the earliest train I could get so that I could spend some time at the farm before the funeral. Dadda and I had drunk a tot of brandy in the kitchen but the Gaffer wouldn't join us and found jobs to do that took him out to the workshed on his own. He didn't speak to me as we drove to the church or after the burial and at the wake we didn't really cross paths until he came into the Gents while I was washing my hands.

He looked at me, in a fashion at least, and stepped up on to the urinal, putting his fag in the corner of his mouth while he undid his flies.

'Why don't I drive you back to the farm?' I said.

He ignored me and pissed with one hand flat on the tiles for support. Most of it still went on his shoes.

'Angela's gone now,' I said. 'I think the wake's over, don't you?'

'They were still serving at the bar last time I looked,' he said.

'You'll be drinking on your own,' I said. 'Everyone's leaving.'

'They can do what they like,' he said. 'I've two nice lasses to talk to.'

'Why don't you just have one more?' I said. 'For Jim.'

'Who? St Francis of fuckin' Assisi?' he said. 'I'm not drinking for him.'

'Why not?' I said.

'I've forgotten about him,' said the Gaffer. 'I've removed him from my mind.'

'What are you talking about?' I said.

'He were weak,' the Gaffer said, ditching his fag end into the trough with the blue cubes of disinfectant.

'He wasn't well,' I said. 'You know that.'

'You don't just give up, though,' said the Gaffer.

'It's hard living here,' I said.

'And what would you know about it?' he said, stepping down and holding the towel dispenser to steady himself.

'I was here for eighteen years,' I said.

'Aye, well, now you're not here, are you?'

'I've not forgotten,' I said. 'I know what it's like.'

'Is that right?'

'I've not abandoned the place,' I said.

'I can hear someone talking,' said the Gaffer. 'But I don't recognise the voice.'

'Don't be like that,' I said. 'I've not changed.'

And then he had me up against the wall with my tie around my neck, his forearm like an iron bar across my chest, his blue eyes on mine.

I started to speak and he pressed the side of my face hard to the cold mirror above the sink.

'Who is that?' he said. 'You'll have to remind me, 'cause I don't fuckin' know him any more.'

My breath clouded the glass and then he let go, opening the door to the smell of cigarette smoke and beer and the music from the jukebox.

When I'd washed my face and rearranged my tie, I found that Dadda and Bill were putting on their coats. They'd given up on the Gaffer and we left him showing the girls from the abattoir a trick with a coin.

I drove Dadda and Bill back to the Endlands through slush and filthy snow. Neither of them spoke. There was nothing to talk about, I suppose.

I don't think anyone, perhaps even Angela, could say that they'd ever really known Jim. He'd always been there at Lambing and Gathering and Harvest, of course, like everyone else, but he was a watcher rather than a talker; happier when he was with his blue-eyed horse or working on the drystone walls with one of his stump-legged dogs and his own thoughts for company. Thoughts that weren't always kind to him, as it turned out.

One afternoon, a few days into the new year, he'd gone up to the moors and put a shotgun under his chin.

~

The Burkitts slid the Gaffer out of the back of the hearse and we arranged the coffin on to our shoulders.

Being the shortest of the four of us, Dadda had been given a small folded towel to wear like an epaulet so as to level the box. But it didn't seem to make any difference, and Bill and I had to walk with a stoop. The coffin itself felt unbalanced, the weight shifting as shoulders dropped or feet adjusted to the buckled paving stones on the path. Even on the smooth tiles inside the church, I felt the casket digging hard into my cheek as if the Gaffer had rolled over and were pressing against the side. But when we came to the gurney at the altar steps, Burkitt took the load off me with ease and placed the wreath Laurel had made on the lid before retiring with his son.

Everyone came to the final lines of 'Abide With Me' and sat down in echoing coughs and creaking wood. From the row behind us, Clive Ward reached forward and put his hand on Dadda's shoulder. The other pews of faces all held the same expression of grim resignation. Death is death but life goes on.

They sat in family groups, some of them intersected now like Venn diagrams where sons and daughters had married, just as the Dyers and Beasleys had been linked by Jeff and Liz. Anderton, Abbot, Dewhurst, Parker, Beckfoot, Ward, Wigton, Earby, Thorpe.

A hundred years earlier, the rollcall would have been more or less the same.

'Nothing like a funeral to bring them out of the woodwork, is there?' said Liz as Betty Ward clanked out an instrumental verse on the antique of a piano and the priest made his way to the lectern.

'Keep your voice down,' said Angela.

'Come on, Mam,' said Liz. 'Most of them wouldn't have given the Gaffer the time of day.'

'At least the bloody Sturzakers aren't here,' said Bill, turning back and facing the front.

'They've got the decency to be honest about their feelings,' said Liz.

'Everyone's just come to pay their respects,' said Laurel. 'That's all.'

'They've come for a gawp and some free sandwiches,' said Liz.

'Let them do what they want,' said Dadda. 'It doesn't bother me.'

He pulled at his collar, desperate to undo his tie. He'd never felt entirely comfortable in anything but his overalls and if it had been even remotely acceptable to come to the funeral in them he would have done.

In the wedding album that had been unearthed the night before along with the others, Dadda looked stiff and awkward outside the church as he squinted into the sunlight on the August day he and Mam had married. But come the reception, the tie was gone and the waistcoat unbuttoned and the sleeves of his shirt rolled up. Mam, on the other hand, looked pleased to be in a dress instead of her dungarees. And they were dancing, my goodness. His hands on her hips, hers on his shoulders. They were people that I didn't know; people that could have been and never quite were.

Their first undertaking as man and wife had been to bring in that year's hay harvest, and there were photographs of them smiling with the same satisfaction and relief as those long-dead Pentecosts who stared from the wall of the Croppers' Arms. My sinewy ancestors in flat caps and bonnets standing in front of a cart groaning with winter feed.

I knew what Dadda was thinking as he and Mam stacked the bales in the hay barn, because I'd thought it too when I'd married Kat. He'd been thinking that the future might just leave them alone. That they might be able to slip through unnoticed and quietly get old in each other's company. They, Tom and Jane, might be a constant that survived cold springs and deluged summers, ferocious autumns and long winters. They would remain, even if the animals perished. And if the valley thrived – as it had done that summer they'd promised to love, honour and obey – then so would they.

'Aye, but a full barn brings an early winter, Johnny lad,' the Gaffer used to say.

It didn't, of course, but none of the Endlands proverbs were meant to be taken literally. They weren't predictions so much as an acceptance of life's capriciousness. A good summer brings with it no assurances of anything. A blizzard can come from nowhere.

It was years before Dadda told me what had actually happened to Mam, but by then she already felt like someone who had nothing to do with me. She'd been crossing the high street in town, he said, and a motorcyclist, taking the bend by the castle too fast, hadn't seen her. They say these things are instantaneous.

~

Kat had made sure that she sat next to Grace and all through the service she gave her as much attention as she could, pointing to the right verse in the hymn book and smiling as she watched her playing with the locket during the sermon.

It was an off-the-peg homily about Jesus as shepherd but delivered with great enthusiasm nonetheless. I suppose the priest thought if he performed well he might at least set one or two souls on the road to salvation. Although I thought his chances were slim here.

They'd all passed this way: Methodists and Baptists, Congregationalists and Spiritualists. And it was the view from Pendle Hill across the Ribble Valley that had conjured up the vision of the *great people to be gathered* in George Fox and his Quakers. But none of these earnest men in their tricorns and frock-coats had ever really had much of a hold, especially in the Endlands. Yet still they came, and outsiders, at least, continued to find God here, just as Nathaniel Arncliffe had done.

An architect by profession, he had helped design many of the mills by which the wool burghers of Yorkshire had made their fortunes. He was a wealthy man himself, but felt no richer in spirit than when he was out on the hills that overlooked his home in Keighley. He had been born into a devout Catholic family – two of his brothers were Jesuit priests at the college by the Ribble – and went to Mass each Sunday morning with his wife and children. By rights, he should have done nothing else but contemplate the mystery of God the Father, Son and Holy Spirit for the rest of the day, but always justified his solitary Sabbath afternoon walks by thinking of them as psalms, each outing an opportunity to offer up praise or meditate on some spiritual puzzle. O Lord, why dost thou? What maketh a man?

The journals he'd kept were all there at Brownlee Hall – a dozen green leather booklets each no bigger than a pack of cards, easily tucked away from the weather under layers of clothing. In forensic detail, Arncliffe had catalogued the buildings and curiosities of the various hamlets and villages through which he passed, and illustrated his descriptions of the heathlands and fields in between with sketches of natural springs and ancient trees, streams and wild flowers, birds and clouds. Always with a westward traction to his feet. A desire to walk, eventually, to the edge of the county.

In those days, the Briardale Valley lay on the very edge of the West Riding – and still did when I was growing up. It was only when those men in smoky committee rooms took their scissors to the map in the seventies that we became Lancastrians.

'We're Yorkshiremen at heart, Johnny lad,' the Gaffer said. 'Yorkshiremen cast adrift.'

Yorkshiremen, just. The old borderline was somewhere along the valley, but no one really knew where. Sullom Wood? Underclough? The Cutting? Perhaps that was what Nathaniel Arncliffe had been looking for the day he got lost on the moors above the Endlands.

A cloudless summer afternoon had quickly turned – as they often do here – and the rain fell with such violence that it forced him to look for shelter. For a miserable hour, he said, he'd walked and prayed until he began to hear the cry of sheep and knew at last, at least, that he'd found pastureland.

A few of the ewes and lambs were huddled by the remnants of a wall while the others watched him blankly from the edges of a pond ringed with holly bushes. He followed the stream that tumbled away into a ravine, troubled by every loose stone, beset with fear, he said, that he should soon become like the poor animal that he saw down in the chasm, fallen from the steep terraces of grass.

In time and with careful footsteps, he reached the valley floor and picked his way across the marshland, heading for the farmhouse that came and went in the drifting cloud. The shepherding family had given him no more than a stranger descending off the moors could have expected, but he was glad of the bread and the apple and the shelter of the hay barn until the storm passed over. And when it did, and the sunlight returned and the birds began to sing in the Wood, he knew that God had wanted him to see this wild garden. That He would bless a man who brought others here to work.

When Arncliffe wrote to Edgar Denning requesting to lease some of the land in the valley in order to build a fulling mill, the wine merchant was amused as much as he was bewildered that anyone should want to try and do business in such a place, and he was happy to part a fool from his money. But that August afternoon he'd been driven from the moors, Arncliffe had watched the river coursing with a determined power as it moved through the rocks and trees, running faster still when it came to a place of deep ferns that the farmers called Underclough. Even a layman could see how its strength might be conducted through the wheel and the shaft and the cog and make a mill here a going concern. There was good trade to be had on this side of the Pennines, too. The finished cloth could be easily transported to Preston and Liverpool and Manchester, and there were a dozen other market towns within half a day's ride that he could sell to.

In 1813, when the mill was nearing completion, Arncliffe built Syke House for himself and his wife and children and the Nine Cottages for his workers, whom he drew from the West Riding villages impoverished by the war with France. Skilled men and women going hungry through lack of bread and lack of work. There'd been riots over food in Sheffield and Leeds and he could understand, even if he couldn't condone, the Luddites going armed into mills to butcher the machines that had taken jobs from strong hands and nimble fingers. Good cloth, said Arncliffe, should have passed through hands from start to finish: from the shepherd shearing the fleece to the merchant teasing the fabric with his thumb. He vowed that he would have nothing in his mill more mechanical than a set of water-powered fulling stocks. The rest of the process would be driven solely by human muscle.

The women pricked their fingers on the tenterhooks and had palms chapped to bleeding by cold water yet not one of them complained. And the dressers he employed to finish the nap might have winced and rubbed in their liniment, but each was secretly proud of having a wrist bent out of shape by years of using the heavy shears; their *cropper's hoof*. To them, said Arncliffe, it was a disfigurement of the upmost beauty, like the bound feet of Chinese courtesans.

The mill thrived, as Arncliffe had prayed it would. Each morning, pleats of weavers' cloth would arrive to be washed of their claggy oils with soap and soda, urine and clay. The fulling stocks beat out the hours of the shift, and each shift was recorded in yards processed. Weekly totals grew into quarterly figures and then to an annual summation that affirmed a healthy profit margin. Enough for Arncliffe to turn his attention to his village, in particular the little church. He dated it to before the Reformation, perhaps a place for the monks who'd come to collect firewood to pray and feel assured that God was watching over them.

Damp had moulded the walls and the missing pieces in the simple arch of stained glass let in finches and sparrows that had built nests in the rafters and turned the chancel into an aviary. It was clear that the renovations would be expensive but it was necessary that his workers should have somewhere to give thanks to the true father who had liberated them from hunger and indigence. That it was called St Michael's was no coincidence either; churches on the edges of these lonely places were often dedicated to the Archangel, he noted. And here it was like a glimmer of light beside the huge darkness of the moorland.

~

When the service ended, we carried the Gaffer out of the church and the Burkitts lowered him into the grave along with all the usual thous and thees and ashes and dust. A little wooden box of soil did the rounds and each of us peppered the lid of the coffin, which was strangely small now that it was deep in the earth.

Laurel sniffed into a handkerchief and Liz comforted her. Bill put his hand on Dadda's shoulder. Kat squeezed my arm. Grace watched the Burkitts rolling up the towelling straps they'd used to steady the coffin's descent and fiddled with the locket around her neck.

Perhaps it was looking at all the long faces, or it was the seriousness of the whole thing, but she started to laugh.

'Quiet, Grace. Show some respect,' said Liz, nudging her and looking over at the villagers who had all turned their attention to a noise they hadn't expected to hear. Laughter during a burial was as strange in the ear as a dirge at a christening.

'What's the matter, Grace?' said Angela. 'What's so funny?'

Grace tried to clench her bottom lip in her teeth, but it quickly slipped out and she laughed again, snorting in her nose.

'Jesus, Grace,' said Liz. 'That's enough.'

'I'll take her across to the pub,' said Angela, steering Grace down the path, following those from the village who'd started to drift off to the wake.

Kat watched them, wondering if she ought to go too.

'Sorry, Tom,' said Liz. 'I don't know what's got into her lately.'

'It's the change,' said Laurel. 'Like I said.'

'Perhaps when our Jeff gets back she'll settle down,' said Bill.

'She'd better,' said Liz. 'I mean imagine laughing here. What the hell is wrong with her?'

'Don't worry about it,' said Dadda. 'It's not as if the Gaffer can hear her now, is it?'

He moved away from the grave first and then the rest of us followed him across the road to the Croppers' Arms.

~

It was a place of grubby anaglypta and carpets the same shade and smell as dishwater. The pendulum clock by the cigarette machine was as pissed in its timekeeping as the men who wandered in every afternoon and stayed until midnight with their dinners and their wives going cold at home. Rusty handsaws and billhooks, horse-brasses and crooked oil paintings of men in red hunting jackets hung on the walls. Above the bar, a pair of antique blunderbusses yawned at each other, their trumpets dull with dust.

The lounge bar was hazed with smoke and by the time Kat and I were through the crowd of black suits near the door, Dadda and Bill were already halfway into a scotch that the landlord, Brian Anderton, had given them on the house. He'd run the pub since before I was born with his wife, Eileen, a sumptuously proportioned, green-eyed Irish woman who often infiltrated my filthy adolescent dreams.

'Over here, love,' Laurel called, and waved Kat to go and sit with her and Angela and the others. Grace had stopped laughing now and sat quietly spinning the locket on its chain as Liz scolded her about some muck she'd got on the sleeve of her dress.

'Go on, Kat,' I said. 'I won't be long.'

I made my way to the bar, receiving comforts from the girls with pineapple hair-dos who worked at the abattoir and then the wrinkled Dewhursts, Parkers and Wards.

'Well, at least he had a decent innings.'

'Glad the owd sod went peacefully.'

'He'd have been pleased with the turnout, wouldn't he, John?'

All of them were hopes for their own endings, of course. We all want to live to a good age, but not decrepitude; not colostomy bags and puréed dinners. We all like to imagine ourselves white-haired and sane, unafraid of death, brown as a shoe, touching the hands of our nearest and dearest as we slip into eternal sleep. We want to go before we have time to know we're gone, as if under anaesthetic. I hope it was like that for the Gaffer. I like to think that if he had realised his heart had stopped beating, then it was only for a second.

~

The bar of the Croppers' Arms was built in a U-shape that allowed Brian and Eileen to move between the lounge and the small tap room, which for as long as I could remember had been under the sole occupancy of the slaughtermen. They tolerated some of the scrotum-faced Methuselahs who came in for the comfortable chairs by the fire, but no one else set foot in there. Apart from the Gaffer who, after he'd finished playing cards, would drift in and ruffle their feathers, flashing his winnings or tapping them up for a drink, depending on the outcome of the games of whist and cribbage.

Looking over, I could see that Jason Earby and Mike Moorcroft were drinking with the other men just off shift. It was incredible to think that Mike was the foreman of the cold store now, a man of authority and executive power. Monkey Moorcroft. The lump of a lad that we used to follow around the playground scratching our armpits when he wasn't looking. We'd always assumed that he would end up marrying Janet Abbot – or Janet of the Apes, on account of her hairy forearms – but she'd been one of the few from my class who'd escaped the valley as soon as they could (even if it was only as far as Accrington) and Monkey had shackled himself to Tracey Parker instead.

She'd been friends with Claire Eaves, who still lived on New Row and worked in the admin office at the abattoir with Irene Dewhurst, who used to let boys put their fingers down her knickers at the Midsummer Fair in exchange for sweets. Their manager was the often-spoonerised Kelly Smith, who – cruel gods – had halitosis and a lisp.

Finally noticing that I was there, Jason and Monkey gave the slightest acknowledgement that they remembered me – that quiet, friendless streak of piss from the Endlands whom Lennie Sturzaker once battered in the churchyard – and went back to eviscerating Davy Wigton about his lack of girlfriend, his lack of prospects, his lack of everything.

They were one of the reasons I left the valley, Jason Earby, Monkey Moorcroft, the Sturzakers. Not because they hounded me out or anything like that, but because it frightened me how easily they'd settled for so little. They'd married girls from school – Sam somehow netting the studious, sensible Cheryl Beckfoot – and followed their fathers into the abattoir as instinctively as the pigs followed each other in from the lairage to the killing floor. And sure enough, Earby, Moorcroft and Sturzaker senior were also there in the tap room, playing darts in a haze of smoke.

'He's got a fuckin' nerve,' said Bill, knocking back the rest of his scotch.

Dadda turned from assembling a roll-up on the bar.

'Who?' he said.

'Who?' said Bill. 'Ken fuckin' Sturzaker. Who do you think?'

'It's a free country,' said Dadda.

'He knew we'd be here,' said Bill.

'He can have a drink if he wants, can't he?' said Dadda. 'Anyway, it's not a day for falling out with folk. Just leave it.'

Bill shook his head as loud laughter came from the tap room and someone started the jukebox going.

'Hey,' he said. 'There's a bloody wake going on in here.'

A few faces looked over but quickly went back to their conversations.

'At least turn it down a bit, lads, eh?' said Dadda.

Jason and Monkey ignored him and carried on taunting Davy until Ken Sturzaker came to the bar.

'Didn't you hear the man?' he said. 'Have some fuckin' respect. Go and sit over there.'

They stopped laughing and looked at us before squeezing in with the other men at the table by the fireplace.

'Switch it off, eh, Brian?' said Sturzaker, and Brian felt around behind the cardboard rack of peanuts for the socket where the jukebox was plugged in.

The music cut out to complaints that Sturzaker quickly subdued. He'd been at the abattoir for so long that his word went on most things, in and out of work. He was a small, ratty man, but it would have been unwise to dismiss him as a weakling; he'd boxed at bantamweight in his younger days and hadn't lost the hardness in his fists.

'I heard about the fire,' he said across the bar. 'Sounded like you had your work cut out.'

'We managed,' said Dadda.

'Any idea what started it?' said Sturzaker.

'You mean who,' said Bill.

Sturzaker smiled and sipped his pint.

'Sounds like you've got summat on your mind, Bill,' he said, lighting up.

'Do I?' said Bill.

'Aye,' said Sturzaker. 'You don't seem your usual cheery self.'

'Well, I am at a wake,' said Bill.

'My commiserations,' said Sturzaker, lifting his glass. 'He were a game owd lad, I'll give him that much. Your Jeff not with you?'

'He's working away,' said Bill.

'Is that what he calls it?' said Sturzaker. 'Last thing I heard it weren't just barrels of beer he were shifting up and down the country.'

'Well, you heard wrong then, didn't you?' said Bill.

'Whatever you say,' Sturzaker said, and took another mouthful of stout.

Like all the male Sturzakers, he'd never seemed entirely well. His father had died young from tuberculosis, and middle age had brought Ken intermittent bouts of bronchitis. His eldest son, Sam – Jeff's inept partner in crime – had venous, translucent skin, his eyes afflicted with the bulbousness of someone born prematurely. And Lennie, of course, hadn't been able to run more than ten yards before he was struggling for breath.

All the Sturzakers lived together in the end house of New Row along with the dogs that Ken bought and sold to make a bit of money on the side. How they'd all survived this long without killing one another was difficult to imagine. But they were like so many others in Underclough, preferring to scrape by than chance it anywhere else. They didn't leave, or couldn't leave, or lacked the courage to leave, and relished the gossip that returned to the valley about those whose escape had ended in failure: the Abbots' eldest daughter, Susan, sister of the hirsute Janet, had been mugged at knifepoint in London as she walked home from work one night; Terry Anderton, Brian and Eileen's son, had gone off to make his fortune in Blackpool and ended up drinking himself to death. For two weeks, he'd lain in his North Shore flat before the hum of flies brought a policeman's shoulder to his front door.

Life away from the valley wasn't all it was cracked up to be. He shouldn't have bothered. He should have stayed put.

No doubt they would have thought the same about me if they'd known how I'd been at the school all term. Distracted, forgetful, late.

So much so, that not long before the half-term holidays, I'd been summoned to the head's office after the last bell of the day.

'I've had a letter, John,' Sweeting said. 'From a parent.'

He didn't like letters from parents. Letters from parents usually made ripples. And ripples spread.

'It's Mrs Weaver,' he said. 'Nicholas's mother. She's rather unhappy.'

'About what?'

'*Nicholas has told me on a number of occasions that Mr Pentecost has not arrived on time for lessons and that the lessons themselves have been found wanting*,' Sweeting read from the letter.

He took off his glasses and sat back in the chair, waiting for me to speak. When I didn't reply, he sighed and shook his head.

'It's just not like you, John,' he said. 'You've always been so – ' he flapped his hand like a fin as he searched for the right word – 'straightforward. I've always been able to rely on your level-headedness.'

Part of me was convinced that it wasn't only the references I'd got from a notoriously unruly comprehensive in Ipswich that had persuaded him to give me the job but that I'd been employed on the strength of my accent too. Sweeting had been brought up in Sheffield and he was proud of telling people that his father had spent thirty years in the steelworks, his mother thirty-five engraving cutlery. His vowels might have been flattened during his scholarship to Cambridge but he was, at heart, a northern working-class boy, and felt himself allied to me in some way.

For him, my accent contained a promise of the worldly,

no-nonsense teaching that Churchmeaders needed, bubble-wrapped in privilege as they were. Foreman-like, I'd stand in my blue coat with a clipboard and stopwatch and oversee the lads' edification from Goods Inward to the final buff of the sleeve on the way out of the showroom.

'You know it's not uncommon for people to burn out in this job,' Sweeting said, practising the bedside manner he'd learned on his management course the previous week. 'Even young men like yourself can lose their way a little.

'If that's how you feel,' he went on, 'there are certain – ' flap flap – 'mechanisms in place which can put you in front of a professional trained in these sorts of things.'

I told him I was fine. Only I wasn't. But how could I have begun to explain why I wanted to go back to the Endlands? And what I owed everyone there.

~

When he came back from taking his turn at the dartboard, Sturzaker looked at me.

'It must seem a world away from you now, all this,' he said. 'I'll bet you're glad you don't live here any more.'

'I've not forgotten the place,' I said.

'Was that your lass you came in with?' he said.

'Yes,' I said.

'Pretty, isn't she, Bill?' he said and pursed his lips. What he wouldn't give.

Bill started to speak for me and Dadda shook his head to stop him.

'Go on,' he said. 'Take the drinks over. I'll be there in a minute.'

Bill looked over at Sturzaker. 'You tell your Vinny I'll be coming to have a word with him,' he said.

Sturzaker watched him go and shook his head.

'My condolences, Tom,' he said.

'Aye, well, he were eighty-six,' said Dadda.

'I weren't talking about the Gaffer,' said Sturzaker. 'I meant having to live with Bill fuckin' Dyer next door.'

He left his fag smouldering in the ashtray and took the darts off Eddie Moorcroft, who leaned against the bar, reading that day's *Gazette*. I saw the headline come and go as he flipped through the pages to get to the sport: the younger of the two children set upon by dogs in Burnley had died.

We sat in Herod's Seat – one of the four booths arranged two apiece on either side of the room. The others were Jezebel, Judas and Job, where on Saturday nights the Gaffer would lose his money and tell either Clive, Laurence or Alun that I'd be down with whatever was owed in the next day or two.

They all liked to keep the amounts they'd won (or lost, or had at stake) from their wives, so if the Gaffer owed them any winnings I'd be sent off on my bike to the village or the abattoir to deliver them the money at work rather than going to their homes. The Gaffer was a better drinker than he was a card player, but a better storyteller than any of them, adept at delaying a hand for so long that no one could quite remember whose turn it was, or exactly who owed what to whom. He'd told everyone a hundred times how the booths had been built using the old benches Nathaniel Arncliffe had torn out of the church during the refurbishments. The windows had benefited too, and over the years when any of the little squares of glass had been smashed they'd been replaced by random fragments of the holy tableau that had once sat behind the altar. Here, the eyes of the Virgin. There a nailed hand.

Grace knelt upon the bench and ran her finger over Christ's wound, tracing the stream of blood while the others argued around her.

'Tell him, Tom, please,' said Angela as Dadda and I sat down. 'He's giving me a bloody headache.'

'I just want to hear Vinny Sturzaker deny it,' said Bill. 'That's all.'

'This is the Gaffer's wake,' said Angela. 'Enough.'

'Let's not argue about it any more,' said Laurel. 'Katherine will think that all we do is fall out.'

'Aye, forget about the Sturzakers,' said Liz. 'We're here to remember the Gaffer.'

We toasted his life and the others in the lounge looked over, chewing on the sandwiches and cakes that Laurel and Betty Ward had brought. A few of them raised their glasses and smiled. Mr and Mrs Abbot who ran the garage out on the road to Mythamwood, the Parkers, the Wigtons, and Alun Beckfoot, who lifted his lemonade and nodded. They were all still interested in Grace and kept their eyes on her when they went back to their conversations.

'They must think we've dragged you up,' said Liz, reaching over the table and pulling Grace away from the window and making her sit. 'What was all that about in the graveyard?'

'I don't know,' said Grace.

'What do you mean you don't know?'

'Auntie Katherine told me to think about what the Gaffer used to laugh at,' said Grace.

Liz looked at Kat. 'Thanks for that,' she said.

'I was just trying to make it easier for her,' said Kat.

'Of course you were, love,' said Laurel.

'I were thinking about a joke he told me,' said Grace. 'I couldn't help it.'

'Of course you could,' said Liz. 'You're not a baby. What do you say to Granddad Tom?'

'Sorry,' said Grace.

'I should bloody well think so, an' all,' said Liz. 'I don't know what the matter is with you at the moment.'

'Don't be too hard on her,' said Laurel. 'It's difficult to know what to do at funerals sometimes.'

'Owt but laughing would have been fine,' said Liz.

'I wish Daddy was here,' said Grace.

'I'll bet you do,' said Liz.

'He has to work, love,' said Laurel.

'I suppose,' said Grace.

'It won't be long now,' said Angela, patting her face. 'A couple of days.'

'Couldn't they have given him time off?' said Kat.

'He didn't like to ask,' Laurel replied. 'They're short as it is and he didn't want them to think he wasn't keen to work.'

'It would have only been for a day,' said Angela. 'I'm sure they'd have let him.'

'I'm only telling you what he told me,' said Laurel, and sipped her gin and tonic.

'The Gaffer's not going anywhere, is he?' said Dadda, re-lighting his roll-up. 'Jeff can go to the church and pay his respects when he comes home if he wants to.'

'Two days,' said Kat to Grace. 'That's not too long.'

Grace sat back in the booth between me and Kat with the orange juice Bill had bought her and sucked it noisily through the straw. The others drew me into a long conversation about Dadda's ram so I only half caught what Kat was saying to Grace. But I was aware that Grace was starting to talk more than she had since we'd arrived back in the Endlands, and after a while she was smiling at Kat as she'd done at the wedding. She shared her drink and asked her about the baby, and when I looked back again, she'd taken off the locket and was holding it by the chain over Kat's stomach.

'Look, Grandma,' she said. 'It's swinging.'

'It'll be a girl then,' said Angela.

'Poor you,' said Liz.

'No, I'm sure it's going to be a boy,' said Kat.

'Why's that, love?' said Bill.

'I just know,' said Kat. 'I can't explain it.'

'It were the same when I were expecting our Jeff,' said Laurel. 'I knew I were having a little lad.'

'Well, either way we'll need them,' said Angela.

'How do you mean?' said Kat.

Angela frowned at her. 'To keep the farm going, of course,' she said.

Kat smiled as though she wasn't being serious.

'What's funny?' said Angela. 'That's your name on the gate, isn't it? Pentecost?'

'Is Auntie Katherine coming to live here now then?' said Grace, thinking that we might have changed our minds since the wedding.

'We can't,' said Kat, stroking Grace's hair when she sagged with disappointment. 'But like I said, we'll come and visit as much as we can, won't we, John?'

'Yes,' I said.

'And you can always come to see us, can't you?' said Kat.

'Can I?' said Grace, turning to face Liz. 'Can I go?' And then it was a dozen questions about where we lived and was it nice and did it rain and did we have a dog and what was our house like and what was our street called?

We lived on a place called Alder Crescent, right in the middle of the bow. We had friends who lived on Beech Drive and Lime Avenue; the Carters were round the corner on Hawthorn Close. All the streets on Meadowfields had been named after the trees they'd uprooted to build the estate. Our neighbours were sales executives and middle managers in supermarkets. Friendly folk with two cars and regular hobbies. Their sons would play football on the square of grass that didn't yet have a nickname and their daughters would roller-skate up and down the street on tarmac that was still black.

Kat liked it there at least.

'But you belong here,' Angela said. 'Both of you.'

'That's kind of you to say,' said Kat, watching the locket moving back and forth. 'You've made me feel so welcome.'

'I'm not saying it to be kind,' said Angela. 'I mean it. One day your Dadda will shuffle off, John, and then what?'

'Angela,' said Laurel. 'It's the Gaffer's wake, not Tom's.'

'But you have to think about these things,' Angela said.

'I'm not going anywhere just yet,' said Dadda. 'Anyway, what would these two know about running the farm?'

'Oh, you don't forget,' said Angela, reaching over and rubbing my hand. 'It's in the blood, this place, isn't it, John?'

'It's stopped now,' said Grace, looking at the locket. 'Can I go and get some more food?'

'Aye, go on,' said Liz.

'And take Katherine with you,' said Angela. 'She's not even eaten enough for one, never mind two.'

Grace took Kat's hand and led her over to the table where the villagers were circling with paper plates.

'Look at them,' said Bill. 'They're like bloody crows.'

'Or magpies,' said Liz, as the girls from the abattoir touched Grace's hair. Those red tresses would be the envy of other women all her life.

While she piled crisps on her plate, Grace gave the locket to Kat so that she could see what was inside. Kat looked over at me, glad that Grace seemed brighter now that the funeral was over, but her smile quickly disappeared when she opened the two halves with her thumbs.

There was a sudden increase in noise as the slaughtermen came out of the tap room, zipping up their coats and looping scarves around their necks for the walk home. As they passed the table, Jason and Monkey reached between the villagers and helped themselves to the sandwiches.

'Those are for the mourners,' said Angela, and Monkey grinned as he chewed one and took another for the road.

'Go on, lads, piss off home,' Sturzaker called to them as he buttoned his jacket and they laughed as he laughed and went out into the street.

'Pity your Vinny doesn't listen to you like that,' said Bill.

'What do you mean?' said Sturzaker.

'You know what I mean,' said Bill.

'You'll have to enlighten me,' said Sturzaker.

'He's feral,' said Bill.

'Feral?'

'Bill, not now,' said Angela. 'Drink your pint.'

'She's got you pegged down, hasn't she, lad?' said Sturzaker. 'And she's not even your wife. I'd have a word with her if I were you.'

'Come on,' said Bill. 'You know it were Vinny that started the fire.'

'Is that what you think an' all, Tom?' said Sturzaker.

'I don't know,' said Dadda, after licking the seam of his roll-up. 'I weren't there, were I?'

'You want to listen to him, Bill,' said Sturzaker. 'He's got some sense.'

'Doesn't it get to you?' said Bill, checking that Grace was still out of earshot. 'To think history's going to repeat itself?'

'How do you mean?'

'Well, you've already one lad in the nick,' said Bill.

'Aye, and we all know who to thank for that, don't we?' said Sturzaker.

'It weren't our Jeff's fault,' said Laurel.

'Course not,' said Sturzaker. 'You cut Jeff Dyer in half and he's fuckin' golden all the way through.'

'Do you mind?' said Liz, indicating Grace, who was squeezing her way back to her seat with Kat, her fingers orange from the cheese puffs she was eating.

'I'm sure she's heard worse, love,' said Sturzaker. 'Living in your house.'

'Just tell your Vinny to stay away from the Wood,' said Bill.

Sturzaker smiled. 'Why? You worried he'd find summat you didn't want him to see?' he said.

'What do you mean?' said Bill.

'Well, you hear things, don't you?' said Sturzaker, tying his scarf.

'What things?' said Bill.

'I don't want to go spreading rumours without proof,' Sturzaker replied, and patted Bill on the shoulder as he went out. 'Watch your mouth.'

~

For the rest of the afternoon and into the evening, Grace and Kat were as thick as thieves and went off around the pub hand in hand looking at all the old photographs. When Kat squatted down to examine some detail, Grace put her arm around her as she'd done at the wedding. In her black dress and her black shoes and with her hair tidied with a tortoiseshell clip, she looked incapable of violence and I knew Kat didn't believe that Grace would have taken a hammer to her mirror without good reason. She had been driven to it. When Grace started to lead her off to talk to the Wigtons, Liz shouted at her to leave Mrs Pentecost alone, but Kat said she didn't mind and it seemed to me that she thought it best to keep Grace away from her mother.

Without really meaning to Dadda got steadily drunk and when he knocked over the table that the Dewhursts were sitting at on his way to the Gents, Angela sent me to pick him up.

'Take him home, John, for Christ's sake,' she said. 'Otherwise we'll be burying two Pentecosts today.'

With Bill's help, Kat and I managed to get Dadda into the Land-Rover, wedging him between us in the middle seat, and I drove back to the farm.

Through Sullom Wood, the trees moved in a blackness that unfolded in all directions, up on to the fells, out on to the moors. Miles and miles of thick night that I don't think Kat had ever known before. Even when we drove through the fens after dark it was at least stippled with a few lights. But here there was nothing and it would have been easy to reach the end of the valley without ever knowing that there were any farms here at all.

When I turned off the lane, Fly and Musket came out barking and their eyes lit up glassily as they put their faces through the railings of the yard gate.

Somewhere along the way, Dadda had fallen asleep against Kat's shoulder and she gently moved him upright, settling his cap on top of his head as if he were a snowman. Hearing the dogs, he came to and opened his eyes and looked at me bewildered.

'We're home, Dadda,' I said.

'You'll need the keys,' he said, opening his suit jacket and peering into the inside pocket.

'I've got them,' I said. 'You gave them to me in the pub.'

'Did I?' he said. 'Not that I know why I'm locking the bloody doors anyway.'

'You're keeping Bill happy,' I said.

'Daft sod,' he said. 'Who does he think's going to come here?'

'It's better to be safe until we find out who started the fire, Dadda,' I said and he gave me a disparaging look.

'It's done with now,' he said. 'It's out. Whoever it were isn't going to come back and start another, are they? There's nowt much left to burn.'

I handed the keys to Kat.

'You'll have to get the gate,' I said, and she got out reluctantly, trying to mimic the tone Dadda had used with the dogs the day before. They ignored her, of course, and she was still trying to send them away when I drove into the yard.

Once I'd parked by the hay barn, I helped Dadda out of the passenger seat and he ran his hand through my hair.

'You're a good lad,' he said. 'My John. And you're better than this bloody place, love,' he said, gently touching Kat's cheek.

'Let's get him into the kitchen,' I said, and Kat took one side and I took the other and we walked him over to the porchway.

'Sit on the bench while I open the door, Dadda,' I said, but he'd already detached himself from Kat's arm and was heading across the yard.

'Where are you going?' I said.

'I need to go and check on the ram,' he said.

'He's fine,' I said. 'Just go to bed, Dadda.'

'He's not been well,' he said. 'I need him in shape.'

'He is in shape,' I said. 'You only looked at him this morning.'

'He's my responsibility now the Gaffer's gone,' he said.

'I know that,' I said. 'But you can't be responsible for him when you've had a skinful, Dadda.'

'Skinful?' he said. 'Give over. I'm fine.'

'John, just let him go if he wants to go,' said Kat, wrapping her coat tighter as the wind picked at some loose piece of guttering on the house.

'I'll bring you some tea then, Dadda,' I said and he raised his hand and went unsteadily to the ram's pen as if he were wearing someone else's shoes.

~

The pen had been built on to the end of the lambing shed out of breeze blocks and corrugated iron, a temporary arrangement that the Gaffer had been meaning to spend time making more permanent for years. Now it was Dadda's job.

I put the tea down on top of the pen wall and watched Dadda inspecting the ram's mouth.

'Did I make an arsehole out of myself at the pub?' he said. 'I didn't think I'd drunk that much. It were Bill kept buying me scotch.'

'No one minded, Dadda,' I said. 'Not today.'

He moved along the trough filling it with protein pellets. The ram grumbled in his chest and nudged past Dadda's thigh to get to his supper.

'You're going to over-feed him, you know,' I said.

'Nay, he needs to build his strength up, don't you, lad?' said Dadda.

He rubbed the ram's fleece and stroked his head. He was a good tup. Broad across the rump; good bollocks too, the Gaffer had said, firm as pears. A Yardley tup. Yardley's of Reeth always sold good rams, traceable all the way back to the original Tan Hill Swaledales. But for a week or so now he'd been listless and sniffy about his food, which was never a good sign. Especially when Tupping was just around the corner.

Dadda patted the ram's back once more and then came to join me on the other side of the gate.

'What was Ken Sturzaker talking about?' I said.

'Sturzaker?' said Dadda, sipping his tea. 'Nowt. He were just winding Bill up.'

'He said something about the Wood.'

'Since when did you start taking any notice of owt Ken Sturzaker said?'

'So he's just protecting Vinny then, is he?' I said.

'Probably, I don't know,' said Dadda. 'Like I say, I've too much to do to worry about it.'

The ram backed away from his trough after a few mouthfuls and snuffled in the straw. Dadda tapped the wall with his wedding ring, wanting a smoke.

'Look, why don't me and Kat stay a bit longer?' I said.

'How do you mean?' he said.

'I mean after Gathering.'

'Haven't you jobs to go to?' he said.

'Not necessarily,' I said.

'You're being cryptic, John,' he said and drank some more of his tea.

'I mean we don't have to carry on doing what we're doing,' I said.

'Perhaps I should get Leith up tomorrow,' said Dadda, leaning over the wall to look at the ram. 'He said to give it a few days. What do you think?'

'I think you're trying to change the subject, Dadda.'

'I weren't sure if you were being serious,' he said.

'Of course I'm being serious,' I said. 'There's nothing to stop us living here.'

'Apart from your lass trying to get up and down the ladder to the attic when she's the size of a bloody whale.'

'We could have the Gaffer's old room,' I said.

'Oh aye,' said Dadda, a still-drunk smile on his lips. 'I can just see her agreeing to that.'

'But unless there's someone to take on the farm,' I said, 'it'll go when you do. Like Angela said.'

'And I told you that I'll be around a while longer yet,' said Dadda.

'We have to talk about it, though, don't we?' I said. 'Now that the Gaffer's gone?'

'Fuckin' hell, John,' he said. 'The soil hasn't settled on him yet. There'll be time enough for all that.'

'Dadda, you know you can't put things like that off.'

'Look, just because I've got a bit of a cough doesn't mean you're going to find me stiff and cold tomorrow morning.'

'It's not about your chest, Dadda,' I said. 'You know that's not what I mean.'

'What then?'

'Look, me and Kat will have a child soon. Wouldn't you rather we raised it here?'

'What is there here for a kiddie, for Christ's sake?' he said.

'It was good enough for me,' I said.

'Were it?' he said.

He looked at me and then back at the ram.

'You've been gone too long, John,' he said. 'Coming here twice a year isn't enough. I don't care what Angela said, she were wrong. Farming's not in the blood, it's in your hands. You've forgotten what it's like day in day out. You can't just drift back to the valley as if you've never been away.'

'Let me come with you to find the deer tomorrow,' I said.

'I'll be all right on my own,' he said. 'It's not summat you can do just like that.'

'So, show me,' I said. 'Teach me.'

'Aye, well, I did try once,' he said.

He turned his attention to the ram again and waited for me to close the door.

~

I'd timed it badly, that was all. I should have waited until he'd sobered up properly. He wasn't thinking straight. He wasn't thinking about anything other than Gathering and his poorly ram and that was understandable. But the future wasn't going to fade like the past. Quite the opposite. It would edge towards him and one day catch him unaware if he wasn't careful. He knew as well as everyone else here that a wall built today saves a flood tomorrow.

Fly and Musket came out and sniffed at my fingers. They were restless and pining, unwilling to leave me alone until I got closer to the house. They both stopped at the rectangle of light that came from the kitchen window and sat down, cocking their ears to the sounds coming from inside.

'It's only Kat,' I said, but when she started calling for me, the two dogs turned away and went to find the darkness of their kennels.

'Oh God,' she said, as I came into the kitchen. 'It's just as bad down here.'

'What is?'

'That disgusting smell,' she said.

'Kat, we're on a farm,' I said. 'You have to expect there to be smells.'

'Perhaps you're used to it,' she said.

'What is it, manure?' I said.

'No, it's not manure,' she said. 'I can cope with the smell of manure. It's like something's died. No, like something that's been dead a long time. You remember that toilet in Spain?'

A shack with a hole in the back streets of some parched little village on the edge of the Tabernas Desert. San Lucas? San Federico? And down in the pit a drowned dog festered with a half-brick tied to its collar.

'I think I'd be able to smell it if it was as bad as that,' I said.

'Perhaps it's coming from outside,' said Kat. 'Go and see, will you?'

'I've just come across the yard,' I said. 'I'd have noticed.'

'Please, John,' she said.

I went out with a torch and looked in the coop against the wall of the house, thinking that perhaps something had died in there. But the chickens were all feathers and terror as the light swept across them.

'Absolutely nothing,' I said, when I went back in and closed the door.

'Don't say it like that,' she said. 'I'm serious. Something's rotting somewhere.'

She looked under the sink, opened the lid of the rubbish bin, sniffed her palms, pulled open the neck of her dress.

'It's me,' she said. 'It's on my clothes. It's on my skin.'

After putting her dress into the washing machine, I ran a bath for her and she got in while it was hotter than she would normally have it to try and get rid of the smell. She slid her body under the water to lie chastely beneath a floating blanket of foam.

'Better?' I said and she nodded.

'What was it, do you think?' she said.

'I don't know. Doesn't pregnancy do something to your sense of smell?' I said.

'Maybe,' she said and rubbed the soap against her thigh where the heat had brought out her scars.

'I think it might just be one of those things you'll have to get used to,' I said. 'Like morning sickness.'

She put her hand on her stomach.

'How can something so small make me feel so strange?' she said.

'It won't be for ever,' I said.

'I'll pop at some point, will I?' she said.

'You'll have to,' I said. 'You'll want to.'

'Do you really have to go out tomorrow?' she said.

'Dadda can't manage on his own,' I said. 'He needs someone with him.'

'Does he?' she said. 'It doesn't seem so.'

'Don't expect him to admit to it, Kat,' I said. 'He'd rather work himself to death before he asked for help.'

'You make that sound like a virtue,' she said, but quickly turned herself in the bath and apologised with a wet, suddy hand on my arm.

'I'd just feel better if you were here,' she said. 'Aren't there jobs you can do on the farm?'

'Look,' I said, 'they'll all be coming over here to make the Ram's Crown tomorrow. Give them a hand. Get to know them a bit.'

'The Ram's Crown?'

'They'll show you what to do,' I said.

'I don't think Liz will have the patience to teach me anything,' said Kat.

'She does like you, you know.'

'John, don't be patronising,' she said. 'Liz couldn't have made it any more obvious at the wake that she thinks I'm an idiot.'

'She was cross with Grace, not you,' I said.

Kat put her chin on my forearm.

'But these deer,' she said. 'You can't just go and shoot them, can you?'

‘It’s a job that needs to be done, Kat,’ I said. ‘Like any other on the farm.’

‘A job?’ she said.

‘What did you expect it was going to be like here?’ I said. ‘Roses round the door and cows in the buttercups?’

She sat up and leaned forward to wash her feet. ‘Of course not,’ she said, even though deep down I think she’d hoped to come to the farm and find Dadda in mustard tweeds like a jolly squire.

‘Then what’s wrong?’ I said.

The soapy water ran down the nubble of her spine as she sponged the back of her neck.

‘Nothing,’ she said.

‘Was it Ken Sturzaker?’ I said. ‘Because you don’t need to worry about him. He won’t bother us up here.’

‘No, it’s not him,’ said Kat. ‘It’s Grace.’

‘But she seemed so much better at the wake,’ I said. ‘Thanks to you.’

‘She’d put something in the locket I gave her,’ she said.

‘Well, that’s good,’ I said. ‘At least she’s making use of it.’

‘John, she had hair in there,’ said Kat. ‘The Gaffer’s hair.’

‘Is that all?’ I said. ‘You had me worried.’

‘Don’t laugh,’ she said. ‘You must admit it’s a bit macabre.’

‘She didn’t cut it off post-mortem, Kat,’ I said.

‘He gave it to her while he was alive?’

‘It’s a token of affection,’ I said. ‘It’s not that unusual here.’

People had always exchanged locks of hair in the Endlands. Brothers and sisters; ageing friends; furtive lovers; schoolchildren finalising some truce in the playground.

Back before the Gaffer’s day, when wedding rings were too expensive, folk from the Endlands would often seal the deal before the priest by winding strands of each other’s hair around their fingers instead. Or if someone was getting on in years, as the

Gaffer had been, then they might pass on one of their curls while they still had any to give. I told Kat that if she went to Brownlee Hall, she'd be able to see the one Nathaniel Arncliffe presented to his son in his last days. A sprig of white bristles pressed under the glass of a gilt-edged frame, with his dates engraved into a copper plate beneath.

He'd passed away teeming with cancer in 1845 at the age of seventy-two, a life that he insisted had been lengthened beyond all expectation by the clean air of Underclough and God's approval of his work. By that time, his son, Richard, had been the de facto manager of the mill for some years, and when Nathaniel died he took the opportunity to make the changes that had always been endearingly resisted. The world was not the same now as it had been when his father had arrived in Underclough, and personal sentiment had to be cut with economic truth. The reality was that all over the West Riding there were mills that could process from fleece to cloth and if Arncliffe's did not expand, if it were not mechanised, then it would close and the heart of the village would stop beating.

Provision would have to be made for three times as many workers. A school would be needed for their children. The lane improved for better access up and down the valley. By this time, Edgar Denning's son, Enoch, had inherited the estate and the letters that Richard had written to him requesting to buy the land that he needed for his *great endeavour* were there in a glass cabinet at Brownlee Hall, full of the observations he'd made during his visits to the rookeries in mill towns across the north of England. He described the brimming cesspools, offered lists of diseases and numbers of dead infants. Every correspondence was crammed with the well-turned aphorisms that men like Richard Arncliffe, men with posterity as well as charity on their minds, took great pride in constructing.

It is those who suffer most who profit least from profit.

An industry that makes corpses of its workforce throws water on its own coals.

There is no greater inheritance one can give or receive than education.

And so on.

After several months of discussion, Enoch finally agreed, once the price had been wrangled upwards, naturally, and the tenter-hooks in the yard were dismantled and weaving sheds built there instead. The mill race – where Lennie Sturzaker would wash up almost a century and a half later – was constructed to pep the river water with gravity as well as thrust, so that it would turn the bigger wheel required to drive the power-looms and carding machines and slubbing billys. And those men with twisted wrists in the finishing room now operated water-powered shears to snip the tufts from the nap.

As the village had grown during Nathaniel's time, there had been other enterprising fellows with money to invest in the valley. The abattoir had opened the year Victoria was born and a company from Lancaster had operated a saw-mill by Sullom Wood for a few years before the practicalities of transporting the timber proved too expensive. The Croppers' Arms had been built in 1830 – the year is still etched into the lintel – and sat opposite the church that Richard continued to repair. An organ was installed. The priest's home, the middlemost of the Nine Cottages, was given a new roof. And within a year of him taking on his father's mantle proper, Richard had erected a statue of St Michael and the serpent within view of the lounge bar windows, so that on Saturday nights, when the last shift ended for the Sabbath, the weavers and carders and cloth-dressers might be reminded that the Devil came in many forms and go home to the good book instead.

Six days a week, the valley rang with the lucrative clatter of the looms, making the peace of a Sunday morning all the sweeter when it came. A day to consider profit of a different kind, one that could not necessarily be counted in pounds, shillings and pence. The fresh smell of woodland, the discreet, efficient sanitation, the diet of homegrown fruit and vegetables meant that the premature mortality of infants and geriatrics that had plagued every slum from Liverpool to Newcastle was virtually non-existent in Underclough. There was little in the way of sedition either. Not like there was in the towns. Places of brick and smoke brought out the worst in people. We were not bees or worker ants, said Richard, indifferent about living in a crush as the tenement and the workhouse demanded, nor were we mushrooms blindly soaking up darkness and wilting away again. We needed space and we needed light. And here in the valley, after Mass, after a good lunch, the millworkers could walk on the fells and the moors, they could swim in the Briar and forage in the Wood for whatever the season offered. They could live as the English should live: with the soil under their feet, and a river in their ear.

~

Kat got out of the bath and dried herself and padded her skin with talc. I began to wonder if Angela might be right about her body. Her boyish hips and her soft little span of abdomen didn't look as though they could possibly cradle a full-term baby.

But she would change, she would swell as the baby swelled. That tummy would balloon, and her little breasts, hanging like apples now as she bent to towel her knees, would grow into gourds.

'You'll look good when you get fat,' I said.

'Can't you say maternal?' she said.

'When you get maternal, then.'

'I can't even imagine what I'll look like in seven months,' she said. 'I can't imagine being weighed down by him.'

'It'll happen,' I said.

'And then when I've got used to him being there,' she said, 'I'll have to push him out.'

'Are you worried about it?' I said. 'The birth?'

'Only a man could ask that question,' she said.

'So, what's the answer?'

'I don't know,' she said. 'I think that I'll be all right but then when I hear what other women have gone through I'm not sure. Twelve hours Liz said it was with Grace.'

'I'll be there with you,' I said.

Not that holding her hand would deliver her from the pain, of course.

'I take it you were born here in the house?' she said.

'I was,' I said.

'That was brave of your mum,' she said.

'Everyone did it then,' I said. 'There were plenty of folk to help.'

'I think I'd prefer a room full of nurses.'

'I turned out all right,' I said.

'You're tough as old boots, aren't you?' she said and stepped into her pyjama bottoms. 'It must be all that farming in your blood.'

'What's making you laugh?' I said.

'The thought of us living here,' said Kat. 'Like Angela said.'

'Would it be so bad?' I said.

'Can you imagine it?'

'Can't you?'

'Oh, John, that's not why you've brought me here, is it?' she said, touching my face. 'Did you want me to fall in love with the place?'

'I want you to see that it's important to keep the farm going,' I said.

'That's your dad's job.'

'I mean when he's not around any more,' I said. 'You're still laughing.'

'I'm just trying to picture Mum's face,' said Kat, 'when we tell her that we're going to raise her grandson on a farm.'

'It'd be good for him,' I said.

'No, it wouldn't,' she said. 'Look at Grace. She's miserable. I don't want our boy to be like that.'

'Grace is like that because of Liz and Jeff,' I said. 'We're not the same as them, are we?'

'Who knows what we'd turn into if we stayed here,' said Kat.

'Angela was right, though,' I said. 'The farm is ours as much as it's Dadda's.'

'I'm not sure your dad would agree,' said Kat.

'Maybe not, but it's true,' I said.

'It will be yours one day,' she said, combing the wetness out of her hair. 'But not yet. Can't we talk about it when it happens?'

When Dadda's time was up, the farm would pass to me, of course, but who was to say when that might be? Twenty or thirty years might go by and then Kat and I would be middle-aged and our boy might well be off finding his own path. The farm would mean nothing to him and I knew that Kat wouldn't want to start a new life here as we stumbled towards pension age. No, we would have to move to the Endlands soon, or we'd never come at all.

The Moors

It rained again in the night but by the morning the clouds were high and grey and a hard wind was roaming the Endlands. It broke like water on the fells and spilled in all directions, shivering the puddles in the yard and racing upwards to the rowan trees and the holly bushes. There was a smell of brine to it too; it was twenty miles to the coast but at this time of year storms could lick off the brackish surface and bring it far inland, seasoning the hills and the moors. After the sweet of the summer came the salt of the autumn.

Driving over the Moss, the track was flooded in places and Dadda switched on the wipers to clear the filthy spray off the windscreen. It wouldn't be long until the door closed on the year and the whole place became inaccessible. But by then we wouldn't need to go there anyway. All the sheep would be down off the moors and the Devil would be back in his hole.

Dadda came to the end of the track and parked the Land-Rover by the pile of wooden stakes and rolls of mesh that were being used to fence off the lower reaches of the path, where Fiendsdale Clough ended and the Briar came into its own. It had always seemed like a miraculous birth, the river, conjured out of the fells high above, made of nothing but damp air and rain, yet suddenly here and loud. It never stops talking, either; always urging itself – *flow, hurry, flow* – to leave the valley and find the sea.

Like so many things in the Endlands, the job of fencing here required frequent repetition. The ground into which the uprights were hammered was often undermined by the surge of water, and high winds could easily tear the wire loose. Before he'd died, the Gaffer had been making repairs with the chickenwire left over from fox-proofing the Dyers' hen coop and the sturdy wooden posts that he'd purloined from the side of the railway line near the town one night. He'd not quite finished, but he'd done enough to keep the sheep from straying during Gathering. Because of the soft grass at the edge of the river and their hesitancy about crossing the marshes, they tended to bottleneck here when we brought them down, and it was easy for one of them to end up being bumped into the water.

At this point, the river wasn't especially deep but it was fast and could carry a sheep quickly out of the reach of our crooks and away into the stony flood plains. Sometimes they managed to scramble on to dry ground themselves but more often than not we'd have to wait for them to drift to the bridge by the Beasleys' farm before we could fish them out. A summer-plump ewe with a sodden fleece took the strength of two men. Meanwhile, the rest of the flock might be scattered over the Moss or straying up the fellsides.

To be truthful, the whole of the path up to the moors needed fencing off, but it was too steep and narrow to get anything but a quad bike up there and so all the wood and wire would have to be carted up in a tag-along trailer a little at a time. Perhaps there was no point anyway. A fence wouldn't last very long in a landslide. They happened pretty frequently too. They still do. It's not unusual for slurries of mud and grass to block the path, and when the rain cuts deep into the upper slopes, the peat slips off the gritstone skull beneath and great wedges of the fellside end up in the clough. If I need to go up to the high pastures I tend to go on foot, just as Dadda used to do and the Gaffer and all those grandfathers whose boots were lined up in the scullery.

Back then, however, it was always on the walk up to the moors when I noticed all the years that I'd spent away from the valley. I fell quickly behind Dadda, sick in the stomach and stiff in the legs. But I'd get used to it again. I'd have to.

He hadn't said anything about the conversation we'd had the night before, but I didn't expect him to have changed his mind. He hadn't spoken much that morning at all; not a word as we drank tea in the kitchen and only a few more as we sat in the Land-Rover. He was being careful not to say anything that might lead on to the subject of my coming back to the Endlands again. He wouldn't have wanted to get into a debate about it. He wasn't one for pondering over things. Like everyone here, the perimeters of what he believed or what he knew had been hardened by experience.

He was waiting for me up ahead beyond the cairns that he and the Gaffer had built to mark the edge of the path when the weather was low. They were more than necessary; it wouldn't have taken much to slip down into the clough and be carried away by the water. The run-off from the days of rain fell fast and white down the broken steps of rock, raising a cold mist that beaded the ferns and grass. By the time I caught up with Dadda I was soaked.

'You all right?' he said, resettling the strap of the rifle on his shoulder.

'I'm fine,' I said. 'It's just been a while.'

'Go back down if you want.'

'I said, I'm fine.'

'We've further to go than the top of the path,' he said.

'I know, I know,' I said. 'Give me a minute.'

He looked at his watch and waited for me to get my breath back.

We were high up now, two hundred feet or more, and the valley opened up all the way back to the village. A toy town of little houses and a tiny church and tiny jackdaws in the school field. And the river turned as a river should, as though a child had drawn its passage through the rocks and reeds towards Sullom Wood.

From up here, the full extent of the fire was clear. For a long stretch beside the river, the trees were as black and wiry as ripped umbrellas. What had once been overgrown was now exposed to the sky. The Greenhollow was gone.

~

Since I'd stumbled across the place, I hadn't stopped thinking about it and when Mrs Broad called my name in class it was to drag me away from the sound of the Falls and the bright darts of the kingfishers. Lennie and Sam and the others laughed when being the centre of attention made me go red in the face, but for the final week of the summer term, they were more interested in eking out the last few tears and tantrums from Davy Wigton and left me alone.

On the very last day, once Mr Cuddy, the headmaster, had finished his assembly and awarded all the prizes (For Reading and Writing, John Pentecost), I slipped out of the playground full of sobbing girls and lairy boys, released, walking backwards and watching the place getting smaller. When I came to the war memorial and Private Philip Pentecost, I turned and ran the rest of the way home.

I don't think there's any better time in a child's life than the weeks between primary school and secondary. The one is over for good and the other waiting at the far side of August to be dealt with later. Those first few days of the summer I was peregrine, desperate to set out on the devotional trail to the Greenhollow as soon as I'd finished my chores around the farm. So far I'd been content to play in the trees and throw things into the river, but I knew that there was more to find down there, there was more that I would be shown.

One afternoon, when a warm wind was bending the thistles and the foxgloves by the river and sweeping dust from the gravel by the lane, I slipped away from the farm before Dadda could find me another job to do and walked past the Dyers' place to the horse field. I sat on the top rung of the gate for a while, willing the two that were drinking from the stone trough to move to the other side so that I could get across to the Wood. But when they'd finished they were in no hurry to go and sauntered through the tall grass, flicking their tails, as they headed to the shade.

Once they were standing out of the sun, I jumped down into the hard-baked ruts and set off alongside the hedgerow. I knew that the wall-eyed horse wouldn't bother me. He was lame in two of his legs and in all the time Jim had looked after him, I'd never seen him move from the far corner of the scrub. He could only watch as I climbed over the fence into the Wood.

On the other side, in the chapel-dark of the trees, it was airless and insecty. Rabbits skittered from bracken to bracken. Pheasants strutted and croaked like dandified guardsmen. The oaks and beeches were in their full green and the light fell as if through a roof of broken tiles.

Down by the Falls, it was cooler under the trees and there was a dampness in the air and on the rocks. I baby-stepped to the edge and looked down into the whorl of foam and form, tracing the thrust of the water away to the stillness of the riverbend, where midges burned like dust in the few rods of sunlight that had managed to find their way through the leaves.

Stepping back, I found a heavy stone and heaved it end over end, until I could push it off the top of the Falls and listen for the crack of it hitting rock underneath the water, but there was nothing. I tried it a second time, now lying with my ear turned to the river. Again, there was only a deep plunge and a crown as though a depth charge had gone off.

For a good half an hour I sat on the lip of the Falls stripped to my underwear, kicking my heels against the rock and watching the twist of white water being formed and formed and formed beneath me. Courage is something you think you have until it's called upon.

In the end, I jumped and changed my mind in the same moment and tumbled in shoulder-first, reaching out for the edge I'd left behind. There was no sensation of breaking the surface, only of being swallowed up entirely and borne away in froth and mud. Floundering rather than swimming, my feet drubbed against the tree roots that caged the banks and my hands caught ribbons of weed, but as the momentum from the Falls diminished, the blizzard of sediment began to calm and I came into a glass-green underworld banded with sunlight. Fish appeared and dissolved again: foil-skinned gudgeon, a school of portly carp, a perch gulping and wriggling away into the forest of water-crowfoot.

The noise of the river was softened here and I would have stayed for longer if not for the strain in my chest and my heart's muffled two-step beating in my ears. A pulsing that grew more insistent as I scissor-kicked to the surface and spat out a mouthful of rotty water. Back in the loud world of the air, I let the current take me under the trailing fingers of the willow trees and into the bend, where the river widened and the water was deep and slow.

The light here was of several different species, sparking in flints as the plapwater hit the edges, spotting the green fur of the moss-stones, webbing across the underside of the branches above me. In places, it hardly penetrated at all and the bank opposite was matted with stalks and seedheads that had become tightly entwined as they'd followed the wandering sunstreaks. Brambles grew in large spools and the ferns and nettles were loured over by trumpets of butterbur that seemed too monstrous for an English wood.

As the warm wind moved along the valley, the skirts of the willows were blown aside and sunlight fell all the way to the bed of pebbles where the sticklebacks gathered. Hundreds of them, spiny and staring.

I dived down and watched them dart from my fingertips to mass again beyond my reach. Every time, they'd do the same thing, quick as a thought. But if I lay still, floating like a corpse, they came back and taught me the ways of their world. How to become truly aware of the current, to weave with its weave, until it was impossible for the water to know who was in control. And so, the fish told me, they could bend whole rivers to their will.

How would it be, I asked them, if I were to live inside the Briar like them? Forever pulled at by the currents and swells; looking up at the rain ripples. And at night-time swimming through ink. Would I be a frog or a fish? No, an otter. An otter, with a spike of muscle for a tail. I tried to imagine how it would be when I changed. Whether it would be a gradual alteration or a sudden gifting of webs and whiskers. The latter, I hoped, and I pictured myself disrobing my old skin like a dressing gown and underneath there being a glistening sebaceous pelt.

And when I dived in, slick as oil, to go hunting in the jades and olives of the sunbright water, there would be plenty to eat. The hanging mobiles of fish. The little nuts of bladder snails glued to the reed stems on the banks. For variation, I'd wriggle downriver and find the estuary and the sea. Herd the lobsters. Worry the mackerel. Sharpen my teeth on cuttlefish. Break crab shells like meringue.

But the Greenhollow would always be my home. I'd know every tree and every bird call. I'd build my holt in the oldest roots and lay down a boundary of oily spraints to ward off rivals. Down in my hole, I'd hear the thudsteps of men well before they appeared with their fishing nets, just as I was able to hide myself away behind the hanging hairs of willow long before Lennie Sturzaker came wading through the undergrowth.

I watched him uproot some of the ferns and thrash a stick against a tree before he opened his jeans and pissed a yellow flume into the river. When he'd finished, he sat down on the bank with his feet dangling over the water and lit a cigarette, smoking it like his dad by pinching the filter between his thumb and index finger. He coughed and sniffed and took a few quick drags before spitting into his palm and dabbing out the butt end to save for another time. For a few minutes, he watched whatever floated down the river, his forearms on his knees, and then lay back in the grass. He didn't move for a while and when the dragonflies and wasps that buzzed around him weren't swatted away I knew he'd fallen asleep.

While I watched him, I was aware of movement on the other side of the river. The undergrowth cracked and a young stag emerged like a broken-off piece of the woodland and came down to the bank to drink.

He lifted his head, the river water a sopping beard, and when he saw me I expected him to sprint off and wake Lennie up. But when I looked again, I couldn't be sure that it was a stag at all. The way it moved its head, or pawed at the mud, it wasn't quite what it was pretending to be. That was how I could spot the Owd Feller, the Gaffer told me.

'Look for an animal trying to be an animal, Johnny lad, and it's probably him. He can't always get it right. That's why he likes to hide himself in a flock, so no one notices.'

The Devil stared at me and I looked away with the same feeling I had when Lennie spotted me from the far side of the playground and picked his way through the other children, assembling some sophisticated insult or devising some means of hurting me without the teacher seeing. But the Devil didn't seem as if he wanted to do me any harm. He seemed more like one of the lonely boys who started at the school now and then and, shunned by everyone else in the yard, always gravitated towards me as a kindred spirit and stuck like a burr.

As the Devil watched me, the same question ran through my mind as incessantly as the river. Did I like stories? Did I like stories?

I answered yes.

And did I want to know another? Did I want to see one played out before my eyes? Not in a book, but here in the Wood.

I did, I said.

I could see a boy die down here, if I wanted to; the boy who was sleeping now in the butterbur. It couldn't be prevented. Nothing could. All time had already run its course. All we ever saw were stories. But I should keep that to myself, along with the trick the sticklebacks had shown me.

The stag finally turned his head away and went up the bank between the willow trees, picking his way through the bracken, leaving the Devil with me, his voice closer to my ear now, speaking into it from the inside.

Come and see the boy who's going to die here, John. Come and look at him.

In my bare feet, I moved along the banks and I stood over Lennie, my toes inches from his outstretched fingers. I watched his fat belly rising and falling under his striped T-shirt where the stolen packet of Players strained against the breast pocket. I watched his eyes moving under the lids as he dreamed, his mouth open and slack.

I'd spent seven years at school with him, but until then I hadn't ever really looked at him so closely or for so long. I hadn't ever noticed the spray of freckles across his nose or the subtle cleft in his chin, like a finger-dent in a lump of dough. His ears were unusually small and his eyelashes as fair as those of the Beasleys' pigs.

He'd have fitted in well with the Tamworths, I thought. I could see him snaffling at the trough with them. Looking up with a dripping snout, wanting more swill.

I touched the bruise on my eyebrow, remembered the smell of his body close to my nose, his silent concentration as he hit me.

I could have dropped a rock on him quite easily. There were plenty by the river. Even a rock of modest size, I thought, would have stoved in his head as if it were as soft as a melon. But if I snuffed him out now, said the Devil, it would spoil the story.

~

Before I'd found my strength again, Dadda had already set off, his hands in his pockets and the rifle across his back. At least now the path levelled out and I could keep pace with him.

For another half a mile it cut along the fellside, rising steadily beside the thundering of Fiendsdale Clough, which high up in this steeper, craggy country was strewn with rockfall and broken trees. In the final fifty yards, the ravine dog-legged to the left and the path carried on up to the peat-haggs that crenellated the ridge like battlements. Here, the sky opened and the wind found us as it came racing across the grass and heather.

Whenever I talked to Kat about the Endlands, I'd tried to describe the moorland to her, but it was impossible to find the right words. Lonely didn't cut it. Nor did barren. It wasn't either of those two things that I really noticed anyway. It was more that there was still so much unknown up there. So much of the old, anonymous earth so close. So much of what wasn't ours, or anybody's.

The moors had never really felt familiar to me and they still don't now. They appear suddenly, too vast and wide to take in all at once, uncoupling from each ridge the eye comes to and drifting away. The land up there doesn't roll so much as swell, like a sea frozen in its wildest uproar, full of deep troughs and dooming walls. If someone were to set off sailing, I say to Adam, they might be able to carry on for ever, the horizon continually replenished with another. But what does that mean to him? He's never seen the sea. He can't picture distance, not really. Even walking to the Moss feels like a long way for him. Imagine walking to the Moss and back fifty times, Adam, I say. A hundred times. Or all day long. That's how far it is across the moors. But he still doesn't understand.

A rabbit lifted its head out of the grass and after a moment of indecision it scuttled away, bursting a pair of red grouse from their hiding place in the heather. They went off low across the moor, rattling out their warning – goback goback goback – and as the silence resettled nothing else moved, only scraps of morning daylight raking over the brown horizon miles away.

Look at a map and it's easy to see how far folk have ventured on to the moors. Farming hamlets like the Endlands are scattered all around the edges, but take your finger a little further and it seems that whatever has been named has been named from a distance: White Heath, Greystone Ridge, Blackmire Edge. And there are pools and bogs and hillocks out in the heart of all the nothingness that have no names at all. The farmers had never gone much further than the edge of the sheep pastures, which stretched almost a mile from where we stood at the top of the valley path to the Wall.

Whoever had lugged the rock up Fiendsdale Clough to build it had been long forgotten, but there'd been a boundary line on the moors of some kind or another for centuries to separate the ewes and the game, the commoners and the rich, tenants and masters, and maybe, at one time, the shepherds and the Devil.

Much of it now was just grassed-over rubble, apart from the small section at the foot of Poacher's Seat that Jim had rebuilt before he'd died. He'd made a proper job of it, as I remember, taking his time to strip everything back to the foundations with his mattock and crowbar, and lay out the copings, face-stones, fillings, through-stones and footings in neat rows so that reassembly would require a minimum amount of confusion and movement.

When Dadda and I came up to check on the sheep, I liked to try and catch the knack Jim had of selecting the right stone each time. I tried to understand how his hands could remember the contours of the one he'd laid down and find its partner with just a few brief touches. Sometimes he made his decision by sight only and worked mechanically, though never quickly, bending and rising and fitting and bending again, already knowing which stone to pick.

I got the impression that he didn't mind someone else being there as long as he wasn't required to engage in conversation, which was fine with me too. Dadda made small talk with him, but it was generally statement of fact or a compliment about the job he was doing, nothing that necessarily invited him to reply.

Which he didn't. He let the knock of the stone's consonants speak for him. When we said goodbye and went back down to the farm with the dogs, he wouldn't watch us for long before he was back bending and rising and fitting again.

It was hard to imagine he'd always been as silent as that. Angela wasn't the type to marry a mouse, nor would someone like that have been much use in the Endlands. I'd always assumed that he must have been different once but no one talked about him enough for me to know if that were true. Perhaps they'd forgotten how he used to be. It was a waste of time to look backwards anyway when there was work that needed to be done now and I think, to be honest, they just let him do whatever seemed to make him happy. Caring for his animals, piecing together his walls.

Mind you, it was only as I got older that I realised they were indulging him. There was no need for the Wall to be rebuilt at all. Apart from the waste of physical effort – each yard repaired required the lifting and shifting of a ton of stone – there was no benefit for the animals either. If the deer came, they'd shoot them, and in any case the presence of the boundary line was so deeply entrenched in the consciousness of the Pentecost sheep, and had been passed down from ewe to lamb for so long, that to refrain from crossing it had become as instinctive as the urge to feed or breathe. There were, of course, always some lambs that seemed to be born clueless, and the dogs would find them lying in the old grouse moor at Gathering picked to bones or as a scum of dirty fleece on top of a bog. But these were few and far between and not worth worrying about.

'There's nowt worse than a lamb that won't heft, Johnny lad,' the Gaffer said. 'You might as well take it to the slaughterhouse and have done with it.'

The sheep that were lying down by the stones watched us closely as if we were the first human beings they'd ever seen, and then, nervous and wide-eyed, they unbent their forelegs and lumbered off, braying for their lambs. They were all fat from the summer, stuffed full of mosscrop and waiting to be brought down for the cleaver or the ram. For them, one year was coming to an end and another was about to begin. It was a busy time for Dadda and I always hated having to leave him when he needed me to stay, even if he pretended otherwise.

He coughed into his fist and brought out a leather hip flask from his pocket.

'It's a bit early for that, isn't it, Dadda?' I said.

He was still rank with the smell of beer and scotch from the wake, still not remotely clear-headed.

'You can't afford to let yourself get cold, John,' he said, taking a nip and then another. 'You can't shoot owt with stiff fingers. And if you can't shoot straight then you might as well go home.'

He hacked again and spat into the grass. It was hard to see how he was going to shoot straight by curing his hangover with brandy either.

'Perhaps we should go back,' I said. 'You're not well. You must have caught whatever the ram's got.'

'Don't be daft,' he said, 'I'm fine,' and scanned the moorland with his binoculars, taking in Poacher's Seat, the acres of brown heather on the old grouse moor, and coming to Top Pond.

In the map book, the Pond, where the headwaters gathered, was marked as the source of the River Briar. It was easy to see why. There was always water here. Even in summer, when the rest of the moor was as dry as a broom, the springtime rain was still seeping down through the peat around the edges of the Pond, keeping the ground wet. It was in the dark, clotted mud that Dadda had found the petal tracks of the deer. And then a day later, he'd seen them feeding on the reeds and grass, quick to huddle behind the bushes when they noticed he was watching them.

‘How many stags were there?’ I said.

‘It were going dark,’ said Dadda. ‘It were hard to tell.’

‘One? Two?’

‘Maybe,’ he said. ‘Maybe more. I don’t know. Here, you’ve got younger eyes than I have.’

He handed me the binoculars and I turned the focus wheel to sharpen the holly thickets that rattled and hushed in the wind, and at the turning of the year were coming into their berry bloom.

‘Well, they’re not there now,’ I said. ‘Perhaps they’ve headed back over to Wyresdale.’

‘We need to make sure,’ said Dadda.

‘But we’ll be Gathering in a few days,’ I said. ‘Then it won’t matter if the stags are here or not.’

‘Aye, and when we come back in the spring we’ll find that they’ve settled themselves in very nicely,’ said Dadda. ‘No, we need to kill them now.’

‘If we can find them,’ I said and gave the binoculars back to him.

‘We’ll find them,’ he said. ‘We just need to be patient. We’ll wait in one of the grouse butts until they come out.’

‘Standing around in the cold isn’t going to do your chest much good, Dadda,’ I said. ‘Why don’t you come back another day when you’re feeling better?’

‘I won’t have another day, will I?’ he said. ‘Not once we’ve gathered the sheep. There’s too much to do.’

‘Dadda, the deer can wait if you’re not well,’ I said.

‘They can’t wait,’ he said. ‘Listen, you won’t remember, but the year after your mam passed away there were a farm over in Wyresdale where foot and mouth went through the whole flock in a day. That poor bastard had to shoot every one of his animals and burn them. I’m not going to let that happen here, John.’

‘I’m only thinking of you, Dadda,’ I said.

'Then think, don't nag,' he said. 'I'm not dead yet.'

Another cough and he picked his way over the Wall and into the deep heather.

~

The grouse butts had succumbed to time and most of them had collapsed in on themselves, though there was one still usable and Dadda climbed down into the arc of stone. The butt was small for two men to stand comfortably together and the smell of our coats was suddenly noxious. Dadda wore the camouflage jacket that hung uncleaned in the scullery all year round and had lent me the Gaffer's oilskin, the one with poacher's pockets sewn inside by Grandma Alice. It was stiff and waxy and impregnated with a rankness that only burning would remedy. But if we were going to find the deer then it would pay to smell like the moorland.

For almost an hour Dadda stood on watch, nipping at the brandy in his hip flask while I shivered and willed him to give up and head for home.

'There,' he said, and handed me the binoculars.

The deer were moving across the moors. A stag and his harem, almost indistinguishable from the autumn colour of the heather.

'Keep your eyes on them,' said Dadda, while he took the rifle out of its leather bag. The bolt-action Remington had belonged to the Gaffer and the story went that he won it in a card game. It was probably true. He'd certainly cherished it like something he'd acquired through sheer luck, something that shouldn't really have been his. I'd often find him polishing the stock with lemon oil or cold-blueing the barrel to prevent it from rusting and to take any glare off the metal that might have given him away to the deer. That summer I'd left primary school, he'd been up on to the moors all the time and killed enough of the stags to stop them using our pastures for their autumn rut. But I knew that he hadn't managed to shoot them all. One, at least, had been able to steal down into the valley and hide in the Wood. With the Devil inside, spurring it on, I supposed that it must have run faster than the others and escaped the Gaffer's gunshots. If I hadn't come blundering into the Greenhollow, then perhaps the Devil would have jumped into one of the animals there instead, or slipped into the heartwood of a willow. But they were toys that quickly bored him. He could make a tree blister with disease or turn a vixen on her cubs and then there was no more fun to be had out of them. A child, however, was a different thing entirely.

I couldn't ever switch off his voice. Even when he wasn't addressing me, he mumbled in the background. And if he sensed that I was ignoring him, he'd remind me that I'd said yes to watching Lennie die and that I couldn't go back on it now. I'd promised. Then, like a boy in the playground taking the sting out of his coercion by pressing all the benefits of it into my hand, he told me it would be worth seeing, it would happen soon too, before the end of the summer, it would be something I'd remember. I needed to see how quickly life went out. One moment everything, the next nothing. And there *was* nothing, afterwards. But I knew that already. I'd look at the porcelain dolls and the glass swans on the mantelpiece that Mam left behind and wait for them to tell me something. But they never did. Not even if I held them in my hand and closed my eyes. The dead were dead. That was why, the Devil said, I shouldn't waste the time I had while I was alive.

Not yet, he said, in answer to the question that I'd only begun to ask. Not for a while. He couldn't tell me how long I would live, otherwise that would spoil the lesson I was about to be given. No one should know when their own death would come, otherwise the world would be wrecked by those with weeks to live and nothing to lose. No, a bit of uncertainty did us the power of good. It was better that we sat in the crosshairs, like the deer on the moors.

Dadda crouched and loaded the rifle with one of the hollow-point rounds, sliding the bolt into place. Two other stags emerged now, the sultan's rivals, waiting on the peripheries for the right moment to make their challenge. The sound of them bellowing repeated on the sharp air.

Dadda took off his cap and laid it down upturned on the ground like a bowl and then, adjusting his position, he brought the rifle to his shoulder and passed the muzzle slowly through the tufts of grass on top of the wall. Now that he had competition, the sultan was alert and lifted his head from the pack of hinds, who had gathered together long-necked and twitchy as the geese on the Moss.

'Come on, you owd bastard,' said Dadda, squinting down the scope. 'Show me your face. Look this way.'

He became completely still. The leather strap hung under the rifle.

'Fingers, John,' he said.

'What?'

'Put your fingers in your ears.'

The sultan's head twitched and a chunk of something red spun off into the air before he buckled into the heather. The gunshot rolled across the moorland, following the rest of the deer as they charged away, rumps and legs, in the direction of Blackmire Edge. On and on they went, the hinds now following the younger of the other two stags, springing over the tumps and bog-moss.

Dadda watched them for a few moments and then pulled on the bolt to eject the case.

'We'll have to follow them,' he said.

Putting the rifle over his shoulder, he climbed out and we set off into a part of the moorland that I didn't know.

~

The sultan stag was a hoary thing, full of nicks and scars, his antlers chipped and bevelled from fighting off rivals. Dadda had hit him just above the eye and the wound had opened up like a little fleshy chrysanthemum. At least he'd died without pain. Hollowpoints are mercifully quick.

His tongue hung limply from his open mouth and the flies that were crawling over the sheep dung had come over to investigate his nose. They murmured and scattered when Dadda lifted the stag's head with his toe.

'Poor owd sod,' he said. 'I don't know why they don't just stay put over in Wyresdale.'

'Something must drive them this way,' I said.

'Like what?' said Dadda, glancing across the moors. 'There's nowt here, is there?'

He looked at the stag once more and then set off, trying to pick out the driest route across the bog that had been churned up by the deer as they ran.

The wind got up and bristled through the dry roots. Watery sunlight spread and receded again. A corner of the sky darkened to slate and promised rain or even hail.

Go up on to the moors late in the year and it's easy to see why it was necessary for the villagers to leave the coffin there if the weather turned and the cloud stooped. Lugging a wooden casket and its contents either back to the valley or over to Wyresdale would have most likely produced a few more corpses. And they were superstitious people, too. They would have thought of those angry spirits whose bodies had been abandoned here by clumsy relatives. They would have remembered the Blizzard and the way the Devil moved on the air. How easy it was to wake him up.

'Aye, but it weren't us, Johnny lad,' the Gaffer said. 'Don't listen to what other folk tell you. They weren't there. They didn't see what Gideon Denning did.'

In 1912 – by which time Richard Arncliffe's son, Jacob, was running the mill – the estate had passed to Gideon Denning, but unlike his predecessors – Edgar, Enoch, his father, Saul, he'd actually made the journey north to see the valley and the moors.

An ambitious man, older than his years, he'd risen through the ranks of Asquith's government and come to occupy an important position in the Foreign Office at not quite forty years old. There'd been a photograph of him at Brownlee Hall that made him look the spit of a young W.B.Yeats: pince-nez, a hawkish nose and disorderly hair. By all accounts, he'd been something of a polymath: a gifted writer, orator, historian and antiquarian. He spoke most European languages, had better than adequate Cantonese and could hold his own in Hindi, Urdu and Bengali. And there were half a dozen other things that he might have easily excelled at if he'd chosen to pursue them: sailing, bridge, photography, cycling, the cello. On his desk in Whitehall, they said, was a chessboard where he'd set out the Budapest Gambit or the Scandinavian Defense as he talked – a reminder to whoever sat across from him that he was already thinking several moves ahead. He liked to unsettle expectations, put others on the back foot.

Which was why instead of taking visiting dignitaries shooting in the comfort of some sleepy estate in Hampshire, he'd bring them up to the Briardale Valley and show them the real England, its heart of peat and stone.

On the wall between the Ladies and the Gents of the Croppers' Arms there were photographs Jacob Arncliffe had taken of serious-looking Indian diplomats in tweeds and turbans, a prince of Swaziland standing uncertainly beside an apron of dead birds, an Arab in his keffiyeh and thawb lined up with the cast of walrus-moustached MPs, consuls, businessmen, High Commissioners, Right Honourables and Lords. A time when deals were done on the grouse moors and the empire was governed to the sound of shotguns.

In those years before the Great War, from the start of the season until the uplands became impassable, the Endlands were loud every weekend with men and dogs and horses whenever a shooting party arrived from Brownlee Hall.

The autumn was a lucrative time for the people in the valley. Jacob Arncliffe's mill-workers made good money acting as beaters and the village boys could pocket more in a month than they'd had in their hand all year if they were nimble in the grouse butts and could load a double-barrel quickly. But it was always the farm lads who led them further afield for the deer. And the Gaffer took at least a shilling a day for guiding the more serious sportsmen over to Far Lodge.

I assume it's still there. No one goes looking for it any more.

Adam asks about it now and again, but I'm glad it's too far away for me to take him. I've only ever been once. I won't go again. It can't rot away quickly enough as far as I'm concerned.

It had been built by Gideon Denning's father on the strength of a passing fancy that he might like to come up to his northern acres and shoot at some point. But he'd never appeared and the Lodge had become a folly and – in time – a place of rumour.

On Sunday afternoons, young folk from the village went up on to the moors to try and locate it out of curiosity, but they found nothing and invariably got themselves lost. Even the Gaffer, who was free to go as far as a child with a healthy disregard for danger might wish to wander, had only stumbled upon it by chance.

'If I'd been walking twenty yards further away I'd have missed it,' he said.

'What did it look like?' I said.

'Like it had been built that morning,' said the Gaffer. 'Strange bloody place, Johnny lad.'

In the old photographs from Gideon Denning's time, it looked a functional rather than pretty place: a long, low building thickly rendered with lime mortar to keep the weather at bay, the doors braced with iron hinges and studded with black nailheads the size of eggs. Inside, there were two rooms: one a dormitory for half a dozen men, the other for eating and drinking.

After he'd found it the first time, the Gaffer went back the following week and then again and again until he could walk straight there every time, whatever the weather. It was a knowledge of the moorland that Denning's guests appreciated when the mist came down and every direction looked the same. They were glad that they had their Little Virgil to guide them.

That was what they'd called him, Little Virgil. It was what Gideon Denning had scribbled in the *Field Guide to British Birds* the Gaffer had been given in thanks for his service. Denning must have known he couldn't read (in fact he was still shaky on a few words up until his death), and assumed that he would think the thing valuable rather than edifying, with its gold embossed lettering and the woodblock prints of hen harriers, red grouse, buzzards and carrion crows. Although, even as a boy, the Gaffer said he knew that it was a present that came with conditions attached. Expensive books were not generally wasted on boys from dirty farms in the arse-end of Yorkshire; it was a reminder that Little Virgil should keep to himself what he'd seen at Far Lodge, especially on those evenings when Denning's old friends from Oxford had come to stay.

The Hellenics, they called themselves; it was the name they'd given to the philosophical society they'd formed during their time at Magdalen. A name that sounded academic enough for them to be able to meet in the upper room of a public house on the Broad without too many questions being asked. Every Wednesday evening at seven, the Gaffer told me, they'd take supper in the parlour bar, read the newspapers, smoke cigars and then go upstairs with two good bottles of claret and try and contact the dead. Denning wore his college scarf around his head and played medium while the others sat at the table with their hands spread and their wine glasses filled. They'd call up Shakespeare and Denning would deliver a sonnet that no one had heard before. They'd tell Cleopatra to make herself known and Denning would paint his eyes and his lips and kiss them all one by one. And at midnight, they'd invite the Devil to their circle for a glass of Château Latour and Denning would make horns with his fingers and chase his fellow undergraduates out into the street.

Years later, when he inherited Far Lodge, he was able to take them to an even better place, miles from anywhere, to play and to drink, especially drink.

'The toffs, Johnny lad,' said the Gaffer. 'You think it's all cups of tea and cucumber sandwiches with them, don't you? I tell you, they put it away like it's going out of fashion. And the women,' he said, 'the women have mouths on them like you wouldn't believe. They'd make a docker blush, some of them.'

'Women went there too?' I said.

'One or two, aye,' said the Gaffer. 'I'll tell you what, the things I saw at Far Lodge after the sun went down, Johnny lad.'

But the pretty book, and the half-crown in the middle pages, instructed him to say nothing about the men who had been taking the opium pipe, the men who had been kissing one another during the séances. What had been spelled out about Mr Denning by the planchette one evening should not be repeated. Nor would it do for rumours to start about the Duke of Bowland's daughter, who'd drunk a thimble of dog's blood and spent the evening on all fours – *her thrup'nies dangling like udders, Johnny lad* – and let the men stroke her as they played canasta.

Most of all he should forget about that night, late in the season, when Gideon Denning, brandied and scotched to slurring point, had read out instructions from an old book he'd brought back from the Levant. And his friends, drunker still, had cut their thumbs and drawn shapes on the door. They were important men and would not wish their names to be mentioned. Nor would they want it reported that someone had come knocking in the small hours, a child by the voice, and they had been too frightened to let them in. They would not want anyone to know, either, that the next day, when they were stalking the deer, there was another with them on the moors. A figure of someone or something, its size constantly growing and shrinking like the firelight shadows in the Lodge, so that when they looked to the ridges behind them, it was impossible to tell how far away it was, or how close.

That was the time the Gaffer had found the small black hand with the six fingers.

'There it were, Johnny lad,' he said. 'Lying in the heather. He's like a snake, the Owd Feller. Sheds his skin.'

'Is that true?' I said.

'Course it is,' said the Gaffer. 'He's always changing. That's why you have to keep your wits about you.'

'Did you show it to the toffs?' I said.

'Nay,' said the Gaffer. 'They were scared enough.'

The Duke of Bowland's daughter, especially, and she'd begged the Gaffer to take them back to the valley as quickly as he could. The others, too, were certain that whatever was following them, whatever they had woken in the night, wanted to do them harm, and now that the weather was coming in they didn't want to be trapped on the moors. If the Gaffer could lead them down to the farm before it turned then there was a handsome tip in it for him and a book about birds that they knew he would like very much.

It was hard to describe the noises that were there behind them as they made their way along the Corpse Road, the Gaffer said. Like crows calling and yet like children crying too. And every so often, the sound seemed to fly over their heads, low enough to make them duck, a hard, loud scraping like metal on stone.

By the time they'd come to the Wall the moors had fallen silent, and in Fiendsdale Clough there were only the familiar voices of rain and water, but none of them spoke until they were in the kitchen at the farm drinking tea and brandy. They hadn't stopped long, enough to dry out in front of the stove, enough to settle their nerves for the drive back to Brownlee Hall, which, a day or so later, Denning closed up for the winter. The servants were released and the doors and windows locked and the chauffeur sent to deliver a book to the end farm in the Briardale Valley.

While the Gaffer was unwrapping the parcel and quietly pocketing the coin that slipped out into his lap, the Devil was wandering from ridge to ridge across the moors. When the rain had come down, he'd lost sight of the ones who'd woken him and he tried to follow their scents instead. But the damp autumn had diluted the trails and they led nowhere. Days went by and then, distantly, he began to catch the sounds of sheep and dogs and whistles that led him to the rubble of the Wall where he hid to watch the shepherds at work. As the sheep brayed and trotted and swerved, two of the lambs peeled away into a mossbog and were soon just white heads crying to be saved. The shepherds went to pull them out with their crooks and the Devil scaled the Wall and caught the ewe closest to him by the horns. His arm around her throat, he pulled her jaw crossways and snapped her neck before she had time to make a noise. Then he cut off the fleece and threw it over his back and went to join the flock as they were driven down into the Endlands.

~

We stopped at the rim of a little hollow and Dadda took out his binoculars again. The deer had settled into a walking pace, pausing now and then to tear at the grass. But they'd got at least a mile ahead of us and were too far away to shoot. The younger of the two stags seemed to have assumed the role of sultan while the other kept his distance and watched.

'Go on,' Dadda said, looking through the binoculars. 'Get yourselves up to the ridge.'

'Won't they hide themselves in the rocks?' I said.

'Nay,' said Dadda. 'There's nowt to eat. They'll go down into the bracken on the other side.'

'Then what?'

'Then we'll be able to pick them off,' he said. 'It's easier to shoot them from above.'

'Do you think we'll have enough daylight?' I said.

'Aye,' said Dadda, looking at the sky. 'We'll be all right. So long as they keep moving.'

But they were content for the moment to stand and feed and the two stags kept vigil on one another, each waiting for the moment when he would have to prove himself. Thumbing on the safety catch, Dadda set the rifle aside and lay down in the heather out of sight. Between the roots were the bilberry bushes that the Gaffer used to pick from while he was out with the dogs, his hands blood red when he got back to the farm. By October, though, the fruits were long gone, like the little birds that had fed on them in the summer. Autumn plays such sad music up there on the moors. There are no meadow pipits, no skylarks. Only the mournful diphthong of the buzzard and the pea-whistle cry of the curlew blown far away to the junction of horizon and sky.

As we kept watch on the deer, a kestrel rose from the bare stems of cotton grass and fluttered so close that we could see its steel hood and butterscotch belly. It fought with the wind for a moment and then settled into an almost perfect stillness and waited for whatever mouthful of meat was quivering in the heather to grow large in its eyes. It had already seen us, of course – it had been watching us since the first gunshot – and knew that if we were a threat then it would only need the twist of a feather-end to take it away from harm.

As a boy, I'd always liked to watch the birds of prey at work. The Gaffer said that they knew the moorland best of all, better than we ever would. They spent their lives peering down at it, scrutinising every inch for signs. The slow unzipping of the water on Top Pond as a rat swam to one of the reed islands. The coming and going of the mother grouse to the nest under the Wall. They knew from the way the grass moved if it was merely the tug of a sudden breeze or the kick-start of a hare. They could swoop or climb on instinct.

'Theirs is a bigger world than ours, Johnny lad,' said the Gaffer. 'They have the sky as well as the earth. You'd like that, wouldn't you?'

'Yes,' I said.

If I hadn't been an otter, then I would have been a hawk.

Dadda brought out his hip flask and took another swig of brandy.

'You sure you don't want some?' he said, wiping the neck on his sleeve.

This time I took it from him and filled my mouth with the stuff, a welcome fire on the tongue and the throat now that the day had started to turn colder.

'You'll be glad to get away from here after Gathering,' said Dadda, pulling up the hood of his jacket. 'Weather like this.'

'We don't have to go,' I said.

'Are we really going to have this conversation again, John?' he said. 'Katherine's a nice lass, but you knew she were never going to want to come and live here when you chose her. That's *why* you chose her, isn't it?'

'Give her a chance, Dadda,' I said. 'She's only been here a couple of days.'

'John, she could stay here for the rest of her life and not feel at home.'

'Mam was new here once,' I said. 'She must have felt the same.'

He looked at me, knowing exactly what I was getting at. 'It were different for her,' he said, and took off his cap and wiped his brow with the inside of his wrist.

'Was it?' I said.

'I mean that folk were different then.'

'I don't think people change,' I said.

'You lot want much more than we ever did,' he said.

'That's not true,' I said.

'It must be,' said Dadda. 'Otherwise you wouldn't have left in the first place, would you?'

'I shouldn't have done,' I said. 'I know that now.'

'Aye, well.'

'You make your bed, do you?' I said.

'Summat like that, aye,' he said, fitting the binoculars back to his eyes.

'You still haven't answered my question,' I said.

He tapped his wedding ring on the casing, itching for a smoke.

'Dadda?' I said.

'It were a long time ago, John,' he said. 'I can't remember how she felt.'

'Come on, you must do.'

'Why do you want to live here?' he said, removing the binoculars and looking at me. 'You never know what's going to happen from one bloody month to the next. Is that really what you want?'

'It's always been like that, Dadda,' I said. 'I know what I'd be coming back to.'

He put his eyes into the rubber cups again. 'It's changed,' he said. 'It's not how it used to be when you were a lad.'

'How's that?' I said.

'I don't know,' said Dadda. 'It just feels like me and your mam saw the best of this place.'

'It can't all come to an end, just like that,' I said.

'Of course it can,' he said. 'Everything does. What do you think's going to happen to Angela's farm? She's no one to take over, has she?'

'She'll have Grace eventually,' I said.

'Come on,' said Dadda. 'She'd never manage that place on her own.'

'All the more reason for me and Kat to come back then,' I said.

Dadda shook his head. 'The Endlands are finished, John,' he said. 'That's it.'

'You're only saying that because of the Gaffer,' I said.

'I've felt like this for a long time,' he said. 'I've got used to the idea. Another few years and then I'll sell up before I get too tired. I'm sure the money would be more use to you than this bloody place, wouldn't it?'

'I don't want your money, Dadda.'

'What do you want then?' he said.

'To pass it on,' I said. 'Like we've always done.'

'Well, I pity the poor bastard you'd lumber with this job,' he said. 'Look at us for Christ's sake, covered in shit and mud.'

'We owe it to the Gaffer, though, don't we?' I said. 'He put his whole life into the farm.'

'You sound like you admire him,' said Dadda.

'Don't you?' I said.

'To be honest, John,' he said, 'I'm glad he's dead.'

The deer began to move on and Dadda gave me a nudge. The kestrel folded its wings and threw its talons into the heather.

It was bereavement talk, that was all. He didn't mean glad. Relieved, maybe, for the Gaffer's sake. Eighty-six was old enough to be still working and he wouldn't have wanted to see him doddering about the valley in his nineties, useless as one of the old dogs that Jim used to look after. Dadda might not have admired him as such, but he could at least see the sacrifice the Gaffer had made to the Endlands. If only because it was equal to his own.

~

We followed the deer for another hour, giving them the space to roam and the chance to forget we were there. When they came closer to Blackmire Edge, they began to skirt around the wide expanse of peat that gave the place its name and head up to the strip of gritstone on the ridge. Wind and rain had peeled away the grass and the peat here and on the other side the moorland fell away from the escarpment to a vale of deep bracken.

'Go on, you bastards,' said Dadda, willing the deer to stop lingering on the skyline and head down the slope.

'Here,' he said and handed the binoculars to me, while he rooted around for a stone.

He threw it as far as he could and the sound of it sent the deer running out of sight.

We followed them and of course Dadda was up the gradient much quicker than I was and waited for me in the rocks. The rain that had been threatening all afternoon finally drifted towards us and by the time I came to where Dadda was crouched on the ridge, it had fingered its way between my hood and collar and found my skin. Dadda passed me his hip flask and I took a couple of swigs, feeling the brandy burning and gassing as I looked down.

A hundred feet below us, the older stag, bison-thick in the chest and throat, had begun to move closer to the harem and let out a deep cow-moan that drifted away as white air. The young stag matched him and shook his antlers as the hinds fed in the undergrowth. Dadda kept the rifle out of their sight and watched them with the rain dribbling off the brim of his cap.

'What are you waiting for?' I said. 'Can't we just get it done and go back down to the farm?'

'Not yet,' he said. 'Wait.'

The rain was puddling around our feet and flowing in miniature waterfalls between the rocks. The cloud drifted lower, momentarily veiling the deer below us.

'It'll be dark soon,' I said. 'Then we won't see a thing.'

'Quiet,' said Dadda and moved along the ridge a little way as the older stag groaned again, drawing the younger male away from the hinds and into the open grassland. For a few minutes they stalked each other, keeping their distance, one lowering his antlers and the other doing the same before lifting their heads again and showing off their voices.

What they saw, or what each sensed in the other, I don't know, but they suddenly dropped their heads and rammed forward at the same moment, their antlers clacking and grating. With their noses close to the ground, they muscled and strained, turning each other in and out of the bogwater, slipping and bracing in the peat. The older stag was much stronger and twisted the young stag's head to the side, turning his ear into the rain. For a while their horns were caught together and they pulled rather than pushed trying to untangle the prongs. When they did, the older stag lost his footing and before he could recover the younger drove his antlers into the side of his face, raking open his throat and tearing out one of his eyes. There was a feeble attempt at retaliation but as soon as the older stag was on his feet again he ran away, breasting through the ferns. The younger stag tipped back his head, gave a bassy affirmation of victory in his throat, and then returned to his hinds.

His defeated rival moved slowly through the bracken, his fur slathered in mud. He snuffled and shook his head to try and dislodge the pain but then his legs gave way and he lay down, his chest rising and falling.

'Let me take the other one,' I said.

'You?' said Dadda. 'When was the last time you held a rifle?'

'I need to learn again,' I said.

'Aye, well, I've a pop-gun back at the farm,' he said. 'You can shoot tin cans off the fence all day if you like.'

'Come on, Dadda,' I said. 'Teach me.'

'I told you,' he said. 'You're best off well away from here.'

'Please, Dadda,' I said, and held out my hands.

He looked at me and then gave me the rifle.

'Hold it steady,' he said, as he slotted a new round into the chamber.

I wedged the stock into my shoulder and Dadda adjusted my hands.

'Here,' he said. 'Set your feet apart a bit more an' all.'

He kicked at my boots and moved me into the right position.

Looking down the sight, the darkening moorland blurred as I

tried to settle the weight of the rifle. I swung past the whole herd before tracking back and putting the young stag's pretty eye in the circle.

'Got him?' said Dadda.

The stag ducked down to tear at the ferns and then lifted his head again, working his lower jaw as he ate. His ear flicked and he blinked away the rainwater, his attention on the hinds.

'Have you got him, John?'

'I've got him,' I said. 'I've got him.'

'Go on then,' said Dadda. 'Before he disappears.'

'All right.'

'Don't tense up,' he said. 'If you tense up you won't hit owt but thin air.'

'I'm not tensing up,' I said.

'You are,' he said. 'There's no creep on that trigger. Just pull it straight back.'

The stag looked up and the crosshairs met on his forehead. But before I could shoot he turned away, distracted as I was by the sound of a voice that drifted in on the wind; a vague and distant cry that quickly died away. However small the noise, it was enough to send the deer bursting out of the ferns, the hinds running close together and the stag behind them.

I tried to keep track of him as best I could but he shuddered in and out of the scope and as soon as the butt of the rifle kicked against my shoulder I knew that I'd missed. While my ears whistled, Dadda took the gun off me, emptied the chamber and loaded it again before the stag was out of range. Following the antlers with the muzzle, his eye wide and unblinking as he looked down the sight, Dadda waited, waited, then fired. The shot struck something and reverberated in the hollow but the stag carried on, splashing through the bogs and losing himself in the mist.

Dadda coughed and spat into the rocks.

'I know, I know,' he said. 'I heard it too.'

It was almost dark by the time we got back to the farmhouse. Musket and Fly came out sniffing at our clothes, smelled death on us and went away to their kennels.

Having been out for so long, Dadda was fretting about the ram but I managed to persuade him to at least change into a dry coat before he went to check on him. As we'd come down Fiendsdale Clough, his cough had got worse and he'd had to stop a number of times at the cairns on the path to catch his breath.

'Who would have been out on the moors in this weather?' I said. 'You don't think it was the Sturzakers, do you? Ken and Vinny?'

'What would they be doing up there?' said Dadda.

'I don't know, poaching?'

'They'd have had their dogs with them,' said Dadda. 'I didn't hear any dogs, did you?'

I hadn't. Just that single, falling cry.

'It were probably birdwatchers,' said Dadda.

'Birdwatchers?'

'Aye, they come over from Wyresdale and get themselves lost,' he said. 'We've found a few behind the Wall before now.'

'There wouldn't be anyone up there birdwatching at this time of year,' I said. 'There's nothing much to see, is there?'

'Look, I don't know who it were,' said Dadda. 'Perhaps it weren't owt at all. But don't mention it to Bill. It'll only make him worse.'

He knocked again on the scullery door and waited for someone to let us in out of the rain.

'I'm coming, I'm coming,' said Angela and we could hear her

humming the tune to 'The Winter King' as she wrestled with the key and the handle. It was what they always sang as they made the Ram's Crown. Out of all the old songs, it's Adam's favourite. The line about the tup doing his business with the ewes makes him laugh.

When the Devil has been and gone,
Jump on their backs, sire, one by one.
Take your crown, oh Winter King,
Fill the ewes and give us spring.

'Jesus,' said Angela, when she finally opened the door. 'Look at the state of you. I hope you didn't get piss-wet through for nowt.'

'Don't worry,' said Dadda. 'We found them.'

'How many were there?' she said.

'Three,' said Dadda, taking off his coat and hanging it as a shapeless fish skin on the hook by the door. 'Three that we saw anyway. There might be more, but they won't come over this way now.'

'And you got them all, did you?' said Angela.

'Aye, we did,' said Dadda, giving me the briefest of looks.

We needn't have worried about telling Bill what we'd heard, as the Dyers had already gone home to talk about reorganising the house. Since Jeff had been out of prison, Laurel, at least, had been hoping that he, Liz and Grace would all come back to live with her and Bill instead of with Angela. Theirs was a much bigger cottage. And anyway, Liz was a Dyer now and it would be the Dyers' farm that she'd be running with Jeff when the time came.

To persuade Liz would be a struggle but Jeff would move quite happily back across the valley to his parents' place and Angela would have gladly carried his bags. She was one of the few people who saw through him and he knew it. Had Liz's union with Jeff on the riverbanks in Sullom Wood that summer I'd left for university not been blessed nine months later by the arrival of Grace, then she would have made sure that she steered well clear of him. Though I suppose it would have been difficult to keep them apart when they lived within sight of each other all the time.

'I don't know why Laurel's bothering to make plans with Jeff in mind, to be honest,' said Angela, taking Dadda's cap and beating off the wetness with her hand. 'If he turns up tomorrow it'll be the first promise he's kept in his life.'

She went back to the kitchen and joined in the loud conversation Grace and Liz were having, the three of them criss-crossing Kat, who sat at the table dressed in Liz's old jeans and woollen jumper. The sleeves were rolled back to thick brown rings that sagged from her wrists, and the neck was so stretched that it almost slipped off one shoulder.

'Where have you been?' she said when I sat down next to her. 'You're soaking.'

'You know where I've been,' I said.

'Until this time?' she said.

'It's a long walk,' I said.

'Why didn't you wake me before you left this morning?' she said.

'I thought you might need the sleep,' I said. 'What's wrong?'

'Nothing,' she said, but I could tell that she was trying to cover her nose without making a show of it. Whatever she thought she could smell the night before had come back and was making her nauseous. It was a phase of pregnancy that would pass and no doubt there would be something else even worse to take its place as the baby grew. It was the curse of the first-time mother. Nothing was familiar. Nothing felt natural. How could it be, when it caused such disruption to the body and the mind?

'Katherine,' said Angela, taking her attention away from me and back to the spread of leaves and flowers in the middle of the table. 'Come on. You wanted to know how to do it, didn't you?'

It was after the first successful Devil's Day just after the Great War that they'd made a crown for the ram, handing the privilege of coronation to one of the children. It had been quite a plain thing in those days, the Gaffer said, nothing more than a small hoop of bent willow wands and hay. But over the years, it's become a much grander creation that takes all day to make, mostly because there is more talk than work. The crown on the table was a large wreath of dried flowers and dogwood stalks, holly prickles and rowan leaves. Acorns in their cups had been carefully tied into the weave of dried hay, with beechnuts threaded on to string and the chain festooned around the rim.

'Look, Granddad Tom,' said Grace. 'What do you think?'

'That's very nice is that, love,' said Dadda, patting the back of his head dry with a tea towel.

'Do you think Daddy will like it, Uncle John?' said Grace.

'I'm sure he will,' I said.

'What time will he be home tomorrow?' she said. 'Will he be there when I wake up?'

'I shouldn't think so, Grace,' said Angela. 'Like this,' she said and showed Kat how to wind the ivy through the green ribbon strapped around the crown.

Kat took over, pricked herself almost immediately on the holly and sucked her finger.

'She'll have to toughen up, John,' said Liz. 'What's she going to be like when she comes back at Lambing if she's fussing over a little cut?'

'I'm not fussing,' said Kat and, for a moment, I wondered if she might drop the baggy jeans she was wearing and show them the scars on her thigh. Proof that she hadn't lived her life unscathed.

'Don't worry, Auntie Katherine,' said Grace. 'I'll show you what to do when the lambs come. You can help me feed the runts.' And she went into great detail about the various weaklings that she'd bottle-fed that spring.

'Tell Katherine another time, Grace,' said Angela. 'Tom will want a bit of peace and quiet after the day he's had.'

'Aye, come on,' said Liz. 'Fetch your coat. Time for home.'

'But I want to practise my magic trick for when Daddy comes,' said Grace.

'Another time,' said Liz. 'Granddad Tom's tired, aren't you?'

'Don't mind me,' said Dadda, putting on his raincoat. 'I've to check on the ram.'

When he went out, Grace moved her chair very close to Kat's, so that their shoulders were touching. The dressing on her hand had come off now and the wound had scabbed over in a three inch crust.

'Do you like magic tricks, Auntie Katherine?' said Grace.

'Yes,' said Kat, doing her best to brighten up. 'Why, do you know some?'

'The Gaffer used to teach me all the time,' she said.

'That must have been fun,' said Kat. 'What were they, card tricks or something?'

'Sometimes,' said Grace. 'Or there's one with a coin.'

'Go on,' said Kat.

'Everyone's seen it,' said Grace.

'I haven't,' said Kat.

Grace leaned to the side and put her fingers in her pocket, teasing out a penny that had the likeness of a Roman emperor crudely minted on both sides.

'Nero?' said Kat.

'Caligula,' said Grace.

'Didn't he marry his horse, or something?' said Angela as she swept the table.

'No, he made his horse a priest,' said Grace.

'And his pig the Pope?' said Liz. 'Where do you get this stuff from? School?'

'He'd roast people alive in the brazen bull,' said Grace. 'And he got his sister pregnant.'

'Did he?' said Angela.

'Aye,' said Grace. 'He cut the baby out of her and threw it on the fire.'

'He couldn't have done that,' said Liz.

'He could do owt he wanted,' said Grace. 'He were the emperor, weren't he?'

'It was no wonder he was mad,' said Kat.

'He weren't mad,' said Grace. 'I think not being able to do what you want makes you mad, don't you?'

'That's a difficult philosophical question,' said Kat.

'It's what me and the Gaffer used to talk about,' Grace shrugged and reached over for the empty water glasses on the table, upturning them and putting the coin under the one on the left.

'Now watch,' she said. 'I'll make it move.'

She covered both glasses with a teatowel that had been left on the back of one of the chairs and when she lifted it again, the penny had switched places.

'Very clever,' said Kat. 'Show me again.'

'That's for kids,' said Grace. 'I can do better tricks. I can read your mind. I can tell you what you're thinking.'

'All right then,' said Kat. 'What am I thinking now?'

'It doesn't work like that,' said Grace, nudging her with her shoulder. 'I have to say a word first. Mummy, will you show her?'

'You don't want to know what I'm thinking,' said Liz, and Angela laughed and they took the offcuts from the Ram's Crown out through the scullery to the compost bin.

'Hold my hands, Auntie Katherine,' said Grace. 'I need to connect to your thought waves.'

Grace clamped her fingers in hers and Kat tried to smile but couldn't help watching Grace's thumb as it smoothed a little circle on her knuckle.

'Colour,' said Grace, closing her eyes. 'Green.'

'That's right,' said Kat.

'Animal. Blackbird.'

'Right again,' said Kat.

'Number. Six.'

'You're very good at this, aren't you?' said Kat.

'Happy,' said Grace. 'Baby.'

'Of course,' said Kat.

'Home. Daddy's house. The vicarage'

'Perhaps once,' said Kat. 'Not now.'

'Fear. The Endlands.'

'I'm not frightened here,' said Kat, looking at me. 'Why would I be frightened?'

'Love. John.'

'Definitely.'

'Womb. Relief.'

'Relief? What do you mean?' said Kat.

'Tick-tock, tick-tock,' said Grace. 'You were worried, weren't you?'

'Sorry?'

'That it would be too late.'

'Perhaps you should go and get your coat,' said Kat. 'I think your mum wants to go home.'

'You didn't like the other men enough, did you?' said Grace.

'But then when you heard the tick-tock you thought that perhaps you should have let them.'

Kat looked at me.

'Leave Kat alone now, Grace,' I said.

'That's why you let John stay after that party, isn't it?' said Grace. 'Tick-tock. Tick-tock. He's the only one who's ever seen your scars.'

Kat stopped wrestling with Grace's hands and looked at her.

'What?' she said. 'What did you say?'

When Liz and Angela came up from the scullery Grace let go and opened her eyes.

'Is she going to be sick, John?' said Angela, nodding at Kat.

'A little cut on the finger and she's white as a sheet,' said Liz. 'Jesus, John, I think you'd better take her home.'

'What do you think of the trick, Auntie Katherine?' said Grace. 'Do you think Daddy will like it?'

'Who told you those things?' said Kat.

'I can't show you how it's done, can I?' said Grace. 'If everyone could do magic tricks then it wouldn't be magic any more.'

'You look worried, Mrs Pentecost,' Liz said, patting Kat's arm as she went past her to get her coat. 'Are you nervous about Devil's Day tomorrow?'

'Perhaps you'd better hide yourself in the sheep pen when the Owd Feller comes,' said Angela and laughed as she gathered up her things.

'I don't know,' said Liz. 'It might be good to have a vicar's lass in the house as bait.'

'I don't want him to eat her,' said Grace, getting off her chair and looping her arm through Kat's.

'He'd go to bed hungry if he did,' said Angela.

She put on her wax jacket and was tugging the zip over her chest when someone started banging on the front door.

Laurel's voice came urgently and then Bill's as he rapped at the glass.

'Bloody hell,' said Angela. 'He'll have his hand through in a minute.'

Dadda must have heard them outside and he came in with Bill shouting and Laurel apologising.

'I'm sorry, Tom,' she said as she came down the hallway. 'I'm sorry for coming over like this.'

'Summat wrong?' said Angela, when Laurel appeared at the kitchen door.

Before she could answer, Bill sidled past her, his coat spattered with blood.

'You'd better get yourself home, Angela,' he said. 'Make sure your animals are all right.'

'Jesus, what's happened?' said Liz, and Grace slid down from the table and stared.

'It's our Douglas,' said Laurel. 'They've torn chunks out of him. When we got back, he were lying there dead.'

'Who'd done that?' said Angela.

'Bloody Sturzakers' dogs,' said Bill.

'What, you saw them, did you?' said Liz.

'No, I didn't see them,' said Bill. 'I didn't need to see them.'

'Were the cows all right?' said Angela.

'Aye,' said Bill.

'And the geese?'

'Aye, aye,' said Bill, distracted.

'You didn't lose any geese?' said Angela.

'No, thank God,' said Laurel and crossed herself.

'How can it have been dogs then?' said Dadda.

'Tom's right,' said Angela. 'If the Sturzakers' dogs had got on to the farm, you'd have a yard full of dead birds.'

Bill dismissed her with his hand. 'I'm going to see them

first thing tomorrow morning,' he said. 'That's it. I've had enough.'

'I still don't think that's a good idea,' said Laurel.

'Aye,' said Dadda. 'Without any proof, there's nowt you can do. Just bury your dog and leave it at that.'

'No proof?' said Bill. 'I've all the proof I need wrapped up in an owd blanket in the toolshed.'

'Oh, stop shouting, Bill,' said Laurel. 'It's bad enough.'

'Well,' he said. 'It's about time we had words with that bastard family.'

'I agree,' I said. 'First the fire and now this.'

'Keep out of it,' said Dadda.

'So you'll come with me, John?' said Bill.

'Of course,' I said.

'You stay put,' said Dadda. 'If anyone's going with Bill, it'll be me. It's nowt for you to concern yourself with.'

'Why would the Sturzakers go to so much trouble?' said Angela. 'It doesn't make any sense.'

'It's obvious,' said Bill. 'This is him warning me off after yesterday, isn't it?'

'You don't know that,' said Dadda.

'The Sturzakers came to our farm, Tom,' said Bill. 'If someone had come here and done this to you, don't tell me you'd just sit back and do nowt. The Gaffer didn't, did he?'

'That's enough, Bill,' said Laurel.

'The Gaffer? What do you mean?' I said.

'Nowt,' said Dadda.

'Let's go home, Bill,' said Laurel. 'I don't want to be away from the farm for too long.'

They looked at one another and then Bill sent Grace to get her coat from the hallway.

When the door had closed, Bill said, 'Well, are you going to tell him then, Tom? You said that you would when he came up for Gathering.'

Dadda looked at Kat.

'She's John's wife,' said Bill. 'She needs to know too.'

'Not now,' said Laurel, pulling his sleeve. 'Another time.'

But Bill stayed in the chair and looked at Dadda again.

'Come on,' said Bill. 'It's better that they hear the truth from us than the crap Ken Sturzaker comes out with.'

'Hold on,' said Liz, gesturing at Kat. 'We hardly know her. We don't know what she's going to do. She's not from the valley, is she?'

'She is now,' said Bill.

'This isn't the time,' said Angela. 'We'll talk about it later.'

'Or not at all,' said Liz.

'I agree,' said Laurel. 'Katherine doesn't need to know.'

'She married into the family,' said Bill. 'She has a right to know, they both do.'

'A right to know what?' said Kat, looking anxiously around the table.

'Tom?' said Bill and Dadda lit his roll-up and looked away.

Bill leant forward. 'Listen, John,' he said, 'something happened after Lambing back in the spring. We've been meaning to tell you, but what with the wedding and everything, it just didn't seem right. And we wanted to wait until you came here so we could explain it in person.'

'What is it?' I said. 'What's happened?'

'I don't think the Gaffer meant to do it,' said Angela. 'He just reacted on the spur of the moment.'

'Aye,' said Bill. 'It weren't really his fault.'

'That boy shouldn't have been here,' said Angela.

'What boy?' I said.

We'd always lambed late, so that new life emerged in better weather and warmer sunlight. That way, within a few days of being born, the lambs could be taken with their mothers up to the high pastures. Down in the valley they got fretful and restless. It wasn't where they instinctively belonged and they seemed to sense it keenly. The Gaffer said that he'd seen sheep all looking up at the ridges of the fells and braying in the same way they brayed when they were hungry. The quicker they were on the moors the better.

But on the middle day of April, the day I'd arrived to help, snow had started falling and not stopped all afternoon. The ewes put their new lambs between themselves and the walls of the bye-field, bearing the brunt of the weather, and Dadda wanted to take them inside. But the Gaffer, looking up at the sky, said that it would do the lambs no harm to get used to the cold and the snow would stop before dark, which it did, leaving the valley strangely luminous when the daylight gave out.

A few days of cold wind kept the snow from thawing, and more lambs came at all hours. The Dyers and the Beasleys took it in shifts to watch the ewes but Dadda, and especially the Gaffer, didn't sleep for more than a couple of hours before they were back in the shed, watching and waiting.

But even when the natural April warmth returned and the snow began to melt away in the valley, Dadda and the Gaffer had to give the moors another day or two to follow suit. It would have been colder up there and the hollows still deep enough for lambs to be lost in.

I'd stayed for a week and once most of the ewes had lambed Dadda drove me to the station and I made my way back to Suffolk. It had been that night when a young man – a boy, really, Dadda said, a boy not much older than the ones I taught at Churchmeads – had come to steal the new-borns. The

Gaffer had been on his own in the lambing shed and, hearing the distress of the sheep outside in the bye-field, he'd gone across the yard to the house and fetched his shotgun from the kitchen.

Kat put her hand over her mouth and closed her eyes. No one spoke for a few minutes until Dadda stubbed out his roll-up and coughed.

'I'm sorry you had to hear that, John,' he said.

'What did you do?' I said. 'Afterwards, I mean.'

'That's enough,' said Dadda. 'You don't need to know any more.'

'Tell me,' I said. 'What happened to the boy?'

'We took him to Sullom Wood,' said Bill.

'And?'

'Jesus,' said Liz. 'Do you really want the details?'

'Who was he?' I said.

'God knows,' said Bill. 'No one's come looking for him.'

Kat had her head in her hands now and was crying. I rubbed her back and then Laurel shushed her and smoothed her hair away from her face.

'It's all right,' she said. 'We're all here for you.'

'I need to go home,' said Kat.

'I know, love,' said Laurel. 'It must be hard for you.'

'I don't understand what's happening,' said Kat.

'God does,' said Laurel, putting her hand on the crucifix around her neck.

'What?' said Kat.

'I prayed for His guidance and He answered,' said Laurel.

She sat down now and looked Kat in the eyes.

'You see, the sins of the world, Katherine, love,' she said. 'They're too much for only a few people to bear.'

'Give over, woman,' said Bill. 'What are you talking about?'

Laurel ignored him and arranged Kat's hair behind her ears. 'Sometimes,' she said, 'God just asks us to share the load.'

Kat shook her head and pushed Laurel's hands away. They all tried to stop her, but she went off up the stairs and into the attic room.

~

I found her sitting on the edge of the bed rubbing her stomach as her reflection came and went in the dangling mirror.

'Swear to me that you didn't know, John,' she said.

'Of course I didn't know,' I said. 'You heard what they said. They kept it from me as well as you.'

'Why did he do it?' said Kat.

'He must have thought he was doing the right thing,' I said.

'God, it makes me feel sick,' said Kat, staring at the floorboards, 'that they all came to the wedding having done that.'

'It was the Gaffer, Kat,' I said. 'Not the rest of them.'

'Come on, they're all just as guilty,' she said.

'What were they supposed to do?' I said. 'Turn him in? The Gaffer was eighty-six. He'd have died in prison.'

'He killed someone,' said Kat, looking at me with red eyes. 'He took someone's life, John. Christ, no wonder Grace has been acting so strangely. The poor, poor girl.'

'She doesn't know anything,' I said.

'She's not stupid, John,' said Kat. 'She knows plenty by the sounds of it.'

'Meaning?'

'What kind of conversations have you had with her about us exactly?'

'I didn't tell her about your scars, Kat,' I said. 'And anyway, I could ask you the same question.'

'As if I'd talk to her about things like that,' she said.

'She seemed to know a lot about it,' I said. 'Is that really how you felt? Did you feel like you had to take whatever you could get?'

'Of course not,' said Kat. 'Don't be ridiculous.' She sniffed and nodded downstairs. 'I suppose they're all wondering what I'm going to do next, aren't they?' she said.

'What are you going to do?' I said.

'We've got to tell someone, John,' she said. 'That's the only thing we can do.'

'And what do you think would happen to this place?' I said.

She looked at me and frowned. 'What are you saying?' she said. 'That we keep it to ourselves?'

'I'm saying that you should think about Grace, even if you don't care what happens to anyone else. No, it's not blackmail, Kat. You'd ruin her life. You know I'm right.'

'We could take her with us back to Suffolk,' said Kat. 'She shouldn't be here. Not with these people.'

I held her face to make her look at me.

'I'm not saying that what the Gaffer did was right, Kat,' I said. 'But it happened and they did what they did. What good would it do to go around shouting about it now?'

'We'd be doing the right thing, John,' she said.

'By whom?'

'Come on, you know what I mean,' she said, taking my hands away. 'I won't be able to live with myself if I don't say anything, and neither will you.'

'Look,' I said. 'It's been six months and no one's come looking for this lad, have they?'

'But someone must be missing him,' said Kat. 'Someone will come sooner or later.'

'Even if they do, there won't be anything left to find in the Wood. Not after all this time.'

She swallowed and smeared away new tears.

'What about this Ken Sturzaker?' she said. 'He knows something. He said so at the wake.'

'He'll have heard half a rumour about nothing much,' I said.

'Sometimes half a rumour is worse,' said Kat.

'That's all Sturzaker ever has,' I said. 'That's why no one listens to him.'

'I still don't think you should go and see him tomorrow.'

'I think Dadda would prefer it if I did,' I said. 'Then at least there'll be two of us holding Bill's lead.'

'I just want to go home,' she said.

'You'll have to wait,' I said. 'We've come to help with Gathering.'

'I can't stay here,' she said. 'Not now.'

'But we're needed,' I said.

'What am I supposed to say to them?' said Kat. 'After this?'

'You don't need to say anything about it,' I said. 'Just pitch in and help. We've got work to do.'

'You're asking me to forget what they've just told me?'

'No,' I said. 'Just to leave it in the past where it belongs.'

She started to cry again, wiping her eyes with the sleeves of Liz's old jumper.

'What right did they have to put us in this position?' she said. 'It's nothing to do with us. Why did they have to tell us?'

'Because we're Pentecosts,' I said.

Devil's Day

It was just unfortunate that the Gaffer had been on duty that night in the lambing shed. If Dadda had got to the bye-field first, or if I'd been there and not back in Suffolk, then it was possible that the boy would still be alive. The slightest hint of noise, a few lights coming on in the house and I'm sure that a novice like that would have turned on his heel rather than put up a fight. Perhaps he would have come back better prepared or mob-handed and tried again, I don't know. Maybe he'd have stayed away from the valley for good. But it wasn't really worth thinking about that now. As I'd said to Kat, we couldn't change anything.

Before she finally went to sleep, she cried for a while longer, telling me that she was glad I'd been at home when it happened, that I wasn't like the others. I didn't say so, but I knew that if I'd been here that night I'd have done exactly the same as them. I'd have helped carry that boy into the Wood.

The following morning, we put the Dyers' dog into the back of Bill's truck with the wooden cages he and Laurel used to transport their birds to the markets at Christmas and Easter. Despite being left in the cold workshed all night, Douglas was starting to smell, but Bill was determined to go to Sturzaker's regardless.

'I don't know what you're expecting him to say,' said Dadda.

'Even if it were his dogs, he's not going to hold his hands up and say so, is he?'

'I want to ask him straight to his face,' said Bill.

'You can ask him any way you want,' said Dadda. 'It won't make any difference.'

'I just want him to know that I know,' said Bill. 'All right?'

He changed gear and slowed to clank over the cattle grid at the start of Sullom Wood. The wind was moving the trees as one body and even over the whine of the engine as Bill accelerated again the noise was loud and vast, like the long breaking of a tide. Leaves skirled in the gusts, sunlight came and went, there was rain in the air as the year edged towards its closure. I didn't want to leave Dadda to face the winter by himself. It was always hard leaving him after Gathering but it would be worse this year. Folk in the Endlands had become used to the rain and the hail, of course, and carried on anyway, but there were times when it was impossible to be outdoors. Times when the cloud came down so low in the valley that the other farms disappeared from view. Then the house would seem empty. Then the ghosts would come. Better that there was talk. Better the sound of a baby crying than nothing at all.

We passed the church – strange to think that the Gaffer was lying there under the blustering larches – and Bill turned over the bridge and drove to the far end of New Row.

Sturzaker's car was hitched up on the pavement, a battered saloon with balding tyres, the back window plastered with stickers, the driver's door a different colour to the rest.

'Good,' said Bill, 'he's in. You let me do the talking, all right?'

We followed him across the road and Dadda reluctantly rang the bell. The windows of the house were fogged with condensation that had mottled the curtains with grey mould. Damp had chewed the wooden sills too and thistles grew in the cracks on the front steps. All the houses on New Row were the same. They must have seemed palatial to the millworkers when they'd first been built but now they would have been better off razed to the ground.

Even at this time in the morning the Sturzaker house was loud with arguments and dogs, and a radio had been turned up to distortion. It was just as well that Mr and Mrs Earby next door were both deaf.

Dadda rang the bell again and Karen, Vinny's little sister, the youngest of Sam and Cheryl's offspring, lifted the nets at the front window and grinned at us before squashing her face against the glass, moving her lips like slugs.

'Jesus,' said Bill. 'They should have neutered the fuckin' Sturzakers a long time ago.'

A shout came from inside and she was hauled away by Jackie, who smiled thinly at us and pulled the lapels of her dressing gown over her cleavage. She called for her husband and the door opened with Sturzaker's face in the crack that the chain allowed.

'What do you want?' he said, trying to keep one of his bull terriers from escaping into the street with his knee.

'A word, Ken,' said Bill.

'About what?' said Sturzaker, looking at the three of us.

'About what's in the back of the truck,' said Bill.

Sturzaker glanced over the tops of our heads at Bill's Daihatsu. 'And what would that be then?' he said.

'As if you don't know,' said Bill.

Sturzaker turned his eyes to Dadda. 'Fuck's sake, Tom,' he said. 'It's half-six in the morning.'

'Just come and look,' said Dadda. 'Then we can leave you in peace.'

The door closed, the chain slid back and Sturzaker came out in his slippers and his overcoat.

Bill opened the back of the truck and lifted the tarpaulin off the dog.

'And?' said Sturzaker

'What do you mean and?' said Bill. 'Never mind fuckin' and. It were your dogs that did this, weren't it?'

'Do you know what he's on about, Tom?' said Sturzaker.

'Never mind him,' said Bill. 'You listen to me. I'm talking.'

'You're talking summat, Bill, aye,' said Sturzaker.

Jackie had come to the door now and called to her husband through gritted teeth. 'Let them come inside for Christ's sake,' she said. 'The whole street doesn't need to listen, do they?'

Holding her dressing gown closed with one hand and restraining the terrier with the other, she held the door for us as we came in.

'Is this about the fire?' she said. 'Ken's already told you that it weren't our Vinny, haven't you, Ken?'

'I did try,' said Sturzaker.

Catching the scent of the farm on us, the little black dog in the hallway strained and barked, setting off the others that came to the gate at the top of the stairs.

'Take this bloody thing into the front room, Ken,' said Jackie, and Sturzaker looked up at her and dragged the terrier away.

Jackie had worked at the Croppers' Arms since the hairdresser's in town had closed down, the darling of the old boys who heaved themselves on to the high stools at the bar to get a look at the contents of her bingo blouse: eyes down, look in. She was one of the rumours that had attached themselves to the Gaffer over the years. Behind the empty beer kegs in the back yard one night, was it? Or down in the cellar between changing the barrels? No one else had noticed, and I hadn't said anything to the others, but during the funeral I'd seen her slip in at the back of church during the second verse of 'O for a Thousand Tongues to Sing' and slip out again before the sermon.

Without the make-up that she layered on for work, Jackie was almost unrecognisable. Her eyes were puffy and her chin cross-hatched with wrinkles. She must have been pushing sixty at least, and helping Cheryl look after Vinny and Karen while Sam was inside was taking its toll. Mind you, she'd looked old ever since Lennie drowned.

'How are you, John, love?' she said, as she took us into the kitchen. 'How's that wife of yours? The Gaffer used to talk about her all the time in the pub, you know.'

'She's fine,' I said.

'She must wonder what she's come to here,' she said, almost tripping over the pair of yapping dachshunds pawing at her shins. Through the window another dozen dogs jumped and barked in a wire mesh cage in the back yard.

It was Karen who had the radio up to its full volume – probably to drown out the dogs and the argument her grandparents were having as we arrived – and she sat at the table with a spoon in her fist scraping out the flesh of a swede. The village children would all be out with lanterns tonight. The doors along New Row done up with spray-on cobwebs and hung with cardboard skeletons.

'Switch it off or take it upstairs, Karen,' said Jackie. 'I can't hear myself think.'

The little girl held on to the radio and pretended not to be able to hear her and it was only when Sturzaker came into the room that she cut the deafening fuzz.

'Bedroom,' he said. 'Go on.'

She huffed and tossed the spoon loudly on to the table before she went out.

Sturzaker waited until he heard her feet on the stairs.

'So your dog gets killed and you come straight here?' he said. 'How does that work, then?'

'Killed?' said Jackie.

'Last night,' I said.

'And you think it were one of Ken's, do you?' she said. 'Well, you're probably right. They're nasty bloody things.'

'Unless they've learned how to undo padlocks,' said Sturzaker, nodding out of the window, 'then it can't have been one of mine.'

'They're not all in cages, though, are they?' said Bill, as more dogs thumped and padded through the bedrooms upstairs.

'The ones I keep in the house wouldn't be able to do that to your dog, Bill,' said Sturzaker. 'Anyway, they're all accounted for. If one had got out, I'd know. They're all listed in the book. I can show it you, if you want.'

The dogs upstairs rumbled back the other way and a tired-looking wolfhound wandered into the kitchen looking for the warmth of the fire.

'How can you know what you've got here?' said Bill. 'You're overrun, man.'

'I have told him that,' said Jackie. 'I did say that, didn't I, Ken?'

Sturzaker got up and opened a drawer in the table. He held up a little leather book and passed it to Bill.

'You count them,' he said. 'If you find one missing, then I'll listen to you.'

'I know they didn't come to the farm by themselves,' said Bill. 'Someone brought them.'

'Someone?' said Sturzaker.

'You know who I mean,' said Bill.

'Do I?'

'Your Vinny,' said Bill, looking through the window. 'I've seen him out walking some of them big fuckers you've got. A couple of those could have torn up our Douglas, no problem.'

'It weren't Vinny,' said Sturzaker, sitting down at the table again.

'How do you know?' said Bill. 'You've no idea what he's up to most of the time.'

'Excuse me?' said Jackie.

'Well, is he here?' said Bill, glancing at the stained polystyrene tiles on the ceiling.

'No,' said Sturzaker.

'There you are then,' said Bill. 'Point proven.'

'He's not been here for a week,' said Jackie. 'He's gone away with Cheryl to see his auntie in Bradford. Didn't Ken tell you that?'

Sturzaker drank his tea and looked at us.

'Sorry to disappoint you, Bill,' he said.

'Come on,' said Dadda, patting Bill on the shoulder. 'Let's go. We've got enough to do today.'

'Hang on a minute,' said Bill, nodding at Sturzaker. 'I'd still like to know where he were yesterday evening.'

'Night-shift,' Sturzaker replied. 'Ask at the abattoir if you want.'

'He's only just got in,' said Jackie.

'I don't usually have pork chops for my breakfast, Bill,' said Sturzaker, indicating the plate of food that Jackie was preparing for him.

Bill handed him back the leather book.

'I'll show you out,' said Sturzaker and got up from his chair.

'Will we see you in the pub, while you're here, John?' said Jackie. 'You and your wife?'

'He's not stopping,' said Dadda, and took me out into the hall.

Another couple of dogs squirmed past us and started barking for food.

'Jesus, Ken,' said Jackie, pushing the smallest one away. 'I won't be stopping much longer here myself at this rate. Can't you get rid of these bloody things?'

Sturzaker cut her off by closing the door with his foot.

'Sorry you had a wasted trip, lads,' he said.

'It weren't wasted,' said Bill. 'I said I wanted to look you in the eyes, and I've done that.'

'And what did you see?'

'That you had summat to do with it.'

'Is that right?' said Sturzaker, unlatching the front door. 'You want your eyes testing, then.'

'Listen,' said Bill, his voice low now that we were standing in the street. 'If owt else happens in the Endlands, I'll be back down here before you know what's fuckin' hit you.'

Sturzaker smiled and shook the dregs of his tea out on to the steps.

'You ever heard of a bloke called Dent?' he said.

'No, we haven't,' said Dadda, trying to encourage Bill to come away.

'Dent?' said Bill. 'Who's Dent?'

'Paul Dent,' said Sturzaker. 'Liberace, they call him.'

'Pouf, is he?' said Bill.

'Because of all the rings he wears,' said Sturzaker. 'One on each finger.'

'Sounds like a pouf to me,' said Bill.

'Well, I wouldn't like to call him that,' said Sturzaker. 'You can't mention his name in a Burnley pub without someone shitting themselves. Proper nasty fucker, he is. You must have read about them two kiddies. The rumour I've heard is it were his dogs that were set on them. Their daddy owed him money, apparently.'

Bill looked at him.

'No?' said Sturzaker. 'I'm surprised you don't know him, Bill, to be honest, the circles your Jeff moves in. Who does he work for now?'

'The brewery,' said Bill. 'You know he does.'

'Aye, that's his job,' said Sturzaker. 'I'm asking you who he works for. Or hasn't he told you? Mind you, best his mam doesn't know, I suppose.'

'Why are you telling me about this Dent?' said Bill.

'I've heard he's looking for a Tranny van that's gone missing,' said Sturzaker.

'You've heard how?' said Dadda.

'Through the lads at work,' said Sturzaker. 'A few of them come from over that way. You know how it is. A mate overhears summat and he tells his mate and he tells someone else.'

'And you listen to gossip, do you?' said Bill.

'Not usually,' said Sturzaker. 'They talk a load of bollocks at our place most of the time. But then I remembered seeing a van come past the house one night a few month back and head down your way.'

'So?' said Bill.

'The thing is,' said Sturzaker. 'I didn't see it come back.'

'I think it's you that wants his eyes testing,' said Bill, and finally conceded to Dadda's hand on his arm.

'I've not said owt to anyone yet,' said Sturzaker. 'I just thought I'd ask you lads what you knew about it first. I mean, I wouldn't want someone like Dent paying you a visit if he didn't have to.'

Before we got into the truck, he called to us across the street.

'Sorry about your dog, Bill. I hope you find the bastards,' he said.

Bill said nothing as we drove out of the village, leaving Dadda to explain that Sturzaker was right. He would have seen a van come through Underclough. The blue Transit van that the boy had intended to fill with stolen lambs.

In the pitch dark of the early morning, he'd left it on the lane and walked the last hundred yards to the farm so as not to wake anyone with the noise of the engine. He'd had a few meat bones to keep the dogs quiet too. But that was about as far as his expertise went.

'I think it must have been the first time he'd come robbing sheep in his life,' said Dadda. 'They were all over the yard when the Gaffer went out.'

'And the van belonged to this Dent?' I said.

'Christ,' said Bill. 'We don't want someone like that turning up, Tom.'

'I thought you said he sounded like a pouf?' said Dadda.

'What if he comes poking about in the Wood?' said Bill.

'And what if he does?' said Dadda. 'He's not going to find owt, is he?'

'Even so.'

'I don't think Sturzaker will say anything to him,' I said. 'He's enjoying all this too much.'

This Dent was his trump card and to play it on a whim would spoil the pleasure he'd get from keeping us on edge.

'I think Sturzaker's told him already,' said Bill.

'Don't talk daft,' said Dadda.

'Well, if it weren't Vinny that set fire to the Wood or killed our Douglas then perhaps it were Dent.'

'I don't think so,' said Dadda.

'You heard what Sturzaker said,' Bill replied, as we passed the war memorial and came into the Wood. 'If Dent set his dogs on those little kids in Burnley, then burning down trees would be nowt.'

‘If he had summat to say to us,’ said Dadda, ‘why wouldn’t he just come and knock on the farmhouse door?’

‘I don’t know, do I?’ said Bill. ‘They’re twisted in the fuckin’ head, blokes like that.’

‘I can’t see it,’ said Dadda.

‘Well, someone’s been to the Endlands,’ said Bill. ‘You can’t deny that, Tom.’

‘What happened to it?’ I said. ‘The van.’

Dadda lit his roll-up and put his eyes on the lane.

‘We burned it,’ he said. ‘And then we pushed it into the Moss.’

Bill shook his head. ‘Fuckin’ hell, Tom,’ he said. ‘What were he thinking, the Gaffer? Couldn’t you have stopped him?’

But he knew that there was nothing Dadda could have done. By the time the gunshot had woken him up, it was all over and the boy was lying dead in the bye-field.

‘Not a word when we get back,’ said Bill. ‘All this about Dent stays between the three of us, all right? I can do without Laurel wringing her bloody hands every hour of the day.’

‘Course,’ said Dadda.

‘And your lass definitely doesn’t need to know, John,’ said Bill.

‘Agreed,’ I said.

‘Have you spoken to her this morning?’ said Bill.

‘She didn’t say much,’ I said. ‘She’s just trying to take it all in.’

‘What will she do?’ said Dadda. ‘Will she say owt?’

‘I don’t think she knows what she’s going to do,’ I said. ‘You’ll have to give her some time.’

‘We need to know,’ said Bill. ‘What if she decides she’s going to tell someone?’

‘You should have thought of that before you opened your mouth,’ said Dadda. ‘If you’d let me speak to John first, she wouldn’t have needed to know at all, would she?’

'Bollocks,' said Bill. 'You wouldn't have told John a damn thing unless we'd made you.'

'Aye, well, perhaps that wouldn't have been so bad either,' said Dadda.

'The lad had to know,' said Bill.

'I'm glad I do,' I said.

'See?' said Bill.

'You tell your lass to pack up her things,' said Dadda. 'I'll take you both to the station this afternoon.'

'I thought you wanted some help in the Wood today?' I said.

'We do,' said Bill.

'We can manage on our own,' said Dadda.

'And what about Gathering?' I said.

'You just get yourselves home,' said Dadda.

'For Christ's sake, Tom, this is his home,' said Bill. 'If our Jeff can float back here whenever he wants, I don't see why John can't stay. Let him work if that's what he wants to do.'

Dadda took another drag of his roll-up and looked out of the window.

~

It had always been like that for Jeff. Always welcomed back. No questions asked. Indiscretions forgotten, as an adult and as a child. In Laurel's eyes he was always taken advantage of, easily led because he was so trusting.

The summer I'd left primary school, Jeff had spent more and more time down in the village with Sam and Monkey and Jason, breaking windows at Arncliffe's and learning how to pocket things in Wigton's when no one was looking. Perhaps such things were initiations, I don't know, but a few weeks into the summer holidays and he seemed to have become a fully-fledged member of their little cabal.

One afternoon, the four of them came thrashing through the bracken in the Greenhollow, following Lennie, making bird calls and baboon shrieks.

'Is this where you've been going all this time then, Thunderbelly?' said Sam, staring at him with his large eyes.

'You been meeting a lass down here?' said Jason.

'Is it Irene Dewhurst?' said Jeff. 'Does she give you a fishy finger?'

Monkey laughed as he picked his nose.

'Is this where you saw the ghost?' said Sam.

'I didn't see a ghost,' said Lennie. 'I said there were someone watching me.'

'Who were it?' said Sam, looking around but not seeing me, of course, sitting cross-legged behind the willow branches.

'Were it the Devil?' said Jason and Monkey laughed again.

'Aye,' said Sam. 'Is that who it were, Blubber?'

'He lives in the Wood, doesn't he?' said Jason.

'Aye,' said Sam.

'No he doesn't,' said Lennie. 'The Devil lives on the moors. Doesn't he, Dyer?'

'That's just an owd story his lot tell their little lads,' said Sam. 'Isn't it, Jeff?'

'Aye,' said Jeff. 'This is where he really lives. He jumps from one animal to another so he can't be caught.'

'What animals?' said Lennie.

'Birds and rabbits and that,' said Sam. 'Whatever's here.'

'Aye, right,' said Lennie. 'You're talking bollocks, the lot of you.'

'Sometimes,' said Jeff, 'he'll jump into people too, if they stay down here long enough. That's right, isn't it, lads?'

'Aye,' said Jason.

'Aye,' said Monkey.

'And you have to look in their eyes,' said Sam. 'That's how you know if they have the Devil inside them.'

He clamped Lennie's face and stared at him.

'Is he in there?' said Jason.

'Aye, look,' said Sam and twisted Lennie's head so that the others could see.

'Those are his eyes,' said Jeff.

'Oh aye,' said Jason. 'That's the Owd Feller for definite.'

'Piss off,' said Lennie and pushed Sam's hands away and then Monkey started them off shouting *Devil, Devil, Devil.*

Lennie shoved each of them in the chest as they closed in and they laughed.

'We have to get him out,' said Sam. 'We can't let him into our house. We have to put him in the river. Then he'll jump into one of the fishes instead.'

'Leave me alone,' Lennie said, and when he tried to duck under Sam's arm, Monkey and Jeff caught him and dragged him down to the mud and shingle. His cries as he twisted and kicked sent the wood pigeons clapping away through the canopy. Chanting again, they pinned him down on his belly and Sam kicked water into his face. Lennie spat and choked, while Monkey and Jason held his hands and Jeff knelt on his back.

'That's it,' said Sam. 'Spit him out.'

'Put his face under,' said Jeff and they edged Lennie forward and Sam pressed his head into the running water.

Monkey laughed as Lennie convulsed and then came up opening and closing his mouth like a fish.

'Has he gone yet?' said Sam. 'I don't think he's gone yet, has he, lads?'

No, the Devil was still there. And so Sam gave him another opportunity to escape into the river. And then another.

When Sam was satisfied, he told the others to let his brother go and Lennie sat on the bank and began to cry.

'Stop it,' said Sam. 'Stop wailing, you big fuckin' baby.'

Lennie put his hands around the back of his head and told him to piss off again. And then Sam was on him, trying to prise his fingers apart, trying to get to his face with his fists. The others watched for a while and then, one by one, they went away.

I wanted to tell Lennie that it would all be over soon. That his story was so close to the end that I could hear the sand grains dropping in the hourglass. Those bruises from his brother's fists, I wanted to say, would still be there when they buried him.

I wanted to tell him that I almost envied him too. Nothing much mattered now. There were so many things that he would never have to worry about. He was going to be spared so much.

~

Back at the farm, Angela's Hilux was parked near the hay barn and on the other side of the kitchen window I could see Liz filling the kettle at the sink. She lifted her hand when she saw us and Dadda went off to see if the ram had eaten any of the food he'd left for him that morning.

As soon as I knocked on the front door, Kat came to open it. I could tell that she'd been crying but she tried to cover it up. There'd been noises outside, she said. She couldn't describe them now. The dogs had been barking at something, too. Yes, she knew that the door was locked and bolted, but even so, she'd been frightened. And then when Angela and the others had arrived that awful smell had come with them.

'It's Grace,' she said. 'She carries it with her, I'm sure of it.'

'Come and sit down,' I said. 'You look like you're going to be sick.'

It was nothing to do with Grace, of course. Kat was still shaken about what had happened back in the spring. All night she'd been up and down to the toilet, pulling on T-shirts and jumpers when she was cold, undressing again when she was too hot, opening the window, closing it, staring at the rafters while Dadda tinkered with something in the workshed. The others had their doubts about her, but I knew that she wouldn't say anything. And she knew it too. That was why she was frightened. She hadn't ever been trusted with so much before.

I took her into the kitchen and sat her down while I poured her a glass of water. She looked uncertainly at Grace, who smiled back at her and spun the locket on its chain.

'I take it Ken Sturzaker told Bill where to go, did he?' said Liz.

'You could say that,' I said.

'Did they bury Douglas?' said Grace.

'They did,' I said. 'Round the back of the house.'

'Well, perhaps that'll be an end to it now,' said Angela. 'With any luck, the Sturzakers will leave us alone.'

Grace stood behind Kat and put her arms around her neck.

'Can we go now Uncle John's back?' she said. 'I want to show Auntie Katherine the Wood.'

Kat tried to drink the water I gave her but she retched and it dribbled down her chin.

'What's wrong, Auntie Katherine?' said Grace, sitting down next to her. 'Is it the baby? Is it making you sick?'

'I felt like that for weeks on end,' said Angela. 'I couldn't keep owt inside me for more than five minutes.'

'I were just the same,' said Liz. 'You wonder why you bother, don't you?'

'Can you feel it moving yet?' said Grace.

'No,' said Kat, mopping up the water with her sleeve.

'Can I try?' said Grace, and before Kat could say no, Grace had her hand on her stomach. 'There's something there,' she said. 'Its heart is beating.'

'Don't be daft,' said Liz. 'It's probably your own.'

'It's too early,' said Angela. 'She won't notice that baby moving for another few months yet.'

'Here,' said Grace, taking Kat's hand and pressing it to her belly. 'I'm right, aren't I?'

'There's nothing,' said Kat.

Grace bent down and listened. 'It's stopped now,' she said. 'I hope it's all right.'

'Of course it's all right,' said Angela. 'Get your coat on.'

'Are you coming then, Auntie Katherine?' said Grace.

Kat nodded and slipped her hand under the shirt she was wearing, trying to find what Grace had been able to feel.

From the farm, we drove down the lane and we met Bill and Laurel in the field by the Wood. It was still sheened from the rain but the edges were dry and we walked in a single line to the trees, our reflections passing one by one over the water in the old drinking trough. Grace held Kat's hand as she led her alongside the hedgerow, telling her how they would come and pick blackberries here in the summer when she came for Harvest. She'd have the baby by then too. And could a baby eat blackberries? Would they like the taste? Did Auntie Katherine like them? She shouldn't eat them after Michaelmas, though. No one ate them after Michaelmas. The Gaffer had told me the same story every year. How the Archangel Michael had thrown Lucifer out of heaven and into a bramble bush. How, in a rage, the Devil had relieved himself on the berries and turned them sour.

'Come the end of September, Johnny lad,' said the Gaffer.

'Whatever's still in the hedges, you leave for the birds, all right?' And he'd tell me about the boys he'd known in the village who came blackberrying after school and stuffed their faces and pissed hot blood for a week.

Angela called to Grace and directed her attention to the geese flying into the valley. They flapped low over the Wood, their calls echoing off the fells, and everyone stopped to watch.

'They come all the way from Iceland, Auntie Katherine,' said Grace and Kat smiled at her and held back so that she could talk to me.

'You know, they haven't said a word about last night,' she said.

'I don't think they wanted to start a debate about it,' I said.

'But it's like they never told us at all,' said Kat.

'What else is there to say?'

'Plenty.'

'I mean, what else is there to say that will make any difference now?'

'I'm worried about Grace,' she said. 'I'm sure she knows much more about what the Gaffer did than she's letting on.'

'No one's told her anything,' I said.

'They wouldn't need to. She's sharp as a tack,' said Kat. 'She worked out that I was pregnant, didn't she? And she obviously overhears things too.'

'Does she?'

'You were there when she was showing me her magic trick, John,' said Kat. 'How could she have known all those things unless she'd been listening to our conversations?'

'We haven't talked about those things since we've been here,' I said.

'Perhaps we have and we didn't realise it,' said Kat.

'I think we'd remember,' I said.

'You explain it then,' she said. 'You can't, can you?'

'What do you want to do about it?'

'I'm just saying that we need to be careful what we talk about,' said Kat. 'Grace is very good at standing quietly in the shadows.'

'She wouldn't be the first child to enjoy spying on grown-ups,' I said.

'It's not a game. There's something not right with her,' said Kat. 'That smell on her. And she keeps staring at me.'

'Kat, if you've not noticed that she has a crush on you by now . . .'

'Not in that way,' said Kat. 'Like she's weighing me up.'

Grace was waving her over and calling her name.

'Just help her enjoy the day,' I said.

It was tradition that everyone spent the morning of Devil's Day in Sullom Wood, gathering leaves and skins of bark, acorns and mossy branches. The stuff that would smoke and stink and get into the Owd Feller's nose to wake him up. It was something for the children to do, something to keep them occupied as they waited for the bonfire and the songs in the evening. Kat was reluctant to leave me, but Laurel took her arm and they went off to help Grace fill the plastic bag she'd brought.

As they went deeper into the bracken, me, Dadda and Bill headed towards the river to try and salvage what we could from the trees that had suffered in the fire. We'd stockpile what we could in Archangel Back and then come down with trailers to take the wood to the farms.

The noise of the river increased as we walked through the trees and came to the fringes of what had been ruined. The rain had dampened down much of the ash to a tar-like sludge that wallowed between the stumps. Some of the trees had been burned to charcoal and whatever came away in the hand crumbled to dust.

Dadda and Bill paced out the range of damage the fire had caused and agreed on it being just over fifty yards. It could have been much worse, but it would still take time to grow back, and would be recorded on the maps for years to come.

'What did they use?' I said. 'Petrol?'

'God knows,' said Dadda. 'It went up quick, whatever it were.'

'Christ,' Bill said, looking along the line of blackened trees. 'It'll take weeks to cut all this down.'

'Were you hoping to do it in a day or summat?' said Dadda.

'I just want to get it done, that's all,' said Bill. 'I don't want to spend any more time in here than I have to.'

He went away to the trees that had been at the peripheries of the fire, the point at which they'd managed to finally dampen down the flames and beat out the blazing undergrowth with shovels. With a look back toward us, he pulled on the rip-cord of the chainsaw and took off the branches of the beech tree closest to him. They fell heavily, lifting a haze of sawdust and ash.

'Go on, John,' said Dadda. 'You go and see to what's left at the top of the bank.'

As I'd suspected, what had once been the Greenhollow had been torn open. The silver birch and willow had lost their leaves, the branches scorched to stiff black wires. Those trees that had been already leaning out over the river had collapsed into the ravine, making an ossuary of white trunks below. The top of the Falls was clogged with thickets of charred boughs and the bank where Sam and the others had pinned down Lennie that muggy afternoon years ago lay heaped with burned wood that still gave off wisps of smoke.

As he'd spluttered and choked at the edge of the river, I'd been convinced that this would be how Lennie died. It seemed inevitable that Sam would be responsible, too, after all the times he'd kicked and thumped his brother at school. But Lennie had a little while longer to live and once Sam had left, he'd sat and sniffed on the riverbank, dabbing the back of his hand on his nose to look at the blood.

When he stood up, he winced like an old man and put a hand to his lower back. He looked in the direction Sam and the others had gone but their voices were still there somewhere in the Wood and he didn't follow them just yet. He could hardly have gone home in the state he was in anyway and he pulled off his T-shirt to wash it in the river. His body was startling to see. Pale and shapeless as the sludge of a burned-down candle. Before long it would be under the earth in the churchyard. No longer his possession. No longer his shame.

Kneeling by the water, he soaked his T-shirt and hung it dripping on a branch. He washed his face and his hands and made his boy breasts wobble as he wiped the mud off his chest.

While he waited for his shirt to dry, he picked stones from the shingle and threw them across to the far bank, raising insects, frightening a rabbit. Then his target became the willow tree where I was sitting, the pebbles ripping through the canopy above me and sending down leaves.

I don't think he saw that it was me, but sensed that there was someone there watching him again and he peered through the branches.

'Piss off,' he said. 'What do you want?'

Looking again, he moved back a few paces and armed himself with a bigger rock.

'Is that you, Sam?' he said, knowing that it wasn't. 'Is that you, you fish-eyed prick?'

He wiped his nose on his forearm and wafted away a bee from his eyeline.

For a moment or two he hesitated, his arm poised, and then he pitched the rock towards me. It clubbed into the branches and tumbled down with twigs and peels of bark. Another one quickly followed, but by then I was already running through the trees to where the river bent and the water was deep enough for an otter to slip out of sight.

And did I know how close I was to seeing the boy die now? the Devil said. Did I know that these were the last few days of his life? These trees, this river, they'd be the final things he'd see. This was the place where the world he'd known would vanish and he'd disappear into silence.

We worked for a couple of hours, sawing and chopping and carrying the timber worth saving the quarter of a mile through the Wood to Archangel Back.

Whether I passed the place they'd taken the boy, I don't know. It could have been anywhere. Under the fallen leaves, in its autumn silence, the Wood seemed as if it had been undisturbed for centuries.

The only thing that moved here was Owd Abraham, ambling slowly through the ferns and stopping to look at us before he pressed on in search of penny buns and butter caps. If he'd come across the boy, then there wouldn't be much left of him by now.

He'd been poor, Dadda had told me. Hardly dressed for the weather. Nothing on him but a few coins and a couple of fags in a squashed packet. His trainers were coming apart and he had that unwashed smell about him like the old fellers in the Croppers' Arms who had no wives at home any more. The tattoos on his forearm of crosses and squares looked as if he'd done them himself.

I felt sorry for him, of course. Who would wish for Sullom Wood as their final resting place? And if he was as young as they said he was, as his ineptitude seemed to prove, then it was a terrible waste of a life.

A boy he might have been, but he wasn't naïve. He must have considered the potential consequences as he drove up the valley in the dark and yet he'd come anyway. All that had happened was the worst thing he could have imagined. He'd gambled and lost. It was no one's fault but his.

He wouldn't have known what he was stealing anyway. What would he have done with a van full of meatless little lambs? No butcher would have taken them that young. Or if they had then they'd have given him next to nothing for them. He'd have left the farm devastated for the sake of a few notes in his back pocket. Dadda knew that well enough. They all did.

By the time we were heading out of the Wood and across the Beasleys' horse field, the others had already gone to pick up the lamb from Beckfoot's, taking Kat with them. She wouldn't have wanted to go, but she needed to spend time with them on her own. The more she got to know them, the more she'd understand why they'd done what they'd done back in the spring. They weren't bad people. They'd done it for the Gaffer's sake. They'd done it because they loved the Endlands as much as he did.

It had to carry on. It had to have a future.

~

Back at the farm, we added a few of the branches we'd brought from the Wood to the bonfire the Gaffer had started to build before he died. It had always been constructed under his supervision into a carefully stacked hive, and he'd often lay a ladder against the mound and climb to the top to rearrange some old pieces of fencing or sawn-up boughs that weren't quite secure enough for his liking. Always with a fag in the corner of his mouth, of course, flickering with the threat of total conflagration as he gave instructions to us below.

Kat came out of the scullery door carrying a bucket with two hands and tipped the brown water into the drain. Since they'd come back from Beckfoot's she and Grace had been skivvying in the kitchen for Angela and Laurel, who always put themselves in charge of preparing and setting out the food on Devil's Day.

As Kat went back inside, she passed Grace, who came out of the house with a tray of tea and a hundred questions. When were we going to light the bonfire and what time would the Owd Feller come down off the moors and could she still sing the song? Did we think that her daddy would be home soon? Would Auntie Katherine's baby be frightened? And what would there be to eat?

It was a day for children. It always had been. It was a shame that Grace had no one her age to share it with. Something she felt more than ever on Devil's Day.

I'd been an only child too, of course, and so were Liz and Jeff, but at least we'd had one another. And even though Jeff ignored me most of the year, he'd side with me at school when the Sturzakers took the piss out of our traditions. Not that it mattered. I looked forward to Devil's Day more than Christmas and they couldn't spoil it whatever they said.

~

The afternoon came to a close in ribs of reddened cloud over the fells. Blackbirds chuttered in the beech trees and the river was loud. For a while, the light glowed coppery around the farm and then the sun began to slide out of the valley, past the holly bushes, over the crags and burning on the ridges.

Once the last of the daylight had gone we went out and lit the bonfire, inserting burning tapers into the base of the stack so that it lit from the inside out. As the wind got to the flames, they pulsed and spread slowly from the heart, casting our shadows as giants on the wall of the farmhouse.

There was still no sign of Jeff, but then I wasn't surprised. It wouldn't have been the first time he'd given his word and then rendered it meaningless. And yet, when – if – he turned up, Laurel would forgive him his trespasses, Liz would let him kiss her and Grace would hang off his neck like a monkey.

'Where is he?' said Grace. 'You said that he'd be back before we started the bonfire.'

'Perhaps he got held up,' said Angela. 'He'll be here soon.'

'I want to show him my magic trick,' she said.

'You can,' said Liz. 'When he gets here.'

'But that might not be for ages,' said Grace.

'Don't sulk, love,' said Angela.

'I'm not sulking.'

'Well, get on with it then,' said Liz, and Grace dipped into the plastic bag she'd filled that morning and began to throw handfuls of leaves and acorns and beechnuts into the flames.

'Sing the rhyme, Grace,' said Angela. 'Don't forget the rhyme.'

Rise, Devil, rise;
Open your eyes.
Wake, Devil, wake;
Eat up all your cake.
Come, Devil, come;
Whisky, wine and rum.

'When *will* he come, the Owd Feller?' said Grace.

'I told you, when he's good and ready,' said Angela. 'He has to walk a long way, you know.'

'Walk?' said Grace. 'I thought he had wings?'

'They're all crumpled up from him sleeping for so long,' said Angela.

'But Daddy will be here before him, won't he?' said Grace.

'He'd better,' said Angela. 'Nobody wants to meet the Owd Feller on the lane.'

The smoke and sparks drifted away towards the very end of the valley and the willow leaves that Grace had collected from Sullom Wood were lofted up on the hot air, burning at the edges, curling and shrivelling into ash.

'She does keep staring at me,' said Kat.

'She isn't staring at you,' I said.

'She is,' Kat insisted. 'Look, just then.'

'She thinks you're pretty, Kat,' I said. 'That's all.'

'I've seen that look on children's faces a thousand times, John,' she said. 'She's planning something.'

Once the bonfire was at full tilt and the heat of it had pushed us back to the damson tree outside the scullery, Angela called time and we went into the house to eat. The dogs were brought in from their kennels and Fly, of course, was over-excited by the privilege of being indoors.

'Perhaps I'd best leave her here tomorrow,' said Dadda, making her lie down like Musket. 'I reckon she'll be more bloody hindrance than help.'

'We can't gather with one dog,' said Angela. 'She's got to learn some time.'

'Maybe Tom's right,' said Bill. 'We don't want owt to go wrong tomorrow.'

'What's going to go wrong?' said Angela. 'The forecast is good, isn't it?'

'I'm not fussed about the weather,' said Bill. 'It's just given what's happened these last few days, I'll be a lot happier once the sheep are down off the moors.'

'The Sturzakers aren't going to bother with us any more now,' said Angela.

'How do we know what that bastard's going to do?' said Bill.

'All right, Bill,' said Laurel. 'What's got into you?'

'Nowt,' he said.

'You seem so touchy,' she said.

'I wonder why?'

'Douglas?' said Laurel.

'Of course bloody Douglas,' he said. 'I lost a damn good dog yesterday just because some bastard had a grudge.'

'A grudge that's now been settled,' said Angela.

'Aye, well, we'll see if it has, won't we?' said Bill. 'When they come and cut up your pigs.'

'That's enough,' said Laurel. 'Don't spoil the evening for Grace.'

The kitchen had been scrubbed clean and the food that Angela and Laurel had made was spread out on the table, savoury and sweet together. Cuts of ham, cuts of beef. Roast heart. A Roman pie. Marmalade pudding. Blackberry crumble. Damson tart. Jugs of custard and cream next to the gravy boats. An abundance and disorder that children always loved. A reminder that the Devil had once tried to starve us and failed.

As well as being the prelude to Gathering, Devil's Day marked the start of winter too and things were always brought to stock the larder in the scullery. Bottles of plums, pots of chutney, bilberry jam. And goose eggs from the Dyers' farm, beetroot from Angela's allotment and the cucumbers that Bill grew in his cold frame were all pickled in four-pint jars and stacked on the slate shelves.

But the centrepiece of the meal was the lamb stew that Angela carried to the table and unveiled in a mushroom of steam.

'It's so nice to have everyone here, isn't it?' said Laurel. 'Well, almost everyone. Isn't it a pity that the Gaffer couldn't have held on for one more week?'

'We'll just have to sing a bit louder,' said Angela.

'And we'll have to get this one learning the fiddle soon, won't we?' said Laurel, cupping Grace's chin. 'Keep all the old traditions going. We should write down all the songs too before they get forgotten.'

'They won't get forgotten,' said Angela. 'We've been singing them long enough.'

'Shall we wait for Daddy before we eat?' said Grace.

'He can catch up when he gets here,' said Bill.

'Aye,' said Dadda. 'Let's start before it goes cold.'

'But we'd better save him some food,' said Grace.

'I don't think we're likely to run out, are we?' said Liz.

'All the same, I'll put some aside for him,' said Laurel, and once she'd dished out a portion for Jeff, she flitted about the table as usual, handing out the plates of stew. Kat made do with vegetables and bread.

We ate for an hour or so, with Grace and Laurel looking at the clock as each minute passed. Twice, Grace went out into the hallway thinking that she'd heard someone knocking, and twice she came back with a face that no one could perk up until Angela told her it was nearly time to sing the song she'd been rehearsing at home.

'I've lit the fire in the other room,' said Laurel. 'It should be nice and warm for us.'

The dishes were left in the sink, the lights switched off and ivy hung on the door handle. We didn't want the Devil in the kitchen. There was too much temptation there and he'd never leave if he got his knees under the table. Over the years, he'd been taught to be grateful for the bowl of lamb stew that we set out for him on the hearth.

Laurel had probably spent more time in the front room than any of us Pentecosts. When Mam died, she'd thrown herself into the role of housekeeper and over the years her charity had become habit. She still came every week to dust and hoover, even though the furniture was hardly ever used. The paisley rug was too good to be soiled by boots, the sofa and the chairs too well-kept for grubby dogs to lie on. It was a room for those rare occasions, like Christmas and Devil's Day, when we changed into clean clothes and work could be put off for a while.

Laurel pulled the velvet curtains closed and ran the backs of her hands down the pleats, admiring the job Mam had done of making them when she and Dadda had been first married. It had been Mam who'd hand-stitched the velvet cushions too, blackened the beams that ran across the ceiling, chiselled off the old tiles that had been around the hearth and replaced them with blue and white squares of Dutch milkmaids and windmills. If Mam lingered anywhere in the house, it was here; perhaps that was why Dadda avoided it.

'She had a beautiful voice, your mam,' said Laurel. She said the same thing every year and every year there were murmurs of agreement around the room.

In one of the albums that had been passed around the night before the Gaffer's funeral, there was a photograph of Mam singing on Devil's Day, her eyes closed, a younger, slimmer Bill standing behind her drawing his bow across the fiddle-strings.

'Can I sing now?' said Grace.

‘We said you could, didn’t we?’ said Angela. ‘Go on.’

Grace got up off the sofa and stood with Bill near the fire. She looked at Kat again and Kat looked at me as if to say, *see?*

‘Ready then?’ said Bill and Grace nodded her head in time as he started and then came in after four.

Come down for a dance and a drink, old boy,
Come down for the sake of your bones.
For the wind will bite and the rain will sting.
Come down for the sake of your bones.
Come down for to filly up your belly, old man,
Come down for the sake of your bones.
Take the wine and the whisky and first bonny lamb.
Come down for the sake of your bones.

There were several more verses, all of which Grace remembered to the letter. When she came to the end, the room was loud with applause and Bill was handed a glass of wine that he swallowed in one go, as tradition demanded. Courage for when the Owd Feller came.

At the reception, the Gaffer had spent an hour singing the old songs from the Endlands, delighting those members of Kat’s family who’d had enough drink to loosen their ties and making those sipping tea half rise from their chairs and peer across the function room at the old duffer making all the noise. He’d gone through the entire repertoire, from tales about honourable thievery:

Come hear the tale of the noble poachers
Condemnèd all to die

to burlesques about counterfeit virginity:

She said she were a maiden pure
With not a thought of sin.
The cherry bowl she tried to hide,
But I could hear the stones inside.

to the rhymes the children chanted as they jumped the rope in the playground:

Poor owd Jacob, run run run.
Fly away home before the Devil comes.
Poor owd Jacob, where did you go?
Here I am underneath the snow.

The Gaffer told me that Jacob Arncliffe's had been the last body they found after the Blizzard, making him the thirteenth to die that autumn. Almost a week of thaw had passed before he emerged from under the snowdrifts, a crumpled thing in a greatcoat, his hat discovered fifty feet away, blown off in the storm. He'd ended up far from the lane in the marshy land next to the river, and they could only assume that the poor man had become disorientated as he tried to make his way home to Syke House.

Planks of wood were laid down on top of the sludge and some of the workers from the mill tried to crawl out and retrieve the corpse with as much dignity as they could manage. Yet the pontoon they'd made was so unstable and the body so weighted with water that in the end they were forced to drag and shove him back to the lane. Their poor Mr Jacob.

And what would happen to the mill now? What would happen to Underclough? Mr Jacob had never married and had no sons to carry on his work. He'd devoted his life to the business and to the village. He was a good man. His own man. He hadn't ever put himself above them, nor did he fawn to the toffs when they came shooting. He'd loved the the valley even more than the other Arncliffes and as Nathaniel had kept his notebooks, Jacob took photographs. Walk the fells or the riverbanks on a Sunday afternoon and he'd be there staring down into his Box Brownie with his pipe in his mouth.

They crossed themselves and prayed for him. But laid out on the verge, there weren't many who could stand to look for long, and eventually someone came with a blanket. Even a week's burial shouldn't have disfigured him so much, certainly not when he'd been packed into ice and snow. It was, they said, as though he'd been stamped on by a bull.

'He might be small, Johnny lad,' said the Gaffer. 'But the Owd Feller has iron hooves.'

'Like that horse at the Show?' I said, recalling the crack of the man's skull, his hands covering his face, the people running and the mare bending down to chew the grass as though nothing had happened.

'Ten times harder than that,' said the Gaffer.

'Is that what killed Jacob then?' I said. 'Not the cold?'

'Aye,' said the Gaffer. 'It weren't the cold that did for anyone. The Devil only brought the Blizzard here to keep us trapped while he had his fun. He's like a child, you know.'

For days they waited for the frost in the graveyard to melt but even a week after the snow had stopped falling it was impossible to get more than the tip of a shovel into the earth. There was nothing else they could do but store the thirteen coffins in the church until they could be taken over to Wyresdale. It seemed scant consolation, but at least they could keep folk safe in death if not in life, and they consecrated the doors and kept the candles burning and marked the caskets with crosses of salt.

Of course, the families of the dead were unhappy that their loved ones would have to be buried elsewhere, but they were glad at least that they didn't have to carry them across the moors where the Devil might be hiding. This was the age of the motor car.

~

'Oh, listen, listen. What's that?' said Angela, as the song we were singing came to an end. 'I heard the gate opening outside. I can hear something in the yard.'

'He's coming,' said Grace. 'Quick. Turn off the lights.'

Laurel got up and flicked the switch and the conversation petered out until there was nothing but the crack of the fire and Gutter Clough spilling past outside. Kat held my hand and tried to avoid looking at Grace, who had seated herself on the arm of the sofa next to her.

'Go on, Granddad Tom,' she said. 'Let him in.'

Dadda went to open the front door and a cold draught followed him back down the hallway. Bill began to play the thinnest note, barely audible at first, but growing louder as he drew his elbow slowly back and forth, now double-stopping in a strange discordant sound. Grace squeezed Kat's shoulder, convinced by every jangling shadow and every settling floorboard that the Owd Feller was coming in through the door. Everyone raised their glasses to him as he passed them and headed for the heat of the fire. And wasn't there an extra shadow on the hearthstone for a moment? And didn't the whisky on the mantelpiece shiver in the glass? And didn't the spoon move in the stew bowl?

Bill began to play 'The Devil's Caper', something like a shanty or a jig that started off slowly and built in pace once everyone was clapping.

Unable to contain her excitement any longer, Grace said, 'Can we start the game now?'

'Aye, go on,' said Angela.

'Where's the blindfold?' said Grace.

'Here,' said Liz, and pulled out a cotton bandage from her pocket.

'What's that for?' said Kat when Grace started to fold it on her knee.

'Well, someone's got to dance with the Owd Feller,' Grace replied. 'Otherwise he won't go to sleep.'

Laurel took the blindfold off Grace and tied it gently around Kat's head. 'It's just an owd custom,' she said. 'A bit of fun.'

'Come on, lady, stand up,' said Angela, helping Kat off the sofa. 'You can't dance sitting down.'

'I don't want to dance at all,' said Kat, going to undo the knot that Laurel had tied.

'Hey, we've all done it, Mrs Pentecost,' said Liz, taking her hands away. 'First Devil's Day after marriage. The Owd Feller loves a married woman. He likes to try and take summat that doesn't belong to him.'

'John, tell them, please,' said Kat.

'Don't you say a word, John Pentecost,' said Angela.

'No one speaks now,' said Grace. 'Otherwise it'll spoil the game.'

'What game?' said Kat.

'You dance with whoever takes your hands,' said Grace. 'And you have to say "Devil" when you think it's him.'

'This is ridiculous,' said Kat and then jumped when Liz held her wrists and began to swing them in time to the music. 'Let me go to bed,' she said. 'I'm tired.'

They took a turn around the sofa and then Liz let go, leaving Kat groping around in empty space, and then startling again when Angela gave Dadda a shove and he gripped her hands in his. Kat squirmed to get herself free but Dadda held her until Laurel took over and affected a kind of waltz across the hearth rug. When it was my turn, Kat immediately recognised the scars and roughs of my palms and extracted one of her hands so that she could touch my face.

'I want to stop now, John,' she said. 'Please. I've had enough.'

But the rules were such that no one could talk for as long as 'The Devil's Caper' lasted so I had to say nothing and let Grace slide in front of me and have the final dance.

As soon as Grace touched her, Kat cried out as if electricity had run up her arms.

'If you think it's the Devil, then say so,' Angela said.

Grace held on to Kat's wrists as firmly as she could.

'You have to say it,' said Grace. 'Otherwise he'll never let you go.'

'John, please,' said Kat, trying to work herself free of Grace's fingers. 'She's hurting me.'

'Just say it then, Kat,' I said.

'Devil,' she said. 'Devil.'

Kat took off the blindfold and inspected her hands. Then when she looked at Grace, she stepped backwards, knocking over the table where several glasses of wine had been set down while we danced. They fell and rolled on the wooden floor, spilling whatever was left in each.

'What are you wearing?' said Kat. 'What's she got on her head, John?'

'Nothing,' I said. 'What do you mean?'

'Why is she wearing that?'

'She's not wearing anything,' said Laurel, trying to hold Kat's shoulders. 'There's nothing there, love.'

'Stop looking at me,' said Kat. 'Why are you looking at me? What is that?'

'What's she talking about, Mummy?' said Grace.

'Take it off,' said Kat. 'Take it off, it's disgusting.'

She grabbed a handful of Grace's hair and pulled it hard. Grace screamed and beat her hands and wrists. Laurel tried to untangle Kat's fingers but Kat put her other hand against Grace's shoulder and pulled again, bringing a fist of hair away with a noise like paper being torn. Grace screamed and shoved Kat aside and Angela held her from behind as she sobbed in great inward breaths. Pushing past me and Dadda, Liz knelt down and thumbed at Grace's scalp. Thin lines of blood were stringing down her ear and beading at the lobe.

'My God,' she said, turning to Kat. 'What the fuck is wrong with you?'

Kat sat down on the edge of the sofa and looked at her hands again.

'Why did she do that to me?' said Grace, turning to Liz. 'It were only a game.'

Liz wiped some of the blood from Grace's neck and smoothed her hair off her forehead.

'Why didn't Daddy come home?' said Grace, pushing Liz's hand away, anger in her tears now. 'You said that he would.'

'All right, all right,' said Angela. 'Shush now.'

'He'll be back soon,' said Liz.

'I hope he never comes. I hope the Devil bloody eats him,' said Grace.

'Go and clean her up in the kitchen,' said Dadda and, putting himself between Liz and Kat, he nodded at the door.

'She'd better be gone by tomorrow, John,' said Liz as she left. 'Take her home.'

Bill finished his drink and then put his fiddle back in the case. Laurel looked at us for a moment and then went to fetch a cloth from the kitchen to soak up the wine that had been spilled.

'Don't you think I'm frightened enough by this place?' said Kat quietly.

'No one's trying to frighten you,' I said.

'Then why would you let her put on that horrible mask?' said Kat. 'What was it? One of their pig's heads or something?'

'Take her to bed, John,' said Dadda. 'I'll drive you to the station tomorrow after Gathering.'

He took another piece of wood and laid it on the fire, so that it would burn through the night and keep the Devil sleeping.

Gathering

No matter how much wine and beer had been drunk on Devil's Day, everyone got up early the next morning for Gathering. Not because the sheep couldn't be brought down later but because no one wanted the Devil in the house any longer than necessary. The sooner we had the flock in the bye-field, the sooner we could shock the Owd Feller out of his sleep and send him back to the moors. And once he was back on the moors we could forget about him and tuck ourselves into the valley for the winter.

The others were there waiting for us when Dadda stopped the Land-Rover at the foot of Fiendsdale Clough, but there was still no Jeff.

'It's not true what they say about bad pennies, is it?' said Dadda.

'We could have done with another pair of hands today, though,' I said.

'We'll cope without him,' said Dadda. 'We always have done.'

Lighting his roll-up, he got out and went to talk to Bill.

Kat stared through the brown rainbows the wipers had smeared on to the windscreen.

'Are you coming then?' I said.

'I can't,' said Kat.

'You're here now.'

'Only because I didn't want to be on my own at the farm,' she said.

'But you'll be on your own if you sit here,' I said.

‘Please don’t make me be with the others,’ she said. ‘Not today. I don’t think I can look at Grace.’

‘It was hot in the room last night,’ I said. ‘You were just tired. That’s all.’

‘I know what I saw, John,’ she said. ‘It was vile.’

She put the heel of her hand to her eye.

‘I must be ill,’ she said.

‘You’re not ill.’

‘Then how do you explain what I saw last night?’ she said.

‘We can go and see the doctor in Clitheroe this afternoon if you’re worried,’ I said.

‘I want to see *my* doctor,’ said Kat. ‘Not some stranger.’

Dadda finished his conversation with Bill and waved us out of the Land-Rover.

‘We need to go,’ I said.

‘If I’ve got to come, then I’m coming with you,’ said Kat.

‘Put your scarf on, then,’ I said.

‘And when we’ve finished, we’re going home, aren’t we?’ she said.

‘And leave everyone else to do the work?’

‘But we only came for Gathering,’ said Kat.

‘Well, things have changed, ‘I said.’

Dadda knocked on the window.

‘Come on,’ he said through the glass. ‘We’re starting late as it is.’

The others all looked at Kat when she got out. Grace had on a thick woollen hat which she pulled down further and went to throw stones into the river. She made a show of it, of course. She wanted to make sure that Kat felt guilty. But she’d live. Lennie Sturzaker had snatched out tufts of my hair often enough for me to know that she’d only have a tender scalp for a day or so.

‘She’s coming with us then, is she?’ said Liz, looking at Kat as she put on her gloves.

'She came here to help with Gathering, didn't she?' I said.

'Well, just keep her away from Grace,' said Liz. 'And me.'

'Oh, give over,' said Angela. 'Grace is all right. We've not time for falling out when we've got work to do. Anyway,' she went on, adjusting Kat's scarf and pulling the belt of Liz's old coat tighter, 'we can't have Katherine sitting about in the cold with a baby on the way, can we?'

'Go on, Grace,' said Liz. 'You get going with Granddad Bill.'

Grace nodded and Bill took her hand.

'I didn't mean to hurt her,' said Kat. 'I don't know what happened.'

'Your mind can play funny tricks when you're expecting,' said Laurel. 'You think all kinds of odd things are true.'

'I didn't,' said Liz.

'Well, you've forgotten then,' said Angela. 'You certainly weren't yourself whenever you were pregnant.'

'Am I meant to feel sorry for her or summat?' said Liz. 'You saw what she did to Grace.'

'And she's said sorry,' said Laurel.

'Just keep your mind on the job,' said Angela.

Liz set off before Angela had finished speaking and caught up with Bill and Grace on the path beside the clough.

'Ignore her, Katherine,' said Angela. 'She's just angry at Jeff.'

'No word then?' I said.

'He'll be here today,' said Laurel. 'He'll have got caught up in traffic somewhere.'

'Hasn't he called?' said Angela.

'I don't think he gets a chance while he's on the road,' said Laurel.

'He must have to stop some time,' said Angela. 'They have payphones at service stations, don't they?'

'Aye, but he'll be tired after all that driving,' said Laurel. 'He'll just want to sleep.'

'I'd have thought he'd want to speak to Grace more,' said Angela.

'He probably means to phone,' said Laurel. 'I don't know why he doesn't. Perhaps he forgets. Please don't make out that he doesn't care about us. He's still trying to find his way. He can't get everything right.'

Bill was calling her and, her cheeks flushed, she put her hands in her pockets and went to join him.

'Where is he?' I said. 'Does she even know?'

'I don't think anyone knows,' said Angela. 'Not really.'

'Bill says he's got mates in Scotland,' said Dadda, opening the back of the Land-Rover.

'Aye, well, he might be best off staying there then,' said Angela. 'Let Liz and Grace get on with their lives here. I'm sick of that bastard breaking their hearts.'

Dadda sent the dogs on their way. They went off immediately, sniffing and nosing up and down the rocks, Fly making a dash up the path, Dadda calling her back and giving her a clip on the nose.

I couldn't blame him for being on edge. Even though the Gaffer had done less and less of the chasing and whistling as he'd got older, he hadn't ever fully handed responsibility for Gathering to Dadda. Organising Gathering was the last thing a hill-farmer in the Endlands let go.

Like all the other Pentecosts, the Gaffer had spent most of his life understanding how to work the dogs and bring every one of the sheep safely down the narrow track by Fiendsdale Clough and over the Moss to the farm. He knew from his own experience, of course, that there was only a certain amount that Dadda would ever learn from watching him, and that doing was the only way to acquire any skill, but he had a possessiveness over Gathering that he couldn't quite shake off. It wasn't arrogance, I don't think, or even the fear that under another's supervision the whole thing would fail, but a reluctance to give up wrestling with the moorland. Go up there and it looks as if it hasn't changed since the glaciers retreated and yet no two days are the same, certainly no two Gatherings. That year it might have been cold and clear, but the one before, cloud had dropped so low as we were going over the Moss that it became almost impossible to separate the track from the marsh and we'd nearly lost some of the ewes.

Every year, like his father and his father before him, the Gaffer would learn a little more about the movement of water, wind, light and cloud; the growth and spread of bog-moss, the deception of peat, the network of furrows that the heather disguised. They were scraps of victories, but enough to keep him coming back to the high pastures despite his age, rather than sitting by the fireside at the farm.

'The moors are different for everyone, Johnny lad,' he said. 'You'll understand them in your own way.'

The moor he knew had died with him. Dadda would have to find his own. And the thought of that had surprised him, I think. He hadn't quite expected to feel like a novice here at the age of fifty-four.

~

Age, aches, lack of sleep, hangovers, bad chests and bad dreams meant that everyone made their way up Fiendsdale Clough at a different pace. The dogs, as always, had the most energy and were well ahead of us within half a minute, their breath steaming when Dadda called them to stop.

'That's it then, Tom,' said Angela, rubbing the backs of her hands as she walked next to him. 'Winter's on its way.'

We'd had the first raw night of autumn and woken that morning to find the kitchen windows covered in cock-feathers of frost. The air still had its night-hardness and the valley was so undisturbed that every sound was as sharp in the ear as it was at source: the river, the trees moving in the Wood, the geese on the Moss. Over the last few days, the flock had swelled in numbers, massing in a chorus of unoiled voices. Hundreds of them were packed together on the islands of rushes and grass that whalebacked out of the ice.

Somewhere underneath the glassy sheets and the black sludge was the van that the boy had driven to the farm. If Dent came, he might stand and look for as long as he liked and find no trace of it.

Here in the clough, we'd already lost the sunlight and walked in a shadow that at that time of year would linger in the ravine all day. The temperature dropped a few degrees more and as the water fell next to us it struck the rocks with an alpine clarity, kicking up spray and noise.

With the path so thick with ice in places, we made slow progress and I was glad that I had the crook in my hand to steady myself and Kat, who followed me in slow, uncertain footsteps.

The shepherds had always made their own crooks in the Endlands over the winter when snow kept them indoors, peeling ash wood for the shank and boiling the horn soft enough to bend it into a serif. The one that I used had been made before Joe Pentecost's time, the ripples on the handle worn down with use. It was proof that men I'd never met had spent their lives working hard to preserve the Endlands for children they'd never know – just as the Gaffer had protected the sheep that night back in the spring. Not because he had any desire to hurt the boy who'd come to steal them but because the flock didn't just belong to him. It belonged to Dadda and it belonged to me and Kat and our children and theirs.

Going back to Suffolk would be like taking each crook and snapping it over my knee.

Our line stretched and broke for a while, leaving Laurel and Angela at the rear, and we came back together in ones and twos, regrouping where the steep section levelled out. This was as far as Angela's body would take her and for as long as I could remember she had been in charge of marshalling the path here when the flock was driven down. She, Laurel and Grace would spread themselves out and make sure that none of the sheep ended up straying too close to the edge and falling into the clough. Grace still wouldn't look at Kat and stuck close to Liz, asking about Daddy and if he was going to be back before they woke the Owd Feller and crowned the ram?

'I'm sure he'll try,' said Liz.

'I want to tell him about Devil's Day,' said Grace. 'He'll want to know everything.'

Now she looked in Kat's direction and made sure that Kat heard her.

'I'll have to show him my head,' she said.

'There's nowt to see, Grace,' said Angela. 'Go on, you go and stand with Laurel. Let your mam go up to the ridge.'

Liz went off with Bill and Dadda, and Kat and I followed several yards behind.

'What's Jeff going to think of me?' said Kat.

'You're assuming he's going to turn up,' I said.

'But what if he does?' said Kat. 'The first thing Grace will tell him is that I pulled her hair out.'

'If he does come home,' I said, 'she'll be so excited that she'll forget.'

'Well, if Grace doesn't tell him, Liz will,' said Kat.

'Don't worry about her,' I said. 'She'll get over it.'

But when we came to the ridge Liz took up her position and kicked the cold out of her toes on a wall of peat and didn't look at Kat as we came past and went to help Dadda and Bill.

The soft, brown uplands that I'd crossed with Dadda only two days before as we tracked the deer had gone. Now everything was metal-hard, compressed by the weight of the sky. And seeing the moors for the first time, Kat couldn't help but stare at the miles that unfolded from where we stood.

In the sharp air, the sunlight picked out the crowns of stone on the distant ridges, making the moorland seem bigger still.

I thought about the voice Dadda and I had heard at Blackmire Edge. Now I couldn't be sure that it had been a voice at all. It didn't seem likely. If it had been someone who'd got lost while they were walking or looking for birds, then they were a long way out on the moors, much further than strangers usually went. And the wind up here shifted sound across such distances that it was easily distorted. We might have heard one of the ewes, or a bird, or it might have been the wind itself.

Down in the shelter of the valley there hadn't been a flap, but up here gusts came in sharp waves blowing the frost from the grass humps and making the dogs blink. Over to the west, clouds were beginning to pile on the horizon, and Bill kept looking over his shoulder as we walked.

'What do you reckon, Tom?' he said.

'We'll be down long before that reaches us,' said Dadda.

'You say that,' he said. 'But remember last year?'

'We've had it worse,' said Dadda.

1947, 1963, 1975, 1981, 1982, they were all chapters in a chronicle of vicious autumns, when ash trees were uprooted in windstorms and the spines of bridges swept away in rising floods; when the Dyers' cowshed lost its roof, our barn its heavy doors; when lightning punched the Beasleys' pig field and killed half the herd.

Certain Gatherings were remembered for what was lost or damaged. Look at the maps – all the evidence is there.

'Still,' said Bill. 'I don't think we should drag our heels.'

'Do we ever?' said Dadda.

'I'm just saying,' said Bill.

'Kat's not going to hold us up,' I said. 'If that's what you mean.'

'I'm sure she wouldn't mean to get in the way,' said Bill. 'But if you're not used to the job . . .'

'Give her something to do then,' I said.

'You stand yourself there then,' said Dadda, looking past her to the Wall. 'Make sure none of them get through.'

Kat made her way over to the large gap between what Jim had rebuilt and the next line of rubble, wading through the heather, her arms spread like a tightrope-walker.

'She'd have been better off on the path,' said Bill.

'She'll be fine,' I said. 'She needs to learn what to do.'

Bill looked at the coming weather again and carried on, following Dadda and the dogs.

The sheep were spread out across the pastureland, their shadows stretched by the low sun, each one giving off wisps of white breath as they cried. The grass they chewed was stiff with rime and the heather brittle. The moorland had sustained them for as long as it could but now they had to come down. Most of the ewes would stay in the bye-field for the ram, but the four-shears – the older girls with the worn-down teeth

– would be taken to auction. Up here in the hills, their lambing days were over, but a lowland farmer with more space and softer grass might get another season or two out of them yet. The males that had been born in the spring – sturdy and rumpish now – would be taken to the abattoir. And the gimmer-hoggs given another year to grow to wombhood before they were tupped.

For years now, the strategy had been to corral the sheep by the ten yards of the Wall that Jim had reassembled at the foot of Poacher's Seat and then flank them on either side with the dogs. That way, when Musket and Fly advanced there was only one way the sheep were likely to go. The difficulty was in scouring them out of all the crevices and hollows in the first place and preventing them from being so terrified that they forgot their hefting and headed over the broken-down patches of wall into the old grouse moor.

Fly was a little over-eager at first and Dadda had to shout to get her boisterousness down to a wolfish tread. Otherwise, the sheep would have been scattered before we'd even started.

Being the elder dog, obedience his first thought, Musket reacted to the calls and whistles as soon as they were made and went over towards Poacher's Seat, snaking his way through the heather humps to the top and then moving the sheep that were grazing there down on to the level ground. As they hobbled along (sheep always look lame when they run) Musket took little diversions into the hidden runnels and peaty troughs to chase out the ewes and lambs, who emerged with the red grouse.

Others were feeding along an isthmus of grass that lay between two mossbogs and Dadda sent me to the far end of it to push the sheep towards the Wall. Musket and Fly were dispatched to the edges of the bogs so that the sheep would not think about making a sideways dash and ending up in need of rescue. Over the years, we'd lost ewes in that exact way, drowned in sludge before we'd got within fifty yards of them.

Musket kept pace with me as Dadda made him do, but Fly was too quickly ahead and with her barking she caused the sheep at the front of the pack to turn into the ones behind. Dadda quickly whistled and shouted and Fly backed off sulkily, allowing the sheep to move again when I urged them on.

A few – mavericks or imbeciles – tried to dart past but I moved quickly, making a fence rail with the crook to bring them back into line. They switched direction, wild-eyed and clumsy, and re-joined the flow, their hooves hollow on the frozen ground.

We worked like this for half an hour or so, flushing the sheep from every dip in the moorland and holding them by the Wall. Kat clapped her hands if the sheep came close but generally her presence was enough to make them double back and slot themselves between the other humps of fleece.

While the dogs kept them bunched together, Dadda made a head-count, and then Bill did the same. They made a second tally, and then I totalled them again.

'I make it sixty-one,' said Dadda.

'Same here,' said Bill. 'John?'

'Sixty-one,' I said.

'That's not all of them, then,' said Bill.

'Nothing like,' said Dadda.

Seventy animals – ewes and lambs – had been sent up in the springtime. It was written in the ledger with the marbled cover that the Gaffer had used for years, the one I still use now. Dadda climbed up on to some of the rubble of the Wall and scanned the grouse moor.

'Go on,' he said and Musket kinked between the stones to go off in search. Fly tried to follow him but Dadda lifted his voice and she stayed put, lying down and watching the sheep which grew more restless as Kat came over from where she'd been standing.

'You didn't let any through, did you?' said Bill.

'No,' she said.

'You sure?'

'She said so, didn't she?' I said.

Musket sniffed his way in and out of the heather but after a few minutes he stood and looked at Dadda with an expression as close to uncertainty as a dog could manage. What was he supposed to find exactly? There was nothing there.

'You take these down,' said Dadda. 'I'll go and look for the others.'

'Don't you want some help?' I said. 'A few more eyes and we'll find them quicker.'

'I've got Musket, haven't I?' he said.

'We'll cover more ground if we all go,' I said.

Dadda looked at Kat and then back at the grouse moor. 'It'll be hard going out there,' he said. 'I've not time to keep waiting for folk to catch up.'

'Come for them tomorrow then,' said Bill. 'They'll be all right for another night on their own.'

'They might be even further off by then,' said Dadda.

'Give them a day and you'll find them back where they belong,' said Bill. 'I'm sure.'

'And what if we don't?' I said.

'They've never gone this far before,' said Dadda. 'Summat's not right.'

'If you come back tomorrow, we can all help,' said Bill.

'We gather every animal on the same day,' said Dadda. 'We always have done.'

'I'm only thinking of you,' said Bill.

'That's what every bugger keeps telling me,' said Dadda.

'We mean it, Tom,' said Bill. 'We've always pulled together, haven't we?'

'Then stay and help us,' I said.

Bill looked up at the low brown clouds. 'Use your head, man. If that comes down you won't see your hand in front of your face,' he said.

'Aye, well, until that happens we'll carry on,' said Dadda.

Bill caught his arm. 'Tom, you've not failed, you know,' he said. 'It's just one of them things. It's not your fault.'

'You still here?' said Dadda.

Bill looked at him and then turned to Kat.

'Leave them to it, love,' he said. 'You're best off coming back to the farm with me.'

Kat shook her head and Bill kept his hand on offer for a while longer before he put his thumb and finger in his mouth and whistled to Liz on the ridge to let her know that the sheep were on the move.

Dadda got the dogs on to their feet and with a noise at the back of his throat he moved them slowly towards the flock in order to peel them away from the Wall. The sheep at the very edges went first, vocal again, and the others followed to converge into a mass of fleece and black heads, braying and moaning, their heads twitching with a woody knock of horns when Fly got too close.

'Can't I take Musket?' said Bill, as he started walking away. 'This lass is a bloody liability.'

'Just keep an eye on her,' said Dadda. 'The sheep know what they're doing.'

Filthy from the mud, their time up here over for the year, they began to stream away towards the ridge, running off the moors as certainly as rainwater.

At Gathering, I tell Adam, two thoughts occur to sheep at the same time. The first is an instinct that jolts them like a spark and makes them run from danger – and danger is in everything but themselves. The second is an urge as deep as the one that usually stops them from wandering past the Wall or readies them for the ram: it tells them that it is time to leave the moors. The growing cold and the shortening days awaken some synaptic conduit that compels them to find shelter and food and they recall in some form the meadowgrass in the bye-field and the path that leads them there.

They resist being rounded up and yet they go so willingly.

'They know they have to, Johnny lad,' said the Gaffer. 'They know that's the end of them if they don't.'

And it set me thinking what death – or rather the thought of death – must be like for them. If it was always there in their minds as a buzzing fly, or if it was nothing so loud as that but more a dull throb, like toothache.

I don't know. Perhaps they have no sense of death at all, perhaps they do what they do without ever being conscious of it, like a tree desiccating its leaves in autumn. I quite envy them really, the simple vessels they have to fill. For them there is only ever the belly the belly the belly, the womb the womb the womb.

~

If the missing sheep had strayed up Poacher's Seat, then they'd have stood out on the exposed slope, and if they'd hidden themselves in the holly bushes by Top Pond, we'd have heard them even from this distance. The most likely thing was that the cold weather had driven them across the grouse moor to the old shooting butts where they could stand out of the wind for a while. Musket investigated each clump of fallen stones and jumped down into the hole Dadda and I had hidden in to shoot the stag, but found nothing and went over to the wall of peat where Kat was sheltering out of the wind.

'I wish I'd brought my binoculars,' said Dadda. 'I can't see a bastard thing up here.'

He was looking beyond the place where the stag had fallen.

'They can't have gone over towards Blackmire Edge, Dadda,' I said. 'We were there only a couple of days ago, we'd have seen them.'

'Aye, but what's made them go off at all, though?' said Dadda, looking again.

'It happens sometimes, doesn't it?' I said.

'Aye, one or two every so often, maybe,' he said. 'But not nine.'

'Perhaps whatever sent the deer over this way from Wyresdale scared them too?' I said.

'They wouldn't have gone towards it, though, would they?' said Dadda.

'Something's made them run,' I said.

He coughed and rubbed his chest. It took longer than usual for him to stop.

'Jesus, listen to me,' he said. 'This is what you'll sound like in twenty years if you come back here.'

'It's just the fags, Dadda,' I said.

'It's nowt to do with the fags,' he said, wiping his mouth on his sleeve. 'It's this bloody place, it cripples you.'

'It's a cough, Dadda,' I said. 'You'll live.'

'Is this really what you want to bring her to, John?' he said, looking over to where Kat was stroking Musket's head. 'Is this what you want for her? Chasing stupid fuckin' sheep around the moors all day?'

'It's a job,' I said. 'There are lots of jobs to do here. If it needs doing, it needs doing.'

'Look at her,' he said. 'A strong wind would blow her back to the farm.'

'Give her six months,' I said, 'and I reckon you wouldn't know she'd ever lived anywhere else but here.'

'Six months?' said Dadda. 'It's not even been six days and the place is making her sick.'

'It's just the baby,' I said. 'Once it's born, she'll settle down.'

'You know there's one person you can't ever fool, John,' he said. 'And that's yourself. Don't waste your time trying.'

He zipped his jacket tighter and pulled up the collar to keep out the wind that came now with a freshly whetted edge.

The stark blue of the morning faded and the sky became overcast. A deeper glooming moved across the moors and then snow began to fall slowly in large feathers. It wasn't unheard of at this time of year, but it was usually no more than a flurry that came on the back of sleet and soon melted away.

'Should we go now?' said Kat, when she came over with Musket.

'It'll pass,' I said.

And if it didn't, then it would be a useful lesson for her. She needed to see how quickly the weather could change up here. She needed to be caught out by it at least once to learn anything.

'I tell you what, the weather here, Johnny lad,' the Gaffer said. 'I've known women less fickle.'

He was right. I've seen it a thousand times.

Stillness turns to storm.

Hail comes clattering from a springtime sky.

A sudden shower, and then a rainbow hoops the bright wet valley.

Winter melts in an hour.

The summer can end in a torrent. Just as it did the day Lennie Sturzaker died.

The heat that had been settled in the valley for weeks finally cracked one afternoon towards the end of August and clouds rolled in so low and so dark that Dadda and the Gaffer came dashing from the bye-field and the three of us stood in the kitchen with the lights on watching the storm.

The brushed concrete slope from the gate to the lane was a weir of rolling white water and the grass was tugged and shimmied like the weed in the river. The drains in the yard choked and the roof of the house shed the rain in wide, spattering curtains. Thunder broke at ground level, beating into the heart of the fells and down into the earth, thudding again when it echoed off the Three Sisters. All afternoon the valley filled like a bowl, but by the evening the rain started to pass away and the cloud lifted and only the wind remained, ruffling the surface of the flood water and shaking the wetness from the trees. Every slope continued to gush and roar and enlarge the river, which flowed with great purpose, deep and brown, carrying away what the storm had flung into its current.

It was Laurel who came back to the Endlands with the news about Lennie Sturzaker. She'd been in the village visiting Betty Ward and on the verge of driving home when the rain started and forced her to stay for the rest of the afternoon. When it finally petered out, they'd just started on a pot of tea, she said, and she didn't want it to go to waste, she said, and Betty was halfway through telling her about her sister's latest infidelities and anyway the lane was two foot under and so she'd stayed put.

As they ate their fruit loaf and rock cakes they heard one of the Beckfoot boys shouting outside and, lifting up the net curtains, they'd seen folk crowding on the bridge. The other Beckfoot lad came out of the butchery still in his apron, followed by Alun in his.

Boots on, Laurel in a borrowed mac, the two of them walked up the lane and joined the Dewhursts, the Earbys and the Parkers, who were all looking over at Arncliffe's. The Beckfoot brothers had climbed down the muddy bank and were balanced precariously on the wall of the millrace trying to reach Lennie as he rose and sank with the crust of litter, his body knocking against the iron paddles of the wheel. At the top of the slope, where the railings were rusted and the village kids got in to play in the grounds and break the windows, Jackie was saying Lennie's name as if she were calling for a cat at dusk. The other women there with her touched her shoulders and her hair. And when the Beckfoots finally managed to get hold of one of Lennie's arms and haul him out she began to scream and no one could watch any more.

Eventually, an ambulance came – always a strange, white creature in the valley – and took Lennie away, passing Ken Sturzaker as he drove back to the village from the abattoir.

'The poor man didn't even get to see his boy,' said Laurel.

'What the hell was the lad doing playing by Arncliffe's in that weather, anyway?' said Dadda.

'I don't think he was,' said Laurel. 'Betty seemed to think that he must have been in Sullom Wood and fallen in there.'

'Aye, well,' said the Gaffer, 'you go nosing about in places you shouldn't and that's what happens.'

'Have some sympathy, Harry,' said Laurel. 'I know you don't get on with the Sturzakers, but still.'

The Gaffer waved her off and lit a fag.

'I think we should at least send them some flowers,' Laurel said to Dadda. 'Something.'

'Aye,' said Dadda. 'Of course we will.'

'And perhaps a card too,' said Laurel. 'We could all sign it.'

'We're not sending them owt,' said the Gaffer. 'The lad shouldn't have been there.'

'No one's saying otherwise,' said Dadda. 'That's not the point, is it?'

'What is the point then?' the Gaffer said.

'They've just lost one of their sons. A lad our John's age,' said Dadda, raising his voice in a way that he rarely did with his father.

'I'm not having them think that we're all crying over him down here,' said the Gaffer. 'We'd be lying to ourselves, wouldn't we, Johnny lad?'

He put his hand on my arm and took another drag.

'Wigton's have flowers,' said Dadda, finding some loose change in his pocket to give to Laurel.

'It doesn't need to be much,' she said, looking at me with a sympathetic smile. 'Just something.'

The Gaffer stood up and sent the coins across the kitchen floor. Then he went out, calling for the dogs.

When the morning of the funeral came around a week later, he took himself off shooting on the Moss and the others made sure they were absent too. Angela kept Liz at home to muck out the pigs and Jim went up to work on the Wall. Bill had been trying to discourage Jeff's association with the Sturzakers for months and Lennie's death seemed a good reason to cut the ties once and for all. Laurel could go and sniffle in the pews if she wanted to. As far as he was concerned the Sturzakers were nothing to do with us. What happened to them was not our concern.

There might have only been three of us from the Endlands

there at the church but nearly everyone from the village turned out. The Wigtons and the Beckfoots had closed for the morning out of respect and those men who worked the same shift as Ken Sturzaker at the abattoir had been given time off to attend the funeral. All the teachers from the school were there too: Mr Cuddy, Mrs Broad and the usually floral Miss Bibby from the Reception class who was wrapped in black and comforting those children who had preferred to sit with her rather than their parents. They were the same age as I'd been when Mam died and could have had no idea what was going on. They sucked their thumbs, bewildered to see Sam Sturzaker crying, and sat mesmerised by the little box near the altar inside which his brother now lay, not asleep but dead. Gone for good. Such permanence they didn't understand.

Once the service was over, Ken Sturzaker, Eddie Moorcroft and the Beckfoot brothers carried Lennie out of the church and into the graveyard. On the other side of the boundary wall the river drifted past, going about its business reasonably now; the only evidence of the storm-swell the flattened ferns and hogweed along the banks. But it couldn't have escaped anyone's thoughts that Lennie must have floated past here already limp and dead, his body just another thing for the river to remove from the valley, the floodwater conveying him past the school field, past Beckfoot's and Wigton's, under the green, echoing bricks of the bridge and on and on until he was caught in the millrace.

As they started to bury him, I wondered what would have happened if he hadn't been snared and the river had carried him out of the valley, out of the hills. I pictured him being passed from the Briar to the Hodder under Mellor Knoll and then rolling in the confluence where the Hodder met the Ribble by the Jesuit College. And then on he'd go, gliding through Balderstone and Salmsbury and Preston, past the mudflats of the Fylde, the river widening and becoming estuary and estuary becoming sea. And I imagined crabs hanging off his fingers, I imagined eels slipping over his neck and the gulls lifting off from the grey waves as he was taken out on the ebb tide and expelled from England.

After the burial, Laurel and Betty set up trestle tables in the school playground, it being the only space large enough to accommodate everyone, and served tea and sandwiches and orange squash. It was only natural that the smaller children – relieved that it was all over and death, whatever that was, could be forgotten – started to play as they would at breaktime, making ones and twos on the hopscotch grid and weaving away from whoever was on. The grown-ups let them. It was nice, they said, to hear laughter on such a sad day.

After an hour or so, the wake broke up and folk started to drift back to their houses. Ken Sturzaker went off to the Croppers' Arms with Eddie Moorcroft and the other men from the abattoir, dragging along the Beckfoot brothers for the drinks they'd been promised after risking their lives in the millrace.

Soon the playground was empty and Dadda held my hand as we went back to where he'd parked.

'Are you all right?' he said.

'Yes, Dadda,' I said.

'Perhaps you shouldn't have come,' he said. 'They're strange bloody things, funerals.'

'I'm fine,' I said.

'You've hardly said a word all morning.'

'I don't know what to say.'

'It won't happen to you, you know,' he said, as he unlocked the door. 'If that's what's bothering you.'

'I know, Dadda,' I said.

'Accidents are accidents,' he said. 'They're rare enough for you not to worry about, all right?'

'Yes, Dadda.'

He tapped his wedding ring on the steering wheel as we drove out of the village and into Sullom Wood, and I almost confessed to him that it hadn't been an accident at all.

~

The best guess we had was that the sheep had gone off along the line of the Corpse Road, following the most obvious route across the moorland. It would have seemed to them like one of the desire lines they cut through the grass to get to water.

We walked for half an hour, finding nothing. The snow was still falling softly but in the trenches between the peat-haggs the wind set the air swarming with flakes that made it hard to see more than twenty yards ahead.

'Perhaps we should go back now,' said Kat.

'Aye,' said Dadda. 'You and John get yourselves down to the farm. I'll be all right on my own.'

'I'm not leaving you up here by yourself, Dadda,' I said. 'I told you that already. What if something happens?'

'Like what?'

'Don't be obtuse,' I said. 'You know what I mean. You might fall or something.'

'I've not fallen up here yet,' he said. 'I'll watch my step, don't worry.'

'John, please,' said Kat. 'I think we should turn around. I don't want to get lost up here.'

'We've only walked a mile or two,' I said.

'It's not the distance,' said Kat. 'It's the daylight. When it's like this it goes dark much earlier. You know that.'

'It's only midday, Kat,' I said, showing her my watch. 'I think we'll be all right for a while yet. You shouldn't be scared of this place.'

'I'm being sensible,' she said.

'Quiet,' said Dadda. 'Listen.'

Kat and I stopped and Musket closed his eyes as the wind parted his fur to the skin.

A faint sheep call came and went and Dadda sent Musket off. He disappeared but barked a few moments later and we found him sniffing at two carcasses close to the edge of the path. Both of the ewes were half buried in the snow, days dead, and their blood had frozen into crystalline veins that webbed the drifts. Crows had evidently seated themselves at the table to gorge on the remains and there wasn't much left of either animal but a mat of plucked-at fleece. Each leg had been stripped to the bone and the sweetmeats dragged out of the ruptured bellies.

'But what would have killed them in the first place?' said Kat.

'Dogs,' said Dadda, holding Musket back from sticking his nose into the wounds. 'When a few of them get together, they can tear a sheep to pieces if they're determined.'

'Oh, God, there's another,' said Kat, pointing past us at Musket who had found an older ewe lying split and strewn on the other side of the track.

The faint bleating came again and Musket blinked at Dadda, waiting on his instruction.

'Go on,' he said, and the dog turned and padded off along the track.

Through the snow a hundred yards further on, he was waiting at the edge of a deep hollow, one of the places that the Gaffer told me about, where tired pall-bearers had stumbled and sent the coffin and its contents thumping down through the grass and rocks.

The call that we'd heard was coming from the shearling sprawled at the bottom, one of the females due to be put before the ram for the first time at tupping. After an awkward fall, she'd ended up on her back and was writhing in the mud and snow to try and get herself upright.

'She's had it, Dadda,' I said. 'Look at her.'

'She's only rigged,' he said and began testing the solidity of the peat near the top of the slope with the heel of his boot.

'You're not going down there, are you?' said Kat.

'Well, I'm not leaving her in pain,' said Dadda.

'Don't you go as well, John,' said Kat, holding my arm.

'Aye, stay here, John,' said Dadda. 'I can manage on my own.'

'It's a long way down,' I said.

'I've been fetching sheep out of cloughs all my life,' he said, 'I think I'll be all right,' and began to make his way down, jabbing his crook into the crusted earth and kicking the frost off the rocks. Despite Kat calling me back, I followed him, clinging on to tufts of grass to keep myself steady.

The sheep moaned and rolled as we came to her. One of her front legs had been skinned to the tendons by the rocks and the other was snapped at right angles. The broken end flailed limply as she tried to get away from us.

'We'll have to leave her,' I said.

'Here?' said Dadda.

'She's not going to be able to walk, is she?'

'The poor lass must be in agony,' said Dadda.

'Not for much longer,' I said. Her fleece was dark with blood.

'I didn't come all this way to find the sheep and watch them die,' he said. 'If I can get her back to the farm, I can get Leith to come and have a look at her.'

'Dadda, you can't carry her all the way back to the valley,' I said.

'So what do you suggest we do, then?'

'There are plenty of stones,' I said. 'Put her out of her misery.'

'Just help me get her on to my back,' he said and gave me his cap and his crook to hold.

He knelt down and between us we managed to arrange the sheep around his shoulders like a stole. Her broken leg flopped in his grip and although she tried to wrench herself free, she settled as Dadda started to climb. In the snow, each step was judicious and I kept close to his back so that I could steady him if he looked likely to fall.

'Was it the Sturzakers' dogs, do you think?' I said.

'I can't see him bringing them this far, can you?' Dadda said.

'They might have got out,' I said.

'You saw the cages in his back yard,' said Dadda. 'They looked pretty secure to me.'

'Whose are they then?' I said.

'I don't know,' he said. 'They could be anybody's. They might be strays from Wyresdale, maybe. Or folk dump them on the moors sometimes. Whoever they belong to, they must be the reason the deer were over this way.'

'We'd better come back with a couple of shotguns,' I said.

'They won't stay long now it's snowing,' said Dadda.

'That's what I'm worried about,' I said. 'They might find their way into the valley.'

'Well, if they do, that'll be my problem, won't it?' he said.

'I'm not going back to Suffolk, Dadda,' I said. 'I told you that.'

He missed his footing and I gripped his elbow to stop him slipping over. He must have felt the sheep sliding off his shoulders and grasped the fleece with his fingers to steady her. Whatever life she'd been clinging on to left her in that moment and her head flopped back and bumped against Dadda's back all the way to the top of the slope.

When Dadda was within touching distance, Kat reached down and helped him up. Blood had stained the back of his jacket to the hem and soaked his hair and neck. Something sinewy and grey dangled from the sheep's fleece and left a spatter-line through the snow as he let it fall off his shoulders.

'For Christ's sake,' said Kat. 'The pair of you almost ended up falling down there yourselves. What would you have expected me to do if you'd broken your legs too?'

'We're all right,' I said. 'Stop making a fuss.'

'Even to me it was obvious that sheep was going to die,' said Kat. 'Why the hell did you bother?'

'I had to try and get her out,' said Dadda.

'There's caring for your animals and there's being reckless,' said Kat. 'Look at the weather.'

'I know what the weather's like,' said Dadda.

'Can we go now?' said Kat. 'The rest of them are only going to be dead too.'

'I'd rather see that with my own eyes before I go back to the farm,' said Dadda.

'We're here now, Kat,' I said. 'We might as well see if we can find the other ones.'

She made me look at her.

'Who are you trying to prove yourself to, John?' she said. 'I hope it's not me.'

'Are you going to help?' I said.

'You promised me we could go home today,' she said.

'I didn't promise you anything,' I said. 'I told you we were coming here to work. This is work.'

'We have work,' she said. 'I have the nursery and you have the school.'

‘That’s over with now,’ I said. ‘It has to be.’

‘What are you talking about?’

‘Now the Gaffer’s gone, we’re needed here,’ I said. ‘These animals are ours. We’re just as responsible for them as Dadda is.’

‘Stop saying that,’ said Kat.

‘But it’s true,’ I said.

‘I don’t care about the fucking farm,’ she said and turned to Dadda. ‘Sorry, Tom, but I don’t.’

‘Hold on,’ I said. ‘Who gave you the right to let it fall apart?’

‘What do you mean?’ she said.

‘I mean it’s not up to you to make that decision,’ I said. ‘You’re a caretaker just like the rest of us. Why should other folk miss out on living in the Endlands just because you don’t want to?’

‘I’m not bringing up our son here, John,’ she said.

‘You don’t have any choice, Kat.’

‘Are you threatening me?’

‘Of course not,’ I said. ‘I mean *we* don’t have any choice. Things have changed. There are obligations we have to fulfil now.’

‘John,’ she said. ‘I can’t say it any other way. I don’t want to be here.’

‘Why?’

‘Are you seriously asking me that question?’ she said. ‘After what the Gaffer did? After what they all did?’

Dadda looked at her.

‘Look, you stay if you want to,’ she said. ‘I’m going back to Dunwick.’

‘You’re acting like a child,’ I said.

‘Leave me alone,’ she said and walked off a little way down the track.

‘You’re not going to persuade her like that,’ said Dadda.

‘I’m not trying to persuade her,’ I said. ‘The decision’s made. She knows it’s the right one.’

'You can't force her to stay somewhere she doesn't want to be,' said Dadda.

'She doesn't know what she wants,' I said. 'That's her problem.'

'It sounds to me like she wants to go home,' said Dadda.

'When she says that, she doesn't mean the house where we actually live,' I said. 'She means the vicarage.'

'So? Let her go.'

'No, Dadda,' I said. 'She needs to grow up.'

The snow began to come down with more urgency and Dadda turned up his collar which was still damp with blood.

'Fuck it,' he said. 'Let's call it a day.'

'But there might be some still alive,' I said.

'Not in this,' he said, sending Musket in the direction Kat had gone.

We followed the prints that she'd left in the snow, expecting to catch up with her within a few minutes. But she'd made quicker progress than I'd expected and even Musket couldn't find her. She wouldn't be lost, though. For now, the Corpse Road was still discernible and as long as she stuck to it, she would soon find the grouse butts and then the Wall. And when she got there, when she'd calmed down, she'd have the sense to stay behind it and wait for us. Then we could show her the way to the top of the path and take her down into the valley. We'd go back to the farm to help the others shoo the Owd Feller from the fireplace and then crown the ram. We'd drink tea and browse the scullery for the food brought over on Devil's Day. We'd watch the snow falling in the yard. Then we'd sit down and make plans.

Sweeting always stayed at Churchmeads with the boarders over half-term so I'd be able to phone him after prep and tell him to expect my resignation. I could hear his voice already, ranging from confusion to persuasion to acquiescence and then philosophy. Well, it was obvious that I hadn't been happy at the school for some time, and life was too short to spend it feeling unfulfilled, and if a man found his life's purpose then he could count himself lucky beyond measure. But he'd be relieved, I knew, that there'd be no more letters from parents, no more ripples. Ah, he'd think, it was a more complicated situation than he'd imagined. I'd been worried about my father being on his own. I'd felt a pull towards family responsibilities. There were genuine reasons for Mr Pentecost's *difficulties* of late. That should appease Mrs Weaver.

We'd have to go and see Kat's family, of course, and Barbara would be devastated when we told her what we were planning to do. Devastated and then angry, and naturally I'd be blamed. The Reverend would be sorry to see her leave the village, but secretly glad that Kat was thinking of her own life rather than her mother's. Rick would laugh at her, unable to imagine Kit-Kat working on a farm. But whatever they said, however they felt, we'd still clear the house and put it on the market. We'd throw or give away what we didn't need and head north for good.

It would be hard for Kat to leave the nursery, of course, but she would have left before long anyway, when the baby came. And her feelings would change, too. They always do. Things that seem so vital never usually are, and they're often replaced by what's truly needed.

When we came to live here, we'd be cleansed of all the old layers. The past that we once had would seem like someone else's.

Which it does now, I say to Adam.

It seems absurd, I say, that I once taught Shelley and Shakespeare, Hardy and Houseman, to boys in deckchair blazers.

On the open grouse moor, the snow had come down thickly and covered the tracks that Kat had made. Dadda headed off straight towards Poacher's Seat, which came and went in the clouds. But the wind rose and everything ahead of us was quickly lost in a whiteout. I could see nothing but the back of Dadda's blood-stained jacket and the divots left by his boots. Musket padded next to me, finding the best route he could, his fur licked into spikes by the wetness of the snow.

He was usually pretty adept at retracing his paw-steps, and like the sheep he could have probably found his way back to the Endlands without much difficulty, but when we came into a deeping that we would have remembered for its complete silence, Dadda called him to stop.

'We must have gone wrong,' he said. 'There are no scars like this on the grouse moor.'

'We can't have strayed that far,' I said. 'We were walking in a straight line, weren't we?'

'When can you ever walk in a straight line in weather like this?' said Dadda.

'We'll have to go back, then,' I said.

Dadda opened his sleeve and looked at his watch. 'It'll start going dark in a couple of hours,' he said.

'I know, Dadda.'

'It's not easy to find the top of the path when the daylight goes.'

'I know.'

He was expelling his doubts, that was all. I knew that he had no intention of leaving before we'd found Kat, but he was right. Darkness closed off the edges of the moors. And even if by luck we came to the head of Fiendsdale Clough, the likelihood of making a descent through the ice and snow on the sheep track without slipping into the gully was remote. We had no torch and we were tired too.

Walking through the snow had sapped the strength from both of us and we waited for a minute listening instead. The silence down there was what I forgot most when I was away from the valley. It was impossible to take it with me back to Suffolk, impossible to notice it anywhere else but here.

It was Musket with the sharper ears who heard the call first and padded off a few steps to investigate.

'It sounds like another ewe,' said Dadda.

'No, that's Kat,' I said.

But when it came again, it didn't sound like either. There was the intonation of words this time, but it was impossible to make out what they were.

'Perhaps it's whoever we heard the other day,' said Dadda.

'Maybe,' I said, the voice sounded just as distant as it came a third time. A decaying note that was too short-lived to pinpoint.

Musket barked and Dadda told him to be quiet. I called Kat's name and started to climb up the rise.

The blizzard calmed now and the snow petered out to a few spindling flakes. When I came to the top of the ravine, I could see that the wind had pushed the snowstorm across the moors, leaving the sky on the horizon in front of us a dirty orange. Musket's nose must have been numbed by the cold. He'd led us in a wide arc so that we were now heading west and not east.

The moor might have been swept clean of cloud, but there was no trace of Kat at all, and nothing looked familiar. It was hard to judge distance, hard to tell whether the white ridges we could see were miles away or a few minutes' walk. I followed Dadda up to a higher viewpoint on the edge of the cleft, but it only gave us more of the same. I shouted for Kat and got nothing back. The voice that we'd heard didn't speak again.

There wasn't much we could do any more but head for the

Wall. So long as we kept the failing daylight at our backs we would be walking in the right direction.

At sundown, the horizon turned to vermilion ribbons that underpinked the clouds and before long a new front came sweeping in. Dusk fell with the snow and from then on we could only try and stick to the line we'd been walking, the two of us calling Kat's name.

By the way the light faded, I should think that Dadda and I must have walked for another hour, though I doubt we got more than a mile. Crossing the moors in the height of dry summer was slow enough, but in snow every footstep was an experience in itself and it was hard to tell whether what we were about to stand on would give way to a yard-deep hole or send the boot skidding off into slush. When we came to the basins in the moor, it was easier to edge down them on the backside rather than on foot, and climbing up the other side was as exhausting as scaling a sand-dune.

We'd worked our way in and out of half a dozen cuttings and troughs and were coming to the top of a particularly steep slope when Dadda bent down and gripped Musket's scruff to stop him from going any further.

'What's wrong?' I said.

He didn't reply and when I'd climbed the last few feet to the ridge to join him, I could see that he was looking down on Far Lodge.

Despite what the Gaffer had told me, I hadn't thought that it would be quite so well preserved. The walls were sound and the roof – surely the first thing that should have gone – held the snow in a rigid tent. The shutters had lost their black paint, but they remained tightly bolted over the windows. It was like one of those

Iron Age bodies they pull out of peat bogs from time to time, with the hair and the skin and the fingernails intact. Something dead but curiously close to being still alive.

'I don't understand,' I said. 'We can't be here if we've been walking east.'

'You saw which way the sun went down,' said Dadda. 'We've been walking in the right direction.'

'How can we have been?' I said.

Dadda looked down at the Lodge again as it was slowly interred in snow. 'I don't know,' he said.

'Do you think we'd be able to get inside?' I said.

'I'd rather we carried on,' said Dadda.

'We're miles from the valley,' I said. 'It'll be pitch black before we're anywhere near the path.'

'Maybe so, but I think that place is best left to itself,' he said.

'Ten minutes, Dadda,' I said. 'Just while this passes over.'

Between us, we kicked away the drifts that had mounded up against the doors until we could push them inwards, enough to get through the gap. The window shutters kept the place in a grey gloom but even in the half-light it was easy to see that the dining room where Gideon Denning and the Hellenics had played cards and drunk their scotch and raised the Devil from his sleep under the moors had been gutted of its furniture. If the marks they'd smeared on the door that night in late October were still there, as the Gaffer had said they were, then they had been long covered in mould and cobwebs.

It was colder inside the Lodge than it was out in the snow and Dadda went over to the fireplace to see if it was usable.

'We'll not get much going in here,' he said.

It was thick with bird shit and the hearth was piled with the remains of old nests. More were probably wedged in the chimney.

All that we had for fuel was a pair of window shutters that had been brought inside at some point to be repaired and left propped against the wall. Dadda stamped them into pieces and we stacked them in the grate and knelt down to try and blow the flames into life. But they smouldered rather than burned and a foot or two from the hearth it was breath-cold.

'She'll have got herself back down to the farm, won't she?' said Dadda.

'I'm sure the others will have found her,' I said. 'They'll look after her until we get back.'

'It'll take us a couple of hours, I reckon,' he said.

'Dadda, we can't go anywhere now,' I said.

'It's only five o'clock,' he said, looking at his watch. 'If we set off soon, we'd be back by seven. Eight at the most.'

'Eight tomorrow morning more like,' I said.

'Give over.'

'Well, talk sense, Dadda,' I said. 'You know what the moors are like in snow.'

'I've lost nine decent animals,' he said. 'I want to make sure the rest of them are all right.'

'They'll be fine,' I said.

'They better not have left them in the bye-field in weather like this,' he said.

'What would you have done?' I said.

'Taken them into the shed, of course,' he said.

'Well, that's what Bill and the others will have done then, won't they?' I said. 'They've all been Gathering for as long as you have.'

'The ram needs watching as well,' said Dadda.

'They have eyes,' I said. 'All of them.'

'Properly watching, I mean, smart-arse,' he said. 'They need to know to call Leith if he takes a turn for the worse.'

'They'll manage,' I said.

'They'd better.'

'What will you do about the ewes?' I said.

'There's nowt much I can do. I've no time to replace them before Tupping,' he said. 'I'll have to wait until next year now.'

'We'll build the flock back up, Dadda,' I said. 'Don't worry.'

He spat into the fire and took another drag of his roll-up and didn't reply.

It wasn't just the nine ewes that had died but their offspring and theirs and theirs. Each death echoed on and on.

'Bill was right, though, Dadda,' I said. 'It's not your fault.'

'It'd be a different story if the Gaffer were still here,' he said. 'I'd never hear the end of it.'

'But he's not here, is he?'

'Maybe not in body.'

'Did he ever bring you here? The Gaffer?' I said.

'No,' said Dadda. 'And he told me that if he ever found out I'd even been looking for it, he'd take off his belt.'

'He never took off his belt in his life,' I said.

'Figure of speech.'

'How was he?' I said. 'After what happened with the boy?'

I hadn't yet really asked.

'He didn't say much about it,' Dadda replied. 'None of us did.'

'Was he worried?'

'Course he were,' said Dadda. 'How could he not be?'

'He told you that, did he?'

'He didn't need to, the amount he were putting away in the Croppers' Arms every night,' he said. 'I don't know, you'd think he'd have laid off it for good after what happened.'

'How do you mean?'

'He didn't mean to kill that lad,' said Dadda. 'He were just trying to put a shot over his head to scare him off. The thing is, he'd been in the fuckin' pub all evening, hadn't he? He couldn't see well enough to piss straight.'

'It was an accident, then,' I said. 'Like you thought it was.'

'That doesn't make it all right, John,' he said. 'It doesn't stop him being a drunken owd bastard, does it?'

'Is that how you want to remember him?' I said.

'How else do you want me to remember him?'

'He was your dad,' I said.

'Aye, but he never liked me much,' said Dadda.

'Of course he did,' I said.

'Then you know less about this place than I thought you did,' he said.

'I never saw you arguing,' I said. 'Not about anything much.'

'That's because you weren't here,' he said. 'He always blamed me for letting you go.'

'But I was the one who left,' I said. 'It was me he fell out with not you.'

'He never thought badly of you, John,' said Dadda.

'He did, Dadda,' I said. 'I know he did.'

'Listen, I lived with him every day,' said Dadda. 'He changed whenever he knew you were coming to stay. He were counting the days last week. I heard him telling Musket.'

I didn't believe him and Dadda could tell.

'It weren't me who put the fancy piss-pot in the attic and hung up the mirror,' he said. 'He thought the world of you and your lass.'

He took off his cap and put it closer to the fire to try and get it dry. 'It's not just the sheep anyway,' said Dadda. 'I've other things to do.'

'All the jobs will still be there tomorrow,' I said. 'And if it's Bill you're bothered about, he's not going to see Sturzaker before he knows we're all right, is he?' I said.

'Sturzaker?'

'Come on,' I said. 'You know he's going to be back down there after what's happened to the sheep.'

'He won't,' said Dadda. 'He's too worried that Sturzaker will tell Dent about the van.'

'Perhaps he's right to be worried,' I said.

'You've changed your tune,' said Dadda. 'I thought you were sure Ken Sturzaker was going to keep us dangling for as long as he could?'

'You know what he's like,' I said. 'If there's some money in it for him, the temptation might be too much.'

'There won't be any money in it,' said Dadda.

'What makes you so sure?'

'It doesn't matter, John,' he said. 'Forget it.'

'I don't understand,' I said.

'Look, Ken Sturzaker's been listening to owd news,' said Dadda. 'Dent's not going to come to the farm.'

'How do you know that?' I said.

He drew on his roll-up and picked a strand of tobacco off his lip.

'Dadda, how do you know?' I said.

'Because he's already been, John,' he said.

'What are you talking about?' I said. 'When?'

'A couple of weeks afterwards,' he said. 'The lad the Gaffer shot were Dent's nephew.'

'Christ.'

'And that goes no further than these four walls, all right?' he said.

'Of course,' I said. 'But how did Dent know to come to the Endlands?'

'One of the other little bastards who works for him told him that this nephew of his had come here to make a few quid for himself on the side.'

He let the smoke curl out of his nose and rubbed the skin under his eye. He was exhausted.

'You know most of the time,' he said, 'I'd say that Ken Sturzaker were full of shit, but everything he told you about Dent were true.'

'How do you mean?' I said.

'Well, he didn't seem right bothered about his nephew. It seemed to me that he thought he got what he deserved,' said Dadda.

'So that was that?' I said. 'They were straight? Him and the Gaffer?'

'Come on,' said Dadda. 'Do you really think a bloke like that's just going to walk away with nowt?'

'So what did he want?' I said.

Dadda looked at me and then at the fire. 'Grace,' he said. 'He wanted Grace. The Gaffer were supposed to take her over to Burnley.'

'But he didn't,' I said, 'so what's to stop Dent coming back for her?'

'Because the Gaffer gave him summat else instead,' said Dadda.

'What did he give him?'

'I don't know,' he said. 'They sorted it out between them.'

'The Gaffer didn't tell you?' I said.

'To be honest, John,' he said, 'I didn't ask.'

~

The snow didn't stop falling and so there was nothing we could do but wait for the night to end. Musket lay over my feet, Dadda smoked his roll-up and soon that amber pip was the only light in the room.

I slept a little – though I don't remember how on the cold floor – and when I woke again daylight was starting to rim the window shutters and leak under the door. Dadda coughed and rolled over.

The wind had dropped and the moors were silent. I listened for a few minutes, wondering if in all that stillness I might hear Kat calling. But she must have been down at the farm. She would be getting ready with the others to come and look for us.

The fire was almost out and I could see Dadda's and Musket's breath as they slept. Without a torch, it had been too dark in the night to search the bunkhouse for anything to burn but now there was enough greyness to at least see that the door had sagged on its hinges and sat a few inches ajar. There seemed to be more brightness in there than in the room where we'd slept and when I lifted the door to open it enough to get inside, I found that one of the shutters had fallen off, letting in the same grubby daylight as the scullery window down at the farm. Outside, it had stopped snowing and under the low cloud the moors stretched away, drift after drift, to the cold sunrise on the eastern edge.

There was nothing much left in the place where Gideon Denning and the Hellenics had slept and screwed. The wooden bunks were gone, the iron coke stove that had kept them warm probably taken for scrap, and all that remained were a few broken chairs at the other end of the room and a powerful smell of decay like there'd been in that toilet in Spain.

The Lodge might have looked solid from the top of the hollow, but it was rotting from the inside out. The rafters had soaked up decades of rain and had grown a blubber of white mould. Over the walls, the plaster glistened with sweat and tall sprays of grass grew where the wooden floorboards had perished. Every plank was streaked black from the leaking roof and looked ready to splinter at the next footfall.

I wondered how long it would take for the whole place to be eaten by the moor. Another hundred years? Two? Maybe longer still. But one day it would be gone. The wind would work the slates loose like old teeth and eventually the rain would finish off what the rising damp had started and gnaw the roof beams until they kinked and fell. The rendering would crack and each winter ice would form in the fracture lines, opening them a little more, levering off the cement in chunks and exposing the brick-work beneath. And that would come undone as well in time and weather. Rain to dissolve the mortar, gales to push the wall into the heather. Perhaps the chimney stack might remain standing for a while, but eventually it would be toppled and its scattered bricks grassed over and then only the fireplace would be left, the bas-relief of grapes and leaping stags around the rim gradually scoured flat. A mysterious structure for future generations to tell stories about.

Someone had been here and recently. A half-empty can of dog food sat open with a spoon inside. There were fag ends and spent matches. Blokes from the village or from over in Wyresdale had perhaps sheltered here while they were out after grouse. Fed their terriers, cleaned their guns, waited for the rain to pass.

But then I came across a car battery, a pair of pliers, a lump hammer, one leather boot and then the other. And the smell in the room was too strong for dog meat.

Behind the scattered chairs, I found someone lying curled up facing the wall, their bare feet turned the colour of aubergines. I waited for them to move or wake up, knowing that they wouldn't. Nobody lay as awkwardly as that to go to sleep. And it was too cold to have spent the night in just a T-shirt.

Standing at the edge of the stain that had seeped from under the body and dried, I recognised the wild hair and the lobeless ear. I knew that bony nose and (even though the fingers were broken) the hand tattooed with *Liz* and *Grace*. But the blood on his skin and on his clothes wasn't his. Jeff lay in the remains of another man's body. A man who had been opened up like the ewes we'd found on the moor.

Musket had followed me in by now and after recoiling from the dog food, he began to sniff through the rags of clothing that had been spread across the floor and the flesh that had been scattered into the corner of the room. He barked and looked at me, waiting for permission to eat the fingers that he'd found, each of them banded with a silver ring.

In the other room, I could hear Dadda stirring and calling for me and after kicking Musket out, I closed the door to the bunkhouse as tight as it would go.

'What are you doing?' said Dadda.

'You were cold,' I said. 'I thought there might be something we could put on the fire.'

'Forget it,' he said. 'We're not staying. We need to go.'

He knew that at first light the others would come out looking for us again and he didn't want them wandering miles across the moorland. It was deep in snow already and there was no telling how much more there was to come.

Spring

Days of heavy rain eventually cleared the drifts, leaving the valley muddy and dank. Christmas came and went and then the true winter arrived in January, when the worst was always thrown at us. The farms were cut off, pipes froze, fences were kicked flat by storms, while Musket caught a cold and had to be nursed like an old grandfather.

The freeze lasted well into February, but then the sun began to creep into the valley and the cloughs became dripping grottoes of snowdrops and dog's mercury. And the river, so long muted by ice, ran loud with meltwater. March gave way to April and the lambs were born into blossom and high cloud. Just as they have been this year.

I'm as bad as Dadda and the Gaffer used to be. I can't leave the sheep for very long. Mind you, Kat's no better. She's less than a month to go with our second child and I tell her to take it easy but she doesn't listen. She's so large, she says, that she can't sleep and she might as well waddle over to the pens and help me with the night shift. She says her presence is calming anyway. The ewes can sense that she's in the same bind as them.

Liz and Grace have been over most days to muck in and Angela, too, though she gets tired in the afternoons and sits with Adam to help him with the bottle-fed lambs. For years, it's been his job to look after the runts (just as it used to be mine), and a few more than usual have come along this year. As always, though, he's a serious worker. He doesn't coo over the baggy suede skin or the comical little bleatings, he's determined to turn these spares into good strong animals. But it's child's work and he's not going to be a child for ever.

Kat mothers him more than she needs to, especially when he's near the sheep. She doesn't like him being in the pens with them at Lambing. She worries that they'll knock him over and trample on him. But he needs to learn and we've made the odd pact of silence so as not to worry her.

Yesterday evening, when we got back from shooting on the Moss, one of the ewes went into labour and only the head of the lamb emerged and not the feet. A bad position for birthing. Their shoulders get stuck. They can die, and the mother too.

I took Adam's hand and led him into the pen and helped him kneel down in the straw next to me. The ewe shuffled and guttered in her throat and Adam backed away a little.

Don't worry about her, I said. She won't bother you if she knows you're trying to help. Can you feel its head?

I moved his hand and he put his fingers to the lamb's greasy face.

I have to push it back in, I said, so we can rearrange the legs. That'll be your job. Don't worry, it'll be easier for you anyway. You've smaller hands than me.

Once I'd manipulated the lamb back into the uterus, I rubbed Adam's fingers with jelly and slid one of his hands through the ewe's vagina. He couldn't stop his face from curdling at the sensation on his skin and the liverish smell, but he didn't say anything.

Can you feel its feet? I said.

Yes, he said.

How many?

Just one.

Put both your hands in, I said. It's all right. Let her make her noise, you're doing her no harm. Have you found the other one?

He had.

But they're slippery, he said.

Move yourself closer then, I said. Get a good grip on the ankles.

He shuffled his knees forward, his cheek almost touching the ewe's rump, his brown eyes wandering and his mouth slightly open as it always is when he's concentrating on something.

All right, I said. You bring it out now.

He retracted his forearms, his skin covered in syrupy blood and clot, and pulled two small hooves out of the maw of the birth canal. The ewe grumbled and tensed and I held her while Adam worked his knees backwards and drew out the lamb into the straw.

Is it all right? he said.

It's fine, I said.

What is it? he said.

A lad, I said.

A twice-born.

Kat went frantic, of course, when she saw the state of him, but I told her that he'd only held the lamb and that I'd delivered it. She didn't need to be worried unnecessarily with a month to go. There are lots of things I haven't told her. She doesn't know that I let Adam use the ear-tagger on the lamb we'll have on Devil's Day later in the year. I didn't tell her that I let him carry the shotgun home from the Moss yesterday. Or that he helped me gut the mallards in the scullery this morning.

When I say to him, that's between you and me, he knows to keep his mouth shut if he wants to carry on learning about the valley. And so it's only when we've left Kat crocheting a baby bonnet in the kitchen and we're out in the yard chaining Jenny to her kennel that he asks where we're really going.

Somewhere you've not been before, I say.

But what about the lambs? he says. What if more come?

Grandma Angela and Auntie Liz are there, I say. And Grace too. They'll look after them while we're gone. Don't worry.

Most days, I try and take him out to the hay fields or the other way to what used to be the Dyers' place. He can't walk quickly, even though he's known the lane all his life. But that doesn't mean to say that he can't walk far. We've always assumed, Kat and I, that he would get quickly tired if we made him try any kind of distance, but why should that be so? His legs, at least, are as good as anyone else's.

One foot, then the other, we inch along the lane. There's a warmth to the sunlight when the wind drops. There is no question that it's spring. All the muddy sloughing of winter is done with now and the river has a leap to it like the lambs in the bye-field.

It's so loud, says Adam, and puts his hand to his ear. To him, water is everywhere. It fills the valley to the brim. It reminds him, constantly, to be afraid.

I can't remember exactly how old he was when his hand slipped out of Kat's and he fell off the stepping stones by the Beasleys' bridge, whether he was closer to three than four, but he wasn't in the water for long. Only the few seconds that it took for the current to sweep him under the concrete span and out the other side where I was cutting back the thistles. Hearing Kat's screams, I'd thrown down the billhook and plucked Adam out by his arm coughing and crying.

For weeks afterwards, we scourged ourselves with what-ifs and imagined all sorts of awful things: the family name on the front page of the *Lancashire Gazette*, carrying a wee coffin into St Michael's, the pair of us drowning for ever in guilt.

Kat went back and forth to the doctor with him, worried about the cut on his ankle from the edge of the stone, worried that he'd damaged his lungs or starved his little brain of oxygen. But he hadn't been under long enough to do himself any real physical harm. It was in his night-terrors that he suffered, and for a good few months afterwards he'd slept in bed with us.

But that was a long time ago and he's nearly eleven years old now. There's no time for him to be a child. All that's gone.

Where are we? he says.

At the deer, I say.

He knows the Dyers' old place by the stag's head carved into one of their gateposts; a finger of masonry torn from the doorway of the church when Richard Arncliffe was overhauling the bell tower. Ever since he was a little boy, Adam's liked to trace his finger round the antlers.

The gate's locked with a chain that's gone rusty and the concrete track up to the farmhouse is sprouting new grass to cover the FOR SALE sign that blew down during the winter. For a while, when she was engaged to a dairyman from Clitheroe, Grace considered taking the place on. It made sense. The buildings they'd need were already there, she knew the land well, and her fiancé had raised his own cattle on his father's farm and had the makings of a good herd. But the relationship had fizzled out, as they tend to do for Grace, and then Farrowing had come around and Angela and Liz needed her, and the idea was abandoned.

Folk in Range Rovers come to look now and then with plans in mind for country living and there was talk a while ago about someone opening a bed and breakfast, but the Endlands are remote, not secluded; watchful rather than peaceful. They're a place of work, too, and these doctors and barristers who come with their families in their Hunter wellies soon see that they wouldn't fit in here. And even someone with deep pockets would baulk at the money needed to renovate the farm. The house wants a hundred different repairs, and the roof of the barn is rusting towards collapse like the corroding stanchions of the cattle shed that still smells of disinfectant. It ruined the Dyers, foot and mouth, when it came to the valley. All their Ayrshires went in a pyre, the same as the Beasleys' pigs, the same as our sheep. I was just glad that Dadda wasn't around to see the farm being switched off.

Because we lamb late, our ewes were still pregnant when those men from the abattoir who'd found slaughter work of a different kind that spring came up to the farm with Leith one afternoon.

They went into the lambing pen with a bolt-pistol and some pithing canes and left it silent. Then we burned what they'd killed. Then we buried the ashes. Then we re-stocked, like Angela did. Then we tried for another baby and now Kat was nearly at full term. A girl this time, she says. As certain of that as she was that Adam was going to be a boy.

We carry on. If the world comes rolling down the valley – and sometimes it does – then we start again. We can look after ourselves. We can feed each other. We have houses that belong to us. The land is ours. Whatever happens, that won't change. We're not like the folk in Underclough, trying to live in wreckage.

It's difficult to explain to Adam the difference between the village now and the village that the Arncliffes knew. I've described the mill to him and told him what it was used for but quite what he pictures I don't know. Wheels and cogs and belts, like the innards of some enormous clock maybe. He knows that it closed when the Gaffer wasn't much older than him, but what's harder for him to understand is that the place really died with Jacob Arncliffe. After the Blizzard, work went on, of course, the looms still racketed from the early hours to the ring of six from St Michael's, though the firm that had bought the business began to struggle and quickly realised that they'd purchased an antique. The following year, the war came and the mill played a small role in the effort, but only a fraction of the building was needed for what they were asked to produce and rooms that had once been bloated with noise now lay empty.

Men left the terrace and the Nine Cottages and on the boats to France wondered if the uniforms they were wearing had been cut from the cloth they'd produced. And, later, if the blankets of their hospital beds had been ones they'd trimmed to size in the finishing room. A few of them returned jumpy and altered, a few as if the whole thing had been an inconvenience, but most came back as names for the mason's chisel. By the time the war memorial had been erected on the roadside near Sullom Wood, the year Gideon Denning sold the Endlands, those photographs Jacob had taken of the river and the church, the weavers hoeing their allotments at the back of New Row, the girls dancing ghost-blurred round the maypole, the farmers with their sickles and their crooks, they seemed old already. Pinned to a time that they could never claw back.

But we don't live like that, Adam, I say. We don't let things get lost. We don't let things get taken away from us. We have the means to keep going. And so we must.

That's what the Dyers forgot, or couldn't see any more.

I sometimes come across Laurel if she's down in the village visiting Betty Ward and she tells me every time what a blessing it was that she and Bill were forced to leave the valley. Bill's more or less housebound now with his arthritis and she's hardly in the best of health either. Imagine if they'd had a farm to look after as well? No, they're happy in Fleetwood. She'd always wanted to go back to where she'd grown up and live near the sea. She has a job in a fishmonger's that pays for a little flat. And when Jeff finally arrived back in the valley, I could tell him that there was a room waiting for him there with a view over the esplanade.

Laurel is the only one who still believes that he'll turn up. She still thinks that Jeff will one day walk through her front door and kiss her on the forehead and sleep in the room that she cleans for him each week. Even Grace resigned herself to him being dead years ago.

The police had looked into the case for as long as they ever look into things when someone goes missing, and it was hard to watch the Dyers going through it all. But better that than knowing what I'd found at Far Lodge.

We don't talk about that night very often nowadays, Kat and I. But it's there in our history and sometimes when it snows I'll catch her daydreaming and I'll know that she's thinking about it.

It had taken Dadda and me an hour or so to walk back to the Wall with Musket, where Bill had been waiting with Fly since it was light enough to see. The sheep they'd driven down the day before were all well in the sheds. The ram was feeding. They'd found Kat wandering near Top Pond, her hands stiff and the blood gone from her lips. But once they'd got her down to the farm and she'd warmed herself and eaten something she was fine; she'd slept too, despite being worried about me and Dadda. It was Grace they were concerned for. She had a temperature.

She couldn't stop being sick. Laurel was looking after her. They'd called the doctor, but he wouldn't be able to get through the snow for hours. Bill had been out with Dadda's tractor and driven a cutting from the Moss to the farm, and on the lane Liz and Angela were clearing the snow, although fresh flakes were starting to come now, adding to the rind that covered all the outhouses.

When we got back, Kat put her arms around me and didn't let go until she realised how cold I was and helped me off with my clothes and ran me a bath.

'I'm sorry,' she said, as we waited for the tub to fill.

'Where did you go?' I said.

'I don't know,' she said. 'I couldn't tell.'

'Why didn't you wait for us?'

'I was angry,' she said.

'Even so,' I said. 'You went off at some pace, Kat. Why?'

'You'll think I'm stupid,' she said.

'What do you mean?'

'I thought I heard someone calling me,' she said.

'Who?'

'It sounded like Grace,' she said.

'Why would Grace have been on the moors?' I said.

'I thought she might have come looking for me with the others,' said Kat. 'Didn't you hear it too? You must have done.'

'I thought it was you,' I said. 'Weren't you shouting for us?'

'I did once,' she said.

'Perhaps that's what I heard.'

'But who did I hear?' she said. 'There was someone up there on the moors who knew my name and it wasn't Grace.'

'How is she?' I said.

'Really not well,' said Kat.

'She'll have just caught a cold,' I said.

'It's not a cold,' said Kat. 'It's something else.'

'Like what?'

Kat lowered her voice. 'When I went to the bathroom earlier,' she said, 'I found her with her fingers down her throat.'

'Is she bulimic, do you think?' I said.

'John, she said she was trying to get rid of the Devil,' said Kat. 'She told me that was why she smashed the mirror. She didn't like him looking at her.'

'That sounds like a fever talking to me,' I said.

'Or she needs a different kind of doctor,' said Kat and switched off the taps.

'Have you told Liz?'

Kat shook her head. 'She's still not talking to me. Get in. I'll go and make you something to eat.'

She closed the door and went downstairs and I climbed into the bath, unstiffening my knuckles, waking numb toes. On the other side of the frosted glass, the snow was falling again. It would keep us stuck at the farm for another day or two at least. Time enough for Kat and me to talk again about staying for good. Enough time for her to understand how important she was. How she was carrying the Endlands in her womb.

~

Is this where you were going to bring me? says Adam, running his finger in the groove around the stag's face. I've been here loads of times.

No, we're going somewhere else, I say. Across the Blackberry Field.

What's there?

You'll find out if you come, won't you?

We walk past the green acre where the Dyers' Ayrshires used to chew the cud and come to the place where Jim had once kept his horses.

I hold Adam's hand as we negotiate the verge to get to the gate that's held ajar by nettles. I squeeze through the gap first, stamping down what I can, and tell Adam to reach out for the wooden edge.

Got it? I say.

Got it, he says.

Pick your feet up when you come through, I tell him, though he still catches a toe on one of the hard ruts and stumbles and feels around for something to hold on to.

I've got you, I say, don't worry. He sort of dangles from my hand for a moment before he finds his balance again.

We follow the line of the hedgerow, Adam treading with care, his free hand catching thistle heads and grass as the wind makes them bow.

We're going to the Wood, aren't we? he says. I can hear it. Is that where you're taking me? I've been to Sullom Wood before, you know.

Not the place we're going to, I say. You want to go somewhere different, don't you?

He nods in that way of his that means he's agreeing but agreeing with uncertainty. He's just how Kat used to be.

Through the mud and puddles, it takes us a good half an hour to reach the fence on the other side of the field. When I was younger I'd been able to scale it with hardly a break of stride. A step, a step, a hand on the rail and down into the fallen leaves.

Let me climb over first, I say, and Adam grips my arm. You'll have to let go, I say. Just for a minute. I'll climb over and then I can help you.

His nightmare, he tells me, is that we'll be out on our walk one day and I'll fall or die (and he knows that mummies and daddies do die because of what I've told him about Mam) and he won't know where he is.

Well, then you shout, I tell him. Someone would hear you. Someone would come.

But he knows that we've walked further today than we ever have and he's lost all sense of distance.

Tell me about the birds you can hear, I say, giving him some distraction while I climb over the fence.

When he was younger, he'd sit on the bench in the yard and copy what Kat and I told him. Hear that, Adam? That's a blackbird. That's a robin. That's a jackdaw.

If the cat ever left a gift on the porch step or in the scullery, then I'd let Adam hold it so that he knew how big one bird was to another. Then he could make comparisons. Sound on its own is tricksy. The wren weighs little more than the egg from which it hatches but fills the bye-field with its song. The great flapping marsh harrier that beats the bounds of the Moss does nothing more than squeak like a hinge.

Birdsong is how the seasons move for Adam. Summer is loud. Autumn downhearted. Winter silent. Spring ferocious.

What's that? I say, as I clamber down the other side. Twink, twink.

Chaffinch, says Adam. And the chaffinch's song is different everywhere. What they sing here they don't sing anywhere else.

Who sounds like he's sawing up wood?

A jay, says Adam. He's angry about something. I can hear a nuthatch too. And that's a mistle-thrush.

But I wish that he could see the light in here this afternoon. I wish he could see the bluebells and the campion and the dog violet.

After a thousand single steps, the trees change from oak and beech to silver birch and willow. And the sound of the river rises loud out of the Greenhollow. A decade on from the fire, things are slowly returning to how they were. The willows that survived at the top of the ravine have thickened and sagged. And in time what is starting to sprout in the shadows beneath them will spread out over the river and meet the branches on the other side, knitting the roof back together. My daughter might one day see the place as I knew it.

Can you hear how big the trees are, Adam? I say. Can you hear the different sounds the leaves make? But he's not listening to me or the trees but the brawling of the Falls downstream.

The slope to the water's edge looks steeper than it used to do and what was once all mud and roots is now wild garlic and wood sorrel.

Put your arms around me, Adam, I say, crouching down next to him. I'll carry you. It's too steep for you to walk down yourself.

If it's steep, you'll fall, he says.

I won't fall, I say, although under the leaves, waiting to catch my foot, are the remnants of what we cut down on the morning of Devil's Day years ago, the bigger boughs still in the process of rotting away and the stumps mossed over.

Adam hangs his little weight on me, with his chin on my shoulder and his thighs clamped around my waist. I can smell the tomato soup Kat fed him at dinner time on his breath and in his hair.

I think: he is real and he is alive.

I think: he is my boy.

I think: the cold fact is that there will be a time when I am gone and Kat will be gone and there will only be Adam and his sister. He can't fear the valley. It can't be unknown to him.

We contour the bottom of the slope for a while, following the flow of the water, until the willows above us become heavier and the shade has stunted the weeds. I lift him over the shallows and carry him to the long flat rock that hangs over the Falls.

If we want to talk we have to talk loudly now. The spray is on Adam's hair and skin. It dribbles off his brow and he blinks it away. His eyes still flinch at water and dust but they have no other use but to give his face a little colour. He carries them like he carries marbles in his pocket.

I used to jump in here, I tell him. When I was your age. I used to come here in the summer. I used to pretend that I was an otter.

But even that doesn't crack a smile. Even the thought that his father was once a boy and liked to play imaginary games.

What would you be? I say.

I don't know, he says.

You could be a frog, I say. Then you could jump in too.

No, he says. I can't.

I won't let you drown, I say. I'm not going back to the farm without you, am I?

Please, he says.

You won't get hurt, I say. There are no rocks for you to land on. Listen, I say. I'll throw in this stone and you'll hear it splash. Listen.

I let it drop and Adam hears it, I know he does, but he still says he doesn't.

I'll get into the water, I say. I'll wait for you to jump in and I'll catch you. How's that?

Can we go home? he says. I want to go home now.

All this is your home, I say.

I mean the house, he says. I want to go back to the house.

Didn't you hear the rock splash? I say. You can't hurt yourself. I won't let you. I survived, didn't I?

After a moment, he nods.

Put your arms up, then, I say, and I pull his T-shirt over his head. His mop of hair gets caught in the neck on the way and then flops down over his ears. He's a slight boy, Adam, all ribs and budding muscle.

I get down on my knees to unlace his trainers. His skin is frilled from the elastic of his mismatched socks. His toenails need cutting. The scar from where he slipped off the stepping stones years before smiles under his ankle bone.

He holds on to me as I stand up and finds my fingers with his little hand, yet to grow.

I'm going to go down and get into the water now, I say. You stay here. It won't take me long.

I let go of him and pick my way through the shallow pools.

No, I say, don't turn around, don't move. Just stand there until I get into the water.

How will I know if you're all right? he says.

Keep talking to me, I say. Then you'll know that I'm still here.

He crosses his arms and rubs the cold from his skin.

You knew Lennie Sturzaker, didn't you? he says.

They still talk about Lennie down in the village. He's the warning that parents give their children about playing near Arncliffe's.

Is that what you're worried about? I say.

I don't understand what happened to him, says Adam.

He drowned, I say. You know that.

But how? he says.

Down in the Greenhollow, Lennie Sturzaker is real, not just a mother's parable. He'd died here in the valley, here in the river gushing past and spilling endlessly over the edge of the Falls.

A few days after I'd watched Sam and Jeff and the others dunking Lennie in the river, the Gaffer sent me to cycle down to the abattoir with the money that he owed Clive Ward from their last card game. Money that Dadda said had been earmarked for the deposit on my grammar school uniform. But the Gaffer had told him not to worry about it. He knew someone who worked at Mosconi's and he'd let us have it on the tick until he won the money back on Saturday.

When I got to the abattoir, the lairage was full of pigs all knuckled together and waiting for the doors to open. Clive Ward was one of the two men in boiler suits standing by the fence on a fag break. I passed him the pound notes through the railings and he stuffed them into the pocket of his overalls.

'Here,' he said, blowing smoke from the side of his mouth and pressing some loose change into my hand. 'Tell the Gaffer I'll see him on Saturday. Make sure he doesn't gamble away that bike of yours.'

He winked at me and flicked the butt-end into a puddle and went with the other man to herd the pigs inside.

By the age of eleven, I'd become expert at cycling through the village at speed, using the slight downward gradient along New Row to take me over the hump of the bridge. On the other side, I'd make pistons out of my knees and feel the twitch in my stomach as I took the sharp bend by Beckfoot's and Wigton's. It had been some time before I'd found the courage to keep my fingers off the brakes and lean into the corner, but if I steadied my nerves then I could freewheel all the way past school, past the Croppers' Arms and the church and only have to start working the pedals again when I reached Archangel Back. Then it was a case of keeping the momentum going, arse off the saddle, and into Sullom Wood.

At first, I thought I must have run into a stone in the road, or caught the front tyre in a rut. There were no puddles in which I could have skidded; the lane was dust-dry.

The handlebars jerked to the right, jack-knifing the wheel, and the lane suddenly rose to meet me. I hit it hard – knee, elbow and shoulder – and the bike went end over end, clattering into the undergrowth on the other side of the lane. It lay there with the back wheel ticking as I picked myself up. My elbow had been torn open and the skin hung off in a flap, dribbling blood down my arm. A fist-sized lump of rock had left a long scratch mark on the concrete, where it had rolled after pranging the spokes.

The bracken rustled and Lennie Sturzaker emerged sweat-stained and red-faced from the humid afternoon.

'Come off your bike, did you?' he said.

The bridge of his nose was black from where Sam had hit him a few days before and there were little cuts all over his neck.

I said nothing and went to retrieve the bike from the ditch. Both wheels were buckled and twisted. It would have to hobble home like me.

'Where have you been?' he said.

'Nowhere,' I said.

'Where are you going now?' he said.

'Home,' I said over my shoulder.

'Not to the Wood?' he said and I felt his fingers jabbing me in the back. 'It were you, weren't it? It were you hiding in the trees?'

I tried to push past him, but he stopped me short.

'I didn't say you could go home, did I?' he said, his palm in my chest this time.

I started to say something – God knows what – but I hadn't got more than a few words out before he put his fist into my stomach, knocking loose every breath of air in my lungs. The bike fell to the floor again and I bent over trying to inhale. I felt him grab hold of my hair and drag me off the lane and down into the ditch. Through the brambles and nettles at the edge of the Wood, he let go and shoved me hard in the back, sending me stumbling on a few paces.

'Come on,' he said. 'Show me where you were hiding.'

Even with a shredded elbow and labouring lungs, I'd have easily outrun him, but the Devil told me that this was the time, these were the last moments of Lennie Sturzaker's life and I had to watch. Every footstep he took through the Wood was one closer to his end. He'd retrace none of them.

'Is there summat wrong with you, Pentecock?' Lennie said. I was his plaything now, as he flicked me in the side of the face and put his knee into mine. 'Do you like spying? Have you built a den, or summat? It's mine now, if you have.'

I could show him the willow tree where I'd concealed myself, I could show him the bank where I was going to burrow out my holt; it didn't matter, he wouldn't possess them for long now anyway. I hoped it would happen quickly. The pain from my torn elbow was knocking me sick and there was no escape from the clamminess of the afternoon. Even in the Wood it was sticky with heat and the tree trunks swarmed with ants. Lennie was breathing heavily as he shoved and prodded me and when he pulled me close to him at the top of the Greenhollow I caught a whiff of his sweat, a rancid smell, as sharp as geraniums.

'Don't think about swimming off, Pansycock,' he said. 'Or I'll be waiting for you at the farm.'

He nudged me down the slope to the edge of the river and when I came to the bottom, I felt his hand on the scruff of my shirt again.

'Come on,' he said. 'Show me where you were hiding then.'

When I didn't move, he turned me around and pulled hard on my ear.

'Doesn't this work, or summat?' he said. 'Have you gone deaf? What are you looking at me like that for?'

I didn't know what to say to him. It didn't really matter now.

'Stop fuckin' staring at me,' he said. 'You're not right in the head, Pentecost. Have you got problems or summat?'

I'd heard about folk dropping down dead on the spot from a sudden glitch in their heart or from some portion of the brain tearing open and shedding blood. Perhaps that was how Lennie would go.

'If there's summat wrong with you,' he said. 'If you've got the Devil in your head, you need to have him taken out.'

He nodded past me.

'Get in the water,' he said.

'Like this?' I said, looking at my clothes.

From his back pocket, he took out a penknife and opened the blade.

'Go on,' he said, pointing with the tip of it.

I went to the bank and down on to the shingle, the back of my head blown with spit. Then with a hard kick in the thigh I was ankle-deep, losing my balance on the weedy rocks underfoot.

'Further,' said Lennie and, squatting down, his belly bulging, he picked up a handful of pebbles. 'Get under.'

He was as accurate now as he had been when he'd knocked me off the bike and stone after stone found the hands that were covering my face and, when he realised I wasn't going to take them away, my ribs, my back, my balls. Then he sloshed into the water up to his knees and had me in a headlock as he'd done that day after school. I don't think he realised, but he called me Sam as he hit me. He called me every name he could think of. He found the eyebrow that he'd opened weeks before and resurrected the pain in a white flash. He thumped at the wound on my elbow. He brought out the penknife again and I managed to fend off the blade once or twice before it sliced through the webbing between my thumb and finger and then went deep in down the side of one of my nails. The Devil had lied to me. Of course he had. Lennie was going to kill me. I was the boy who was going to die down here in the Greenhollow, not him. Squeezing tighter, Lennie leaned back and stood me upright in a position where he could draw the knife across my stomach. His nose snuffled close to my ear and I could smell beef crisps and fag smoke on his breath as he tried to twist his hand out of my grip. Death wouldn't be quick at all. Not like it was for the lambs we took to the abattoir after Gathering – a warm pulse of electricity to the brain and then a knife through the windpipe as quick and clean as a paper cut. The way Lennie was hacking at me with the blade, I'd be left to leak to death from a dozen trickling wounds.

The loose pebbles underfoot made both of us stumble backwards, and searching around for something solid to stand on as we moved further out into the river, one of my feet found a lump of rock and I toppled backwards on to Lennie. His legs buckled under my weight and I felt his hold on me disappear.

His voice became muffled as we went under the surface and were pulled away in the water. His fat hands swept through the murk in front of me, cadaverous-looking already, then one of his trainers kicked aimlessly, the shoelace trailing, then coiling. But after that, I lost sight of him in the silty green and swam across the ply of the current to the bank, where I pulled myself out, my clothes plastered to my skin.

A few moments later I saw him surface much further along than I'd expected. Where the river bent, he managed to catch hold of the dangling willow branches and he made one or two efforts to try and pull himself out. But I'd seen him on the gym rope at school and he couldn't ever heave his bulk any more than six inches off the mat.

He wasn't all that far from the bank and as I went along the edge of the river I watched him trying to grab the roots that ribbed out of the soil. But the water jostled and turned him so that he was always reaching backwards.

He caught sight of me and started to shout when he slipped under, one hand patting the water. I sat in the roots and watched his face emerge again, his lips puffing like a woman in childbirth, his free arm thrashing about in my direction in the hope that I would take it. But that wasn't how the story ended. I couldn't save him. I couldn't change what was meant to happen in the world.

He let out a single cry, his eyes wide with the realisation that he'd come to the end of his life, that death was going to happen to him now, and then the river plucked him from the branches and took him away. An elbow, a hand, a foot broke the dark surface and then disappeared again.

I felt the Devil move inside me, preparing to leap, the way a cat crouches to scale a fence. He sprang into the trees where the jackdaws were waiting, slipping into one of them and flapping away. Then the rain began, striking the dry acres of the wood, making the leaves nod, falling through the clearings, thickening the river.

~

Tired and warm, I fell asleep in the bath and woke to find it tepid and Laurel calling for Grace. When I dressed and went down to the kitchen, Laurel was on her tip toes looking out of the window at the snow coming down in the yard.

'Is she upstairs?' she said.

'No,' I said. 'Why?'

'She's gone,' said Laurel. 'Katherine's looking for her.'

'I thought she was sleeping in the front room?' I said.

'So did I,' Laurel replied. 'But when I went in with some tea for her, she wasn't there.'

'You go and fetch the others,' I said. 'I'll see if I can find her.'

She wasn't in the workshed or the haybarn. Nor was she in the shed with the ewes and lambs. When I looked in on the ram's pen, Kat caught me by the door and held my arm.

'What's wrong?' I said and she nodded to where Grace was leaning on the bars of the gate and watching the tup grunting and pacing. The Ram's Crown lay in pieces on the concrete.

'What's she doing?' I said. 'She's supposed to be resting.'

'I don't know,' said Kat. 'I found her in here pulling the crown apart.'

'Grace?' I said and Kat prevented me from going closer to her.

'Don't,' she said. 'Leave her.'

'It's freezing in here,' I said. 'If she's not well, then she needs to be back in the house.'

'There's nothing physically wrong with her,' said Kat. 'She's not got a cold. I told you what she said to me.'

A flint of light wandered over the wall and then caught Kat in the eye as Grace looked at the piece of glass in her hand, a shank from her broken mirror.

'I thought Liz had cleared it all up?' said Kat.

'God knows.'

'Where is she?' said Kat.

'Laurel's gone to fetch her,' I said.

Grace looked at her reflection in the splinter and then stared up at the ceiling with tears in her eyes.

'He's telling me to kill the ram,' she said. 'He's telling me to stick it.'

She turned and looked at Kat.

'Oh, Grace, there's no one there,' said Kat. 'It's not a real voice.'

'He's telling me to cut its throat,' said Grace. 'He's telling me to cut yours too and Uncle John's.'

'You'll hurt your hand again on that glass,' said Kat. 'Why don't you put it on the floor?'

'Now he's laughing,' said Grace.

'The doctor's coming,' said Kat.

'Not in all this snow,' said Grace.

'Perhaps your dad might be back soon,' said Kat. 'You'll want to see him, won't you? Why don't you come and wait for him in the house?'

Grace caught herself in the mirror again and shook her head.

'What?' said Kat.

'He's saying that if I don't like him inside me then I'll have to cut him out,' said Grace. 'But I don't want to.'

'No, no, don't,' said Kat, going over to her now. 'The doctor will get rid of him for you.'

'With the magic word?' said Grace and smiled as she climbed up on to the bottom rung of the gate and leant over to look at the ram again. He stared back at her, his nostrils opening and closing, his white breath mixing with the gentle steaming of the haybales.

'It wouldn't hurt him too much,' Grace said. 'If I get him in the right place, it'll be quick.'

'Grace, come down,' said Kat. 'Come inside with me and John.'

She smiled again and did as she was told.

'Just here, Auntie Katherine,' she said, pulling down the scarf Kat was wearing and pressing her fingertips under the angle of her jaw. 'If I do him there, he'll bleed like a tap.'

Kat swallowed and found my hand with hers.

'Stop,' she said. 'Please, Grace.'

Grace put her hand on Kat's cheek instead and kissed her.

Outside in the yard, Musket and Fly began barking with a hostility that I'd never heard in them before. Their chains tensed, chinking as a deeper voice yelped back at them. A nose and a set of teeth wedged open the door of the pen and a large dog came in making so much noise that Grace put her hands over her ears.

It wasn't Ken Sturzaker's but one of the strays that were up on the moors. Part of the pack that had killed the sheep and come across Dent at Far Lodge. One of Dent's own dogs, maybe. One that he'd been intending to use on Jeff. I don't know. It didn't look as if it had eaten properly for some time. When it barked at us, its skin moved over rib rather than muscle and its legs were sore with rot from wandering about in the mud. It was the one that was always shunted aside from the kill and only got to lick up blood or chew on bones. The ram backed away braying and muttering.

The dog recoiled a little when I clapped my hands and shouted, but was determined to get to the ram and put its front paws on the gate, wedging its face between the bars.

'Whose is it?' said Kat.

'I don't know,' I said.

'Perhaps you should let it in,' said Kat, putting her arms around Grace. 'Then at least it'll be trapped.'

'I don't think Dadda would ever forgive me,' I said.

'Wouldn't he rather it took the ram than us?'

'It's not going to go for us,' I said.

'It's starving,' said Kat over the dog's barks. 'Look at it.'

A brush sat against the wall and even though I wouldn't be able to beat away a dog that size with it I thought the noise of the handle on the metal gate might send it packing. But it only made the dog's voice louder and it chased the wooden pole until it was tight in its jaws.

'You're just provoking it,' said Kat. 'Let go.'

The dog pulled the broom out of my hands and thrashed it against the wall of the ram's pen before turning its attention to Grace. There was something about her that it didn't like. A smell of threat. The same smell that Kat had noticed, perhaps.

Grace waved the dirk of mirror in front of her but the dog caught her forearm in its teeth, puncturing the skin as Kat and I tried to push it away. Skinny as it was, the dog was strong and even a kick to its ribs didn't stop it clamping down. Grace screamed and cried for Jeff. She shouted for Kat to help her. And as she called out, the dog's voice began to change. The deep growl in its throat was replaced by a whining noise and then it finally let go and backed away, its eyes closed and its mouth wide open as if it were gagging on something. Kat put herself between the dog and Grace, hurriedly untangling the scarf she'd been wearing to wrap the bleeding holes. But she heard it, I know she did, because she looked at me and wanted me to tell her that it wasn't true.

The dog was crying just like Grace was crying.

It was sobbing like a child.

The door to the shed opened and Bill, Angela and Liz appeared, followed by Dadda who came in loading his shotgun. In a voice more accurate now, the dog turned and growled at them, stretching its mouth wide when it barked. Dadda took a few steps further inside as he closed up the shotgun and waited until the dog was closer, almost by his feet, before he fired.

The dog's noise shut off and it lay against the breeze block wall with its tongue hanging and its head spilling like a cracked pomegranate. Dadda looked at it and then stepped over the body and went into the pen to calm the ram. Liz pulled Grace away from Kat and unravelled the scarf to look at the wounds.

'Jesus,' she said.

'Bring her into the house,' said Angela. 'Tom has some iodine.'

'She needs to go to the hospital, Mam,' said Liz.

'The doctor's on his way,' said Angela. 'Let him look at her first.'

Having heard the gunshot, Laurel came in and Angela caught her arm before she could stumble into the dog.

'Good God,' she said, crossing herself. 'Are you all right, Grace, love?'

Liz showed her what the dog had done.

'Was it after the ram?' said Laurel.

'I think so,' said Dadda.

'It must have come down off the moors,' said Angela.

'And not for the first time,' said Bill.

'Is this it?' said Laurel. 'Is this what killed our Douglas?'

'It must have been,' said Bill and took hold of the dog's back legs and began to drag it out into the snow.

'Come on,' said Liz, pressing her fingers to Grace's back. 'Inside.'

'Quick,' said Angela.

'They'll get infected,' said Laurel.

Before the three of them could take her away, Grace held Kat's wrist. 'Stay,' she said.

And she did. She stayed for Grace. At first, at least. She was worried about her. She wanted her to know that she was there. But then she stayed for me. She stayed for Adam. She stayed for everyone else here. She could have left if she'd wanted to but she didn't. It was her decision. An instinct was uncovered that she didn't know was there. Then there was nothing else to discuss. Like the sheep coming down at Gathering, she knew where she needed to be.

But more than that – after the glimpse she'd had of him grinning like a pig, after the voice on the moors that had led her astray, after what she'd seen in the ram's pen – she'd come to understand what I meant when I said that the Devil was real. Not the soppy Owd Feller in the songs, or the thing Gideon Denning and his friends thought they'd woken at Far Lodge. There was nothing to wake anyway. The Devil has been here since before anyone came, passing endlessly from one thing to another. He's in the rain and the gales and the wild river. He's in the trees of the Wood. He's the unexpected fire and the biter of dogs. He's the disease that can ruin a whole farm and the blizzard that buries a whole village. But at least here we can see him at work. He'd jumped from the stag into me and from me into the jackdaws. From a wall-eyed horse into poor Jim Beasley. From the Gaffer into Grace when his heart packed in. From Grace to a stray dog off the moors.

Where he went after that, we didn't know. But then Adam was born. A blind kitten that stayed blind. But Kat didn't run. She didn't scoop him up and take him away. She realised that what we pass on in the Endlands isn't only the privilege of living here, but the privilege of living itself. Seeking out the struggle, I mean, rather than hiding from it. Inoculating ourselves with fear.

Little doses and we find courage.

Adam looks as though he's staring at me from the top of the Falls. He shivers again and wedges his hands under his armpits.

Can you still hear me? I call to him and he nods. You know the pearl-fishers? I say. Remember what I read to you the other night? They're not frightened of the water, are they?

He's at that age when boys are ravenous for superlatives. The fastest this, the heaviest that, the tallest, the longest. Not that any of it means much to him but the numbers sound impressive enough in comparison: the greyhound is fast – ah, but the cheetah.

The pearl-fishers dive a hundred feet or more on a single breath, don't they? I say.

A hundred and fifty, he says.

If a fathom is six feet, what's that in fathoms? I say, giving his brain something else to think about other than falling and drowning and Lennie Sturzaker.

Down here, away from the breeze, there is a little warmth in the air, and, with my shirt folded, I can feel it on my back. Good for that ache in my shoulder that the ointment hasn't touched.

Twenty-five, says Adam.

That's twenty-five of me, I say. Fifty of you.

He considers himself from head to toe and tries to imagine dropping his own height time after time down into the ocean. I unbuckle my belt and thumb open the fly-buttons on the jeans that have seen better days.

Do you remember? I say. That there's a point where they don't have to swim any more? They don't have to do anything. Gravity takes them down and it's like they're flying underwater. Do you remember that? I say, and he nods.

My jeans with the shirt and my socks rolled into my boots, I hold the hand of a willow branch and step down into the shallows of the river, one foot and then the other finding the weedy stones. The water is still winter cold, but I keep my cries to myself. I don't want to scare Adam any more than he already is. I wade out until I'm up to my waist and then call to him.

Adam, I say, I'm in the river now. I'm down below you. When you jump, I'll be here, you'll feel my hand before you know it.

He stands absolutely still and says nothing.

I won't let the river take you away, I tell him. I'll catch you. I won't let you drown. But you have to make sure that you jump away from the edge, I say. Don't fall off, but jump.

And for a moment I have to ask myself if I've ever seen him jump. I don't think I have. But perhaps only because he's scared of landing awkwardly on the ground. Leaping into open water, it doesn't matter, the surface yields and the river cradles.

You'll have to bend your legs, I say. You'll have to think you're a frog. You have to crouch and spring, Adam. Move a bit closer, I say, and of course he can't. Slide your feet forward until you can touch the edge with your toes, I tell him. Take your time. There's no rush. Although I can't feel my legs any more and the lapping water has sent my balls retreating to my stomach. Use your arms to balance, I say. The rock's flat, you won't trip.

Daddy, he says.

You're almost there, I say. Another step.

His whole body lurches to the side as he moves but he keeps himself upright and first one foot and then the other comes to the rim of the Falls.

Can you feel the edge now? I say.

He nods and keeps his arms out by his sides. Even without being able to see, he senses the great open space in front of him.

Now bend your knees, I say, bend your knees and lean over. And when you feel yourself falling, you push yourself as far out as you can and I'll be here in the water waiting for you, I'll catch you. Don't be scared of this place. This is your valley. Can you hear me? I've not gone anywhere. I've not left you. I'm here.

And he jumps.

My boy jumps.

And he comes down through the green light.

My boy jumps and my daughter kicks in the womb.

The wind comes and stirs the willows and the silver birch. It shakes the holly and rowan on the fells, rising and rising to the edges of the moors.

There is a rightness to the valley at this time of year. After the long winter, it has found itself again in the baritone of the ewes and the treble of the lambs; in the infectious restlessness of the chiff-chaff and the wren.

The lapwings are in the hay fields chasing off the jackdaws.

Dozens of them rolling and falling in this time of territories. And their cries are full of joy, as though at every turn they come upon their own endless freedoms afresh.

Promise, it all says. Promise.

Like every spring.

Acknowledgements

Thank you to all the wonderful folk at John Murray for all their hard work and support. You've enabled me to write for a living. I couldn't have asked for more than that.

Many thanks to Sara Marafini for designing another iconic book cover. To Becky Walsh, Caroline Westmore and Morag Lyall for their help in editing the final draft and to Amanda Jones for managing the production. To Joanna Kaliszewska for selling the novel abroad.

Thanks to my publicist, Yassine Belkacemi, for keeping me busy around the country and promoting the novel with such passion and commitment. To my agent, Lucy Luck, who is always there to help in every way – from astute editorial advice to various life crises. And to my editor, Mark Richards, for all his patience on the long road and his constant faith in my writing.

Lastly, thanks to Ben and Tom: you kept me going even if you didn't know it. And to Jo, not only for her unwavering encouragement throughout but for often seeing the light more clearly than I was able to.